and mamma

Bright Tomorrows

Also by Kate Alexander

FIELDS OF BATTLE
FRIENDS AND ENEMIES
PATHS OF PEACE

Bright Tomorrows

KATE ALEXANDER

Macdonald

A Macdonald Book

First published in Great Britain in 1985 by
Macdonald & Co (Publishers) Ltd
London & Sydney

British Library Cataloguing in Publication Data

Alexander, Kate
Bright tomorrows.
Rn: Tilly Armstrong I. Title
823'.914[F] PR6051.L363

ISBN 0-356-10980-1

Photoset in North Wales by
Derek Doyle & Associates, Mold, Clwyd
Printed in Great Britain by
Richard Clay (The Chaucer Press) Ltd,
Bungay, Suffolk

Macdonald & Co (Publishers) Ltd
Maxwell House
74 Worship Street
London EC2A 2EN
A BPCC plc Company

I. Shoddy Yesterdays

Chapter One

It was March, and wet. The narrow streets of Jarrow gleamed dark and sullen in the fading light. An old newspaper flapped in the gutter, gathering round it a pile of debris: a gnawed apple core, cigarette ends, an empty matchbox, a bottle top. A paper boat, launched before the rain drove all the children indoors, sailed down the stream with the face of Ramsay MacDonald at the helm, only to be wrecked against the headline, 'Means Test Protest'.

In the yard behind numbers 1 to 5 Launcelot Terrace the cobbles were humps of black and silver. In the space between the two privies which served the five houses a boy crouched for shelter. He was cold, wet and hungry, but he wouldn't go inside, where there was food and light and warmth, because the party going on in number 3 was to celebrate his father's marriage to Bessie Baillie and Ben Harcourt wanted no part of it.

The back door opened and a shaft of light shone across the yard. Phyllis Baillie, the younger of Bessie's two daughters, ran out – squealing as she realized that it was raining harder than she had thought. She was a heavy girl of nine who suffered from catarrh to such an extent that all her consonants were blurred, making her speech unintelligible to anyone whose ear was not accustomed to it.

She saw Ben and stopped with her hand on the iron latch of the privy.

'Wha' you doin' ou' 'ere?' she asked.

'Mindin' my own business,' Ben replied.

Phyllis flung open the door and disappeared inside. Ben heard a rush of water and then the sound of the chain being pulled. Phyllis came back, still pulling her knickers more comfortably into place under her frock.

'You comin' in?' she demanded.

'No.'

She went back into the house, but as Ben had expected his father appeared in the open doorway and called, 'Ben? You there, lad? Come away in. You'll get wet through.'

Reluctantly, Ben went towards him. Andrew Harcourt put his hand on his son's shoulder, knowing what was wrong with him, but incapable of explaining the step he had taken.

'It'll work out all right, he said awkwardly. 'You'll see. More comfortable all round and a home for Bess and the girls, too.'

'Don't want them in our house,' Ben said, rubbing a grimy fist across his nose.

'It's their house as well now. Bess'll be a good mother to you.'

'She's not my mam!'

The inner door opened and Bess erupted into the kitchen in time to hear what Ben had said.

'I'm your stepmother and I'll treat you like you's my own,' she announced. 'No more lurkin' around in wet. You'll catch your death. There's a fire in the parlour, tea and a bit o' cake. Get in there and stop worrying your father.'

There were half a dozen people in the front room: Ben's two new stepsisters, Phyllis and Elsie; Bessie's sister, Ethel, and her husband, Stan, and their baby; and one of Andrew's workmates from the shipyard and his wife. There were empty beer glasses standing about and one cheese sandwich on a plate. Ben took it and went to sit in the corner, gnawing at the bread hungrily.

His mother had died ten months earlier, giving birth to a baby, a little girl, who had survived her mother by no more than an hour. Until Gwyneth Harcourt had died, Ben's life had been happy enough. They had been poor, but better off than many of their neighbours. Andrew Harcourt had been in work and a good, generous husband to his ailing wife. He had given her most of his weekly wages and had carried the coals in from the yard for her after she became pregnant. Ben knew that his father had not been above putting the broom round the kitchen when Gwyneth was feeling poorly, but that memory filled him with shame; it was not the way for a man to behave and would have brought down scorn from Ben's mates if they had known about it.

Everything had fallen apart when Gwyneth died. Ben's Welsh granny came up from Cardiff and cried her way round the house, but after a few weeks of unmade beds, burnt potatoes and beer bottles under the sink she had departed, taking with her the cream lustre tea-set inscribed 'A Present from Llandudno' on the grounds that it had been a wedding present from Gwyneth's brother and belonged in her family.

'We'll be better off on our own,' Andrew had told Ben. 'We'll manage.'

And manage they did, but the heart had gone out of the house. It was no longer a home, it was just a place to eat and sleep. Andrew took to ordering Ben off to bed and going down to the pub in the evenings, and that was how Bessie had captured him.

He was looked on as a good catch. A decent, honest man, and still hanging on to a job when most men in Jarrow were out of work. Number 3 Launcelot Terrace was a house worth having, too. Two up and two down, and water laid on in the kitchen. The outside privy, shared with the neighbours, was no drawback in Bessie's eyes, not after the two rooms she had been living in with her daughters, up three flights of stairs, every drop of water to be fetched from a standpipe outside, and the slops to be emptied from a pail each morning.

Andrew was lonely and Bessie, full-bodied and high-coloured, was a satisfying armful. She would keep his house clean, cook his meals, do his washing and look after Ben, as well as keeping Andrew's bed warm in a way he'd been missing for a long time with Gwyneth being so ailing. He shut his mind to the things he did not like about her: her loud voice, her grossness, a streak of vulgarity that grated on him. Compared to Bessie, Gwyneth had been a fairy woman, insubstantial and romantic, with a vein of melancholy in her and a touch of Celtic poetry.

Ben was like her, with black hair and grey eyes as clear as the light reflected from the rain-washed hills of Wales. He was a clever youngster, too; if he could get an education he might go further than the shipbuilding job his father held down, skilled man though Andrew was.

Inevitably, even though the wedding was a festive occasion, the talk drifted towards work, or the lack of it. Bessie's brother-in-law, Stan, was unemployed. He and his wife, Ethel, sat close together, with the baby on Ethel's knee. There was something defensive about their attitude. Although nothing was said, Ethel already knew her sister's opinion about her fecklessness in getting herself pregnant and having to marry a man who could hardly provide for himself, let alone a wife and child.

'Palmer's will come through all right,' Andrew said. 'It's a good yard. They'll not close it down while there's the chance of an Admiralty contract – which I hear there is.'

'Aye, man, so we thought in South Shields until National Shipbuilders Security came along and closed us,' Stan said bitterly. 'A right good name they've got! Whose security d'they mean? The bloody owners, that's who!'

'Language!' Bess said, coming in from the kitchen with a big brown teapot in her hand. 'I'll have no swearin' in my house, Stan Bewley. We'll cut the cake.'

A fruit cake, its top sprinkled with sugar, was enough of a novelty to fetch even Ben out of his corner. He stood at the table, his eyes on the flashing knife, his mouth watering, and Bessie had sufficient good feeling in her to give him the first slice.

'I felt anxious until it was cut,' she admitted. 'Aye, I had my doubts. A long time since I had the baking of a proper cake, but the oven in this kitchen gives a bonny heat, though I'll be more satisfied when I can get at it with a bit o' black lead and a scouring pad.'

She looked round complacently, with the satisfied feeling that she had done well.

'I've started on the house,' she said. 'I gave it a scrub earlier in the week, but I was that vexed when I saw the state of the step when we got back from church today. If I'd given it a thought I'd have got one of the girls to come round and whiten it special, but I did it only yesterday and I didn't think it'd have been stepped on the way it has.'

'I'm sure you've no call to feel ashamed, hinny,' Mrs Foxley said soothingly.

'I've told Andrew and Ben they'll be usin' the back door from now on. I can't be forever out the front cleaning the step.'

There were not enough cups to go round. Ben had to have his tea in a chipped enamel mug. He sat with his hands clutched round it, grateful for the warmth to chase away the chill of his damp clothes.

'I'd counted on that bonny tea-set Gwyneth had locked up in the cupboard,' Bess said. 'You could've knocked me down wi' a feather when Andrew told me her mother had taken it. He were too soft wi' her. I'd not have let her have it, but there, I wasn't in the picture then. It were given as a present, weren't it? You don't go takin' back presents, do you?'

Ben scowled into his mug. He, too, had hated to see the cream lustre tea-set disappear into his granny's bag. Once in a while his mam had unlocked the cupboard and let him hold one of the cups and he had turned it in his hands, fascinated by the colours gleaming on the surface, the sprays of lilies-of-the-valley and the sprawling lettering across each piece. But he was glad it had not fallen into Bessie's big, careless hands.

He began to feel sleepy, but it was not possible for him to go to bed. He had been turned out of his upstairs bedroom. Phyllis and Elsie would sleep there now. Ben was to have a camp-bed in the parlour and, because there was company, it had been bundled out of the way behind the sofa and would not be made up for him until they had all gone.

The baby woke up and began to cry in a thin, complaining way.

'She's hungry,' Bess pronounced. 'Take her into the kitchen and feed her, Ethel.'

Full of curiosity, Ben slipped off his chair and made as if to follow, but Bess caught him by the shoulder and spun him round.

'Ethel don't want you watching her,' she said. 'Go and sit down and be a good boy.'

Phyllis sniggered and her sister kicked her under the table.

His father smiled at him, an awkward, apologetic smile. 'That's women's work, lad,' he said.

As soon as the door had closed behind her sister, Bess turned to Stan.

'No prospect of a job?' she asked.

'You ought to know better than to ask,' he said. 'No, I've got no hope of work round here. I'm thinking of goin' south.'

There was a stir of interest, especially from the men. Fred Foxley and Andrew were both employed at Palmer's, and both still in work, but Stan had been at another yard which had closed three years earlier, and none of the men who had been with that company had yet found jobs.

'You'll not leave Ethel behind,' Bess stated.

'I'm not deserting her,' Stan said, nettled by the suspicion in her voice. 'It makes no more than sense to go where the work is. I'm a carpenter. I've got a trade that don't depend on shipbuilding – or needn't. We canna go on living like we are. It's not fair on my mum an' dad. It was good of them to tak' us in, wi' the babby an' all, but it canna go on.'

'What does Ethel say about it?' Mrs Foxley asked.

'She doesna want me to go,' Stan admitted. His shoulders sagged. He looked defeated. 'She wants to come wi' me, but the fare's more'n we can afford for the two of us.'

'Lodgings are dear,' Andrew said. 'I've heard of some that went south and had to come back because they couldn't keep themselves and send home to their wives as well.'

It hung on the air unspoken, the thought that Stan had done badly in landing himself with a wife and a baby to keep.

'Pity you didn't go long since,' Andrew said, and Bess stirred restlessly, knowing that he was thinking that both the baby and the marriage might have been avoided if Stan had gone south sooner.

'Ethel's got no sense,' she said. 'I'll talk to her, get her to see it's best for you both if you go off to earn a livin'.'

'I've a cousin lives in a place called Watford,' Stan told her. 'He's in the building trade and he wrote to Mum and said he could get me a job. His firm's startin' a new housing estate this summer and, him being a foreman, he thinks he could slip me in.'

'They don't know they're born down there,' Fred Foxley said.

There was a murmur of agreement, touched with scorn; they all shared the old resentment against the soft southerners who had captured the country's wealth.

Ethel came back into the room. The baby against her shoulder was drooling milk from a slack mouth, her eyes closed into slits, half asleep again.

When she saw them all watching her Ethel looked round nervously and Bessie said, 'Stan's been tellin' us he's the chance of a job and you're holding him back. Dinna be a fool, hinny. Let him go.'

'Not wi'out me!' Ethel clutched at the sleeve of Stan's jacket. 'Dinna go an' leave me, Stan.'

'It's aye that or stay out o' work,' Stan said. 'You'd be all right wi' Mum an' Dad. Bess here'll keep an eye on you and give a hand if you're anxious about the bairn.'

'That's right,' Bess agreed.

Ethel said nothing, but tears gathered in her eyes and rolled silently down her cheeks.

'Dry up, do,' her sister said. 'It's not the end o' the world, sayin' goodbye to your husband for a bit. Now there's a fine thing to say, and me only married today! Anyone for another cup o' tea? You won't say no, Ada, will you?'

It was late before they all went home, later still before Ben's bed was dragged out and made up. He lay in it, dazed with tiredness but alert to the unaccustomed sounds around him. It was a funny thing, sleeping downstairs. He could hear footsteps and voices in the road outside in a way he had never noticed at night before. The air in the room smelt frowsty from the smoke of the men's cigarettes, not cool and clean as it did upstairs. Them rotten old girls had got his room and they'd already torn his picture of King Kong off the wall. His dad and Bess – he'd been told to call her Mum but so far had managed to avoid it – were over his head. He heard the rhythmical squeaking of the bedsprings without understanding the significance of the sound, but connecting it dimly with the new marriage. Eventually he fell asleep.

Gradually, Ben got used to the change. Bess was not unkind,

though she found him less easy to understand that her own two girls and she had to give him a cuff or two before she could bring him round to calling her mother. Ben spat it out eventually and after the first time it came more easily. Elsie, the elder of his stepsisters, who was twelve years old, almost ignored him, but he found Phyllis a plague. She would tease him and then complain when he was goaded beyond endurance and struck out at her, and she brought Bess's heavy hand down on him more than once.

Bess was in her element, scouring and cleaning, shouting across the yard to the neighbours. She struck up a feud with the woman two doors away, accusing her of leaving the lavatory dirty, and the insults they exchanged acted like a tonic on Bess. The only thing that worried her was the rumour that began to go round that there would be no reprieve for Palmer's.

'I've heard the talk,' Andrew admitted when she asked him about it. 'But I'll no believe we're finished. We're a goin' concern. It's only last July we launched the Duchess. A yard that can turn out a ruddy great warship canna be written off overnight.'

'No smoke wi'out fire,' Bessie said. 'There must be something in it. Can't you find out? What's the Union doin'?'

'What do you expect them to do? Call us out on strike?' Andrew demanded.

'They ought to keep you in the picture,' Bess persisted. 'If Palmer's went ... eh, it don't bear thinkin' about. Half the town's out o' work already and that'd mean the rest would follow.'

The days dragged on. There was a feeling in the air that no one dared put into words – what had happened before could happen again. Other companies had gone under, other yards had been shut down. There was too much shipbuilding capacity; the National Shipbuilders Security had been formed to rationalize the industry, and the axe might fall on Jarrow as it had on other places in the north east.

They waited, breathing again as each week went by without the notice going up, but always with the nagging anxiety at the back of their minds. Bess began to be mean with her spending, hoarding spare coppers in an old jam jar by the side of the kitchen clock. Not that there were many of them, with five mouths to feed. She was exasperated by the way Ben suddenly began to shoot up.

'I'm feedin' you too well, that's what,' she said, only half joking. 'New boots you'll have to have, I suppose, but I'll let down the sleeves of that jacket and you'll have to mak' do. Don't let me catch you playing rough games, tearin' your trousers, because you'll not get another pair, an' that's flat.'

That was the night that Andrew came home and stood in the doorway, turning his cap in his hand, unable to speak. Bess sat down with a thump on the kitchen chair.

'It's come then,' she said.

'Aye.' Andrew wiped his hand across his forehead. It made Ben feel sick when he saw that his father's hand was shaking.

'We've all been turned off,' Andrew said. 'Every last man of us.'

Chapter Two

Bert's Transport Café stood by the side of the Great North Road, some sixty miles south of Tyneside. A wide, dusty yard in front provided a good pull-in for the lorries which travelled north and south. Bert had been dead for eight months, but Lily Manley kept the place going, shutting her mind to the things that needed doing which were beyond her strength and capability with only a part-time woman to give her a hand.

The café still looked bright and inviting, the weather boarding painted in blue and white stripes, with the name boldly displayed across the front in yellow on a black background. There were red and white check cotton curtains at the windows and matching oil cloth on the tables. Lily still got down on her hands and knees every morning and washed the dark blue linoleum, though she doubted whether the customers noticed; what mattered to them was that the food was good: hot, freshly cooked and quickly served.

In days gone by Lil would not have had time for looking out of the window, even at four o'clock in the afternoon, but the Depression had affected more than the men who had been thrown out of work. Factories closed meant fewer lorries on the road. Only three were parked in the yard, and only four men sat inside the café having a late dinner.

Lil leaned her elbows on the counter and eased her weight from one aching foot to the other. There were two people coming down the road. Lil looked at them and thought: tramps. Then she looked again. Not the ordinary kind of tramps. The woman, not much more than a girl really, was carrying a baby; the man was pushing a battered perambulator loaded with a collection of household goods. There was a canvas tool bag lashed to the top of the pile, which put them into the new class of drifters: on the road, but looking for work.

One of the lorry drivers muttered a goodbye and went out. Lil saw the man she had been watching leave the pram and go to speak to him. She guessed he was asking for a lift, but the driver shook his head and jerked his thumb towards the north, not the direction they wanted.

The girl sat down on the grass verge, the baby on her knee. She lifted its dress and began to change its napkin, replacing the sheet of newspaper it had been wearing with a fresh one handed to her by the man. The man took the soiled paper to the ditch and dropped it in, then he lit a match and bent over it. There was a flicker of flame, a plume of black smoke and it was gone. The girl was wiping her hands on a tuft of grass. They spoke together. She shook her head, but he seemed to be insisting, and they came towards the café.

They sat in a far corner when they got inside, anxious not to draw attention to themselves. The girl looked exhausted. Her shoes were covered in dust and had never been strong enough for tramping the roads. The baby lay on her lap, awake but apathetic. The man came up to the counter and, not looking at Lil, asked for a cup of tea. One cup. Lil gave it to him without comment, knowing that they were going to share it between them. He counted the coppers out as if reluctant to part even with that meagre sum.

When he got back to the table the girl had taken a feeding bottle out of the bag she had brought in with her. There was nothing in it but water. She glanced round furtively, as if she thought she might be stopped, and then took the nipple off the bottle and tipped in a spoonful of sugar. She put it to the baby's mouth and it began to suck greedily.

The man took a mouthful of the tea and then pushed the cup over to his wife. Another lorry driver got up to go, but although the man looked up, the driver forestalled him by remarking, 'I'm off to Glasgow. See you on my way back, Lil.'

A fly buzzed over his greasy plate. Lil collected it and put it down on the counter. Then she went over and sat down at the table with the young couple, lowering herself thankfully on to the wooden chair.

'On your uppers?' she asked.

'Just about,' the man admitted.

'Where are you from?'

'South Shields. We're walking south, lookin' for work. Thought we might pick up a lift.'

'You'll do no good with this pair,' Lil said, jerking her head towards the remaining drivers. 'With two of them in the cab there's no room for passengers. Besides, it's against the regulations.'

'I know ... but I thought, mebbe ...'

'They might risk taking a man on his own, but not a woman and baby, not to mention the pram. Nowhere to put it. What's your trade?'

'Carpenter, but I can turn my hand to most things.'

'How long you been out of work?'

'Three years.'

Lil turned her attention to the girl and the baby.

'Girl or boy?' she asked.

'Girl,' the mother answered.

'How old?'

'Four months.'

'Been married long?'

There was something about the way they avoided looking at one another that told her the whole story, even though the girl said quickly, 'Just over a year.'

A dole marriage and, no matter what she said, the baby probably already on the way. No business of Lil's. A delivery van drew up outside. Lil got heavily to her feet.

'How about doing some washing up in return for a square meal?' she asked. 'There's a pile waiting in the kitchen out the back.' She glared at the man. 'I don't care which of you does it, but if I was you I'd let my wife sit here and have a rest.'

Stan Bewley was on his feet while she was still speaking. Ethel made a half-hearted protest that it was woman's work, but he put his hand on her shoulder and pressed her back into her seat.

The dirty dishes had been stacked untidily, but the sink was clear and there was plenty of hot water from the geyser. He worked slowly and methodically, anxious not to smash any of the thick white china. Lil looked in with some more plates and cups just as he was letting the last of the water run away.

'Don't bother with these few bits,' she said. 'Wipe up and stack the clean dishes on the table while I dish up your dinner. Sausage, egg and chips, O.K.?'

They had two sausages each, sizzling and brown, a fried egg and a pile of crisp yellow chips. Without saying anything Lil removed the plates they had wiped clean with bread and slapped down two dishes of apple tart and custard.

'Give me the bottle and I'll make up some milk for the baby,' she said. 'What's her name?'

'Josephine. We call her Josie,' Ethel said. She pulled back the edge of the blanket that covered the child's head and revealed a smooth pink scalp with a new growth of sandy hair, sparse and fine as floss silk.

'Pretty little thing,' Lil said politely, though her private opinion was that the baby was a miserable shrimp. 'You're not feeding her yourself?' she asked when she had handed over the mixture of cow's milk and water she had heated up.

'I was till we started walkin',' Ethel said, 'but since then my milk's been poor. We never thought of that. It's been right worrying the last couple o' days.'

'Where are you making for?'

'London, 'less Stan finds work anywhere on the way.'

'Got anywhere to stay tonight?'

Their silence answered her. 'Come with me,' Lil said to the man. 'Stan, is it?'

'Stan Bewley. We're no' looking for charity, missus.'

'Don't worry. I don't give anything for nothing.'

She led the way out of the back of the café. The back yard was small, and cluttered with broken boxes and discarded cartons. Two chairs, one with a broken leg and the other with its back splintered, lay drunkenly on their sides. The fence had collapsed inwards.

'The place is a mess, no need to tell me that,' Lil said. She kicked disparagingly at a pile of black droppings. 'Blasted sheep get in now the fence is down.'

At the bottom of the untended garden there was a long

wooden van.

'Came from a circus,' Lil said. 'Used to belong to the trapeze act. I let it out to casual farm workers when the harvest's on. Not much of a place, but it's a roof and there's a couple of bunk beds. There's a cold water tap you can use in the outside lavatory.'

'We couldn't pay more'n a couple o' bob,' Stan said.

'Who said anything about money? Clean up the yard for me. Mend the fence. I don't know whether those chairs could be saved. It'd be worth more than a night's lodging to me if they could. Take it or leave it.'

'We'll take it, at least for tonight.'

'I'll expect a day's work out of you tomorrow, mind. I'll throw in your food, of course.'

They were still there at the end of the week. The yard was tidy, the fence was mended, the chairs were back in use; Stan's bowed shoulders had straightened and there was colour in Ethel's face. Her flow of milk had improved and the baby seemed to be thriving.

'I'd keep you on permanent,' Lil said. 'But my helper will be back from holiday next week and the profits won't stand two extra.'

'I canna work for nothin', not even wi' food and lodging,' Stan said.

'I'm not asking you to. You can leave Ethel here while you go south, if you like. It's not much of a place, but it's better for her than tramping the road.'

'I'll put it to her,' Stan said. 'She'll mebbe not want to stay, wi'out me, not knowing where I was.'

Lil said nothing. She had already taken in Ethel's weak dependence on her husband and guessed that Stan had tried to leave her behind in her home town while he travelled in search of work and had been defeated by her tears.

'Tomorrow's Sunday,' Lil said. 'Better stay till then. We might get a bit of extra custom tonight.'

It was ten o'clock at night and they were on the verge of closing when the first of the cars zoomed into the dusty pull-in: a red sports car driven by a dark-haired young man with a girl beside him and another young man perched on the back of the seat between them.

'Bangers and mash for nine, Lily,' the driver of the car called out.

'I'm just closing, Mr Pemberley,' Lil grumbled.

The girl unwound a scarf from her head and followed him into the café, trailing it carelessly in the dust behind her, her other hand pushing the waves of her blonde hair back into place.

'Don't be a spoilsport, Lil,' she said. 'Piggy and Brian and Fleur are right behind us and we bet them we'd get here first and have the sausages sizzling in the pan before they'd cleared Bloggs' Corner. Come on, look lively, there's a darling. And put the kettle on for tea as well.'

Ethel had left the baby in the battered perambulator in a corner of the café while she and Stan cleared up in the kitchen. The girl swooped on it, her attention distracted by this novelty.

'I say, Lil, you've been holding out on us! When did you have this?'

'Don't be silly, Miss Marigold. You know very well it can't be mine. It's a little girl belonging to some people who've been helping me out this week while Maggie's away. They'll be off tomorrow, poor things, walking down to London to look for work.'

'How absolutely ghastly! Isn't the baby sweet? Can I pick her up?'

'That you can't. Go and sit down and behave yourselves, the lot of you.'

'If we do, can we have our bangers and mash?'

'I suppose so. But I won't have you hanging around until midnight. I've been working since six o'clock this morning.'

'Are your poor old feet killing you, darling? I'll come behind the counter and help you.'

'Oh, no, you won't! You're more trouble than you're worth. Sit down and keep your friends in order. Here come the rest of them by the look of it.'

'Quick, quick, Lil – sausages in the pan or we lose our bet.'

When Ethel looked out of the kitchen the café was full of young people, all talking at the tops of their high, assured voices, the young men in sports jackets or blazers, the girls in summer frocks, their lips and fingertips brilliantly painted, their hair waved and curled.

'They turn up every now and again on a Saturday night,' Lil explained. 'It's a craze with them. As long as they don't put off my regulars I humour them.'

She was busy with the frying pan as she spoke, the sausages already beginning to sizzle.

'The girl – the first one who came in – is Miss Marigold Berringer. I was in service in her dad's house before I married Bert, so I've known her since she was a baby. She's engaged to marry the young chap with the sports car, if he doesn't kill the pair of them before they can get to the altar. They're not a bad bunch. Silly, but there, what can you expect when they've never known what it is to want?'

Stan and Ethel, carrying plates round, found themselves being questioned by voices that seemed to come from all directions at once.

'You're not really *walking* to London?' Marigold demanded. 'Not actually walking all the way?'

'If we have to,' Stan said. He was bothered by the attention he and Ethel had attracted, not sure how to counter the open curiosity of these careless young people.

'We must *do* something,' Marigold said. She leaned her elbows on the table and propped her chin on her hands, her cheeks flushed, her hair ruffled, frowning heavily with concentration. 'Harry, darling, think of something. Can't we have a whip round? I've got ten bob I could spare.'

'Doesn't really solve the problem, does it? What the chap wants is a job – like thousands of others. You don't appreciate how bad the situation is, Marigold.'

'Yes, I do. I read the papers, too. I'll have to speak to Daddy. I say, Stan, what time are you leaving in the morning?'

'Straight after breakfast.' Her easy use of his Christian name threw Stan into even greater confusion.

'Don't go too early. I'm going to talk to my father about you ...' Her attention was claimed by the adjoining table.

'Marigold! Stop solving the unemployment problem and help us with the clues for the Tennis Club treasure hunt. They've got to be fairly difficult and rather rude.'

'But if we all know them beforehand ...'

'Committee Members aren't eligible to take part, so put your dirty little mind to work.'

Stan looked helplessly at Lil. Lil shrugged her shoulders. 'She may remember, and it may do some good, but I wouldn't count on it.'

Stan and Ethel were half a mile down the road the next morning when a car skidded to a halt in front of them.

'I told you I was going to speak to Daddy,' Marigold Berringer said reproachfully. 'I've sold him the idea of taking you on as a sort of odd-job man, Stan. Provided he likes the look of you, that is, and I don't see why he shouldn't. There's a horrid little cottage to go with the job and not much money, but if you're interested, turn right at the next junction, then up the drive at the big gates and Daddy will see you at twelve o'clock, after he's read the lesson in church. I promised I'd go and support him so I'll have to fly.'

Two hours later Stan and Ethel were looking over the cottage that went with the job on Colonel Berringer's estate.

'It feels damp,' Stan said.

'It's a roof,' Ethel replied. 'And it's all ours, not sharing wi' anyone.'

She looked out at the trees which crowded round and shivered.

'Lonely, isn't it?'

'We don't have to take it. The job's not what I really want – more rough gardening and labouring than carpentry.'

'It's work,' Ethel said quickly. 'You'll be gettin' a wage. And we canna turn it down, not after they've been so kind to us.'

'If they'd really wanted to do us a kindness one of that bunch in the café last night could've offered to run me down to Watford so's I could have taken up the job my cousin told me about.'

'Leavin' me behind?'

'Lil would have kept you for a week or two,' Stan said patiently. 'I'd have sent for you soon as I'd got the fare together.'

‘I couldn’t ha’ travelled on my own,’ Ethel said with conviction.

Stan gave up, defeated by a mentality that could face the rigours of a walk hundreds of miles long, but not a train journey alone.

‘We’re stuck wi’ it now,’ he said. ‘Have to mak’ the best of it, I suppose.’

Chapter Three

There was silence in the town. Ben no longer woke in the morning to the sound of studded boots ringing on the stones outside. On the river bank the tall cranes stood unmoving, there was no clang of metal plates, no ring of hammers, and there were no teeth-chattering drills, no white-hot rivets flying through the air, no cheerful shouts from high on the keel to the dock below. The turgid water slurped against the empty berths, the silt gathered, the metal began to rust.

The slow days became weeks, the weeks became months and the months turned into hopeless, workless years. The men gathered in groups on street corners, talkative in the early days, but more apathetic with every week that went by and hopes of a re-opening of the shipyard faded. They exchanged a few laconic words and leaned against the wall, hands in their pockets, puffing on cigarettes laboriously put together from the shredded ends of previous smokes.

When the pubs opened the men who had the price of a drink in their pockets moved towards the doors and those who could not raise enough for half a pint hunched their shoulders and looked indifferent.

Andrew Harcourt, with a wife and three children still at school, could rarely afford the warmth and company inside the Black Bull, and it went against the grain to accept a treat from a mate who was better off when he knew he was unlikely to be able to stand a round even on the day he drew his dole. But he did sink his pride and accept on the day that Fred Foxley won a pigeon race and received his prize money.

'Ten shillin'!' Fred said. 'I've given five to Ada and I'm sore in need of a bit o' grain for the birds, but there's enough for a pint for you an' me, Andy. How about a game o' dominoes?'

Someone had bought a newspaper and was reading it slowly. After he had finished with it he would pass it on.

'Lot of talk about the hunger marches,' Fred commented.

'Organized by a bunch o' Commies,' Andrew said. 'We dinna want to get mixed up wi' them.'

'Only people tryin' to get owt done,' another man put in.

'Mayor Thompson's been speaking up for us and o' course there's our Ellen.'

There was a brief flicker of interest, a reluctant smile, at the thought of red-headed Ellen Wilkinson, who had just become Jarrow's Member of Parliament.

'She's a bonny fighter, I'll give her that,' Fred conceded.

'Aye, but it's all words,' Andrew said.

They played almost in silence after that, their eyes fixed on the black oblongs and coloured dots, big, skilful hands moving the dominoes with unexpected deftness.

At last Fred leaned back in his chair, admitting defeat.

'You play a canny game, Andy,' he said. 'Will you try another?'

Andrew glanced at the clock on the wall and reluctantly drained the final mouthful of the beer he had nursed through the last half hour.

'Nay, I'm off home,' he said. 'Bess has a job she wants me to do.'

When Andrew reached home, Bess was still at the ironing board.

'I've all but finished,' she said. She smoothed the flat iron over a pillow slip edged with coarse cotton lace and added it to the pile of clean washing on the table. With careful hands she folded it all up in a clean sheet.

'There! That's for Mrs Duncan. Put it in bottom of the barrow and cover it up wi' a bit o' sackin', 'gainst prying eyes. An' dinna come away wi'out she gives you the money. I've told you the way she served young Ben last week. Seven an' sixpence that woman owes me for the two weeks. Tak' the boy wi' you and face her out wi' it.'

She looked with disfavour at Ben. His bony wrists stuck out of the worn cuffs of his jacket. Skinny as a starveling, for all he'd got the appetite of an elephant, and useless when it came to demanding what was due to Bessie for her work even though he was nearly nine years old.

'Neither of my girls would have let themselves be put off the way he were,' she said bitterly.

'I'll see to it,' Andrew said, not relishing his use as an errand boy but recognizing the necessity of collecting the debt that was due.

There was a knock on the back door. Andrew and Bess looked at one another.

'Go out the front,' Bess said urgently.

Andrew picked up the unwieldy bundle, but before he could escape the latch was lifted and a man walked in.

'I didn't hear mysel' ask you in, Mr Baxcombe,' Bess said.

With some presence of mind, she placed her bulky body between the man and Andrew.

'I could have sworn I heard you,' Mr Baxcombe said. He was short and thin, with restless eyes and a greasy lock of hair which was constantly falling into his eyes and being tossed back.

'Good day to you, Mrs Harcourt, and to you, too, Mr Harcourt. By, man, you've an awkward load there. Let me give you a hand.'

'It's just a bit o' clean washing Andrew was about to tak' upstairs,' Bessie said quickly. 'Get away out from under my feet, Andy.'

She was too late; Mr Baxcombe had twitched back the covering sheet.

'Fine lace-trimmed linen you have there, Mrs Harcourt.'

'I was in service afore I married first time,' Bessie said quickly. 'I'd some good things given me.'

'Embroidered table-cloths, too!' Mr Baxcombe said admiringly. 'And what's this? A night-dress you can fair see through! Eh, man you must think you're going to bed with the Queen when you see your missus dressed up i' that.'

'That's enough!'

Andrew put the disordered bundle down on the table and Ben shrank farther into the corner, frightened by the white line of anger round his father's mouth.

'It is an' all! You've been workin', Mrs Harcourt. Workin' and not declarin' your earnings. There's penalties for that, y' know. I'll have to report it to the Unemployment Assistance Board.'

'Report away! I canna declare what I havena' had,' Bessie said triumphantly. 'I've not been paid for that load o' washin'. You can write it down at three-an'-sixpence, though I'd think shame to be so petty mysel'.'

'An' what about the previous weeks?'

'Wha' previous weeks?'

'Fine washing's been seen on your line for the past month or more, Mrs Harcourt.'

'Oh, has it so? There's few round here'd know good from bad. I did a wee bit washin' for a lady this week and this week only. She'll mebbe ha' some for me next week, she'll mebbe not. If she does I'll let you know. A cryin' shame it'd be if the Government paid out a penny piece more'n was owed us.'

With her hands on her hips, flushed and combative, she faced the minor official from the Unemployment Assistance Board, while Andrew stood by rigid and silent, knowing that this was a fight best left to Bess.

Mr Baxcombe looked away uneasily and his eye fell on the jam jar full of coppers Bess kept by the side of the kitchen clock. He picked it up and weighed it in his hand.

'There's about five shilling' in there,' Bess said quickly. 'Rent money! Wi' the three-an'-sixpence I'll get for the washin' I'll just ha' enough. You'll not call that savings, I hope!'

Mr Baxcombe put down the jar and turned away. As he brushed past Andrew he caught the smell of beer and remarked, 'You can still find money for drink, it seems.'

Andrew's hand shot out. He caught hold of the front of the other man's coat and held him fast, forcing him to look up into Andrew's face.

'I was treated by a mate,' he said. 'No, I canna' find money for drink! Nor I canna' find money for food either! Nor for clothes! Stand up, Ben. Stand up, and let the man see your fine tweed suit.'

Ben scrambled to his feet and stood, awkward and ashamed, pulling at the sleeves of his jacket. His trousers, cobbled up roughly from an old pair of his father's, were hoisted up by braces with no stretch left in the elastic and held in at the waist by a belt from a woman's frock.

'These are hard times,' Mr Baxcombe said weakly. 'I'm doin' no more than my duty.'

Andrew made a noise of contempt and derision and let him go.

'Duty! Aye, well, you've found what you came for, now get out of my house!'

They watched him go, discomforted for the moment, but already putting it behind him; it was no more than the most recent of many such encounters and one which, on the whole, he could put down on the credit side, since the report he had been given had proved to be correct and he would be saving the Assistance Board some few shillings this week, with the possibility of more to come if Bessie Harcourt went on taking in washing.

'Tie up the bundle and tak' it round to Mrs Duncan,' Bess ordered Andrew. 'And mind you get the full seven-an'-sixpence out o' her! That way we'll still be a few bob to the good in spite of interferin' busybodies!'

When the possibility of a march from Jarrow to London began to be talked about Andrew held off at first, until he learned that it was to be for Jarrow men only, organized and run by the town itself, not by the National Unemployed Workers' Movement, which had already staged several hunger marches.

'It's to be kept small,' he told Bessie. 'Two hundred men, no more.'

'You'll not go,' she said.

'I will if I'm asked.'

Bess said no more, but her opposition was unceasing until the very day that the marchers set out.

It was a Monday morning, the fifth of October 1936. Andrew was whistling as he laid out his shaving tackle at the kitchen sink and propped up the cracked mirror in a better light. Bessie thumped the cups and plates down on the table in silent frustration at having her wishes ignored, but she had made one concession to the long march that her husband faced.

'I've got you a boiled egg to your breakfast,' she said. She began hacking at the loaf of bread, cutting off thick slices and spreading them with margarine. The three children kept quiet, all of them knowing better than to provoke Bess while she was steaming for a fight. Ben took one of the slices of bread and began stuffing it in his mouth. With any luck, if he got it down quickly, he might get a second one. The tea in his mug, dark brown and sweetened by condensed milk, was too hot to drink.

'If you've not finished scraping your chin in two minutes I'll eat your egg mysel',' Bessie said to Andrew.

He wiped his chin with the towel, hung it behind the back door and tipped his shaving water down the sink. As he seated himself at the table he looked brighter and more alert than he had for months.

'Always the same,' Bessie grumbled. 'Men go off an' have the fun while the women stay at 'ome.'

'It'll no' be fun,' Andrew said patiently. 'It'll be a hard slog.'

'Aye, you'll walk your boots through, no doubt.'

'We'll mend them as we go. It's all organized. Somewhere to sleep every night, though it'll be the bare floor in some places.'

Ben slid his hand towards the bread board, but Phyllis was watching him.

'Ma! Ben's takin' ano'er slice!'

He got a smart rap on the knuckles with the bread knife.

'You've had your breakfast, y' greedy wee pig. Wash your face and get along to school.'

'I'm going to see Dad set off,' Ben said quickly.

'Skiving off fro' school, is it? I thought you was so keen on the education?'

'Dad?'

Ben looked at his father imploringly and Andrew nodded.

'It's not ev'ry day you can see a bit o' history bein' made,' he said.

'History!' Bess's tone was scathing, but for all that she put on her hat and buttoned her coat round her and went down to the Town Hall to see the men lined up for review by the Mayor.

They were as smart as they could manage: flat caps and mufflers and boots mended and polished, with rolled waterproof capes over their shoulders; but there were few among them who looked as if they had the stamina to walk three hundred miles.

'Naff heads!' Bessie muttered, but there was something about the men's look of steady determination that silenced the most obstinate critic.

The long line set off, with the Mayor and councillors and Ellen Wilkinson, her red hair blazing, to set them on their way. Ben waited for his father to pass, then he ran out from the crowd on the pavement and walked by his side. Andrew took his hand and squeezed it in a rare expression of affection, but when they reached the edge of the town he told the boy to leave.

'I could come all the way,' Ben pleaded. 'I could, Dad!'

'It's no' an outin' for bairns,' Andrew replied and, seeing the moment of sympathy between them slipping away, Ben turned back.

The families followed the progress of the march through the reports in the daily papers, even Bess gradually beginning to feel proud of the interest it was arousing and the admiring accounts about the good organization and discipline behind the men's effort. Far more than other hunger marches, this Jarrow Crusade seemed to touch the imagination of the nation, and efforts were made to help them which cut across all the barriers of class and politics. In Leicester the Co-operative Society's boot repairers sat up all night to repair the men's battered boots; in Harrogate the officers of the Territorial Army looked after their welfare; in Leeds the owner of the local newspaper provided a free meal – with beer; and in Barnsley the municipal baths were thrown open to the marchers.

They slept in drill halls, and schools, and casual wards, with usually nothing to lie on but the bare floor; the field kitchens provided by the Boy Scouts went ahead and prepared a mid-day meal and if the weather was fine they sat down for a blessed rest while they ate it; on wet days they ate standing, huddled under their mackintosh capes.

They arrived in London on the third of November, in soaking rain, and the petition they carried was presented to Parliament the following day. Andrew told his family about it when he arrived home by train on the fifth.

'We thought it'd be more of a ceremony,' he admitted. 'Still, we did it, that's what counts. And there was a fine big meeting wi' a bunch of M.P.s – all parties, mind you, Tories as well as Liberals and Labour. Mayor Thompson, he told them straight. He held up his chain of office for them all to see. The links are made like a cable, wi' an anchor for the badge. "Symbols in gold", he said, "of the cables and anchors of the thousand ships we built in Jarrow." He told them as 'ow it was owin' to National Shipbuilders Security that Jarrow shipyard was closed. "Ships for Britain's food and her defence will be made in that famous yard no more," he said. "God grant the time may not come when you Members of Parliament will 'ave need to regret that you allowed the scrapping of this great national asset in the interest of the private profit of a bank's shareholders." Aye, he told 'em. It were a bonny speech.'

'Fine speeches fill no bellies,' Bess said. 'What d'you think to this steelworks there's talk about?'

'Less than the newspapers do. It'll be fine, if it comes off, but it'll give no more'n a few jobs.'

He was looking well, fitter than he had for a long time, with an air of purpose about him and a vigour that came from long hours of exercise in the open air and a feeling of having achieved something, compared with the long, hopeless hours of boredom. It was a feeling of well-being that lasted until he went to collect the next week's dole money.

When he came back the old look of despair was back on his face. He put the money down on the kitchen table. Bessie stared at it.

'Is that all?' she asked.

'Aye. They stopped our money for every day we was away on the march. We weren't holdin' oursel's available for work, they said. Work! What work? There is no bloody work!'

Chapter Four

The steelworks that had been promised to Jarrow proved to be no more than a small works making tubes giving employment to some eight hundred men and boys, a far cry from the great integrated works which had been envisaged. Another year dragged by, with no work for Andrew or men like him, and the situation in the Harcourt family was not eased when Elsie found a job, only to have the amount of her wages docked from the allowance paid to Andrew.

Occasionally Bess heard from her sister, usually a scrawled single sheet of lined paper full of complaints about the miseries of living in the country.

'Moan, moan, moan – an' she's got a house to hersel' and her man's in a steady job. There's no satisfyin' some,' Bessie said, lifting up the lid of the grate and stuffing Ethel's latest note into the fire. 'Are you goin' to sit there all day warmin' yoursel', Andrew? I could do wi' a load o' firewood if you'd get off your backside and go lookin' for it.'

Andrew went out without a word, too dispirited to argue. He seemed to have shrunk in the last year. Ben noticed it; or was it only that Ben himself continued to grow like an undernourished weed seeking the sun?

Nineteen thirty-eight brought a change and though they all deplored the reason for it with their lips, in their hearts they were thankful that the international situation demanded a British rearmament programme. Andrew haunted the Labour Exchange and the shipyard gates, driven by the necessity to be on the spot in case he might be wanted.

They were all in the kitchen on the afternoon when he came back and blurted out, 'I've bin taken on at Maxton's!'

'Y' old job?' Bess asked.

'Aye. Riveter. I start Monday.'

Ben's stomach churned with a mixture of fright and embarrassment as he saw his father's face begin to work. Andrew sat down heavily at the table and put his head down on his folded arms. Phyllis giggled. Automatically, Ben put his hand under the table and gave her a vicious pinch.

'Gi' up, y' silly ha'p'orth,' Bessie said. She stood up and touched Andrew briefly and awkwardly on the shoulder. 'I'll mak' a cup o' tea.'

Knowing that his father was back in work gave Ben the courage to bring up something that he knew was going to be unpopular.

'My teacher wants me to tak' scholarship exam,' he said.

He saw his father begin to turn the idea over in his mind, but Bess's reaction was swift.

'You can put tha' idea right out o' your mind,' she said. 'Addlin' your brain wi' learnin'. It's no' for the likes of us. An' I'll no' keep you at school 'til you're sixteen. If there's work to be had you'll start at fourteen, same as my two girls.'

'It'll do no harm to let lad tak' exam,' Andrew said. 'As for stayin' on at school, we'll see about that if 'e gets through – which I doubt.'

Ben took the examination and was successful, but he was not allowed to take up the place at secondary school which he had won, and that for a reason that filled him with fury.

'You'll know soon enough, so I may as well tell you,' Bess said. 'There's another bairn on the way.' Her lips twisted in bitter anger. 'You'd have thought I'd be safe enough, at my age. I'm fair disgusted about it. So, there'll be no more talk o' scholarships and uniforms and no wages comin' in 'til you're turned sixteen years. Thank God your father's in work and Phyllis of an age to start.'

'I don't know who'd employ her,' Ben said rudely.

'She's got a place in the tobacconist's that's re-openin' near docks. Aye, both my girls will be earnin'. But I'll no' spend their wages on turnin' you into a gentleman, and that's flat!'

She was feeling miserably unwell and angry at having been

'caught'. It was not going to be an easy pregnancy, not when she was over forty. She seized on Ben's wish to progress to higher education and made an issue of it, chivvying Andrew relentlessly until he, already feeling guilty because their celebration of his return to work had given her an unwanted child, and half persuaded that extra schooling was a waste of time for a working class lad, wrote a laborious letter to Ben's headmaster refusing permission for his son to take the place he had gained.

Four months later, too late to be of any benefit to Ben, Bess gave birth prematurely to a baby boy who did not survive. To Ben, advancing uneasily towards puberty, it seemed both offensive and wildly unfair that his father and stepmother should have conceived a child at their ages, and that he should have been robbed of his chance in life by a dead baby. A typical bit of woman's business, it seemed to Ben, involving messy, mysterious sex and unfulfilled promises.

He took no account of Bess's genuine, if short-lived, grief over the loss of her baby. She had said she didn't want it, so what call was there for her to snivel because it hadn't lived? Too young and ignorant to comprehend the frustration of an abortive birth, Ben wrote her off as a hypocrite. In all the years since his father's remarriage he had never reconciled himself to his stepmother, shrugging off her rough attempts at kindness. He knew himself to be superior to either of her daughters. Phyllis, in particular, with her sniffling nose and sneaky ways filled him with loathing.

It was a dislike that turned to black hate when she began to make sexual advances to him. He was twelve years old and well grown for his age, for all his unhealthy skinniness, and Phyllis was fourteen. Ben already knew that she had a reputation at school for letting the boys touch her in an unseemly way. One boy had boasted of having handled her breasts and Ben gave him a black eye for it, since any slur on Phyllis was a slur on the family.

They were alone in the house one Saturday afternoon, Ben reading a book and Phyllis darning a pair of stockings ready for the start of her new job the following week, when she snuggled up to him and put her hand on his leg. Without looking up from his book, Ben shoved her away, but Phyllis persisted, sliding her hand up his thigh in a way that gave him an unpleasant thrill.

'Gi's a go, Ben,' she whispered.

'Don' know what you mean,' Ben said, obstinately looking down at the printed page.

'Yes y' do. Go on. There's no one 'ere bu' us. I won' tell.'

Her fingers moved insinuatingly against his crutch. Ben, sickened and yet excited by a stirring of sexual awakening, kept still for a moment, then his disgust overcame his curiosity and he flung her hand away.

'Silly li'l bugger. Bet y' don' even know 'ow to ge' it up,' Phyllis taunted.

'Yes, I do!' Ben said quickly, though the truth was that the working of this part of his body had only recently begun to dawn on him.

'Show me then.'

'I wouldn't touch you with a fifty foot barge pole, and I wouldn't let you touch me neither,' Ben said. 'Dirty cow. I know what you bin doin' with the other boys. They can 'ave you, I don't want you. Go and find someone of your own sort.'

He flung out of the house, walking blindly along the dingy streets in an effort to outdistance the disturbance she had caused him.

But Phyllis had her revenge. Later that evening, Bess fetched Ben a ringing blow across the head.

'I'll thank you to leave my Phyllis alone,' she said. 'Bin tryin' to touch her up, haven't you? She told me all about it. Filthy little swine. I'll have no goings on o' that sort under my roof, and you scarce out o' your cradle! I'll tell y' father, that's what I'll do!'

To Ben's bitter shame, Andrew also spoke to him. Ben tried to explain what had really happened, and he knew that his father believed him.

'Best keep out of 'er way,' Andrew said. He hesitated. 'Women,' he said. 'They're funny cattle.'

In September 1939, when the war they had all expected the previous year finally broke out, it brought a separation that was as welcome to Ben as it was to his stepmother.

'Evacuation,' she said. 'They're talkin' about it for all the bairns. What do you say to sendin' Ben to stay wi' our Ethel?'

'I want to go wi' my mates,' Ben said.

'You'd no' be wi' your mates if you'd gone to that fancy school you wanted so much,' Bess pointed out. 'I'd as soon send you to Ethel as to a stranger. There'll be an allowance paid and why shouldn't Ethel have it? It'll be welcome, from all I hear. She was aye a feckless lass and Stan's not progressed in the world, stuck away in that backwater.'

Money was easier now, with Andrew and both the girls working. Bess decided to deliver Ben herself and pay her first visit to her sister since Ethel and Stan had left home in 1933.

It was a journey that involved a train and two buses, and then a walk down a lonely lane that made Bess look back over her shoulder uneasily.

'I'd 've gone melancholy mad if I'd bin forced to live 'ere,' she said. 'No wonder Ethel's always got the megrims when she writes.'

She found her sister in floods of tears.

'By, lass, you're not still at it, are you?' she asked. 'You were cryin' when we parted and you're cryin' still, seemingly. Wha' ails you?'

'Stan, Stan! He's joined up!'

'He never 'as! If that don' beat all!'

'He always hated it 'ere, blamed me for makin' 'im stay. I'll no' stop in this cottage on my own, that I won't. Tak' me back to Jarrow wi' you, Bessie!'

'Wha' about our Ben? After me bringin' 'im all the way from Jarrow? He'll be company for you, another face about the place.'

'He's naught but a lad,' Ethel said scornfully.

'Ben! Go outside and play wi' your little cousin while I talk wi' your aunt,' Bess ordered.

'She's no' my cousin and yon woman's no' my aunt,' Ben muttered.

Predictably, that remark brought Bessie's heavy hand round his ears. Still smarting, he wandered out into the small garden. Hemmed in by dark trees, the little cottage seemed to crouch close to the ground, overwhelmed by the heaviness of the surrounding greenery. In one corner a little girl was playing, singing a wordless song to herself as she piled up stones to outline the walls of her imaginary house. Josie Bewley was six years old, not a pretty child, with the sharp features of her mother and the sandy colouring of her father, but she was small and friendly and she seemed pleased to see Ben.

'Are you my cousin Ben what's coming to live with me?' she asked.

'I s'pose so,' Ben said, reluctantly accepting the relationship everyone seemed determined to thrust on him.

'I'm six. I go to school, but the school's shut up because there's a war on. You'll go to my school, too, but you'll be with the big boys.'

A car came bumping down the rutted track and drew up at the gate. A tall, blonde woman wearing slacks and a sweater got out.

'Hello, Josie. Is your mother inside?' she asked.

'Yes, an' my Auntie Bessie. This is my cousin, Ben, who's coming to live with me. Can Nicola come and play?'

'Not today, darling. Hello, Ben. I heard you were joining us.'

Her smile as she passed them got no response from Ben except a long stare. 'Who's she?' he asked Josie.

'She's called Mrs Pemberley and she lives near here an' she's got a little girl called Nicola, but she's only four.'

Inside the cottage Marigold Pemberley was unfolding her plans for running the war in her small corner of England.

'Do stop crying, Ethel! My husband's gone into the Navy, too, but I don't intend to sit around moping. I've got a marvellous scheme for helping the war effort. Now, you don't want to stay in this cottage on your own, do you?'

'I wan' to go home!' Ethel wailed.

'Well, I must say I think that would be foolish, if you mean you want to go back to Tyneside. Don't you agree, Mrs Harcourt?'

'I dunno where she'd go,' Bessie said frankly. 'It'd mean takin' Ben back, for one thing, and with him and my two girls, an' me an' Andrew in the house, there's no room for Ethel and the little 'un.'

'Exactly. Now do listen, Ethel, while I explain my idea. I'm going to close up my house and come back to live with Daddy at the Hall. We're going to run it as a hostel for Land Girls.'

'Where does Ethel come in?' Bess inquired.

'I want her to live in at the Hall and help me to run it. I've persuaded dear old Lil to close her café and come and do the catering. What do you say, Ethel? You'll be doing something useful to help defeat Hitler and you certainly won't be lonely.'

'I'll think about it,' Ethel said. 'I must ask Stan. What about the bairns?'

'Plenty of room for them. You'll all fit into the old kitchen quarters.'

'Long way for them to go to school,' Ethel said, obstinately determined not to be talked into the scheme too quickly.

'About half a mile farther than it is from here. The little boy can see Josie gets there and back safely.'

'S'pose it might be all right,' Ethel admitted.

'My sister'll think it over and let you know,' Bessie said.

Marigold Pemberley looked dissatisfied, but since it seemed that she was not going to persuade Ethel to fall in with her plans on the spot, she prepared to leave them to discuss it between themselves.

'Do try to talk her into it, Mrs Harcourt,' she said to Bessie. 'After all, I really can't leave her here to be miserable and I can't see any other answer.'

As soon as the door had closed behind Marigold Bessie said, 'Proper Lady o' the Manor, isn't she?'

'It was her that got Stan the job in first place,' Ethel said. 'She's into everythin' – Women's Institute, church flowers, cricket teas, runnin' the fête.'

'Aye, I could see she was the managin' sort. Now, I'll tell you something, hinny. You'll no' go up to that Hall of hers wi'out she pays you a wage. She'll have you turned into an unpaid skivvy, wi'out you stick up for y'sel'. Mind wha' I say, now.'

'I s'pose I'll have to do it,' Ethel muttered.

'It's no' such a bad scheme,' Bess admitted. 'There'll be a bit o' life about, which is more than you can say for this God-forsaken corner.'

It took a week or two to arrange, but by the time the village school re-opened Ethel and the two children had moved into Berringer Hall.

His first sight of the Hall gave Ben a jolt. It was not so much its size, though it was far and away the biggest house he had ever seen, nor its grandeur, nor its fine surroundings; it was something more than that. It gave him the same feeling as he had experienced once when he had heard an unaccompanied male choir singing a tune which had touched his Welsh blood: a thrill in the pit of his stomach which spread out through his body in tingling waves, right down to his toes and fingertips.

It had been built in the mid-eighteenth century in a severely classical style and at that time had been considered no more than a modest country house for a gentleman. Now, with the stone weathered to shades of grey and cream, and a patina of golden lichen, the symmetry of its façade softened by a blaze of Virginia creeper, it was thought of as a gem of domestic architecture.

Ben, Ethel and Josie had approached it from the rear, so that his first view of it was from the garden side. Ben thought the smooth green lawns, the rectangular pool which reflected the house, and the clipped yew hedges dull, for a garden, and yet even to his untutored eye there was an essential rightness about it as a setting for the house.

'What's it like from the front?' he asked.

'I've never been roun' there,' Ethel admitted. 'I always come up the garden path and go in side entrance.'

Ben stared at her incredulously, unable to fathom a mind so lacking in curiosity.

'I'm going to have a look,' he said, and darted off before Ethel could hold him back.

The front was grander than the back. There was a gravel drive sweeping up to the front door, three shallow, semicircular steps, and a pillared portico. Facing the house was another lawn and, in the centre of it, an ancient cedar tree, its branches almost touching the ground.

The sound of uneven footsteps on the gravel behind him made Ben look round warily. A tall, middle-aged man with grey hair and a white moustache was coming towards him. He was very upright, but with a stiffness in one leg which caused it to drag a little. He was carrying a gun in one hand and a couple of dead rabbits in the other.

'I don't know you, young fellow. What's your name?' he asked.

'Ben Harcourt.'

'Harcourt? That's not a local name.'

'I've come to live with me Aunt Ethel, 'cos o' the war.'

'Ethel Bewley? My daughter tells me she's persuaded Ethel to come up to the Hall to give us a hand, so you'll be living here, will you?'

'Seemingly. Are you the gaffer?'

'That about describes me,' the man admitted gravely. 'I'm Colonel Berringer.'

'You in the Army?'

'I was. Caught a Blighty one in the last war. They won't let me into this scrap. Still, I dare say I can make myself useful, if only by turning out a bit of extra food. How old are you, boy?'

'Twelve.'

'Old enough to do your bit. Know anything about gardening?'

'No.'

'No reason why you shouldn't learn. We always used to start the gardener's boys off at twelve, I remember.'

'If you want me to work, you'll 'ave to pay me,' Ben stated.

'Fair enough. We'll discuss terms when we see how much time you can give me. What are you doing round the front of the house?'

'Lookin' at it.'

'Fine old place, isn't it? Not what it was, of course. Can't keep it up like we did in the old days. Still, I wouldn't like to see one of Hitler's thugs living in it.'

An agitated voice was heard calling, 'Ben, Ben!'

'That's me Aunt Ethel,' Ben said, not moving. 'She's not really my aunt at all and that bairn o' hers is no' my cousin.'

'Really? All the same, you'd better go. She's probably anxious to know where you are.'

Ben gathered the spittle into his mouth and spat satisfyingly on to the gravel. Looking up, he caught the look of shock on Colonel Berringer's face and was gratified.

'I'll go when I'm good an' ready,' he said.

'You'll go when I tell you. Quick march!'

The rasp in his voice took Ben by surprise. Hunching his shoulders he sauntered towards the side of the house. He did not know how accurately Colonel Berringer read his thoughts as he walked away, obedient but taking his time about it. A Bolshie young devil, but good material was the Colonel's summing up. He had liked the way Ben had held up his head and looked him in the eye when he spoke. He was stirred by an old regret that he had never had a son, that his daughter's only child was a girl. Not that Colonel Berringer would have exchanged Nicola for all the Ben Harcourts in the world. Still, it would be good to have a boy about the place.

Ben found Ethel flustered, but not displeased by the arrangements that had been made for them in the big house. She and Lil had the kitchen, the scullery, the former butler's pantry and the housekeeper's room between them. The only drawback was that all their bedrooms were up on the third floor and Ethel, determined to find something wrong, insisted that she was worried in case Josie woke up and wanted her while she was still downstairs.

Ben had a small attic bedroom to himself. He looked out of the high window over the limitless expanse of empty countryside and was suddenly stricken by homesickness. At that moment he would have given anything to be back in crowded, dirty Jarrow. He wanted the streets he knew, the friends he had left behind. He would have welcomed a sight of Bessie, even of Phyllis or Elsie. Above all, he wanted his father.

His lips quivered. Sitting down on the narrow iron bedstead he pushed his knuckles into his eyes, telling himself that men did not cry. Perhaps his dad had cried when his mam had died, but Ben had not known about it. He had only once seen his dad break down, that time when he had just got his job back. Ben had been embarrassed, but remembering it now he understood the inexpressible relief that had overcome Andrew. It made Ben feel closer to his father than ever before, but it also made him miss him more.

'Have you got a stomach ache?' a small voice asked in an interested way.

Ben looked up, blinking furiously. She was a little brown-haired thing, even younger than Josie. She was watching him with her head tilted on one side, her face screwed up in sympathy.

'No,' he said curtly.

'Did you fall over and cut yourself?'

'No.'

'Where does it hurt, poor boy? Shall I kiss it better?'

'I don' like it here. I wanna go home. I wan' my Dad!'

'You can have my handkerchief, if you like.'

Ben took the tiny scrap of linen and blew his nose. She climbed up on the bed beside him, kneeling by his side, put both arms round his neck and planted a smacking, wet kiss on his cheek. Ben pushed her away, but not roughly, and felt obscurely comforted.

'Who are you?' he asked.

'My name is ...' she paused and took a deep breath, '... Nicola Rosemary Hope Pemberley.'

'Wha' a mouthful! Is your ma that Mrs Pemberley that made us all come an' live here?'

'Yes, we're all going to live with Grand-dad until Daddy comes home from the war. My daddy's in the Royal Navy. He's got gold rings on his sleeve and he goes to sea in a big ship. What does your daddy do?'

'He builds the ships,' Ben said.

'Did he build my daddy's ship?'

'He might a' done,' Ben said cautiously. 'He puts in all the rivets that hold the ship together.'

Nicola looked impressed. 'He must be very clever. Will you come downstairs and play with me now?'

New impressions crowded in on Ben. Space and greenness and clean air. Strange noises in the night. An owl hooting had him out of bed and ready for flight. There were squirrels in the woods and birds he had never seen before. When he sighted a fox he took it for granted that it was a dog. He discovered the art of removing warm eggs from beneath a hen and saw a cow milked for the first time. And he started school.

The school house was in the village, a good half-hour's walk even for Ben, but it took longer than that because he had to slow down for Josie's short legs. On the first day he was taunted about his strange accent and fought his tormentor in fierce, determined silence until they were separated by Miss Flanders, the schoolmistress. 'Ole Fanny Flanders', the older boys called her scornfully.

'We've a new schoolmaster starting next week, to take the place of Mr Smith, who's gone into the Army. I only hope Mr. Tredegar will be able to keep you in order,' she scolded them.

Ben and the other boy eyed one another surreptitiously and then grinned. Honours were about even. Ben was accepted.

When they assembled the following Monday morning Paul Tredegar was on the dais with Miss Flanders. They saw that he was short, barely as tall as she was, and the girls noticed his handsome head, the thick, waving brown hair and dark eyes, his finely chiselled features; it was not until he moved that they saw that he was crippled.

Paul registered the ripple of interest that went round as he limped forward. They were more open about it than a crowd of adults would have been and in some ways he was glad about that. As soon as he was alone with his class of older boys and girls he dealt characteristically with their morbid curiosity.

'You've noticed that I have a disability,' he said. 'I'll tell you about it to save you the trouble of asking questions. I have a diseased hip and a deformed foot. I was born like this. I had treatment as a child and an operation, but it didn't help much. It is sometimes painful. When it is, I am exceedingly bad-tempered. I'm warning you, don't play me up on one of my bad days.'

'Who's going to take us for games?' one of the boys asked.

'I am. I can't run, but I get around fairly fast, and I know as much about the rules of football as any man.'

'What were you doin' before you come 'ere, mister?' Ben asked.

'Call me "sir" or "Mr Tredegar". I was private tutor to a couple of rich boys whose parents have sent them to America for the duration. There was an opening here, replacing a man who was able to go off and fight, so I took it because it seeemed a useful thing to do. Right, that's enough about me. I see from the timetable that our first period is to be spent on English. The best way to find out how much you know of your native language is to get you to write me an essay.'

'What's an essay?' one of the girls asked.

'A composition,' Ben answered her, despising the question.

'Quite. A composition. And we'll take those two old faithful perennials, "What I did in my holidays" and "What I want to be when I grow up": you can take your choice. Who knows what a perennial is?'

'A flower that comes up every year,' someone supplied.

'Right. And these are two subjects that come up every year. See what you can do with them. Put your full name and your age at the top of the sheet, then the title you've chosen. Write neatly and watch your spelling.'

He gave them half an hour, quelling restlessness and whispers by a quick glare from his dark eyes, and used the time to examine the textbooks that were available to him. Old-fashioned, as he had expected, but then he was not required to give these children more than a basic education. A far cry from the two spoilt brats he'd had in his care for the last three years. He glanced round the room. Most of the heads were bent over their exercise books. Some of them seemed to be making heavy weather of it. The girl with her nose almost on the page ought to have her eyes examined. One boy appeared to be writing very little, the one who had asked him where he'd been before he came to the village. An alert, good-looking youngster, with a spark of intelligence in him. A pity if he turned out to be lazy.

Paul returned the exercise books the next day, scrawled over in red with corrections. He picked out one or two common mistakes and put them up on the blackboard, explaining the grammatical errors and faults in punctuation. Another time he would try to instil an idea of interesting narrative, but it had been a couple of dull titles he'd given them and they had done their plodding best with them. All except one boy. Paul's lips twitched as he looked down at the exercise book he had kept back. When they broke up at mid-morning he called Ben Harcourt to him.

'I see you attempted both subjects,' he said, opening the

book. 'I've given you two out of ten marks for neat writing, and I was tempted to award another one for originality. For terseness your two essays can hardly be beaten.'

Ben watched him warily. He had expected to be reprimanded, had even looked forward to the status it would give him in the class. This amused, almost conspiratorial attitude puzzled him. He looked down at the page without saying anything.

Under the heading, 'What I did in my holidays' he had written 'Nothing': under 'What I want to be when I grow up' there was again one word, 'Rich'.

Paul pulled another exercise book towards him. 'You did well in arithmetic,' he said. 'All these answers are correct.'

'I've done all tha' ole stuff before.'

'Then you're rather more advanced than the other boys of your age. You've come from a different school, haven't you?'

'Aye. Jarrow.'

'An interesting place. Who was the most famous man who ever lived at Jarrow?'

'Sir Charles Mark Palmer.'

'No! Long before his day.'

'Oh! Ven'rable Bede.'

'Precisely. The Venerable Bede. Learning, my lad! Learning! That's what Jarrow was famous for and will be long after its shipbuilding days are forgotten. I can't say you're a credit to its tradition when you turn out stuff like this. What do you know about the Jarrow March?'

'My dad was on it.'

'Then I may have met him. I was still an undergraduate in nineteen thirty-six and I turned out to help the marchers on their way.'

He tossed the sheet of paper scantily covered with Ben's handwriting across the desk.

'I can't let you get away with this, you know. Write me an account of what you remember of the Jarrow March. At least two sides of foolscap and I want it by the end of school tomorrow.'

He got what he demanded and read it with the mounting excitement of a teacher who has discovered a pupil with a good brain.

'Did anyone ever suggest you ought to go to a grammar school?' he asked.

'I passed scholarship, but I couldn't go,' Ben said.

Something of his bitterness showed in his face and Paul did not press for reasons. Poverty? Probably. That and sheer pigheaded prejudice against higher education.

'Why do you want to be rich?' he asked idly.

'So's I can buy a house like Berringer Hall.'

'You really do mean to fly high! What about your socialist principles?'

'I ain't got none.'

'What! Not even with the example of what the capitalists did to your father in front of your eyes? But I was forgetting, your ambition is to become a capitalist yourself. Are you prepared to work?'

'I'm going to work for Colonel Berringer, in the garden.'

Paul Tredegar looked impatient. 'I mean school work. I'm prepared to give you, and anyone else who shows promise, a bit of extra tutoring.'

He got a muttered admission from Ben that 'he wouldn't mind', but Paul had caught the flash of interest in the boy's eyes and recognized behind his ungracious manner the frustration of a clever child held back by his circumstances.

Paul's predecessor had been a married man, and his wife and baby were still occupying the house which Paul ought to have taken over. The school buildings included living quarters, but they were inhabited by Miss Flanders, who became flustered to the point of incoherence at the idea of sharing with an unmarried man. Paul was lodging, none too comfortably, in a village house when Marigold Pemberley descended on him and rearranged his life with an assumption of authority that tickled him even while he resented it.

'I've taken Ethel Bewley up to the Hall to live for the duration,' Marigold said. 'So her cottage is empty. You can move in any time. A *bit* isolated, but I don't suppose you will mind that, will you? I expect you'll be glad to get out of the village.'

'What will happen when Mr Bewley comes home on leave?' Paul inquired.

'Naturally he will join Ethel at the Hall,' Marigold said. 'You don't think he'll object, do you?'

She opened her eyes very wide, surprised at the idea, which had obviously not occurred to her. They were very blue eyes, large and slightly unfocused, because Marigold was long-sighted and not prepared to wear spectacles. She was twenty-seven and in the full flush of her beauty, a golden girl, very tall, with long straight limbs, striding swiftly around the domain she considered her own.

'Valkyrie,' Paul murmured.

'I beg your pardon?'

'I was thinking how popular you'd be if the Germans came. A true Aryan type.'

'What a horrible thing to say! I wouldn't be popular because I'd meet them with a machine-gun in my hand.'

'A battle maiden,' Paul pointed out.

'Not exactly a maiden, with a husband and a baby,' Marigold retorted. 'You do talk nonsense, Mr Tredegar.'

'Paul.'

'Paul,' Marigold conceded. 'Is it true you were with the Danecourts before you came here? Imagine them sending their two brats off to the United States!'

'It won't do the boys any harm to be separated from their parents,' Paul said, with a delicate nuance of meaning that made Marigold snort in involuntary laughter.

'I know exactly what you mean,' she agreed. 'Margot is really *too* much. All the same, a village school is a bit of a come down for you, isn't it?'

'There are compensations.'

'I hear you're taking a special interest in young Ben Harcourt.'

'I think he's got considerable potential.'

'Daddy seems to have taken to him, too. You must come up to the Hall and meet Daddy. Dinner next Thursday evening?'

Mr Smith had never been invited to dinner at Berringer Hall, and neither had Miss Flanders, but without anything being said Paul had been accepted as coming from the same class as the Berringers. It was one more thing that marked Paul out as being different, that and going to live alone in the

Bewley's remote and inconvenient cottage. He made himself comfortable enough with a few bits of furniture bought in the local market town, his radio, a powerful gramophone and a mass of books and records.

Ben came to see him one afternoon in late October and stood motionless in the doorway, enthralled by a meandering river of beautiful sound, until Paul motioned him to a seat.

When the music was finished Ben asked, 'What was it?'

'Bach's Double Violin Concerto.'

Paul got up and removed the records and put them away in their sleeves. He did not bother to ask whether Ben had enjoyed the music, that was written all over the boy's face. Extraordinary, that the thirst for a new experience, a different culture, had not been battered out of him by the circumstances of his life.

'Mrs Pemberley sent me down wi' a load o' logs for you,' Ben said. 'I've got them in the barrow outside. She said you'd be cold in the evenings without a proper fire.'

'Mrs Pemberley thinks of everything,' Paul said in amusement. 'Do you want to hear some more music?'

'Haven't got time,' Ben said. 'I told you I was helping the Colonel in his garden. Besides ... I want to remember that bit you just played. Can I have a book to read?'

'Help yourself from any bookcase except the glass-fronted one; those books are too precious to lend out.'

'I dunno what to take.'

'Have you tried Dickens?'

'Christmas Carol,' Ben admitted.

'Like it?'

'Not much. All them ole ghosts. Soppy.'

'Hm. Are you mature enough for Nicholas Nickleby? Perhaps not. Try David Copperfield. And for a bit of light relief you can have some Robert Louis Stevenson – Kidnapped, that will do.'

All that winter and on into the spring Ben devoured the books Paul lent him. His attic bedroom was cold, but he huddled the bedclothes round him and read on, sometimes late into the night. The only trouble was that he was inclined to get tired and fall asleep, no matter how hard he tried to keep his attention on the printed page. The third time Ethel discovered that his light had been on all night she took the problem to Marigold.

'Addling his brain wi' books,' she said resentfully. 'And the electricity left burning! The waste of it!'

'That's bad,' Marigold agreed. 'I'll speak to Ben myself.'

She tried to put it to Ben in a way she thought he would understand.

'It doesn't help the war effort, Ben, if we waste electricity.'

They were going through difficult days. The retreat from France was over, and Dunkirk had lit a flame of defiance in Britain, but overyone knew that the worst was still to come.

'I've only got about a year,' Ben said. 'Got to read all I can while I got the chance.'

'I don't understand,' Marigold said. 'What do you mean, you've only got a year?'

'I'm thirteen,' Ben explained. 'Next summer when I'm fourteen I'll leave school and start work. Back home in Jarrow, I s'pose. Not much chance of readin' there.'

'I see.' Marigold wrinkled her forehead, acknowledging that this was a problem she had not previously considered. 'I'll talk to Mr Tredegar about it.'

She swept down to see Paul in his cottage the following evening. It had been a brilliant summer day and now that the sun was sinking the sky overhead was a deep blue, fading to gold and rose.

'Just the colour of your eyes,' Paul remarked.

'What?' Marigold was pulled up short, not understanding.

'The sky above us. I was just thinking it was the same blue as your eyes when you hove into sight, Juno.'

'Oh, don't call me Juno! It sounds so ... so buxom.'

Paul gave a shout of laughter. 'Sometimes, I think by accident, you produce the mot juste! Buxom *exactly* describes Juno!'

'So call me something else, such as my own name. Now, what I've come to see you about is Ben. What's going to happen to him when he leaves school?'

'A clerical job probably. An office desk, evening classes until he gets a girl, then early marriage, a few struggling years until he can afford a house, a family and ambitions for them that he never fulfilled himself.'

'It sounds so *dreary*!'

'Ben's father might think it an improvement on what he's had.'

'I supoose it would be a step up,' Marigold said doubtfully. 'Not the sort of life I would want.'

'Is it so very different from the job your husband was doing before he went into the Navy?'

'But Harry was a *manager*!' Marigold said, opening her eyes very wide.

'That makes all the difference,' Paul agreed gravely. 'Obviously I must try to turn young Ben into a manager, too.'

'Do you think you could? He is bright, isn't he? Anyway, as long as you're going to watch out for him I can put it out of my mind. I seem to have so many people on my hands these days.'

'Why don't you let them fend for themselves?'

'I think one ought to help if one can and I look on Ben as one of our own people now. I do like people to be happy,' Marigold said with a wistfulness that at once touched and exasperated Paul.

Her attitude seemed to him to be so outdated as to be positively feudal, and she was not, in his opinion, well qualified to deal with the problems that came her way. She knew hardly anything about life outside her own closed circle and she lacked the imagination to envisage it. When she came up against poverty, suffering, bereavement, she was affronted. Paul suspected that her desire to help people arose more from a dislike of feeling uncomfortable than from a real understanding of misfortune. But even though he thought her obtuse, he saw that she did a lot of good. Her ruthless rearrangement of people's lives did work more often than not, and she was highly regarded in the village.

What made him savage, with himself more than with her, was the realization that, in spite of the shortcomings he saw quite clearly, he could not help reacting to her physical beauty. She was accustomed to it, he saw that too. She had always lived inside a shining bubble of admiration: a pretty child, a popular girl and now a lovely woman. She displayed herself, even to him, whom she did not regard as a proper man. Paul had seen, with the part of his mind that kept a morbid watch for it, the shadow that crossed her face when he got to his feet and limped across the room, the way she looked away. It was something else she would have put right, if she could, and he saw her impatience because it was outside her power.

He wondered sometimes whether she knew how much he desired her, but on the whole he thought that she lacked the insight to understand that his sexual appetite was as strong as any man's, perhaps all the stronger for being suppressed. He despised himself for toying with the idea that her lack of awareness was because she had never been properly awakened. His jealousy, when Harry had been home on leave, had been savage, but he had thought Harry a dull dog, no fitting mate for his splendid golden goddess. If she had turned to Paul, with his intense passions and depth of understanding, he could have given her a fulfilment she would never know with Harry.

It was a fantasy that faded almost as soon as it was born. For one thing, Paul believed that Marigold never would turn to him and, besides that, he was not at all sure that she really had the capacity for deep emotion he was attributing to her.

He tried to get her to stay and have a drink with him on that golden summer evening, but Marigold was busy, as ever, with her multitude of trivial tasks. Paul stood at the door and watched until she was out of sight amongst the trees. When he turned back indoors he felt inside him the stirrings of a mood he dreaded.

He sat down very carefully by the empty fireplace. His hip ached. Sometimes he welcomed that because the pain kept the other trouble at bay, but today it would not be denied. Hovering always at the edge of his consciousness was a wall of darkness. He felt himself beginning to shrink, while the blackness moved forward until it hung over him like a great wave, but not a wave of water which would have crashed over him and brought him back to reality. It was a mist that seeped round him, diminishing him until he saw himself as a tiny mannikin in an empty, lifeless world, seated with his legs dangling over the edge of a cliff, waiting for the moment when it would not be possible to stop himself from falling.

Nothing helped him. Drink brought oblivion, but he had learnt that he would wake the next morning with the depression still on him and bodily sickness added to his trouble.

He got to his feet, every movement an infinite labour. Sometimes, if he were obstinate, he could walk it off, pushing himself to a standstill of total fatigue. That he was able to make himself get up was a sign of hope, but the effect of that brief moment of initiative faded as he plodded through the woods, scarcely knowing where he was going, just putting one foot in front of the other.

On the far side of the trees there was a lake which had been used for years as a bathing place. The weeds had been cleared and there was a rough wooden hut for changing and a jetty and plank for diving. When Paul reached it that evening the low rays of the setting sun were on the water. There was hardly a breath of air, and the surface was so still that it could have been a bowl of solid metal. The pool was neglected now that the men were away at the war and the rushes had begun to grow again. They stood stiffly, silhouetted against the light. One leaf from the overhanging trees drifted down and floated on the water.

There was an explosion of movement. A naked boy, his body silver against the gold, ran with the instinctive grace of an untaught athlete along the diving board and flung himself into the water in a shower of fire. Ben had discovered the pleasure of swimming. It was a clumsy dive and the way he floundered through the water was more like a puppy than a fish, but the wild abandon, the joyousness of his movements struck Paul to the heart.

He stepped back into the shadow of the trees. He closed his eyes and saw again the free, naked body, capering at the edge of the water like a dancer. Never for me, Paul thought; never for me, the free movement, the pride of a perfect body, the spontaneous pleasure. He leaned against the rough trunk in an agony of grief for everything that had been denied him. The force of the sobs he tried to suppress made him retch. He doubled up, holding his stomach. When, at last, the moment had passed he straightened up, conscious that a change had taken place. It was a familiar pain, something he had gone through before, to be faced and acknowledged and reduced to its proper place in his life, and it had displaced the other, more terrible, shadow. For the moment the depression had receded. He had been saved from the ultimate despair.

Chapter Five

Until the summer of 1941 Marigold enjoyed the war. She was in her element organizing the local war effort, busier than she had ever been as the bored wife of a young executive, and thriving on it. It was a joy, too, to be back at Berringer Hall. Marigold had not taken kindly to her four-bedroomed villa on the outskirts of the nearby market town and had always seized every opportunity to return to the village. Now she was back running her father's house as she had done ever since her mother had died when Marigold was sixteen and she felt she had returned to the life for which she was suited.

She did miss her husband, or told herself that she did; but when Harry got leave it was exciting and romantic, even more so than it had been in the early days of their marriage. She dramatized their meetings and partings, but once Harry had gone she settled back happily into the life she had chosen, fortified by a glow of satisfaction at being able to rise above the misery of separation, rather than sitting around moping like Ethel Bewley.

The news was bad, of course, but Marigold took very little notice of it since she was untroubled by any doubts that the British would win in the end. She was equally sure that Harry would come through unharmed, until the telegram came telling her that he had been lost at sea.

Marigold could not believe it. Her mind refused to accept that such a thing could happen to her. It was not until Stan, who had been serving on the same ship, came home with his broken arm in plaster and insisted that he had seen Harry go down that she could be persuaded that there was no hope of him being found drifting on a life-raft or even turning up as a prisoner-of-war.

'You'd think no one else had lost a husband in this bloody war,' Ethel said to Lil Manley.

'Miss Marigold never could stand being thwarted,' Lil said. 'She'd made up her mind Mr Harry was going to come through all right and it comes hard on her finding out she's wrong.'

'It's wee Nicola I'm sorry for,' Ethel said. 'She can't make out what's come over her mum. The poor little thing'd be downright neglected if it wasn't for you 'n me.'

She shivered suddenly. 'My Stan gets the plaster off his arm next week. If they pass him fit he'll 'ave to go back. She don't think of that.'

When the news came through that Stan had been posted from a shore unit to another ship Ethel was inconsolable.

'Do control yourself, Ethel,' Marigold snapped. 'The war has still got to go on, you know.'

Ethel waited until she had flung out of the kitchen and then complained, 'She's got no heart. You'd think she'd enter into my feelings.'

'You've still got a husband to worry about,' Lil pointed out. 'Only natural if it irks her to see you grievin'.'

'What's she going to say when she hears I'm expecting?'

'Oh, that's what's the matter with you, is it? Well, she can't turn you out, that's for sure. Cheer up, Ethel, do! This is as good a place as any to have a baby. At least it's safe.'

Ethel braced herself to tell Marigold her news the next day. She saw the look of exasperation that came over Marigold's face and shrank back, even though Marigold managed to restrain herself from saying anything too cutting.

'I suppose it was only to be expected,' she said. 'It's going to be very inconvenient, but if you'll carry on working as long as you can, I'll get someone extra from the village for the last couple of months.'

Her mouth quivered. 'Harry wanted a son,' she said in a low voice. 'But I didn't think it right in wartime when there was so much for me to do.'

She managed to make it sound like a sacrifice, though the truth was that she had had no desire to bear another child. It was something that she and Harry had disagreed about and she preferred now to forget that she had once been determined to frustrate his wish to add to their family.

'Good job she didn't have another, considering the way she treats the one she's got,' Ethel said. 'Nicola's moping for her dad, as anyone can see except her mum, seemingly.'

'She's only six, too young to take in what's happened,' Lil said, but she spoke uneasily. There was something unnatural about Nicola's silence. It was better to believe that she was lacking in understanding than to acknowledge the depth of suffering behind her huge dark eyes.

Josie showed herself at her worst over Harry's death. She had always teased Nicola, but now her tormenting had a savage edge to it. She pulled Nicola's hair and threw her school books about, ran away from her in the woods and refused to allow her to join in games on the grounds that she was too little. What Josie would not admit, even to herself, was that her bad behaviour sprang from fear. What had happened to one sailor could happen to another and Josie had always been closer to her father than her mother. Nicola's white, patient face was a constant reminder of the chances of war and Josie, with all the force of her rebellious nature, fought against the knowledge that she, too, could lose her father.

Only Ben understood what Nicola was going through. Looking back, he remembered the blow that had fallen on him when he had been the same age. It was an awkward thing for a boy of fourteen to comfort a little girl of six, but when he came on Nicola sitting on the stairs one day her dark eyes enormous, clutching her stomach as if she had a pain, he sat down beside her and put his arm round her.

Her little body felt rigid. Nicola seemed to be holding her breath in case she did the wrong thing.

'I was your age when my mam died,' Ben said. 'I remember ... everyone kept telling me to go away and play. Daft thing to say.'

'Nobody won't talk to me,' Nicola whispered. It was the first thing he could remember hearing her say for days.

'They think you're too little to understand,' he said.

'I know daddy's dead and he won't come back any more,' Nicola said. 'He's been killed in the war. Drowned in the sea.'

She crept a little closer and Ben's arm tightened round her. In a very low whisper Nicola asked, 'He won't come up out of the pond, will he, Ben?'

'Christ! No, of course he won't! He was drowned miles and miles away in the sea. Whatever put an idea like that into your head?'

'Josie told me a ghost story about a body coming out of the water covered in weeds.'

'I'll break every bone in her bloody body.'

'You do swear a lot,' Nicola said admiringly. 'She didn't say that about Daddy; I thought of it for myself.'

'Your dad went down with his ship,' Ben said firmly. 'He won't come back and haunt you. He … he loved you.'

'Then why did he go away and get himself killed?' Nicola demanded.

She burst into a storm of tears and Ben, faced with an unanswerable question, could only hold her awkwardly until she became quieter. The tension had gone out of her, and her body was slack and soft in his arms. Ben felt the same tenderness for her as he had discovered when he had been given an orphan lamb to hold.

They stayed like that, on the stairs, until they heard Marigold's hysterical voice calling Nicola's name. Nicola sat up with a sigh. Ben found a grubby handkerchief, wiped her face and made her blow her nose. He sat and watched as Nicola stomped slowly down the stairs, a tiny, stoical figure, and he had the uncanny feeling that in responding so obediently to Marigold's cry she was picking up the burden of her mother's grief as well as her own.

He tackled Josie the next time he got her alone.

'Lay off the kid,' he ordered. 'She's got enough to bear without you being rotten to her.'

Josie tried to shrug it off, all the more defiant because she felt guilty.

'Time she learnt to stick up for herself, 'stead of running to you,' she said.

'She's only six and she's been brought up soft,' Ben said. 'You an' me, we can take care of ourselves, but Nicola's different; she needs looking after.'

'It's not fair,' Josie protested.

'No more'n it's fair for you to torment the kid, just because you're tough and she's not,' Ben retorted. 'If you want to fight with someone, try me.'

'You! You're always smarming round sweet little Nicola,' Josie said angrily.

'She's only a baby.'

'Two years younger than me, that's all.'

'You seem older,' Ben said.

That pleased her, and so did his assumption that they were two of a kind. She had an unwilling admiration for this tall boy who had risen effortlessly to the top place in the village school. She behaved outrageously to get his attention, willing him to look upon her as the boy she would have liked to have been instead of a despised girl.

'Nicola likes playing soppy games with dolls. She can't throw a ball straight and she can't catch,' Josie said, trying to push Ben into further admissions that she was Nicola's superior.

'You can only catch soft balls,' Ben said, cutting her down to size again. 'I should have thought you could have played a few games with Nicola, just to help a bit.'

'I'll play with Nicola and her dolls' house if you'll take me with you when you go scrumpin',' Josie tried to bargain with him.

'I don't go scrumping!' Ben said quickly.

'Get away! I've seen you with the apples up your jersey like some fat old woman with bouncy tits.' Josie giggled at his outraged face.

It took a lot more arguing, but the next time Ben climbed the orchard fence in the neighbouring farm he gave Josie a boost and took her over with him. Apples lay scattered on the grass, but Ben said in a hissing whisper, 'I'm not putting up with rotten old windfalls.'

'I can climb trees,' Josie said quickly, and climb them she did, breathless with excitement and fear, especially when the dogs began barking in the distance. There was a rush of scampering feet in the long grass and, looking down, Josie saw one of the farm dogs below her. He was puzzled, not quite sure whether he had found an unwanted intruder or not, but he gave an experimental growl and then, with growing conviction, began to bark vigorously until he was silenced by a well-aimed apple from Ben. The dog yelped and retreated.

'Come on,' Ben called from his neighbouring tree. 'Time to get out.'

Josie obeyed him with more haste than care, snagging her frock and grazing her knees on the rough bark. With Ben keeping the dog at bay she scrambled over the fence, hampered by the apples she had tied up in the skirt of her cotton frock. Ben followed her and they fled, just in time to avoid one of the farm workers who appeared to find out what all the noise was about.

Out of breath, terrified and wildly happy, Josie pounded after Ben as he ran through the woods. They collapsed in a small clearing at the foot of an old oak tree.

'What we goin' to do with all these apples?' Josie demanded. 'I've got more'n you!'

Ben forgave her that small boast. She had been a good companion and she'd done well for a kid of eight, and a girl at that.

'Eat the ones we feel like eating, and make a cache of the others,' he said. 'I'll find a box to put them in. Here, you can have this one. It's the biggest one I've got.'

Josie munched her way blissfully through the apple he gave her, even though it was not perfectly ripe, and it never occurred to Ethel to wonder why her daughter was doubled up with stomach-ache later that night.

Marigold went on being sullen and difficult to live with, but she did not give up any of her feverish activity. Gradually she noticed that people were no longer treating her with special consideration and she resented their forgetfulness of her recent widowhood. She expected to be told how brave she was and it shocked her when her fortitude was overlooked.

She turned to Paul for comfort, not caring that he should see her with her face blotched and puffed with tears since he had no importance for her as a man. Paul did try to console her, aching to hold her in his arms even while his reason recognized the immature quality of her grief; she was more like a spoilt child wailing over a broken toy than an adult woman mourning a dead man.

'Harry was *special*,' Marigold insisted one evening in his cottage.

'I know he was,' Paul said steadily, but in his heart he thought that what had made Harry special in Marigold's eyes was that he had belonged to her.

Outside the November evening was closing in. The fir trees which crowded round the cottage seemed to be drawing the darkness towards them. Paul had not lit the oil lamps because even in that isolated spot it was necessary to get up and draw the black-out curtains before showing a light. He had given Marigold tea and then, when she asked for it, a stiff whisky out of his one precious bottle.

'Give me another drink, Paul,' Marigold demanded abruptly.

'Don't you think you ought to be going home? It's getting dark. I'll see you on your way.'

'I don't need seeing home. I've been walking through these woods alone since I was a child. But I don't want to go yet. Give me another drink. Say something nice to me. Make me feel better.'

'Nothing I can say will bring Harry back,' Paul said.

He poured her a generous whisky and was worried by the avid way she drank it down.

'As for saying something nice, there's only one thing I can say and I doubt whether you're ready to believe it yet: you're a lovely young woman with years of life in front of you and you will get married again.'

'No! How can you suggest such a thing? And I'm not even pretty, not any longer. I'm a hideous old hag. Look at me!'

'I am looking at you. Golden girl, you are the loveliest thing that ever lived.'

His voice was unsteady and he regretted the words as soon as they were spoken. It was almost dark and only a flicker of firelight illuminated his handsome head and dark, intent eyes. They were sitting on the battered sofa he had bought in a second-hand shop, drawn up close to the fire for warmth. Paul moved closer and took Marigold's hand in his, removing the glass from her fingers.

'You don't need this. Alcohol isn't the answer.'

'It helps me to go on,' Marigold said in a broken whisper.

Almost imperceptibly she leaned towards him and Paul's arm slid round her shoulders.

'Did you mean it?' Marigold asked. 'Am I still beautiful?'

'Beautiful, desirable. Dear God, don't you know how I feel about you?'

He could hardly breathe, but he forced himself to keep calm until the moment when she allowed their lips to meet and then he had such an explosion of desire for her that he knew she could not remain unaware of it. He felt the shock that ran through her and went on holding her, no longer gently but with fierce passion. He expected her to try to struggle out of his embrace, but instead Marigold shuddered once and then lay passive in his arms while he caressed her.

Neither of them was conscious of being disturbed by any movement outside, nor did they see the white glimmer of a face looking in from the darkness at the firelit room, and yet something suddenly roused Marigold from her voluptuous torpor. She sat up with a shudder.

'Let me go!' she demanded.

'But darling, I'm not going to hurt you,' Paul protested.

'It's disgusting! I must be mad! If you hadn't made me drunk I would never have let you touch me.'

'Damn it, Marigold, be fair! If whisky goes to your head you shouldn't have insisted on drinking it, but you're not in the least bit drunk. You turned to me for comfort, I understand that …'

'You make me *sick*! Taking advantage of my grief. You know I wouldn't look at you if I hadn't been beside myself with unhappiness. I've always tried to treat you the same as everyone else, but you're *not* the same, and I think it's despicable, worming your way in when my defences are down.'

'In what way do I differ from any other man?' Paul asked, very quiet and still.

'Oh, Paul! It's beastly of you to make me say it, but you are different, you know you are. Harry was so perfect …'

'Physically perfect, whereas I am a cripple.'

'You said it, not me,' Marigold pointed out.

'It was in your mind.'

'All right then, it was. I like everything about me to be beautiful, I'm sensitive like that. I've been grateful for your sympathy, but in future please remember I can't bear to be touched by a man who is ... twisted, distorted ...'

'I'll remember,' Paul said. 'Oh, yes, I'll remember.'

He had always thought her unimaginative, but nothing had prepared him for this cruelty. She was lashing out blindly, wanting to hurt him because she was ashamed of her moment of weakness, but she had no real understanding of what she was doing to him, because in her heart she believed that he must think about himself in the same way.

'I'd better go,' Marigold said uncertainly.

She opened the door and peered out. 'What a ghastly, cold winter. The wind is bitter.'

'Bitter,' Paul agreed.

Marigold looked back. He was standing quite still, his head silhouetted against the fading light from the window. She had a moment of regret. If only the rest of him had been as handsome.

When she had gone Paul lit the lamp and adjusted the black-out with meticulous fingers, but he moved mechanically, fending off the moment when he would have to face the horror that was waiting for him. He was stunned to discover that any human being could inflict so much pain and then walk away unknowing. His touch disgusted her. She saw nothing of the spirit that lived in him, only the twisted body.

Paul wrenched open the door of the cottage and stepped outside. The wind tore at his jacket, but he was unconscious of the cold. There was darkness all round him, not the gloom of the woods, but the inner shadow that had swept over him while he was disarmed, unable to resist it.

Without knowing where he was going, he walked the same path that Marigold had taken, the path he had followed once before, the one that led to the lake. That time, too, he had grieved for his imperfect body, but he had been released by Ben's lovely freedom. This time there was nothing for him but decaying leaves etched in rime and water the colour of pewter.

He had been closer behind Marigold than he had realized and she heard his footsteps on the path. She made a grimace of distaste and hurried on. In her haste she was careless. She tripped on a tree root and was flung violently to the ground. Her ankle was badly twisted. At first it was so painful that she thought it was sprained, or even broken, but as she sat on the ground rubbing it the pain began to subside.

Paul reached the lake and stood looking blindly over the sullen water. Then he walked out on the jetty. There was a film of ice on the damp wood. His foot slipped and he paused, then he went on. The diving plank was narrow, too narrow to be safe for a man wearing a clumsy surgical boot. He walked right to the end, peversely satisfied at having done it safely. Then he realized that there was no way back. There was no handhold, nothing on which he could brace himself as he turned, and there was ice under his feet. It had come, the moment he had always known was waiting for him. No way to go now, except forward and down. Paul closed his eyes and took a deliberate step forward into empty space.

Marigold, still sitting on the ground nursing her ankle, heard the splash. It was too loud to be mistaken for anything other than someone falling in the water. Paul had been behind her. He must have missed his footing. An accident, a stupid, unnecessary accident. She scrambled to her feet, wincing as she put the damaged ankle to the ground, and then, limping as fast as she could manage, she went back the few yards to the lake.

There was nothing to be seen but great ripples on the surface. She saw the marks his footprints had made in the frost on the wooden jetty and followed them out to the beginning of the plank, but then she paused, realizing, as Paul in his agony had not, that it would be dangerous to trust herself to that narrow slippery surface, especially with a painful ankle. She sat down astride the diving board and edged forward, but even when she reached the end there was nothing to be seen. If he was there, and she knew that he was, he was far below the surface.

She inched her way back to the jetty and took off her coat and skirt and shoes. Clinging with one hand to the wooden struts underneath she lowered herself into the water. It was cold, so cold. The shock of it drove all the breath out of her body. Gasping and shuddering, she took one hand away from the supporting crossbar and moved her arm with a feeble swimming motion under the water. A slimy weed stroked her bare hand and Marigold snatched it back, clinging once again to the jetty.

It was no use, she could not dive into the dark, still pool. In any case, it must be too late. If he had not surfaced he must be caught under the water. The memory of his heavy boot made her shiver even more violently. Even if she found him, she would not be able to raise him. She felt her way back, along the side of the jetty until she reached the bank.

As she tried to lever herself out of the water, Marigold heard someone running through the trees. She called out feebly and the next moment a boy's hand closed round her arm and hauled her out of the dragging water.

'I heard something … a splash,' Ben said. 'Was it you? Did you fall in?'

'Paul … Mr Tredegar,' Marigold said through chattering teeth. 'I didn't see what happened. He must have fallen. I can't reach him … I tried … Ben, run for help.'

Ben let go of her with an abruptness that left her staggering. Without a word he threw off his jacket, pulled off his shoes, ran to the end of the diving board and dived, as Marigold had not dared to do, straight down into the darkness.

Marigold crouched on the muddy grass, shaking all over, waiting for him to come up. When he surfaced she stood up, but Ben only drew one long breath and then he went down again.

A second time he came up through the icy water, and this time he struck out for the edge of the pond.

'I found him, but I can't raise him,' he gasped. 'You'll have to come and help me.'

'It's too late, he's been down too long,' Marigold said with a dull acceptance of the inevitable that drove Ben nearly mad. He turned away to make one more fruitless attempt while Marigold felt around and found the clothes she had discarded. She forced her wet feet into her shoes and huddled her coat round her, not bothering to put on her skirt. Her ankle was still painful. While she had been in the water she had forgotten about it, but now she found it difficult to stand.

When Ben came out of the water once more she seized hold of him.

'I told you it was no use,' she said. 'Give up. Come back to the house and we'll get some men to drag the pond.'

Ben shook her off, loathing her touch.

'How did it happen?' he demanded. 'You were with him. How could he have fallen in?'

'I wasn't with him. I left him at the cottage,' Marigold protested.

'I know you were *there*,' Ben said. 'I saw you.'

The light was too dim for Marigold to see the way he was looking at her, but she could hear the accusing note in his voice. What had he seen? What had he heard? She had nothing to be ashamed of, Marigold told herself uneasily. In any case, this common child had no right to criticize her.

'I left long before Mr Tredegar,' she said. 'And would have been home by now if I hadn't tripped and sprained my ankle. You'll have to run on ahead and sound the alarm. Go on, don't stand around – hurry.'

Ben turned and left her. Marigold heard him, as she had before, running through the trees. She limped slowly after him and as she went she began to make up the story she would tell.

Chapter Six

Paul Tredegar's death brought to an end the extra schooling he had won for Ben. They had both hoped that it would be possible to extend it until Ben was sixteen, but now, only six months after his fourteenth birthday, Ben was left without his champion. Until a replacement for Paul could be found Miss Flanders had too much on her hands to cope with tuition for Paul's protégé. Besides, she had no great liking for Ben Harcourt. Her nervous manner irritated Ben and he was surly with her. Once the stimulus of Paul's interest was removed he stopped working, lounging insolently at his desk, a disruptive influence on the younger children, who looked up to him because of his age, his looks, his arrogant manner and the heroism he had shown in trying to rescue their schoolmaster.

Inwardly, Ben was raging. Marigold had made her story of a casual call at the cottage sound very plausible, but Ben knew what he had seen when he had looked in at the window. Paul had thrown a fresh log on the fire and by the flickering light Ben had seen the couple clasped together on the sofa, the firelight gleaming on Marigold's bright hair. Not much doubt about who that was. He had turned away with a feeling of sour disgust, but his curiosity was awakened, too. He remembered the way Phyllis had tried to experiment with him, more than two years ago, and screwed up his face at the memory. All the same, he was not sure that he would have turned her down now, just for the sake of finding out what it was about.

Because he had felt disturbed he had hung about in the woods, scuffling through the fallen leaves, picking up bits of fallen branches and hurling them through the trees above him, trying to distract his mind from what he had seen and fighting against a temptation of which he was ashamed to go and have another look through the window of Paul's cottage.

When at last he had returned the cottage had been empty. Annoyed at having missed his opportunity to see Paul, Ben had set off for Berringer Hall and that was when he had heard noises for which he could not account coming from the swimming pond. If only he had gone back sooner, he might have been in time to save Paul from the accident – an accident which Ben could still not understand.

He lay face downward on his bed on the day of Paul's funeral, his hands clenched on the quilt, fighting to control the tears that scalded his eyes. According to Marigold, she had made repeated attempts to reach Paul, but Ben discounted almost everything she said. For one thing, there had not been time for her to do much more than get into the water and, for another, he had seen later when she arrived in the kitchen of Berringer Hall, shaking with cold and hysterical with shock, that her hair had been dry, which meant that she had not even put her head under the water.

'Rotten bitch,' he muttered. 'Stupid, bloody woman. I'll get even with her one day, see if I don't.'

He sat up, cheered by the thought of revenge, and scrubbed at his eyes with a grubby hand, but inside he still grieved, not just for Paul, but for the chance that had been taken away from him of improving his life.

The person who most sympathized with him was Colonel Berringer, but even he was unable to provide the education Ben needed. He did suggest keeping the boy and employing him at Berringer Hall, but Marigold was so furiously opposed to the idea that he dropped it.

Ben took the news that he was to leave school and go home to Jarrow at Easter so quietly that Ethel was lulled into thinking that he was pleased about it.

'It'll be nice for you to see your dad again,' she said.

'Why? Does he want to see me?' Ben asked.

'Don't talk like that. He sent you that nice pair of socks for Christmas, didn't he? And he has written.'

'Twice a year,' Ben said, but he knew he was being unfair. His father was no hand at letter writing, and at the time of receiving the letters Ben had been deeply touched by Andrew's carefully written, stilted notes, knowing that the pen, the ink, the writing paper and envelopes must have been specially bought for the purpose.

He paid one last visit to Paul's cottage before he left. Once he was back in Jarrow his one consolation, the books Paul had lent him, would no longer be available, and to Ben it seemed only sense to secure a few of them for himself before Paul's sister, his only living relative, came up from Cornwall to clear everything away.

The cottage was locked up, but there was a window with a faulty catch which provided easy access. Inside, the place still seemed full of Paul's presence: his pipe and pouch of tobacco lay on a table by the side of his armchair, the battered leather bag in which he carried home school work stood on the floor by its side, the fireplace was full of dead, white wood ash and there was still a record on the gramophone turntable.

The light was dim and Ben dared not light the lamp. There were books all round the room, but he had already borrowed many of them. The ones he could be sure of not having read before were in the glass-fronted bookcase. Without trying to make out the titles in the fading light Ben took out an armful and dumped them into the sack he had brought with him. When the top shelf had been emptied he paused. Better not be greedy and risk getting caught. The shelf looked strangely bare; it was far too obvious that something was missing. Ben picked up some volumes at random round the room and crammed them into the bookcase, then he closed the door and locked it with the tiny key.

His sack of books got Ben into trouble with Bess as soon as he was home in Jarrow.

'Dirty old load o' rubbish,' she said. 'What d'you want wi' them?'

'Mr Tredegar gave them to me,' Ben said. 'I'm going to read them.'

'Who's Mr Tredegar when 'e's at 'ome?'

'My schoolteacher.'

'Him that was drowned? A funny business that, by all

accounts. Did he do it on purpose?'

'Prob'ly Ben drove him to it,' Phyllis suggested with a giggle.

She eyed him surreptitiously. No one but Andrew had visited Ben at Berringer, and that only once, during the past two and a half years. They were all taken by surprise at the change in him. He was taller, broader, much better looking, and he talked different, almost posh.

Ben gave her a black look. Nothing about Phyllis had improved, in his opinion. She had grown, too, but mostly outwards, and she now had round, bouncing breasts and buttocks that twitched jauntily as she walked.

'Old books can be worth money,' Andrew said. 'Pounds, sometimes. It was good of the man to give them to Ben an' if the lad wants to keep them I see no reason why he shouldn't.'

He cleared his throat, ill at ease with this tall boy, and yet unexpectedly moved by his return.

'Good to have you back,' he ventured to say. 'Gives me a bit o' support in a house full o' women.'

'Your sister Elsie's walking out reg'lar,' Bess informed Ben.

It was on the tip of his tongue to make the old protest that she was not his sister, but he let it go. Instead, he tried to show an interest in the news.

'Going to get married?' he asked Elsie.

She must be about nineteen, he thought. About time she got hitched or she'd end up an old maid. It would give them a bit more room in the house, too, but even Elsie's departure would not allow Ben to have his bedroom back, not while Phyllis was still at home.

'She's getting engaged first, with a proper ring,' Bess said.

It was of immense importance to her, that ring. There had been no money to spare from either of her husbands for frivolities like engagement rings.

There had been changes in the household since Ben had gone away. With Andrew, Elsie and Phyllis all working there was sufficient money coming in to keep them in comfort. Bess and Andrew both had armchairs to sit in and there was a wireless. Ben, fiddling with the knobs, tuned in to something he recog- nized: Bach's Double Violin Concerto. He stood immobile, flooded with grief, until Phyllis reached over and clicked off the set.

'Horrible caterwauling,' she said. 'I don't know how anyone can pretend to enjoy listening to someone scraping at a cat's guts.'

'You'll go down the Labour Exchange first thing in morning an' sign on,' Bess ordered Ben. 'Unless you can ask about a job at the yard for 'im, Andrew?'

'What d'you say, lad?' Andrew asked.

'Seems a bit of a waste after all that fancy schooling,' Elsie said.

'All what fancy schooling?' Ben demanded. 'I only had a few extra months.'

'From the way that schoolmaster of yours wrote to your dad we thought he was takin' a special interest in you,' Bess said.

'He did give me extra tuition,' Ben admitted.

'Extra tuition,' Phyllis mocked him. 'Proper Eton an' Harrow, ain't we?'

By the following week Ben was working, not in the yard, as his father had expected, but as an office boy.

'One of the white collar workers,' Andrew joked. 'I'd rather you'd gone for an apprenticeship, lad. That way you'd always have had a trade to fall back on.' He felt proud, but uneasy. There was something about the way Ben fixed things up for himself without talking them over first that worried him. True, the lad had been away and must be feeling strange now that he was home again, but that did not altogether account for his independence, nor for the way he detached himself from everyone else when they sat in the kitchen in the evenings and went off to read on his own in the front room.

He did other things that were alien to the Harcourt family, too. He joined the Public Library and he signed up for evening classes.

'It'll help me get on,' he said briefly in answer to Andrew's questions.

'It may help you,' Bess snapped. 'But I didn't look to see your first week's wages go on school books, that I didn't! Who's feedin' you, that's what I'd like to know?'

'Now then, Bess, we've enough comin' in to keep the lad for a week or two,' Andrew pacified her. 'It's to his credit that he wants to spend 'is money on education, surely?'

In an anxious attempt to please his son he brought home half a dozen bricks and a plank of wood, rubbed the wood down and varnished it, and made up a rough-and-ready bookshelf. He had his reward in Ben's gruff, 'Thanks, Dad' as the boy arranged his books on it.

The books he had taken from Paul's cottage were a disappointment, nothing like as readable as the ones Paul had picked out for him. One of them was even in Latin, though that one was pretty to look at, bound in leather and written on something heavier and smoother than paper, with brightly decorated initial letters and trailing flowers and leaves down the margins. Ben liked to handle it, even though the strange old writing defeated him. He had it in his hand one day when someone he remembered from the past came to see Bess. Ben couldn't recall his name, but he was sure he didn't like him.

'You'll mebbe remember Mr Baxcombe,' Bess said. 'Used to be with the Unemployment Assistance Board when times were hard, but he's gone back to his proper trade of buildin' now. Doing very nicely at it, too, aren't you, Mr Baxcombe?'

'None so bad,' Mr Baxcombe admitted.

'Bomb damage,' Bess explained. 'This rotten old place is still standin' – more's the pity – but we've taken a knock or two and that leakin' roof is due to air raids, as I'm sure you'll agree, Mr Baxcombe.'

'I'll tak' a look at it,' Mr Baxcombe said cautiously, but from Bess's satisfied look Ben guessed that the roof would be treated as bomb damage even though he knew, Bess knew, and probably Mr Baxcombe knew, too, that it had been faulty long before the outbreak of war.

Mr Baxcombe reached out and took up the book Ben had laid down on the table. It seemed to Ben that he stiffened.

'Where did you get this, lad?' he asked.

'My old schoolteacher gave it to me,' Ben said.

'You don't say! What made him do that?'

Ben shrugged. 'We got on all right. He's dead now.'

'It's a pretty thing,' Mr Baxcombe said. 'Yes, a very pretty thing. There's people would give good money for a book like that.'

'Andy said somethin' o' the same sort and I didna believe

him!' Bess said. 'How much do you reckon it'd fetch, Mr Baxcombe?'

'I know a man might give five pounds for it, if you'd let me have the handlin' of it.'

'Five ...! D'you hear that, Ben? By, if that don't beat all! You'll be able to 'ave a new suit to go to work in. Take it, Mr Baxcombe, and see what you can do for us.'

'No!'

Ben snatched the book back from Mr Baxcombe's clutching hands.

'It's my book and I won't have it sold.'

Bessie's wrath raged over his head long after Mr Baxcombe had left them, but Ben was adamant. Even Andrew thought he was being unreasonable.

'I daresay it's a nice memento, but you have to be reasonable, lad,' he told his son. 'Five pounds in the hand is more use to you than an old book stuck in the bookcase.'

'If Mr Baxcombe offered five pounds it's probably worth ten,' Ben said.

'There's something in that,' Andrew admitted.

The following day Bess searched in vain for the strange old book. Ben had got her measure; he took it to work with him and locked it up in the drawer where he kept the stamps and petty cash.

Ben found working in the office of the great shipbuilding firm of Maxton's a strange experience, right outside the tradition in which he had been reared, and he secretly agreed with his father's judgement that the work he did was trivial and unimportant. All the same, it was the way ahead. Ben kept a still tongue in his head, watched everything that went on and worked diligently, and he began to see that on the fourth floor of the building where he worked, far from the post room where he spent his days, decisions were taken that affected thousands of men like his father and influenced the war and the history of the world.

The war dragged on, a constant nagging worry at the forefront of everybody's mind, with moments of danger and grief, and even more of tiresome, petty inconvenience. To Ben, who remembered the hard times, it was obvious that the fighting had brought prosperity to his father and his mates. No fear now of being unemployed; there was ample work, and chances of overtime, which put money in Andrew's pocket. The irony of it was that because of wartime shortages there was little on which he could spend it.

Soon after his sixteenth birthday Ben was moved out of the post room and given a job as a junior clerk.

'I've moved one floor up,' he said to his father. 'Only three to go and I'll be a director.'

It was 1943 and agitation was growing for the Allies to invade Europe. 'Second Front Now' said the chalked messages on the rough brick walls. Britain was filling up with American troops. What were they there for if it wasn't to fight?

In his lowly position in the great shipping firm Ben dimly perceived something of the long, slow process of building up the great stocks of fighting material that was necessary before Hitler's bastion of Europe could be stormed.

In June 1944 it came at last: D-Day and bitter fighting in Normandy. For the first time Ben began to think that the war might end before he was old enough to join in the fighting. He moved up another step in his work and became absorbed in processing orders for raw materials, with a special interest in the vast tonnages of steel rolling out from the mills to be turned into ships.

At home, he said little about what he did. His father asked occasional questions, but Bess was uninterested as long as Ben handed over the twenty-five shillings a week he contributed to the household expenses. He resented the fact that this left him with only five shillings to spend on himself and when he was given a rise of half a crown he kept quiet about it, which was not a wise thing to do in a community where everyone knew everyone else's business.

'My friend Polly that works on the telephone at Maxton's says you've all been given more money,' Phyllis told him.

'Does she?' Ben said.

He looked cool about it, but inside he was furious. He still disliked Phyllis as much as ever. Her tonsils and adenoids had been removed and she spoke more clearly than she had as a child and without the horrible snuffling that had offended him, but he still shied away from her, both repelled and attracted by her blatant sexuality.

'Polly's got half a crown, so I 'spect you got the same,' Phyllis persisted. 'If you'll tak' me to the pictures tomorrow night I'll not tell Mum you're keepin' the money to y'self.'

'I'd as soon give it to her as to you,' Ben said.

'I'm not askin' you to pay for me; just to come to the pictures wi' me. Aw, c'mon, Ben. It's Humphrey Bogart.'

'What happened to all your boyfriends?'

Phyllis giggled. 'Jim found out about Mick an' Mick found out about Georgie. My name's mud wi' all o' them at the moment.'

'I bet it is.' Ben hesitated. It wasn't such a bad bargain and it was a film he wanted to see.

'Just this once,' he said suspiciously.

'A'right, a'right! Anyone'd think I'd got the plague!'

They queued up in the darkness outside the cinema and were lucky enough to get in within ten minutes. Inside, Phyllis snuggled up against Ben, but he moved away. She persisted putting her hand on his thigh and squeezing the flesh on the inside of his leg. He had a vivid recollection of this happening before and he was just as reluctant now as he had been then, except that now he was older, his body was developed and he knew more. In spite of his reluctance to give an inch to Phyllis an uneasy excitement awoke inside him.

When the film was over they stumbled out into the black-out. Phyllis clutched at Ben's arm and he did not throw her off. They turned away from the dimly lit street into an alley-way. Phyllis stopped, leaned against the wall and pulled Ben towards her, with her arms round his waist under his jacket. Her full breasts were pushed against his chest, her breath was warm on his cheek. Ben put his hands behind her on her buttocks, but when Phyllis tried to kiss him he tore his mouth away, disgusted by her wet, searching tongue.

Phyllis took her hand away from his back, fumbled with the front of her dress and drew out one of her breasts. For the first time Ben felt the weight and roundness of a woman's breast in his hand. He bent his head and put his lips to the nipple, feeling it grow as he sucked at it. Phyllis made a moaning noise. Her pelvis was moving rhythmically against him. Ben felt himself growing, big and hard.

'There's a bit o' ground a few steps up,' she whispered hoarsely. 'C'mon, it's better lyin' down.'

She knew exactly what she was doing. Even at that moment Ben's mind registered that. He followed her blindly, and not only because it was too dark to see what he was doing. Phyllis took off her knickers and lay down with them under her head, her skirt rucked up to her waist.

'Nearly lost a pair once, feelin' round in the dark afterwards,' she remarked. 'C'mon, slowcoach.'

For one moment Ben was afraid of his own inexperience, but Phyllis solved that. With an expert twist of her hips she guided him into place and Ben was away, on a ride that carried him into realms of sensation he had never known before. He still didn't like her, and nothing was going to persuade him otherwise, but that didn't stop it being good. Without realizing it, he threw into that first, inexpert coupling all the aggression he suppressed every day in his unsatisfactory life. Phyllis cried out and clung to him fiercely.

'Coo, you're a proper tiger,' she said admiringly when they were still.

Ben rolled away from her. He felt drained and, more than that, disgusted with himself. He'd given in to her. The little bitch had been after him ever since he got home and she'd won.

'It was a'right, weren't it?' Phyllis demanded 'By, I didna know you'd got it in you, Ben lad.'

She sat up, brisk and efficient, pulling her knickers back on, rearranging her clothes.

'You might say somethin',' she complained. 'Such as "Thank you very much, Phyllis, that were real nice".'

'Will you be all right?' Ben asked abruptly.

'What d'you mean?'

'Babies an' that.'

Phyllis gave a shout of laughter. 'Who, me? I've known how to avoid that since I were thirteen.'

Ben walked home with her without speaking again. He

disliked intensely the feeling that Phyllis had led and he had followed. What was more, he had known in his heart that she had intended something like that to happen when she had asked him to take her to the pictures. He had known and had shut it out of his mind. He had never had a girl and he had wanted to know what it was like and Phyllis had guessed that he would be easily tempted. She was more than willing, she was downright eager. So what harm in using her to find out what he wanted to know? None, except that he persisted in feeling that she had taken something from him that he had not really wanted to give. An old Bible story came into his mind. He felt like Samson after Delilah had been at him. Was it always like that? It couldn't be, or the men wouldn't be so eager to go back for more. One thing Ben was sure about, he wasn't going to be put upon like that again. What he wanted he would take, but no woman was going to use him to give herself a cheap thrill.

At the end of the next week Ben said abruptly to Bess, 'I've had a half a crown rise. I'll split with you – one and sixpence extra for you and a shilling for me.'

He looked at Phyllis as he spoke and saw that she had got the message: no more blackmail. She tried it on, of course, as he had known she would, rubbing herself against him unnecessarily, throwing out insinuating remarks, even creeping in to him one night when she had been out with a girl friend and suggesting she should join him in the narrow camp-bed on which he had to sleep in the front room. Ben rebuffed her in hissing whispers and she went away in an offended huff. It was a relief when she found a new boyfriend, though it was hard to bear the scorn with which she treated Ben after that.

A relief, too, when his call-up papers came and he could get away. He chose to go into the Army, to his father's surprise.

'I suppose it's because we've had such a lot to do with ships,' Andrew said. 'It seems more natural to think about joining the Navy.'

'I've seen enough of ships,' Ben said. 'I prefer dry land.'

Before he left the office he turned out the drawers of his desk and came across the old *Book of Hours.* He had not exactly forgotten about it, but he had grown used to seeing it half buried under a pile of papers. Now he took it out and looked at it, struck all over again by the freshness of the colours and the strangeness of the little faces peering out from the foliage that decorated the margins. He suspected that it might be worth a great deal more than the ten pounds he had once mentioned. He could take it to a bookshop and find out, or perhaps to the library. In the end, feeling awkward and a bit of a fool, he went to a Newcastle museum.

The official who came to see him was polite but cool, until he held the book in his hands, then he became more enthusiastic.

'Very nice,' he said approvingly. 'English, of course. Fifteenth century. It's been rebound, which is a pity, though the binding is quite good in its way. Late sixteenth century, I would say. How did you come to acquire it?'

Ben had anticipated that question. 'My old schoolmaster gave it to me,' he said. 'He died soon after.'

'He gave you a considerable treasure.'

'If I wanted to sell it ...'

'Take it to one of the major auction houses. Not having the original cover detracts from its value, of course, but I'm prepared to say you could think in terms of four figures rather than three.'

It took Ben a moment to grasp that. Four figures. He was talking about thousands. At least a thousand pounds.

'I've just been called up,' he said. 'It's a bit of a poser to know what to do with it for safety.'

'Leave it with us,' the man suggested. 'On loan to the museum. We'll take good care of it, might even make you an offer for it when you come back.'

Ben left the museum in a state of shock. It was years now since Paul Tredegar had died and no one had queried the whereabouts of the *Book of Hours*, so presumably his sister hadn't known about it. What about the other books he had taken? Were they all worth money? He had a dim recollection of Paul refusing to lend him the books from the locked bookcase because they were too precious. No wonder! Only for one fleeting moment did Ben consider the idea of trying to return the books. It would involve him in too many difficult explanations. Besides, Mr Tredegar had wanted him to get on in the world: the best thing Ben could do was to look upon this windfall as if it had been an unexpected legacy.

In May 1945 the war in Europe ended. In August two atom bombs were dropped on Japan and hostilities in the East stopped. By that time Ben was in Germany with the Army of Occupation.

It was a strange experience to be part of an Army that did no fighting and to be surrounded by the beaten enemy. The Germans had been masters of Europe but now they were laid low indeed, their cities razed to the ground, their men cowed, and their women ready to barter anything for an extra scrap of food or a few cigarettes.

Ben watched and waited and then, when he saw his chance, went into the bartering business. It was not black market, he told himself, not really. He didn't deal in stolen goods, at any rate not knowingly, and he set his face against the trade in medical supplies. He swapped what was surplus to his own requirements for the things the Germans were willing to part with, and sometimes for the favours of the girls involved, but there was no profit in that and he usually regretted being parted from his stock-in-trade with nothing to show in return but a few minutes' pleasure.

He accumulated a hoard of souvenirs, such as watches and small pieces of jewellery; nothing too precious, but always things that were portable and easy to dispose of when he was on leave. He emerged from his years in the Army fitter, harder, more experienced than when he went in, and with a taste for bargaining and making a profit.

It made his job at Maxton's, when his National Service came to an end and he went back to it, seem slow and dull. It was not the same as it had been when he had felt that he was helping the course of the war, and the pre-war clerks who had seen real service were scornful of the 'little boys' who had played at being soldiers in a country their workmates had already defeated.

Ben found himself working under a man who had been doing the same lowly job as Ben himself before he had gone into the Army five years earlier. Ben was quick-witted, with a natural flair for organization; the older man was slow, anxious about his position, and quick to resent advice. Ben, a little too sure of himself and proud of his new maturity, was the wrong subordinate for a fussy plodder. He lacked both patience and tact and the clashes between them were a constant irritation to them both.

The only thing that brightened his life was that Phyllis was at last getting married and leaving home.

'I'll be able to have my bedroom back!' he exclaimed, when he was told the news.

'You're a fine brother!' Phyllis told him. 'How about saying "Congratulations" or "Hope you'll be happy" before you think what you're getting out of me gettin' hitched?'

'Sorry. I wish you all the best, of course,' Ben muttered.

'You're a strange lad, that you are,' Phyllis said. 'It's what – fifteen year? – since me an' Elsie turned you out of that bedroom, but you still think of it as yours.'

'Who's the lucky man?' Ben asked quickly.

'Ernie Baxcombe.'

'The son of that man who used to work for the Assistance Board?'

'Mr Baxcombe's in a very good way of business in the building trade. He's done all right for 'imself, and Ernie'll do better, you'll see.'

Ernie Baxcombe was a sleek-looking young man, with the same sharp features as his father. Looks like a ferret, Ben thought distastefully when Phyllis brought him home. Still, he was taking Phyllis off their hands, which was something to be thankful for.

'How are you finding things at Maxton's?' he asked Ben.

'Well enough.'

'Satisfied with your job?'

'I wouldn't say that, but I hope for something better when we've settled down.'

'If you ever want to make a change I might have an opening for you.'

'Good of you,' Ben said, but Ernie missed the sarcasm in his voice.

'Dad an' me are doing very nicely,' he said. 'I've got plans for expansion. I'm qualified, you know; got my chartered surveyor's exam. I wasn't able to fight, owing to health, so I made the most of my time while I could. You're a smart young chap, with a bit of class about you. You might do worse than come in with us, though what we're really after is someone with a bit of capital.'

'I'll keep it in mind,' Ben said.

Ernie's remark about looking for someone with capital stayed in his memory. His dealings in Germany had left him with a profit of nearly two hundred pounds. On top of that he had his *Book of Hours*, but what he still did not know was how much it was worth. Nor was it quite the right time to find out. Post-war Britain was still in the doldrums. He was unlikely to find a good buyer until things improved. He would keep it until he really needed the money. As for joining up with Ernie, he was not keen on the idea, even though he saw that what his new brother-in-law had said was true: his firm was making money hand over fist.

His job became more and more depressing. He scanned the noticeboards, hoping for a chance to get away from his present department, and when the post of Personal Assistant to the Chairman of Maxton's was advertised it came to Ben in a flash that this was the chance he needed. It would take him out of clerking and into management. He would get an insight into life at the top and it was a stepping stone to better things.

He knew that he was up against stiff competition, but he believed that he could do the job. True, some of the duties mentioned in the job description he was given set him back a bit. He had to admit that he had not had much contact with Government departments, except at a very lowly level, nor did he know how to approach a Minister's Private Office, but to Ben these looked like things he could pick up rapidly if someone would just show him the ropes. More worrying were the hints about social arrangements. Lunches and things, Ben thought vaguely: not really in his line. Still, the Chairman had a secretary who had been with him for years. She would be able to put him straight about things like that.

He was optimistic when he passed the first hurdle and was

given a preliminary interview before a panel of three men, but their talk did not go well. He wanted them to judge him on his personal qualities, on his keenness and his confidence that he could learn the job. Instead, they hammered away at his family background, his limited education and his lack of wide experience. Try as he would, he could not seem to get through to them that he had risen above the circumstances into which he had been born. Most damning of all, they had in front of them a report from his superior which Ben knew could only be unfavourable.

He went back to his desk sour with defeat, but he had made a better impression than he feared and at least one of the panel had been struck by his argument that a grass-roots assistant would bring a fresh insight into the Chairman's office. The three men argued it out afterwards.

'Completely unsuitable,' the first of them said. 'At the very least the post calls for a university education.'

'He's got some good qualities, but of course this level of management is way above his capabilities,' the second agreed. 'All the same ... I think we should let his name go forward, if only to encourage other ambitious youngsters. The Chairman may think it worthwhile to see him – in the name of democracy, if nothing else.'

Since Ben had not expected to get any further with his application the news that he was to see the Chairman revived all his old hopes. He had always believed that if he could get an interview with the man at the top he stood a chance of convincing him that Ben was the right man to serve him.

By the time the Chairman saw Ben he had already seen three other candidates and had made up his mind which one he wanted. It was a waste of his time to see Ben, a piece of softness of which he was rather ashamed. He managed to spare Ben a quarter of an hour, not realizing that Ben knew he had spent three times as long with each of the others. He was kind, and it would have been better if he had been hard. Ben saw through the well-meant effort to let him down lightly and raged at the condescension it represented. His fury put a glitter into his eyes and added a crispness to his responses that interested the Chairman. All the same, the lad was not right for the job, he had no real understanding of what it entailed; he might go far, but not as the Chairman's own Personal Assistant.

When Ben received a letter two days later politely telling him that he had been unsuccessful it was no more than he had expected.

'Damn them,' he said softly, crumpling the letter up in his hand. 'Damn them, they knew all along I wasn't going to get it.'

His reaction was all the more acute because he had seen that job as his way into the world he wanted to reach, the one in which he was sure he could do well. To Ben it seemed that he was like a bird unable to fly because of oil on its wings. He was held down, earthbound and unable to get free, when with absolute conviction he knew that he belonged in a different atmosphere, soaring in clearer air. Being Personal Assistant to the Chairman would have taken him into an environment where he would have been at home. Once there, he would have held his own. In three months he would have mastered the job, in six he would have been doing it better than anyone had before, in a couple of years he would have been ready for promotion. But they wouldn't let him get off the ground.

Paul Tredegar had seen what he was made of, but Paul was long dead. Ernie Baxcombe had had an inkling, too. A repulsive little man, but a money-maker. He and Phyllis owned the house they lived in, he had managed to wangle himself a new car at a time when there were few on the market, Phyllis was flaunting a fur coat. His father's business hadn't brought in profits like that until Ernie took charge. Coldly, Ben weighed up the benefits of joining Ernie against his reluctance to be associated with the Baxcombe family. It was not an attractive prospect, but better than wearing away his days as a clerk waiting for dead men's shoes and one small step at a time up the ladder.

What Ben wanted was a chance to prove himself; a position which would earn respect from other men of his kind, the ambitious men, the go-getters. And he wanted money. Enough to buy him the marks of success. A fine house. The memory of Berringer Hall came into his mind and he dismissed it with a wry smile, for he no longer believed he could buy a house like that. A beautiful wife. No hurry to get married, but when he did he wanted a woman who would turn heads and arouse envy. A family? Plenty of time to think about that. He was only twenty-one. He'd like to be able to do something for his present family, at least for his father. Travel, a fast car, good clothes. But they were a small part of his ambition. What he wanted was to be top.

He would have to break away from Maxton's. The profit from his German transactions would be enough to buy his way into the Baxcombe enterprise and if it looked like being worthwhile he would sell his *Book of Hours* and put up the money for a more ambitious project.

It would be time enough to reveal that he could put his hands on more substantial capital when he had had a chance to find out how much he could get out of a partnership with Ernie. It was going to be a partnership, Ben was quite clear about that. There would be no question of him being a junior member of Ernie's staff, not once he had learnt the ropes. For the time being he would keep his eyes open and his mouth shut, but once he had grasped the nature of the business Ernie could move over and make room for Ben.

II. Josie

Chapter Seven

By the time Stan Bewley came home from the war, at about the time Ben went off to Germany, his son Teddy was four years old and Josie was twelve. Like Ben, Josie had taken the local scholarship examination and had passed, but unlike Ben she had had friends on hand who had insisted that she must take up her place at the grammar school.

'Don't be silly, Ethel,' Marigold said, with the sharpness that had become habitual. 'Of course Josie must have her chance.'

'It'll mean staying at school till she's sixteen,' Ethel muttered.

'And a very good thing, too. She's a bright child. She'll do far better in life if she has a decent education.'

A letter from Stan clinched the matter. He was full of enthusiasm for his clever daughter's success, and Ethel was silenced.

She became vocal once more when she heard Stan's plans for the future once he was out of the Navy.

'Go to Australia?' she said disbelievingly. 'You must be out of your mind!'

'No, I'm not. It's the only answer, lass. Europe's finished. I want a fresh start, somewhere where there's a bit of space and some sunshine.'

Josie knew something was up when, instead of being happy at having her husband home and out of danger, Ethel wept unceasingly day after day. Josie's sharp little nose twitched with curiosity. It took her no time at all to get the news out of her mother, but Ethel was disgusted when Josie was delighted.

'What about your grand new school you're so keen on?' she asked. 'You won't take that to Australia with you.'

'There'll be schools there just as good. I think it's a wizard idea. When do we go?'

'You'd better ask your father. You'd think he'd be glad to settle down, after all we've been through,' Ethel complained. 'We could go home! There's work on the Tyne now.'

But Stan set his mouth obstinately when this argument was repeated to him.

'I'll no' go back to Tyneside,' he said. 'And I'll no' stay here, either.'

'Mrs Pemberley wants us to go on living at the Hall,' Ethel said. 'We'll be letting her down, and she's been good to us all through the war.'

'Aye, and you've been useful to her, too,' Stan said. 'I'm looking for something better than being a living-in handyman. I want a fresh start and that's what we'll get in Australia.'

'I'll never settle.'

'Then you'd better stay behind.'

The wail that Ethel set up sent him out of the room, slamming the door behind him. As soon as he had gone, she dried her eyes. The way he had spoken had frightened her. He might mean it. Anything was better than being left in England, with a husband in Australia.

The long process of applying for emigration began and Ethel was surprised by the businesslike way Stan set about it. He had changed, there was no doubt about that. She began to feel proud of his new spirit of independence, even though it worked against her.

'We've got to report for medical examination,' Stan said one morning.

'Treating us like a lot of cattle,' Ethel said. 'I suppose we're all healthy enough, though you'd never think a morsel of food passed our Josie's lips, growing like a beanpole and about as much flesh on her.'

Little Ted, in spite of being a wartime baby, was a plump, ruddy-faced little fellow; Josie was a scarecrow by his side. She showed few signs of developing into a woman, even though she had suddenly shot up, tall, pale and drooping, like a weed growing in the shade of the Berringer woods.

'She's outgrowing her strength,' Ethel said. 'Perhaps the

doctor will give her a tonic.'

But the doctor's verdict on her daughter when it came, reduced Ethel to terrified silence: Josie had tuberculosis.

It was Stan who discussed plans for sending Josie into a sanatorium. Ethel never opened her mouth. It was not until they were on their way home, sitting side by side on the top of the bus so that Stan could smoke, that she said in a whisper, 'Oh, Stan! Oh, Stan!'

'There was a lot of it about when I was a boy,' Stan said. 'One of my uncles died of it, I remember. You would have thought Josie, being brought up in the country since she was a baby, would have escaped.'

'There's never been anything like that in my family,' Ethel said quickly. 'Oh, Stan, what are we going to tell people?'

He did not understand her at first, then he began to see that Ethel looked upon Josie's illness as a disgrace, something to be concealed if possible. The way she shuddered away from talking about it forced him to take on himself the task of telling Josie the news.

Josie fixed her un-childlike eyes on his face, noting the lines of worry and bitterness that were beginning to show.

'Can't I get better in Australia?' she asked. 'You said we'd get lots of sunshine and fresh air. Isn't that what I need?'

'They won't take us,' Stan said, his voice dull with the disappointment he was trying to conceal from her. 'Leastways, they won't take you and we can't go without you.'

As it began to sink in Josie drooped, overwhelmed by the guilt of frustrating his hope for a brighter future for his family.

'I'm sorry, Dad,' she whispered.

'Not your fault, hinny. It's prob'ly been in you since you were a baby. You had a bad start in life, and that were no fault of yours. It's a blow, I'll admit, but we'll come about.'

'Am I going to die?'

'Not you!' Stan said, startled by the directness of the question. 'You'll go into this hospital they told us about today – a grand place, right up on the moors – and come out fit as a fiddle. Us Bewleys are tough folk, just you remember that, young Josie.'

Josie disappeared into the sanatorium for a year and grew

away from her family, just as Ben had grown away from his. The hospital routine began to seem like a natural way of life, the slow monotonous days, the cold fresh air that swept through the wards, the insistence on rest, the medicines she had to swallow, the X-rays and examinations. She had lessons with the other children, but she knew that she was falling behind.

Always at the back of her mind was the recollection that it was her illness which had prevented her family from taking up a new life in Australia. She dreamed about it sometimes – stretches of empty beach with great waves rolling towards the shore and crashing in a torrent of foam; her mother and father and little Ted, all sun-bronzed and somehow bigger than they were in real life; harmony between them, and herself fit, strong and pretty, her mother's right hand, her father's favourite. Clever, too; even in her dreams Josie valued her brains higher than her looks. She would carry off prizes and everyone would be proud of her; she would be the first woman Prime Minister of Australia.

Reality broke in when Ethel wrote and said they were moving out of Berringer Hall, back to the little cottage in the woods.

'If I had my way we'd go back to South Shields,' Ethel wrote. 'But your dad has lost interest in making a change. I don't like this place and never have, but it's a roof of our own. You may as well know there'll be another brother or sister for you when you come home. Dad sends his love. He's gone down to the pub, leaving me on my own as I do not feel up to it in my condition, and anyway can't leave Ted.'

Josie screwed up her nose as she read the letter. Mum going on, as usual. She did not much like the sound of what was waiting for her when she went home. No word of anyone coming to see her, but it was an awkward journey and she did not really expect it. Money must be tight, with another baby on the way. Josie was conscious of a faint, puritanical disgust. She had developed while she was in hospital, putting on weight, beginning at last to show signs of developing a figure, and starting her periods, but her new maturity did not extend to any real understanding of the relations between a man and a woman. Her feeling about the child her parents had conceived was that they ought to have had more sense.

Stan went to fetch her when she left hospital. He looked like a stranger, bigger and more thickset than Josie remembered him. She had a moment of panic when he stood in the doorway, thinking he might not know her. She had outgrown the clothes she had worn when she went into the sanatorium and had been given a dress and coat which Josie strongly suspected had belonged to a girl who had died. Better not to think about that. The coat was a good navy wool and the frock was only a bit on the short side. Josie had shot up even more during her weeks in bed. She was still sandy-haired, sharp-featured and angular. Not attractive, but memorable for her grey-green eyes and fierce intelligence.

She took a tentative step forward and Stan held out his hand. In her relief Josie gave him a hug, clinging to him more demonstratively than she would have done in the past. He felt solid and dependable, but Josie was quick to notice that he smelled of drink.

'You've been on the beer,' she remarked, as she unwound her arms from his neck.

'By heck! You sound just like your mother. I brought a sandwich with me and had a pint with it while I was waiting for it to be time to collect you. Let's have a look at you. You're taller than ever, a proper young lady. How do you feel?'

'I'm perfectly all right now. Must be, or they wouldn't have let me out. How's Mum?'

'She's fine. And the new bairn's a grand wee boy.'

Josie made no comment. Her opinion of the baby remained unchanged. All the same, when she arrived at the cottage and Ethel put her new brother into her arms Josie was surprised at the thrill his soft weight gave her.

The cottage seemed cramped and dark after the big white hospital wards with the ever-open windows. There were damp nappies over a clothes horse by the fire. Josie began to feel stifled. When Stan lit a cigarette she cleared her throat and her mother looked at her with a frown.

'I thought you'd got rid of that cough,' she said.

'It's only a tickle from the smoke,' Josie said quickly.

Stan ground out his cigarette and Josie muttered, 'Sorry, Dad.'

The next day Josie walked up to Berringer Hall to see Nicola. It was an awkward meeting. They had begun to grow apart before Josie had gone away and now they seemed to have little in common, even though Nicola was pleased to see her.

'I'm being sent to boarding school,' she said. 'Can't say I'm looking forward to it very much, but Mummy is keen for me to go to her old school. She's getting married again, did you know?'

'Mum told me.'

'He's called Raymond Wadsby and he's a Member of Parliament,' Nicola said. 'Mummy wants me to be called Wadsby, too, but I'd much rather not and Grand-dad says I don't have to if I don't want to.'

It sounded vaguely unsatisfactory, as if Nicola did not much relish the idea of her new stepfather. Just like her not to come out in the open and say so. She'd always been a funny little stoic. She caught Josie watching her and flushed, looking away.

'I expect it will be all right,' she said. 'I don't know what to call him. I rather draw the line at "Daddy" or even "Father". Do you remember the way Ben used to call his stepmother "Bess"? I see why now. He wrote to me twice while he was in Germany. I suppose he must be home now.'

'He wrote to me, too. So did you. It was good of you. My mum and dad aren't great letter writers. I think you told me more about what was happening than they did.'

'I would have come to see you, but Mummy wouldn't let me. Will you keep in touch while I'm away at school? I hope to spend some of my holidays at Berringer, but Mummy and … and my stepfather will have to be in London most of the time while Parliament is sitting and he's got a house in Coryleigh for his constituency work, so I suppose I'll spend most of my time there. You could tell me what's going on in the village. I'll always think of this as my real home.'

'I'll write,' Josie promised, but in her heart she thought that Nicola would soon forget her once she began to make new friends. They had never really been close. It had been Ben who had been Nicola's protector. Nicola's life, the way she talked about a house in London and another in the country, of Members of Parliament and constituencies, seemed more alien now than it had done when they were children. Then it had not been important that it was Josie's mother who washed the floors and Nicola's mother who walked over them with impatient feet on her way to a committee meeting. Josie thought about Marigold, married to a Member of Parliament, and suppressed a grin. She'd be in her element, running people's lives.

Josie went back warily into school life. She was fourteen years old and the months she had lost had been crucial. As she had feared, she had fallen behind in some subjects, though she seemed to have read far more than most of the other girls. She was a curiosity to them; they wanted to hear all about her months in hospital and Josie saw that what they were really hoping for were morbid details of lingering death. Some of them shunned her and she guessed that their mothers were nervous of infection, which made her scornful. She flung herself into her work with a sort of feverish despair, knowing that she must catch up if she was ever to make anything of her life.

Her teachers found her a curious mixture of backwardness and maturity. Her long illness had brought her on in some ways, especially since she had been brought into contact with older women in the hospital, but she had also been isolated, both in the sanatorium and at Berringer Hall, and she was strangely out of touch with the obsessions of the other girls. Boys might not have existed as far as Josie was concerned, nor did she show much interest in the fashions in clothes, films or music.

When she had been home a few weeks she asked, 'Dad, are you still going to try to get to Australia, now that I'm cured?'

'The time for that's gone past,' Stan said. 'Your mother's heard too many tales of people going out there, not being able to settle and coming back.'

He glanced at the clock and Josie saw with a sinking heart that he was going off to the pub. Stan had picked up a liking for male company during his time in the Navy. He was not a heavy drinker, but whereas he had been contented to stay at home in the evenings before the war, and perhaps had felt himself too much of an outsider to be accepted by the village men, his years of mixing with all types on the ships in which he had served had made him more sure of his welcome. He had something in common now with the other men who had been away to war and he found that they, too, had difficulty in settling down now that they were home.

Ethel grumbled, but the truth was that she was as glad of his room as of his company. They rubbed along well enough, but she had got used to doing without him during the war and she did not appreciate how much Stan's experiences had broadened his mind. There was a lot of bickering, but few real rows. She disliked the cottage, but it was a roof, and a familiar roof, and Stan was in regular work. To Josie it seemed a poor existence, this dull acceptance of second best. People ought not to live like that, neither happy nor unhappy, just taking what was handed out to them. She nibbled the end of her pencil, frowning fiercely, dreaming of a day when she would deliver them all out of this circumscribed life into a better world.

Her return did give Ethel a little more freedom. She and Stan were able to go to Phyllis's wedding, leaving Josie in charge of Teddy and little Wally for one night.

'It were a real good do,' Ethel reported afterwards. 'Though I'd say Phyllis would have done well to lose a bit of weight before wearing white satin. The Baxcombes aren't my cup o' tea, but young Ernie seems to have his head screwed on right. He'll get on in the world if anyone does. Our Ben's turned into a fine boy – fine looking, that is. I didn't think much of his manners. Very toffee-nosed. Not a word to say for 'isself.'

After that one visit they heard little of the family in Jarrow. Neither Bess nor Ethel was a letter writer and it was only births, deaths or marriages that drew a letter out of them.

There had been a time when Josie had believed that she might get to a university, but as her sixteenth birthday drew near she began to realize that she would have to forget that ambition. Ethel was growing restive, impatient for the day when Josie would start to repay her parents for her extra schooling. She did not take kindly to the idea of a secretarial course which would extend Josie's schooldays by another six months.

'You'll be nigh on seventeen before you're earning,' she complained. 'I was bringing home wages by the time I was fourteen.'

'Six months isn't long to learn shorthand and typing,' Josie said. 'I'm lucky to be offered a free place. Most of the girls on the course will be paying for it.'

'Let's hope it leads to a decent job,' Ethel sniffed. 'There's few enough chances round here.'

Since this was true Josie did not reply. If she went on living at home, and she could scarcely afford to do anything else on a beginner's salary, then the best she could hope for was an opening in an office in the local market town.

She was still brooding over it when Ethel had a letter announcing a visit from Ben.

'Doesn't ask if he can come, you'll notice,' Ethel remarked. 'Just says he'll be here on Saturday and no question whether it'll be convenient or no.'

'We never go anywhere, so why should it be inconvenient?' Josie asked.

'That's enough lip from you, thank you, madam. I wonder what he wants?'

'Something to do with Dad,' Josie said, reading the letter.

When Ben arrived on Saturday Josie was stricken into a most unusual silence. It was the first time she had seen him since he had left Berringer as a boy of fifteen. Now he was twenty-two and she would hardly have recognized him. Had he always been so good-looking? It gave her a curious jolt, as if someone had thumped her in the stomach. He had grown tall, and better built than he had been as a boy, dark-haired, with a well-shaped head, high cheekbones and a thin, straight nose. He had always had those strange, light eyes that seemed to look right through you, but as a child she had never noticed that the clear grey was set off by a darker line round the iris, and by lashes as thick and soft as a girl's. He had changed in other ways, too. There had been a sensitivity about the younger Ben, something Josie had once scorned as softness, shown by his gentleness towards little Nicola, which was missing, or at least hidden, now.

He stopped just inside the front door, looking round as if in search of something familiar, and Josie remembered that the last time he had seen the cottage Paul Tredegar had been living in it. Was Ben thinking the same thing? If so, he did not remark on it.

'I won't waste time making you guess why I'm here,' he said. 'I want to know if you'd be interested in a job, Stan.'

Not 'Uncle Stan', Josie noticed, and saw from the way her mother pursed her mouth that she had been struck by the same thing.

'Depends what it is,' Stan said.

'I've gone into business with the Baxcombes. We've bought up a row of houses – damn near derelict, but I think we can save them – and we plan to do them up for letting. We need some good workmen. Interested?'

He waited, but when Stan did not reply, he added, 'If it worked out all right I'd see you were made foreman. I know you can turn your hand to most jobs so you ought to be able to oversee other men.'

'You!' Stan exclaimed. 'You're nothing but a young lad. What say would you have?'

'I've put up the money for this project. I'm in charge. Like it or not, I'd be your boss. It'd mean moving.'

'Where to?' Ethel asked.

'Ferryhaven.'

'That's within spittin' distance of home!' Ethel exclaimed.

Ben smiled slightly. 'Do you still think of Tyneside as home, after all these years?'

'I do that! Oh, Stan, take it!'

'Hold on, hold on. There's things to be talked about first. Like money and how long the job'll last.'

'I'll see you're all right,' Ben said. He glanced at Ethel's eager face and at Josie, burning with curiosity, and added, 'Walk down to the village with me and I'll buy you a pint while we talk it over.'

By the time they returned it was all settled. Stan would go on ahead of the rest of the family and start work and they would follow as soon as the first of the renovated houses was fit to live in.

'Will Colonel Berringer let us go on living in the cottage if

Dad's no longer working for him?' Josie asked.

'That might be a difficulty,' Ben admitted. 'I'm going to walk up to the Hall this afternoon and talk to him about it.'

'I'll come with you,' Josie said. 'Nicola's there this weekend for her half-term.'

They walked up through the woods, past the pond where Paul had drowned. It was overgrown with weeds, the rushes standing thickly round the edges. The wooden diving board had rotted and collapsed into the water. Ben stood and looked at it, his face sombre.

'You were still at Berringer when Mr Tredegar's sister cleared out his cottage, weren't you?' he asked. 'What did she do with all his stuff?'

'She only came once,' Josie said. 'She had a quick look round and said it was all shabby old stuff, which it was, and it could go to the Salvation Army.'

'What about his books?'

'Miss Flanders took some of them for the school library and we burnt the rest of them.'

'*Burnt* them?'

'Mrs Pemberley said she wouldn't have the fusty old things and Nicola and I helped her put them on the bonfire.'

'Damn stupid woman.'

'You never did get on with her. Did you know she'd got married again?'

'I always thought she would.'

'Why are you interested in the books?'

Ben turned away from the water and walked on. 'Some of them were worth money.'

'Did Mr Tredegar say so?'

Ben took a moment or two to reply. 'He said some of them were too precious to lend out,' he said.

He lapsed into silence, but there was something about his expression, half exasperated, half smiling at some secret satisfaction, that made Josie suspicious.

'Did you keep some of the books he lent you?' she probed.

'He gave me one or two,' Ben said in an offhand way that failed to deceive her.

'And they turned out to be valuable?'

'I never said that!'

'Go on! You look like the cat that's swallowed the canary. And where did you find the money to go in with the Baxcombes? I bet you sold Mr Tredegar's books.'

'I did a bit of trading in Germany and got enough together to satisfy Ernie Baxcombe. Two hundred pounds.'

'Not bad,' Josie said admiringly. 'Now tell me about the books.'

'Nothing to tell.'

'My God, it's like getting blood out of a stone trying to make you talk. Look, this is Josie, remember? We used to tell one another secrets when we were kids, didn't we? You can trust me.'

'I don't know that we were ever that close,' Ben retorted. 'You were a cantankerous little blighter. Nicola was my pet.'

'True enough,' Josie admitted. She waited, not unhopefully, sensing that Ben was bursting to tell someone a piece of news that was too exciting to be kept to himself.

'All right, I'll tell you,' Ben capitulated. 'I put Mr Tredegar's books up for sale. Most of them were only worth peanuts, but the *Book of Hours* was a real treasure. I got twelve thousand pounds for it.'

Josie was too awestruck to say anything at first. 'Twelve thousand pounds!' she breathed at last. 'Ben, it's a fortune! What are you going to do with it?'

'Multiply it by ten to begin with.'

Again she was silent, doing sums in her head. 'That'll be a hundred and twenty thousand pounds!'

'That's right. When I've made my first hundred thousand I'll know I'm on my way.'

'Where to? Becoming a millionaire?'

'Why not?'

Josie felt excited, almost frightened. He was so cool about it, so matter of fact, as if he only had to will it and it would happen. Looking at him sideways, seeing his hard, clear profile against the dark trees, taking in his air of self-containment, Josie shivered.

'Mr Tredegar never gave you a book that was worth that amount of money,' she said. 'You nicked it, didn't you?'

'Better for me to have it than for it to be chucked into the fire.'

'All the same ... twelve thousand pounds!'

'Mr Tredegar gave it to me,' Ben repeated. 'Don't you ever say any different, or I'll wring your neck.'

'As if I would! Anyway, I reckon you're in the clear. The reason the sister didn't want any of his stuff was because she was engaged to marry an American. She must be long gone by now.'

'He would have wanted me to have it,' Ben persisted.

'Perhaps he would. He was daft enough for anything. Was it really an accident, the way he died? All the kids at school said he killed himself for love of Mrs Pemberley.'

'I didn't think anyone knew about that!' Ben exclaimed.

'Oh, Ben! He was always mooning over her! Of course, I took care Nicola never heard what they said.'

'I should hope not! You still keep friendly with Nicola?'

'We don't see much of one another,' Josie admitted. 'She's away at school and we only meet if she happens to visit her granddad. Once Dad gives up working for him I expect we'll lose touch.'

'How do you feel about moving?'

'Suits me down to the ground. There'll be much better openings for me in a town.'

'What are you going to do?'

'Learn shorthand and typing and go into a bloody office.'

'What do you *want* to do?'

'Make things better,' Josie said slowly.

She was conscious of a mounting excitement as she put into words for the first time something that had been at the back of her mind for a long while.

'I want to work for people like my mum and dad. Give them better lives.'

'Politics?'

'I want to be a Member of Parliament,' Josie said in a nervous rush.

She was relieved when he did not laugh at her ambition, only said in his cool way, "Why not?" but then he spoiled it by adding in a way she thought unnecessarily flippant, 'Vote for

Josephine Bewley – our first Lady Prime Minister.'

They entered Berringer Hall by the garden entrance, through the little wicket gate that led from the woods into the kitchen garden, up the old brick path between the rows of cabbages and carrots. Ben stopped when they got their first proper sight of the house.

'It looks a bit run down,' he said.

'There's been a war on, didn't you know?' Josie said.

'I remember it as being the most beautiful house I'd ever seen.'

'It's a fine place, if you like that kind of thing. I'd just as soon see it turned into flats for the workers,' Josie said, getting back at him for his gibe about being Prime Minister.

'Vandal!'

They were laughing as they left the kitchen garden and met Nicola.

'Josie! How nice!' she exclaimed. She looked doubtfully at Ben and he waited, still smiling.

'It can't be Ben?'

'It is,' he said. 'Didn't you know me, Nicola?'

The colour came up into her face. She looked pleased and confused and very young. She must be about fourteen, Ben calculated, a slip of a girl, only half developed, with something of her mother's features but her father's richer colouring. A brown girl, her fine skin the delicate colour of brown eggshell, her eyes wide and dark. Sweet and vulnerable and shy.

'It's been a long time,' she protested. 'I remember you as a big boy who held my hand when we came through the woods.'

'I really came to see Colonel Berringer,' Ben said, still watching her. 'Do you think he'd spare me a few minutes?'

'I'm sure he would. Come into the house.'

Josie followed them, piqued at being forgotten, but as soon as Ben had gone with Colonel Berringer into his study Nicola turned to her again and Josie was mollified, even though it was Ben Nicola wanted to talk about.

'I didn't remember him at all! Isn't that awful? Of course, he's a man now and he was quite a young boy when I last saw him, and I was very little.'

'He's handsome, isn't he?' Josie asked in an offhand way,

wanting to know whether Nicola saw him in the same way as she did herself.

'Very!' Nicola said, colouring all over her too-open face.

'He says he's going to turn himself into a millionaire.'

Since she saw no reason to keep it a secret, Josie plunged into the news about the change that was coming into her life.

'You'll be going away then,' Nicola said. 'I shan't see you again, or ... or Ben.'

'Probably not,' Josie agreed. 'Never mind, you must have heaps of other friends.'

'I quite like some of the girls at school,' Nicola admitted. 'There's nobody else round here, though.'

'What about your proper home?'

'It's so unsettling, moving about with Mummy and Raymond between London and Coryleigh, and when I'm at home for a long time in the summer we usually go abroad.'

She took Josie into the kitchen and fetched some lemonade and glasses – three glasses, Josie noted – and they carried them out to the terrace where the sun was warm enough for them to sit on one of the old stone seats. When Ben came back to join them he accepted a glass of lemonade and stood leaning against the parapet, looking over the neglected garden.

'These urns used to be full of pink geraniums,' he said.

'I try to do a bit of gardening when I visit Granddad,' Nicola said. 'It will take a long time to bring it back to what it was.'

'Never mind that, what did Colonel Berringer say about us staying on until Dad's got a house ready for us?' Josie demanded.

Ben did not answer immediately. The talk with Colonel Berringer had been cordial and yet it had left a disturbing impression on Ben's mind. The old man had been interested to hear how well Ben had been doing and for once Ben had let himself open up, almost to the point of boasting about his success. The colonel had begun to smile and Ben had broken off, regretting a frankness that had sounded brash, but the colonel's only comment had been, 'Don't try to be too clever, young Ben.'

The shrewdness behind his smile had made Ben feel uncomfortable because it hinted that Colonel Berringer guessed how close to the wind Ben and Ernie had sailed on some of their deals, but he put the thought behind him and in answer to Josie's question he said briefly, 'He'll let you keep the cottage for three months.'

'That's because you asked him,' Josie said. 'He always had a soft spot for you.'

'He's aged since I saw him last,' Ben said. He glanced at Nicola and decided not to say any more. 'It was a bit of a blow to him, losing Stan.'

'It would be,' Josie agreed. 'Dad does a bit of everything, even gardening, though not the flower beds.'

'Could you tell me more about your plans?' Nicola asked diffidently.

'There's a housing shortage,' Ben said. 'To begin with, I mean to reclaim old houses that have been damaged or neglected. After that, I need to get hold of some land and start developing.'

'It sounds very ambitious,' Nicola said.

The admiring way she was looking at Ben irritated Josie. It was stupid to be so uncritical, so bowled over by a handsome face and assured manner.

'If I go into the Labour Party and you become a capitalist, we'll be on opposite sides,' she said.

Ben looked at her and a spark of antagonism passed between them as they both realised she was being deliberately provocative. When he replied it was seriously, even grimly.

'I aim to lift myself out of poverty by my own efforts, not by relying on any political party,' he said. 'You may not like the way I go about it, but I'm not worried about that. I'll fix my own standards.'

'That's dangerous,' Josie said.

She would have enlarged on what she meant, but Ben interrupted her.

'That's my message,' he said. 'Live dangerously!'

Nicola laughed with excitement and exhilaration, but Josie shivered when Ben turned his head and smiled at her. There was something calculating about the way he looked at Nicola, something intent and watchful. A strange young man, her cousin Ben, who was not really her cousin at all, quite different from anyone else in the family. Sharp as a knife. Hard and bright, with the glitter of steel in his eyes. Dangerous.

Chapter Eight

Ferryhaven was a small town, close enough to Newcastle to be called a suburb, independent enough to resent being overshadowed by its great neighbour. The Bewley family settled into it as if they had been born there. The house fulfilled Ethel's ambition to be semi-detached, being at the end of a terrace, and it was more spacious than the cottage in the woods had been. There were three bedrooms and the two boys moved in with one another, giving Josie a room to herself at last.

Since there seemed no help for it, she took her secretarial course and studied with fierce concentration. Her shorthand speeds were the highest in the class, she typed like a demon and she had no difficulty in grasping the elements of book-keeping. As soon as she had finished the six-month course she was snapped up to work in the local council offices.

'Just what I wanted,' she said. 'I can study the way things are run so that I'll know all about it when I stand for the council myself one day.'

Stan thought she was joking, but Josie was serious. She joined the Young Socialists and gave them all her spare time. Her room was always littered with pamphlets and she took an active part in meetings. If there was a debate going, Josie Bewley would be on her feet and arguing, her quick intelligence and ready tongue earning her victories which were not always deserved. She knew she had the reputation of being too hard on the slower-witted and she tried to keep a check on herself, but she was too impatient to suffer fools gladly.

Stan went on working for Ben and Josie gathered that the business was thriving. As time went by her father had to spend more and more time away from home on distant sites.

'As bad as during the war,' Ethel said, but she wasn't really grumbling, not with the money Stan was bringing in and the comfortable home they had round them.

It took Josie a long time to realize that she was as much in a rut as if they had stayed at Berringer Hall. For four years it was enough to master her job and make a move up the promotion ladder, to meet her socialist friends and argue with them, to take notes of speeches and push leaflets through doors, and then quite suddenly Josie woke up to the fact that her cronies were dropping away, mostly because they were starting to get married. Josie was contemptuous when she saw their revolutionary fervour change to an obsession with three-piece suites and housing quotas.

'About time you found yourself a boyfriend,' Ethel remarked more than once. 'That's the third wedding you've been to this year. There won't be anyone left if you don't brush your ideas up.'

'I've got better things to do than moon about with a boy,' Josie insisted.

The scowl on her face did nothing to improve her looks. She was as skinny as ever, but these days she was wiry rather than sickly. Her body was angular, her face was bony, and her sandy hair had not benefited from an attempt to give it a permanent wave. What Josie had was personality. She made herself noticed and, having been noticed, she was remembered. She was only half aware of having something that distinguished her from the crowd, and as far as her family were concerned it just made her difficult to live with, but Josie was beginning to feel confined. Something in her needed to stretch; she had to get away.

She was twenty-one and it ought to have been possible to leave home, but the idea was so far outside everything Stan and Ethel were used to that Josie could hardly bring herself to suggest it. Besides, where would she go? London? The idea did not attract her, but it had to be somewhere at a distance to give her the excuse for living independently. She scanned the newspapers for openings and when she saw the advertisement for secretaries to work for the World Health Organization in

Geneva it was as if she had known all along that this was what she wanted.

It fulfilled all her requirements: distance from Ferryhaven; involvement in an organization which was doing some good in the world; a limited contract, so that she could come home at the end of two years and take up her political ambitions again; what sounded like a excellent salary; and the chance to better herself. Travel would broaden her experience; mixing with foreigners, especially people from less privileged countries, would help her to understand their problems; she saw herself at the centre of a group of clever expatriates, all working for a better world.

It was a heady picture and it carried Josie through all the difficulties she had to face, from Stan and Ethel's disapproval, stemming mostly from their ignorance of what the job involved, to cynical remarks from Ben about the amount of money that was wasted on useless projects abroad.

It was only by chance that he heard about the job when he called in unexpectedly to see Stan and Ethel appealed to him to try and make her daughter see reason.

'Still trying to change the world, Josie?' he asked. 'You won't see many results working in a bureaucracy in Europe. You ought to become a missionary.'

'Religion is the spearhead of colonialism,' Josie said.

'I thought it was the opium of the masses?'

She glowered at him, knowing she had been a fool to let him needle her into trotting out a stock phrase. He was looking repulsively prosperous. He was driving a car, for one thing, a sleek grey Jaguar. His suit was well cut, his shirt was pristine white, his tie was silk and his shoes were Italian.

'That set you back a pretty penny,' Ethel said, fingering the sleeve of his jacket.

'I look on it as an investment,' Ben said. 'Have you decided to become Secretary General of the United Nations, Josie? I thought you had your sights set on being our first woman Prime Minister.'

'That's right, laugh!' Josie said. 'No one takes me seriously because they think I'm too young and I'm perfectly aware that I lack experience, thank you. That's why I need to get away and do something that will stretch me.'

'Is your health up to it?' Ben asked and she saw that he was no longer teasing her.

'I've had a check-up and the results were negative. I should be in the clear for the rest of my life. Those months in the sanatorium made a difference to me, though. I fell behind too far ever to make up the ground I'd lost.'

She glanced at her father and added, 'And I ruined Dad's hopes for a new life in Australia.'

'That's an old story,' Stan muttered uncomfortably.

'I haven't forgotten. I always meant to do something for you and Mum to make up for it, but you're comfortably settled now, and Mum likes it here, so ...'

'You feel free,' Ben said, watching her.

'That's right,' Josie admitted.

'I don't know why you don't settle down and get married like other girls,' Ethel burst out.

'Chance would be a fine thing,' Josie retorted. 'Nobody's asked me – not that I'd take them if they did. I want something different out of life.'

'You'll regret it one of these days,' her mother threatened her. 'No use talkin' to you. You'll go your own gate, that's for sure, and nothing I can say will stop you.'

'I think it's a good idea,' Ben said. 'Go after your job in Geneva, Josie, and good luck to you.'

He gave her the tiniest flicker of a wink and she saw that he had realized, just as she had, that that one decisive statement from him had had more effect on her parents than all her own careful arguments.

Geneva was a grey city. Not at all like Josie's idea of Switzerland. No chalets, only tall stone buildings. A gunmetal lake, and a thick layer of cloud pressing down on top of it. A bitter wind that blew up the valley, a wind with a cutting edge to it that froze the hairs inside her nostrils and made the bones of her face ache.

She hunched her shoulders inside her coat as she made her way across the Pont de Mont Blanc. She had been told that she ought to take the tram, not try to walk while the Bise was blowing, and now she saw why. It was January and she had been in Geneva a month. The World Health Executive Board was meeting and for the three weeks it lasted the secretarial pool were required to work in shifts. Josie had been put on the five o'clock to midnight shift, but the previous day there had been a late meeting and a rush of translation work and she had not left the Palais des Nations until two o'clock in the morning. She was living in a small *pension* and she had not been able to sleep late. Madame wanted her *pensionnaires* at the breakfast table by eight o'clock and out of their rooms by nine so that they could be cleaned. In any case, Josie had an appointment to view a studio flat in the old town. She hoped that it would be suitable and affordable because she was beginning to long for a place of her own.

Grand' rue when she reached it was narrow, cobbled and steep. As Josie began to climb the hill the carillon in the cathedral, hidden somewhere at the top, began to play a tune and then to strike eleven o'clock. Josie wrinkled her nose disparagingly. It was all very picturesque, no doubt, but if one had been available she would have preferred a bright new apartment near the Palais. Something modern and labour-saving, and never mind the historical background.

She was half prepared to turn the place down as she walked up the twisting staircase to the first floor, but once she was inside she found a pleasant and well-appointed apartment. It was the usual studio – a bedsitting room, a kitchen and a bathroom. The furniture was heavy and old-fashioned, but the fixtures were new. Josie looked longingly at the yellow bathroom. A bathroom of her own, almost unimaginable bliss. The smallness of the kitchen did not bother her, since Josie had no intention of becoming a gourmet cook. The rent was a little more than she had hoped to pay, but not unmanageable. Within half an hour she had agreed to take the flat and to move in at the weekend.

When she went in to work that afternoon Josie was warmed by the interest the other girls showed in her new apartment. They were a good crowd, friendlier than she had anticipated, and very ready with advice for a newcomer. It was because of their encouragement that Josie had decided to rent a place of her own rather than go on living in the *pension* or lodging with a family, and now that she had committed herself she was glad of it. She would be able to return some of the invitations that had been showered on her to drop in for coffee in the evenings. In particular, she would be able to repay Letty, who had had her to lunch on Christmas Day, and Mona, who had asked Josie to her New Year's party.

It was as well that she liked the girls because Josie found the work boring, just as Ben had warned her she would. In her heart she was outraged at being required to go into the typing pool for two months, but everyone assured her that it was the best place to pick up an idea of the work of the Organization.

'And for getting a chance to go abroad,' Mona told her. 'This year the World Health Assembly will be in Geneva, but quite soon we've heard it will be in the United States. You won't get anyone applying for a job outside the pool that year!'

Josie, with her fast speeds and accuracy, was soon a popular figure with the translators and précis writers. Everything that was said at one day's conference was delivered to the delegates at their hotels the following morning, translated into the working languages of the Organization. It made the girls groan when the taxi drivers who collected them from the Palais after a gruelling evening's work pretended to believe that they were involved in an endless round of parties.

'Mind you, there are "delegates' girls",' Mona remarked. 'I don't know how they keep it up. Has anyone invited you to help him improve his English, Josie?'

'Is it likely?'

Mona looked at her thoughtfully. 'You don't make the best of yourself,' she said. 'You ought to go to my hairdresser and have that mop of yours cut.'

'It does need something done to it,' Josie admitted. 'I washed it under the tap with toilet soap because I couldn't get to the shop to buy a shampoo. Still an' all, even a decent cut isn't going to turn me into a raving beauty.'

'You could wear clothes well, if you'd only take the trouble. You're tall and slim ...'

'Skinny, you mean.'

'A clothes-horse. Honestly, you ought to make more of an effort.'

Josie hitched her baggy skirt round so that the pleat was in the centre instead of over her hip.

'As soon as I get settled I'll give this a press,' she promised.

'Oh, Josie, honestly ...! Put it on the scrap heap and buy yourself a new one.'

They had been chatting during their coffee break. As soon as they were back at work Josie was sent to take dictation from a man she had not met before.

'Who's Mr Rattray?' she muttered to Mona as she collected her notebook and pencil.

'Dominic Rattray. Oh, boy! God's gift to the female sex, if you don't mind them looking scruffy – which is obviously no drawback in your case. Irish, but brought up in France. Went to the Sorbonne. Speaks French like a native, also Russian and one or two other languages. Charms the birds off the trees and the girls into his flat – which is in the Old Town, like yours. Not to be trusted an inch, but practically any girl in the pool will swop places with you if you don't feel like taking dictation.'

'I ought to be safe with him with my looks.'

'Not a bar where our Dominic is concerned. He'll try his hand at anything!'

Because of the way Mona had spoken about him, Josie went warily to her meeting with Dominic Rattray. She doubted whether he would take any special interest in her, but the possibility of being exposed to the automatic charm his reputation would demand made her cautious.

When she first set eyes on him he seemed a fairly ordinary young man, not at all the sleek ladykiller she had been expecting. In his late twenties, she thought; probably tall, though it was difficult to tell from the way he was sitting, sideways on his chair with his heels hooked over the rung, hunched over the pad he held on his knee. Because of this side view the first thing she noticed was his profile: a beak of a nose, and a long chin. Not a good-looking man, then; or not in any conventional way. Scruffy he certainly was. He had a thatch of thick brown hair, long and untidy, and he wore shabby corduroy trousers, an open-necked shirt and a shapeless sweater with a hole in one elbow.

He waved a fine, ink stained hand towards the chair and said, 'Sit down while I collect my thoughts. Am I right, now, in thinking you're new?'

He turned his head and looked at her inquiringly, his forehead wrinkled, and Josie saw that, of course, Mona had been right. The force of his attraction would have taken your breath away if you didn't happen to be level-headed, sceptical Josie Bewley. Blue eyes, that was unexpected, and all the more striking because his skin was deeply tanned. A most beautiful speaking voice. Just a trace of Irish in it, almost undetectable, but there.

'I arrived at the beginning of December,' she said, suddenly realizing that she had not answered his question.

'Your first Christmas away from home?'

'No,' Josie said, thinking of her year in hospital.

Dominic Rattray shuffled together the papers he had been reading.

'We are going to try to make sense of the thoughts of a gentleman from Cambodia who appears to speak no known language, including Cambodian,' he said. 'Are you ready, Miss ... but I haven't asked your name!'

'Bewley.'

'Spelt after the French fashion and pronounced after the English?'

Josie gaped at him.

'B-e-a-u-l-e-i-g-h?' he spelt out.

'Oh! No, strictly plebian, like me. B-e-w-l-e-y.'

'And none the worse for that. And the Christian name?'

'Josephine. I'm usually called Josie.'

'Josie Bewley. Josephine Bewley. The balance is better with the full name. I shall call you Josephine.'

'I'd rather you called me Miss Bewley.'

His delighted grin embarrassed her. 'You've been warned about me! I'm on the English pool's list of dreadful fates. I'm quite harmless, I assure you, provided I'm not provoked. This animal is not to be teased. Understood?'

'I don't go in for that sort of thing,' Josie said. 'I'm here to take dictation.'

'Then let us begin work.'

He dictated for half an hour with clarity and speed and by the time he had finished Josie felt more respectful towards him. He took one telephone call while she was with him, speaking, as far as her untutored ear could tell, in flawless French.

'How many languages do you speak?' she asked.

'French and German like a native, Russian and Arabic passably, enough of most European languages to be polite.' He paused and looked at her and added smoothly, 'And, of course, Irish.'

'Irish?'

'Erse.'

'Oh, yes,' Josie said blankly. 'You come from Southern Ireland, then?'

'I do, though I've seen little enough of my native land.'

'You go home sometimes?'

'Home is wherever I happen to put my foot down, though I keep a base here in Geneva. Have you found somewhere to live yourself?'

'A flat in Grand' rue,' Josie said with satisfaction. 'I move in at the weekend.'

'Then we'll be neighbours. If we bump into one another I'll buy you a drink.'

His smile was a dismissal, and so was the way he picked up a document from his desk.

Back in the typing pool Mona raised her eyebrows inquiringly.

'You've got that dazzled look,' she said. 'The Rat strikes again!'

'Rat?'

'As in Rattray. Where is he taking you and when?'

'He didn't invite me and I wouldn't have accepted if he had. He's got a good mind; I admire him for that, nothing else. Mona, I think I will get my hair cut. Tell me how to get to your hairdresser.'

A fortnight after she had moved into her new flat Josie saw Dominic Rattray walking ahead of her in Grand' rue. He was not hurrying, but his long legs took him easily up the slope.

Josie stayed a few steps behind him all the way, until he stopped to look in the window of the *confiserie*. To catch his attention she would have to touch his arm. Would he recognize her if she did? Josie dithered and then passed on by.

She scolded herself for it afterwards. It would have been the most natural thing in the world to speak. What had stopped her? Not shyness, that was something that had never troubled Josie. Not his reputation, that was of no interest to her, except that perhaps she feared he might think she was chasing him, just like all his other conquests. That was it, she decided: she didn't want him getting the wrong idea about her.

New experiences crowded in on Josie: dining in restaurants and taking it for granted, drinking wine, trying new foods. She discovered something she had never heard of before called yoghurt and liked it, ate her first slice of melon, learned that there were more vegetables in the world than she had suspected and that chicory was called *endive* and could be eaten cooked – and slightly bitter – or raw and crisp in salads. Salad dressing, too, was oil and vinegar mixed together, not something white out of a bottle, while *pommes frites* were not to be compared with soggy chips.

Mont Blanc came out from behind its curtain of cloud and stood, white and impressive, on the horizon. Josie went ski-ing, floundered helplessly in the snow and was disgruntled by her poor showing. She joined an exercise class to tauten up the muscles that ached so much after her day on the nursery slopes and she began to feel fitter than she had ever done in her life.

She almost forgot Dominic Rattray. Almost, but not quite. She caught glimpses of him in the Palais des Nations, she gathered from a passing reference that he had been in New York, and every time she left her flat she half expected to run into him.

When they did meet, in the *boulangerie* early one morning, both buying *croissants* for breakfast, Josie was disgusted to realize that her throat had gone dry. She smiled, more tentatively than she would normally have done, and was relieved when he responded.

'My new neighbour! Well, it's hardly the hour for drinks,

but I brew a fine cup of coffee. Let's pool our croissants and have breakfast together.'

'I mustn't be late for work,' Josie said nervously.

'I'll drive you in.'

He caught hold of her elbow and steered her out of the shop, two doors down the street and up the stairs. His flat was bigger than Josie's, with a separate bedroom. She caught a glimpse of an unmade bed and, in the kitchen, an array of unwashed dishes.

'You'll excuse the mess,' Dominic said. 'I'm between women at the moment.'

He chuckled at the look on her face. 'Cleaning women,' he explained. 'Do you employ a *femme de ménage*?'

'Good heavens, no! I can manage for myself.'

'Splendid girl. Now, do I have a clean cup and plate? I do! Butter, marmalade – English – I'll say one thing for the English, they make the only marmalade. Coffee coming up, black as sin and hot as hell. I hope that's the way you like it?'

'I'd prefer it white.'

'I must cure you of that.'

He sat down opposite her, his vivid face alive with amusement.

'We agreed on Josephine, didn't we?'

'It's what you said you'd call me.'

'Stop bristling like a hedgehog. Tell me, do you ski?'

'I've had a shot at it, but I wasn't any good.'

'You must persevere. I'll take you to Les Avants this weekend.'

'I don't think …' Josie began automatically.

'For the day on Sunday.'

'I haven't the right gear.'

'How did you manage before?'

'I borrowed some clothes and hired boots and skis.'

'Then do the same again.'

Josie looked at him helplessly. He was shovelling *croissant* into his mouth, apparently oblivious to her misgivings, but then he looked up and she saw the laughter in his eyes.

'Why are you bothering with me?' she demanded.

'It's the challenge,' Dominic explained. 'Can I make those

prickles lie down? Talking of prickles, I like the new hair style.'

Josie ran her hand over her smooth, short hair, which still felt strange to her.

'You certainly notice everything,' she said.

'It's a vast improvement. So, we're going ski-ing on Sunday? Meet me at the bottom of the stairs at eight o'clock.'

He drained the last of his coffee and stood up. 'Right, we'd better be on our way.'

'Aren't you going to clear the table, or wash up?' Josie asked.

'I'll get around to it this evening.'

Josie looked with distaste at the cluttered kitchen, then something about the way he was watching her made her hold back the words that had almost escaped her. Damn him, she wasn't going to fall for that. If he wanted his housework done, let him pay for it.

'O.K., I'm ready,' she said.

'I knew you were different,' Dominic said. 'Most of the girls I meet want to mother me.'

'Is that why you go around looking so out-at-elbows? To get sympathy?'

'I don't care what I look like, and it doesn't worry me if the dishes aren't washed either.'

As he followed her down the staircase outside the flat, he added softly, 'I'm quite clean underneath.'

Remarks like that made her shy away from him, but he rarely fell into the mistake of making them. On the ski slopes he was businesslike, helpful and, when he demonstrated his own skill, a revelation of physical co-ordination. By the end of that first Sunday Josie was tired, sore and unbelievably happy. She sat beside Dominic as he drove them home at a cracking pace, hardly speaking all the way home, lost in a dream that was coloured blue and gold and dazzling white.

Outside her flat Dominic slipped an arm round her shoulders and Josie leaned towards him for a long kiss, her lips slightly parted, her body totally relaxed.

'I've had the most marvellous day,' she said as they drew apart.

'Mm. But you've still got a lot to learn,' Dominic said.

'I know that. Will you ... can we do it again?'

'Ski-ing or kissing?'

'Ski-ing, of course.'

'I go every weekend when I'm in Geneva. You can come along next week if you like.'

'Yes, please.'

'On one condition.'

'What's that?'

'We go on Saturday and you spend the night with me.'

'No! Dominic, you must see that I *can't*.'

'Why not?'

'I'm not ... I haven't ...'

'You're a virgin. Well, of course, I knew *that*.'

'It's wrong.'

'Nonsense!'

'Are you in love with me?' Josie asked desperately.

'You intrigue me. I think you have a lot of temperament hidden behind that defensive wall. What I'm offering you is tuition. You'd enjoy it, just as you've enjoyed the ski-ing. Damn it, girl, you've got to lose it some time. Better with me than with some blundering oaf who doesn't know what he's doing.'

'Without love it seems so ... so cold-blooded,' Josie said.

Dominic chuckled. 'No, I'm not cold-blooded,' he said. 'Au contraire! Kiss me again, mignonne, and then go away and think about it. We'll meet on Wednesday evening and talk it out over dinner.'

He held her more closely for their second kiss. Even through the thickness of their ski clothes Josie was conscious of the hardness of his body. Lovely long bones and not a spare ounce of flesh on him. She shivered as his lips moved down from her mouth to her throat.

She pulled away from him.

'It's certainly an improvement on the Young Socialists,' she said in a shaky voice.

Dominic shouted with laughter. 'Ah, Josephine, you're a girl after my own heart! What a pair we'll make!'

'That remains to be seen,' Josie said.

She bought a new dress for their dinner on Wednesday, even though her bank balance was depleted by the things she had got for the flat and her ski-ing clothes. At the back of her mind she knew that if she had meant to refuse to go with him on Saturday she would not have agreed to meet him in the middle of the week. Dominic knew it, too, and she resented that confidence in him. Half of her was appalled by the step she was contemplating; the other half wanted it so badly that she could hardly bear to sit opposite him without reaching out to touch him.

'How do you do it?' she asked. 'Put this glamour on a girl, I mean?'

'It's the Irish in me,' he told her solemnly. 'I've kissed the Blarney stone.'

'And everything else you can lay your hands on since,' Josie said. 'Someone told me you were brought up in France. Is that true?'

'Quite true. From the age of eight to eighteen, and then back again later to the Sorbonne.'

'But ...' Josie wrinkled her forehead, working out dates. 'You must have been there during the war?'

'I was.'

'Was your family interned?'

Dominic's eyebrows rose in exaggerated surprise. 'But, my dear, we were neutral,' he pointed out softly.

'I was forgetting,' Josie said.

'Most English people do. Now, to go back to something more interesting: will you be Mrs Rattray on Saturday night or shall I be Mr Bewley?'

'I haven't said yes yet.'

'Not yet,' he agreed.

'That was a give-away word to use, wasn't it?' Josie asked. 'It shows that I'm thinking of giving in.'

'I hope you will. The time is ripe for you, Josephine Bewley, and I'm the man to bring you into flower.'

'A fine, poetical way of putting it.'

'A touch of poetry will do you no harm.'

With her eyes on the red wine in her glass Josie said in a low voice, 'You'll not make me pregnant?'

'To be sure I won't.'

To her surprise, he changed the subject, leading her to talk about her life at home. Perhaps he thought her question had been a tacit admission that she would sleep with him, but Josie was still conscious of a divided feeling within herself.

The food was delicious, the wine was heady. Whatever faults he might have, such as being a heartless seducer, Dominic knew how to turn himself into a delightful companion. He laughed at her jokes and capped them with his own ready tongue. She was frank about her circumstances at home, but it seemed that he had none of the class consciousness Josie was ready to suspect in men of his type.

'Do you mean to make a career in Geneva?' he asked.

'No, my real ambition is to go into politics, but I felt I'd never been anywhere or done anything or even been properly educated. This is my chance to expand my experience.'

'And here I am offering you the chance to do just that,' Dominic commented, and went on so quickly that she had no chance to reply, 'What sort of politics? Left or right?'

'Left!' Josie said, genuinely shocked. 'With my background how could I possibly be a Tory?'

Dominic chuckled at her vehemence. 'So you're a member of the Labour Party? Or have you committed yourself to Communism?'

'I couldn't quite swallow Communism,' Josie said. 'I mean, the theory is right, but it doesn't seem to work, does it?'

'A perfect system needs perfect people,' Dominic said. 'Something we haven't got around to producing yet.'

'What about your own opinions?'

'I'm with you on the lefthand side of the great divide and I'd like to see a United Ireland.'

'Does it matter to you?' Josie asked. 'You've spent most of your life out of Ireland, haven't you?'

'I've a sentimental attachment to my own soil. It comes of being an expatriate.'

'If you really care about it why don't you go home and work for what you believe in?'

'I can see I shall have to give you a few lessons in the realities of Irish politics. I do what I can, in my own way.'

He smiled and touched her hand. 'You're coming with me

this weekend?'

'Suppose we see somebody we know?' Josie said, still evading the question.

'Not likely in the little village I'll take you to, but what if we do? We're not breaking any law.'

'It's difficult for me to think about it in that way,' Josie said gloomily. 'I've got a bourgeois mentality.'

'Shake it off! You'll lead a much fuller life if you break free of these out of-date ideas.'

'You're bound to say that. It's all to your advantage,' she pointed out.

'Josie, I don't lack for women. Come with me or not, just as you please, though if you decide against it I'll feel very, very regretful because I think it's an experience that will be good for both of us, but don't imagine that I have to descend to coaxing you in order to get a woman into my bed.'

'If I don't come, will you take someone else?' Josie asked.

She thought that Dominic hesitated and it made his answer seem all the more convincing.

'Not this weekend. I'd be too disappointed.'

That was what tipped the balance in his favour. Josie said nothing that would commit her, but she knew that her decision had been made.

The restaurant was only a few yards away from Josie's flat. They wandered back up the street, their arms round one another, and Dominic saw her up the stairs to her door. Josie unlocked her door and turned to him, her eyes bright and her lips soft, anticipating his kiss.

Dominic put his arm round her shoulders and turned her round, pushed the door open wider and stepped inside.

'And what made you think I was going to wait till Saturday?' he asked.

Chapter Nine

Whatever Dominic might say, it was not possible, in the enclosed community in which they lived, to keep a love affair secret. Josie found that everyone who saw her with Dominic took it for granted that they were sleeping together.

'The only question is, how long will it last?' Mona remarked. 'And I can tell you the answer to that, too – not as long as you would like.'

'Meaning Dominic will get tired first?'

'Meaning just that, ducky.'

She gave Josie a long, puzzled look.

'You're wondering what he sees in me?' Josie suggested.

'His previous girls have been less independent,' Mona admitted. 'On the whole, I would have said Dominic preferred his women not to think, except about him.'

'We talk a lot. He's lending me books.'

'What about?' Mona asked.

'Politics mostly. We have some very interesting discussions.'

'The mind boggles,' Mona murmured 'All the same, I have to hand it to you, I've never heard of him doing that with anyone else.'

Josie did not feel it necessary to reveal that Dominic might value her for other qualities. She had proved an apt pupil in bed and he showed no signs of getting tired of her there. The revelation of her own sensuality frightened her at times. Where had it come from, all this fierce pleasure in her own body? Why had she never experienced it before? Dominic insisted that it was because she had been waiting for him.

'La Belle au Bois Dormant,' he said, running his finger idly over her spine. They had made love and Josie was sitting up, her long bare back towards him, while Dominic still lay prone.

'Not much "belle" about me,' she said.

'You have an attraction all your own now that you've shed your middle-class morality.'

'I haven't altogether,' Josie said. 'I'd still hate my family to find out about us.'

'They'd look on you as a fallen woman?'

'Indeed they would!'

Dominic laughed and pulled her down beside him again.

'Fall a little farther,' he suggested.

Josie hated him being away from Geneva, but she had to put up with it. Dominic went wherever the conferences were being held and sometimes he was gone for three or four weeks at a time. Her life was suspended until he came back. She tried to use the time constructively, catching up on chores in her flat, trying to keep some sort of social life going with the other girls, but it was difficult to take any real interest in anything until he returned, by which time she was full of nervous tension and desperate for reassurance that he still wanted her. Was he faithful to her while he was away? Josie doubted it, but it was a question she never dared ask: she was afraid he would answer truthfully.

He never suggested that they should live together and he rarely spent a full night with her, except when they went away at weekends. As for marriage, Josie had always known that was not on the cards. In spite of her obstinate insistence that she was the equal of any other woman, in spite of the books she read and the tastes she cultivated for his sake, there was still a gulf between them. It was his class and breeding that gave Dominic his fine disregard for public opinion. Josie, for all she tried to pretend otherwise, still worried about what other people thought about her; Dominic never gave it a thought.

His attitude towards the political questions that were still her great concern puzzled Josie. His ideas were far more radical than her own, but what Dominic was interested in was the system, the theory. Josie argued passionately about the wrongs of individuals whereas Dominic took what he insisted was the larger view.

'Let's have a rest from the suffering poor,' he demanded one day.

'But it was you who told me to read that book about South America,' Josie protested. 'Now that I've read it I want to talk about it.'

'You talk altogether too much,' Dominic said. 'I've enjoyed feeding that hungry little mind, almost as much as I've enjoyed satisfying your equally hungry body, but you run the risk of becoming a dead bore, my dear, and that's something I can't tolerate.'

'What would you like me to talk about?' Josie asked in an even voice. 'The weather? Very nice for the time of year, isn't it?'

'Ah, now, I've offended the girl,' Dominic said, but Josie was more hurt because he was laughing than because of his previous remarks.

She felt a chill. She had thought that Dominic valued the exchange of ideas between them as much as she did and now it seemed that he had only been indulging her.

She was even more resentful when Dominic put his arm round her and began to coax her to make love. She could not help responding, partly because she was helpless under the spell he wove round her with his hands and lips, and partly because she wanted to believe that his impatience had been a momentary thing arising from his desire to get her into bed, but at the back of her mind there was a doubt, the first stab of fear that a terrible unhappiness was waiting for her.

They struggled on for another six months. Almost before she was aware of it the anniversary of Josie's arrival in Geneva was on her.

'Only another year,' she said.

'Will you extend your contract?' Dominic asked.

'I doubt it.'

She waited for Dominic to urge her to consider a longer term in Geneva, but he looked away and said nothing.

'Will you miss me when I'm gone?' Josie asked, striving to speak lightly.

'It's a long way ahead,' Dominic protested. 'Yes, I'll miss you. I'll look you up when I'm in England.'

'As a change from the girl you'll no doubt be keeping here by that time?'

'That's right. Josie, I've never pretended to you. I like women too much to tie myself down to one.'

'Or even one at a time. When you visit England do you look up the girl before me?'

'The girl before you was French. Don't ask me about her. Jealousy, ma chère, is something that has no place between two people like us. We're both free and what either of us does when we are apart from one another has nothing to do with the other one.'

I'm not free, Josie thought dismally. I'm not free, because I love you. I don't want to, I despise myself for it, but I still love you.

All she said out loud was, 'I'm going home for Christmas this year.'

'Enjoy yourself,' Dominic said carelessly.

Josie grimaced. 'I doubt if I will,' she said.

She felt even more out of place at home now in spite of her desire to hold on to her origins. She had been lavish with her presents, with an inward wry amusement because she recognized that she was spending money out of guilt over her relationship with Dominic, as if an expensive hand-embroidered blouse would stop her mother finding out about it, and she resented the grudging way her generosity was received, even though she understood the reason for it, the fear that money wasted on frivolities might be wanted in the future for more basic needs.

'You've got money to burn, seemingly,' Ethel said.

'I'm well paid and not being liable for tax is an advantage,' Josie said. 'All the same, Geneva is an expensive place to live.'

'You've improved yourself, I'll say that. You look quite smart.'

The ten-day visit went off quite well, but by the time Josie went back to her studio in Geneva she knew she would never be able to live at home again. She had outgrown that crowded, quarrelsome, all-in-together life.

What was she going to do with herself? Her contract expired at the end of November, which looked a long way ahead, but if she intended to extend it she would have to give notice in advance. All of a sudden the decision began to seem uncomfortably near.

The Executive Board came round again and Dominic was settled in Geneva for the whole month. They started ski-ing together again and the physical accord between them was renewed. Josie felt more comfortable with him than she had been before Christmas. And then, in the middle of the month, Dominic's mood suddenly changed. He became moody and irritable in a way that was quite foreign to him.

Josie called round at his flat to talk about arrangements for the weekend and at first could not get any reply to her ring. She put out of her mind, as she had done many times in the past year, the idea that if he had really wanted her in his life he would have given her a key, and would have asked for a key to her flat. She was about to go away when the door opened.

At first she thought he was ill. Then, taking in his flushed face, fumbling movements and slurred speech, she exclaimed disbelievingly, 'Dominic, you're drunk!'

'What of it? Haven't you ever seen a man who's had a drink too many before?'

'But it's so unlike you! There must be something wrong. What is it?'

'Nothing. Stop interfering.'

Josie had stooped down and begun to clear the floor, which was littered with thrown down newspapers.

'I'll trip over if I leave this mess,' she pointed out. 'Darling, do tell me what has happened to make you get into such a state.'

Dominic collapsed on to the sofa, his arm thrown along the back, his head turned against it.

' "The times are out of joint",' he muttered.

Josie had assimilated enough Shakespeare to pick up that quotation.

'Well, you weren't born to put them right,' she pointed out. 'I'm the one who worries about the state of the world – and lately you've shut me up when I talk about it.'

She glanced at the crumpled papers and added, 'Personally, I think the way Krushchev has spoken out about what went on under Stalin is the best thing that's happened in years. A real breath of fresh air.'

'It'll cause a lot of trouble,' Dominic said in the same muffled voice. 'The Americans will say "we told you so" and all the satellites will start revolting.'

'Perhaps the new regime will give them a bit more freedom,' Josie suggested, reassured by the way he seemed to be prepared to talk about something outside himself.

'They can't do that. Can't you see? One small crack, then a real chasm, then the whole system will fall to pieces.'

Josie perched herself on the arm of the sofa and stroked his head. The softness of his hair and the delicacy of the skin beneath it were strangely touching.

'You haven't told me what made you get into this state,' she said.

Dominic sat up abruptly, shaking off her soothing hand.

'It was nothing. I felt depressed. I thought I was going down with 'flu. I had one cognac too many trying to ward it off.'

He stood up unsteadily. 'Go and make me some coffee, there's a dear girl. I'll put my head under the cold shower.'

'That won't do your 'flu much good,' Josie pointed out. 'Daft ha'p'orth!'

When she brought up the subject of ski-ing at the weekend, he was evasive.

'If you don't want to go, say so,' Josie said at last in exasperation.

'I don't know how I'll be feeling,' Dominic pointed out.

'Take a couple of aspirin and go to bed,' Josie advised. 'I'll come round tomorrow to see how you are.'

'No, don't do that. I'll be all right. I'm not sure about ski-ing. If you haven't heard from me by Friday go on your own.'

Josie tried to argue with him, but the remnants of the brandy still clung to him and made him obstinate. When she left him she felt far from satisfied, either about his state of mind or his health, but she had learnt in the past year not to stay when he did not want her.

They struggled on together through the year and Josie shut her eyes to the fact that Dominic was seeing other girls. They were temporary, she was permanent, and she and Dominic had always agreed that they were both free to go their own way.

Not that there was anyone else for her. It was a very one-sided arrangement.

It was a troubled year. Dominic had been right when he had prophesied trouble in the Russian satellite countries. There was unrest in Poland and Hungary, but what dominated the year for Josie was Suez.

She found herself at odds with most of the British in Geneva, who took the line that the attempt to re-possess the canal had been inevitable and would have succeeded if the British and French had not been let down by the Americans, who failed to support their action at the United Nations. Josie argued fiercely on the other side. Dominic was away and she wanted him back, not for the sake of his lovemaking, but because she was sure he would agree with her. In a fury of resentment, Josie saw the way the eyes of the world had been focused on Suez as directly responsible for the Russians seizing the opportunity to intervene in Hungary.

It was November and near the end of Josie's two-year contract, but she had arranged to stay on for an extra three months to cover the Executive Board. She still had to tell Dominic about that and on his reaction depended her decision whether to apply for a longer extension.

One cold evening when Josie had stayed in to listen to the wireless, picking up the news in English and French, her doorbell rang some time after ten o'clock. Josie exclaimed impatiently, not wanting visitors so late in the evening. The last person she had expected was Dominic, especially Dominic abominably drunk.

'Have I go' the right address?' he inquired, lurching forward. 'Josie! Only girl I know with any political ac … acumen.'

'If you're talking about Suez, I'm absolutely sick about it,' Josie said. 'Though I don't see any call for getting drunk. You can come in, but only for a few minutes.'

'Suez! Don' care about that. Bloody English. Serves them right. Kill a few of them off, good thing.'

'Well, thank you very much! Sit down. I'll make you some coffee.'

'Don' wan' any coffee.' For one moment his speech cleared

and he looked at her directly. 'Give me oblivion.'

'If you mean more brandy, not likely! Coffee's what you're getting, my lad, and a piece of my mind when you're in a fit state to listen to it.'

He drank the coffee when she brought it in from the kitchen, but it only seemed to make him withdraw into himself.

'Come on, what's this all about?' Josie asked, when she could bear his silence no longer.

'I'm in pieces. Broken up. Thought you might understand. Only girl I know who might. All my life I've believed. In France, in the war, the only people in the Resistance who got anything done were the Communists. I helped. Wasn't supposed to. Neutral. I had a promise in return, aid for Ireland. Bloody English. I hate you, you know. You thought I loved you, but I didn't.'

He giggled, an obscene little noise that made Josie shrink back. 'I screwed them,' he said with satisfaction. 'One after the other. And they loved it.'

'So did you,' Josie said through stiff lips. 'Don't try to pretend to me that you were thinking about anything but your own selfish pleasure. Are you telling me you've always been a Communist?'

'I *believed*,' Dominic repeated. 'Hope of the world. The only thing left after religion let us down.'

'Why didn't you tell me?'

'I was trained. Keep it a secret. Come when we call you. Help when we need you. I did what I was told. Now ... it's too much, it's too much. It's more than I can bear.'

He put his head down on his hands and to Josie's sick horror he began to cry. She strained to hear what he was saying.

'They sent the tanks in. I *saw*. They were just kids ... kids like I was, proud of themselves, patriots ... *believing*.' He raised his head and looked at her. 'I was *there*!'

'In Hungary?'

'Of course. What am I going to do? I was sick in January, hearing what Krushchev said about Stalin, confirming all the stories, but I came round to agreeing with something you said – a breath of fresh air, a new era. If that isn't true, how can I go on?'

'To begin with, you can stop thinking about yourself. Dominic Rattray has a crisis of faith. So what? Pick yourself up and find another creed to live by.'

'Ah, the wonderful English common sense. But I'm not an Englishman, my dear. I'm a wild Celt and the heart is broken in me entirely.'

'I know better than to believe you when you start talking like a stage Irishman. Half of what you say about the way you feel is true, but the other half is play-acting.'

'It was playing my part that kept me going. My reason for living. Take it away and what do I have? I look inside myself and see nothing but emptiness. I can't live with that.'

He stood up and Josie saw that he had sobered. Even now, shocked as she was, her instinct was to put her arms round him and comfort him. She shrank from the knowledge of his long deception, but he was in torment and she still responded to his need.

'Don't go,' she said. 'I still love you. Stay with me.'

'A generous offer, in the circumstances,' Dominic said. 'I wonder if you realize how much I resent it? No, thank you. I'll go my own way. I shouldn't have come. I always see these things too late.'

He left without another word and Josie let him go. A terrible oppression was bearing down on her. It was the deliberate lying, the realization that in all their long intimacy he had never been frank with her, that made her feel stunned.

She thought that she could understand how he had come to commit himself. A young and ardent boy, caught up in the adventure of the Resistance, a patriot with romantic dreams of a country he hardly knew, it must have been easy to recruit him. What was almost unbelievable was the way he had gone on playing his secretive game. More clearly than ever before Josie saw that Dominic was not a mature person and she suspected now that it was his hidden life which had stopped him from growing up and facing reality.

He must be wondering now whether she would give him away. Would it matter greatly if she did? It would certainly hamper his visits to the United States and that would make a nasty hole in Dominic's income. It was an unpleasant thought that one reason he had kept quiet about his beliefs was that it would stop him making money out of a regime he despised.

More unpleasant motives suggested themselves to her unquiet mind. Treachery. Subversion. But now that he was disenchanted all fear of anything like that must have disappeared. She would have to talk to him, tell him that she would not say anything about his past, reassure herself about the way he meant to behave in the future.

The following week, after a solitary ski-ing session and no word from Dominic, Josie was walking down one of the long corridors on the ground floor of the Palais des Nations when she saw him coming towards her. She lifted a hand in greeting and stopped. Dominic gave her a faint smile, as if they had been a couple of barely acquainted strangers, and walked straight past her.

Josie stood where she was, too shocked to move. The stream of people in the corridor, going to and from the cafeteria for their coffee break, parted round her and joined up again. She could hear voices, laughing, talking in half a dozen languages. Someone spoke to her and she turned and went back to her desk.

She went to Dominic's flat that evening, but his door did not open to her persistent ringing. She telephoned him, but he did not reply. She went to his office the next day and he was there, dictating.

He looked up and said, 'Sorry, busy just now', and waited for her to leave.

The girl with the pad on her knee sat with her pencil poised, ready to continue. Josie went out of the room and very carefully closed the door behind her.

When she got back to the pool she saw Mona looking at her with concern. Josie made a twisted, pitiful attempt at a smile and then she said, 'It looks as if I've lost Dominic. Who is it? Do you know?'

'Brenda,' Mona said reluctantly.

Brenda was a new arrival, a little, plump-faced girl with a bubbling laugh, round eyes which always looked surprised and very highly coloured cheeks.

'But she's just a kid!' Josie exclaimed.

'How old were you when you first met him?' Mona asked drily. 'Josie, I did warn you.'

'I know. Are you sure – about Brenda?'

'He's started taking her out. I don't think it's gone any further than that yet.'

'Perhaps it's only a passing thing. It's happened before and he's come back to me. He can't just mean to drop me, without saying anything, after all we've been to one another.'

The pain was almost unbearable. Day after day she tried to speak to Dominic and he evaded her. Every night she went to bed totally exhausted and after ten minutes of lying in the dark she snapped awake, every sense alert, all her muscles tense, reliving the times they had spent together, trying to see where she had gone wrong, what she had done to turn him against her. And all the time she knew the answer: Dominic had given himself away to her. He had been weak and he resented her knowledge, both of his secret commitment and of the way he had broken down. He needed a new love to build up his pride, a frivolous, uncritical little giggler who would please his senses and never look at him with a critical thought in her head. What distressed Josie was her belief that she could have been of far greater help to Dominic than silly little Brenda. Surely if they had talked it through together they could have arrived at some solution to his moral dilemma? She would have given him love and understanding and support – if he had wanted any of those things from her.

Josie lost weight and her sandy hair was lank and lifeless, but pride kept her from totally neglecting herself. Somehow she kept on her feet, she forced food past her unwilling lips, she worked, she talked to people, just as if she were still alive, not wandering in a pain-filled limbo.

Her contract was coming to an end, for that at least she could be thankful. She refused to extend it further and began to make arrangements for her return to England.

'I'll be glad to get away,' she admitted to Mona.

'You've behaved better than some other girls in similar circumstances,' Mona said. 'No public scenes. You'll be glad of that when you've recovered a bit more.'

'You've been a good friend,' Josie said.

'Fellow feeling,' Mona said deliberately.

'Mona! You don't mean ... you and Dominic?'

'Did you never wonder how I came to know so much about him? It happened in my first year and it only lasted a few weeks. You lasted longer than anyone and I began to think ... but he'll never change now.' She sighed and added, 'Poor Dominic. He's clever, charming, on the face of it the child of good fortune, and yet ... there's something lacking in him.'

'I never knew him,' Josie said slowly. 'I thought I did, but all the time he was hiding himself from me.'

'That's it,' Monica agreed, but Josie could see she had no idea what she really meant. 'He gives nothing, except the temporary use of his body.'

Josie shivered. 'Let's never talk about him again. I'm getting over it – I think.'

Chapter Ten

As soon as she got back to England Josie went to see Ben. The size of his offices surprised her, and so did the fact that he had a secretary who was not at all disposed to let his cousin in to see him without an appointment.

'What did you expect?' Ben said in response to her grumble. 'I'm a busy man. What can I do for you?'

'You're the property king around here,' Josie said. 'I need somewhere to live. Small and cheap, but independent.'

'Found yourself a job?'

'I'm going to work for a solicitor.'

'Locally? Not very exciting after two years abroad.'

'He's a councillor and I hope to pick up some useful tips. I'm going to combine it with doing some constituency work for our M.P.'

'So you've revived your ambition to get into Parliament?'

'I never gave it up. I don't regret my two years in Geneva. I've learnt a lot, my horizons are broader now, I've found out things about myself that perhaps I needed to know ...'

Her lips quivered and she looked down, despising herself for the weakness the memory of Dominic brought on.

'What went wrong?' Ben asked quietly.

'I made a damn fool of myself over a man, if you must know. Well, that's behind me now. I've had my great love affair and got over it. It's not something I'll go in for again ...'

'No?'

'No. I'm going to get down to the work I really want to do. The only thing is ... I can't live at home, not with Mum nagging at me all the time about being an old maid. If she riles me I might blurt out that I'm no maid and that will really put the cat among the pigeons.'

Her chin was jutting forward aggressively and her nose had turned pink with the effort of keeping back the tears. To her immense surprise, Ben came round from behind his desk, sat on the arm of her chair and put his arm round her. For one moment she allowed herself the luxury of leaning against him. Two slow, difficult tears ran down her cheeks, then she pulled away and wiped her eyes.

'Don't be *kind* to me,' she said in a fierce whisper. 'Just find me somewhere to live, a place of my own.'

'I'll do that,' Ben promised. He tilted back her head and looked down into her blotched face. 'I can't ever remember seeing you cry before, not even when we were kids.'

'I took a bad knock, but I'm getting over it.'

In another moment he'd have her telling him all about Dominic and Josie was determined not to give in to that temptation. In an effort to get away from her troubles she said, more lightly, 'Crying's something I leave to the feminine types, like Nicola. I don't suppose you've had any news of her lately?'

'I wouldn't call you unfeminine. You've changed. You used to look like a stringy alley cat, now you're more of a starving lioness.' Ben got up and moved away. 'Yes, I see Nicola when I'm in London.'

'She isn't too grand to know her old friends, then?'

'She's the same sweet kid she always was. Pretty, too.'

'Is that why you take her out or is it because her stepfather's Raymond Wadsby, M.P.?'

'Wadsby's got nothing to do with it. I doubt whether he knows Nicola sees me, nor her mother either.'

'Nicola being deceitful? That sounds out of character. You've corrupted her, Ben. I bet our Marigold would be furious if she knew pretty Nicola was wasting time on you. Hardly a Deb's Delight, are you?'

She saw from the way his mouth tightened and the time he took to answer that she had annoyed Ben, and she took a perverse pleasure in it.

'Equality for all may be your watchword, but it's Nicola who puts it into practice,' Ben said at last. 'She's never hinted that

I'm beneath her notice, and neither should she, considering the size of the operation I control.'

'You and Ernie Baxcombe.'

She saw the look of distaste that crossed Ben's face and asked curiously, 'You don't really like him, do you?'

'I don't, but keep that to yourself, too. One of these days I mean to break away and be independent. At the moment I can't do without Ernie.'

Once she had settled down into the local life again Josie began to understand what Ben had been talking about when he had spoken of the size of the firm he and Ernie had built up. In her job in the solicitor's office she saw many transactions in the local property market and more often than not the sign that went up on vacant tracts of land 'Acquired for clients' meant 'Sold to Baxcombe & Harcourt'. She began to hear talk of a new council estate and was not surprised when the larger part of the land required for it proved to belong to the same company.

'Do you think Ben and Ernie knew about the estate in advance?' she asked her employer.

'You may well ask!' he said. 'I dare say they did. Or else it was the other way round. The siting of the estate depended on where Baxcombe and Harcourt had an interest.'

'Corruption?' Josie wrinkled her nose distastefully. 'I don't think ... I would have said Ben was straight.'

'Would you? Then by all means keep your illusions, my dear Josephine.'

He was a dry stick and Josie found it hard to like him. She did her job conscientiously, but her heart was in her spare time, unpaid work for Cy Maple, the Labour Member of Parliament.

She had renewed her contact with the Young Socialists and had begun to work towards having her name put forward as a candidate for the local council. She was hurt to discover that some of her former associates were suspicious of her because of the time she had spent abroad, and secretly a little scornful at the way they seemed to have stood still while she was away.

'I suppose two years isn't all that long,' she remarked one day in the dusty hall they used for their meetings. 'But it still takes me by surprise to find that everyone I knew has gone on living in the same place, doing the same job.' She picked up a leaflet. 'Writing the same words.'

'You've grown away from us,' one of the young men remarked. 'The way you look ... glossy, not scruffy like you used to – like the rest of us. And you're ambitious. Most of us are content to do our bit at the grass roots. Josie Bewley wants to get into Parliament and makes no secret of it.'

'A councillor by the time I'm twenty-five and into Parliament in my thirties,' Josie agreed. 'Why not? Everyone's always saying the Party needs new blood.'

Cy Maple was far more sympathetic, perhaps because he had already achieved the goal she was aiming at.

'You've got the right background,' he said. 'I'm fair sick of all these Oxbridge intellectuals. A good working class family and your roots going back to the hard times in the thirties. You know what the Labour Party's all about. You've got it in your blood. Stick to it, lass. I'll back you when the time comes.'

There was a shipping strike looming. Josie was heart and soul on the side of the shipworkers. She was indignant when one of the girls in her office tried to argue the other side.

'You try supporting a wife and four children on eight pounds ten shillings and six pence a week,' she said. 'And that's the wage of a skilled man. There's plenty of men who haven't got the sort of skills my Uncle Andrew has, for instance, who are managing on seven pounds two and sixpence.'

'They get overtime,' the other secretary said weakly.

'That they do! There are men just about making ends meet by working until half past eight twice a week and doing two shifts on Sunday. Doesn't give much time for family life, does it?'

Josie did see some merit in going to arbitration, but when Cy pointed out that if, every time the Unions put in a claim, the employers chose to go to arbitration the normal negotiating machinery would grind to a halt, she saw his point. Because she identified so closely with his viewpoint she was as disappointed as he was when, after all the speeches and marches, the dispute was referred to a Court of Inquiry.

Her heavy involvement left Josie little time to visit her family. She told herself she was not needed. Her mother and father were in good health and moderately prosperous. The boys were growing up and doing well at school, though neither of them had Josie's intellectual curiosity. They were a closely knit family without her; she felt almost an outsider.

Her mother continued to harp on her unmarried state.

'I've told you before, I don't mean to get married,' Josie said patiently.

'A lonely old age, that's what you're laying up for yourself. I dare say the truth is you've got someone you don't want to tell me about. There's no tellin' what you get up to, stuck away in that flat on your own.'

'I live like a nun,' Josie said.

It was the truth, but not the whole truth. She met few men who attracted her, but when she did Josie was alarmed by the violence of her reaction. No one had made love to her since she parted from Dominic, but it was not true that that part of her life was over. It was not so easy, she discovered, to live a life of chastity since Dominic had so thoroughly aroused her. She was more attractive to men than she had been in the past, too, and she felt uneasily that it was because they sensed the strength of her latent passions.

One of the men who looked like giving trouble was Cy Maple, which was a complication Josie could have done without. He was in his late forties and married, with children. His wife kept close to home and was rarely seen with him in public. Josie liked him, she found his politcal aims sympathetic, she admired his solid achievements, she even acknowledged to herself that his strong, burly body and florid good looks were not unattractive to her, but all the same she shied away from his hints that they had a lot in common, and she came to resent his even broader hints that he could be of use to her.

She had let herself get too close to him at the time of the shipping strike, but at that time she had been newly returned from Geneva and still raw with hurt over Dominic. She had thought herself safe from ever being attracted to a man again, but as the months went by and she realized that this was not true she became more wary in her dealings with Cy, giving generously of her time and help, and accepting his advice in return, but keeping it as impersonal as she could manage.

It took her two years, but in 1959, at the age of twenty-six, Josie was adopted as the Labour candidate for the south-west ward of Ferryhaven and elected to the council.

Cy, who had spoken on her behalf and campaigned for her, was with her when the results came through. In exuberant delight he swung her off her feet and kissed her on the lips. To the onlookers it was no more than a moment of extravagant pleasure because his protegée had been successful, but Josie was conscious of the undercurrent of sexual desire that flowed between them.

He ran her back to the small, cluttered flat she had found two years earlier with Ben's help. When they arrived he got out and followed her up the stairs, not asking but taking it for granted that she was going to ask him in. They were both still brimming over with excitement, laughing and talking, too restless to sit down.

'The only thing I've got to celebrate with is the tail end of a bottle of Cyprus sherry,' Josie said, rooting about in the corner by her cooker.

'If I'd had any sense I would have laid in a bottle of champagne,' Cy said. 'I knew you'd get in. I *knew* it.'

He took hold of her and this time they were without the restraint of watching eyes. As their lips met he made a strange noise, like a grunt, and clutched her to him. Without leaving go of one another they stumbled towards the bed in the corner, their hands pulling blindly at their clothes. As they collapsed on to the bed Cy raised his head.

'Bloody hell, I'll have to take my shoes off,' he said.

Josie laughed and slipped away from him to throw off the rest of her clothes. The light still blazed in the middle of the ceiling. Josie lay down and closed her eyes against its glare.

The first time since Dominic. It was different, not the rapier-like finesse she had come to expect from him. Coupling with Cy was like being assaulted with a bludgeon. He was powerful, though. He was marvellous. Josie threw back her head in an ecstasy of pleasure and fastened herself to him with arms and legs, swept away by the pounding throb of their two bodies.

An hour later Cy had gone and Josie was glad of it. It gave her a chance to think. She wondered now how she had managed to hang on for two years without a man in her life. It had been good and she had wanted it as much as Cy, perhaps more. It was something that was going to happen again, now that she had admitted her need.

I must be careful, she thought. I mustn't get pregnant. And I mustn't cause a scandal. Cy thinks we'll carry on, but I'm not so sure. I don't like him having a wife and kids. I don't suppose it's the first time he's been unfaithful to her, but all the same I don't like it. I can't give up working for him, not yet, but it will have to come. Being on the council, attending committee meetings, looking after local people, I can't do all that and my job and be his unpaid secretary as well. I'll break with him gradually. I don't want him thinking I used him to get elected and then dropped him.

She went down the corridor to her shared bathroom and as she wandered back she thought about her situation. Back in the bedsitter she turned out the light, dropped her dressing gown on the floor and rolled wearily between the tousled sheets.

You're a cold-blooded bitch, Josie Bewley, for all you've got a fire between your legs, she told herself. She turned over on her back and opened her eyes wide in the darkness. I know where I'm going and I mean to get there. I don't intend to be put off because I can't escape from being a woman. If Cy wants me, he can have me – occasionally. But only as long as it stays a secret. No one is going to say I got to the top by letting myself get laid. If I choose to go with another man, that's up to me. I'm an adult woman and I'll do what I think is right for me.

As she thumped her pillow and prepared for sleep one more triumphant thought slid into her mind: I'm a councillor! Next stop, Westminster!

III. Nicola

Chapter Eleven

When Nicola met Ben again at the age of fourteen she had no real recollection of him, but from then on he was seldom out of her thoughts. The hero of every book she read took on Ben's likeness, it was to Ben that every love song on the radio was sung. She hardly dared hope that he would think of her, but to her surprise Ben did keep in touch. It was only in the most desultory way – a Christmas card, a postcard when he went on holiday – but it was enough to keep him alive in Nicola's memory until she was old enough for them to meet in London when Ben was there on business.

Nicola's memory of her father was almost as dreamlike as her memory of Ben, but she knew that somewhere in her childhood there had been a period of unclouded happiness. She thought of her life as having been divided into three parts. There had been 'before Daddy was killed', which she scarcely remembered; there was 'before Mummy married Raymond' and there was 'since Mummy married Raymond'.

The middle period had been disturbing, with Marigold given to violent changes of mood and bouts of tears, but they had lived at Berringer Hall and Nicola's affection for her grandfather had given her a feeling of stability. When Marigold married Raymond Wadsby her daughter was old enough to see that it was good for her mother to have a husband and if she had chosen any other man Nicola would have accepted a stepfather gladly, but it was not long before she came to believe that in marrying Raymond her mother had made a profound mistake.

He was not long out of the Army when he had met Marigold, just about to re-launch himself into the career in the

City he had taken up before the war, and to stand as Conservative candidate for the constituency which included Berringer. He was the younger son in a family where the elder boy had always outshone him, but this brilliant and dearly loved son had been killed in the war. On Raymond had fallen the burden of trying to make up to his parents for a loss which they saw as irreparable. He had laid his marriage to Marigold Pemberley at their feet as hopefully as a dog retrieving a ball. She was beautiful, well connected, with money of her own – surely this would enhance him in their eyes? – but Marigold's lack of intellectual depth, well suited to Raymond's limited understanding, had condemned her to his mother's faint, unexpressed contempt. She could in no way compare with the fiancée of the dead son, and once more Raymond had fallen short.

Because he saw that his parents did not value her, Raymond came to look on Marigold with their eyes. More than that, he turned to a consolation that had always been available to him and became a womanizer who would make a pass at anything in skirts, including his own young stepdaughter.

He was a good-looking man, still in his thirties, exactly the same age as Marigold. He held himself well, the result of his years in the Army, and prided himself on keeping fit, playing squash and golf, and swimming every morning in the summer in the pool he had installed in the garden of the house he and Marigold had taken at Coryleigh. It was in the swimming pool, when she was little more than fourteen, that Nicola woke up to the fact that her stepfather was handling her unnecessarily as he taught her the finer points of a new stroke. She looked at his handsome, flushed face under its plastered cap of wet hair, the way his eyes seemed to glisten as if they, too, were wet, the way he ran his tongue over his lips, and felt a shiver of repulsion run over her. Above all, she was aware as she clambered out of the water and he followed her, that his scanty swimming trunks did nothing to conceal his state of sexual excitement. She never swam with him again.

After that she watched him and saw that he rarely missed an opportunity to touch a woman, however unattractive. Nicola felt she could scream in company sometimes when she saw the squeezes that went with the handing over of a glass the intimate cupping of hands to light a cigarette, the little stroking movements on a bare arm, or even neck, as he passed a chair. Did her mother see it too? Nicola was sure that she did. Sure, too, as she grew older that, Raymond was consistently unfaithful to his wife, without love, without discrimination. Nicola was deeply contemptuous of him and, because she blamed Marigold for having chosen him, almost as scornful of her mother.

When Nicola left school she had a year in Paris. On her return to London she took a job as a receptionist at an art gallery, more because her mother thought it suitable than because it interested Nicola, and shared a flat in Kensington with two other girls, escaping every weekend to visit her grandfather.

'You lead such an odd life,' her mother complained. 'You never go anywhere, you never see anyone ...'

'I went to a film and a play last week, and I came to your cooktail party,' Nicola said.

'But you slipped away and went home on your own, though I know Eddie Vancourt asked you to dine with him. I asked him specially for you and it's terribly disappointing, darling, when you turn down the opportunities I try to make for you.'

'Eddie is so wet he positively drips.'

'But rolling in money and the chance of a title one day.'

'Think of all the long years of being married to Eddie before I had the pleasure of calling myself "Lady Vancourt".'

'What about that nice American?'

'I don't want to leave England.'

Nicola twitched back the cuff of her jacket and managed to get a quick glance at her watch. Nearly six o'clock and she would have to leave soon if she was to avoid meeting Raymond. She had called in to see Marigold at her mother's special request, carefully fitting in her visit on her way home from work in the knowledge that she would probably get away without having to see her stepfather and that Marigold would be too preoccupied with the evening's entertainment to give her full attention to the post mortem Nicola guessed she wanted to hold on the previous week's party.

'Darling, the reason I wanted to see you is that we simply must talk about plans for your twenty-first birthday,' Marigold said. 'It's only a few weeks away and you're showing no interest.'

'I don't want a big fuss.'

'You know I've got it all arranged to give a party for you at Berringer, just like I had. Such a lovely setting and we can invite some dreary constituency people, which will be useful for Raymond.'

'I thought the party was for me.'

'Of course, but Raymond's career is so important and Berringer Hall is still impressive, in spite of being run down. He says you're to have a beautiful new dress and charge it to him.'

'I can pay for my own clothes.'

'Not very gracious of you, darling. Raymond does try to please you and you aren't at all nice about it. Don't hurry away; stay and have a drink with him.'

'No, I must go,' Nicola said, standing up. 'If you're really keen on this party then, of course, I'll fall in with what you want. I'll let you have a list of the people I'd like to invite.'

Her mother, too, got to her feet. For a moment they stood side by side, reflected in the looking glass over the fireplace. A faint, dissatisfied shadow crossed Marigold's face. She was still a good-looking woman, but in her mid-forties she had discovered a regrettable tendency to put on weight. Automatically, she tensed her stomach muscles and lifted her chin. Her hair was still the colour of ripe corn, but it owed some of its brightness to a rinse these days; her eyes were just as blue, but there were delicate lines at the corners; her skin, carefully tended, was as smooth and fine as porcelain, and yet, with all these remnants of her beauty still about her, she lacked the bloom that belonged to Nicola with no effort at all.

'Youth,' Marigold said. 'You think it will last for ever, but it won't. I'm warning you, Nicola, if you don't make the most of your chances now you may regret it for the rest of your life.'

Nicola laughed and kissed her mother on the cheek. 'I'll keep it in mind,' she promised.

She ran down the stairs from the first floor drawing room of the narrow house her mother and stepfather rented in the division bell area. She thought she had escaped meeting Raymond, but as she reached the hall the front door opened and he came in.

'Not going already?' he asked. 'How disappointing. I came home specially early when Marigold told me she was expecting you this evening.'

Since Nicola knew that he would not have left the House of Commons if there had been any business to keep him there she discounted his remark as one of the little untruths with which Raymond eased his way through life. With the adroitness of long practice she avoided the arm laid casually across her shoulders. Leaning towards him she brushed her cheek against his and stepped back.

'Terribly sorry, must dash,' she said, and was gone out of the door before he could detain her.

She was seeing Ben that evening, that was what gave wings to her feet as she hurried down the road. It was one of his rare visits to London and he had asked her to meet him for a meal. She wondered where he would take her. Somewhere quiet, that was certain. Neither Nicola nor Ben was anxious to run the risk of encountering Marigold or any friends who might inquire about her handsome escort. No need to dress up, but on the other hand she adored making herself look beautiful for him.

She had washed her hair before she went to work that morning. As soon as she got back to the flat she ran a bath and flung in handfuls of bathsalts. Carefully, she went through the ritual of preparation: the scented bath, the talcum powder, the splash of toilet water. She caught sight of herself in the mirror, the skin of her body flushed from the warm water, and considered gravely her small, tilted breasts, the long smooth sweep of her back, her slender waist and the delicate roundness of her buttocks. Would Ben ever see her like that? She longed for it, but although he kissed her and told her she was lovely he had never taken their lovemaking any further, and Nicola hung back, proud and sensitive, waiting for him to lead the way.

By the time he arrived her eyes were huge with the strain of anticipation. Her hair was brushed and shining, her nails were newly painted, she had touched her face with the small amount of make-up she needed. She wore a sleeveless dress of apricot-coloured linen with a neat little jacket to go over it.

Ben took both her hands in his and stood back to look at her at arms' length.

'You look good enough to eat,' he said.

With a gentle tug he pulled her into his arms and kissed her and Nicola clung to him with an eagerness that gave away both her inexperience and the way she felt about him.

'Sweet, lovely girl,' Ben said unsteadily. 'One of these days, if you go on looking so gorgeous, I'm going to lose my head completely.'

His head, not his heart. There was a droop to Nicola's mouth as she waited for him to tell her what they were going to do that evening.

'I thought we'd get out of London and have dinner in the country,' Ben said.

Nicola wondered how he came to know the quiet country hotel to which he took her. It was no accidental choice. Ben drove there without consulting a map; their table was booked; and he knew that there was a terrace with steps down into the garden, even that the grass sloped down to a stream where they could stroll until they were called to their table.

'You're so well organized,' Nicola said.

'I like to plan ahead,' Ben admitted.

'Is that the reason for your success?'

'Of course.'

He smiled, but she sensed that he did not like the reference to his business life. He never talked to her about it. Perhaps because he liked to relax when he was with her?

It crossed her mind that Ben might have brought her to this charming, out-of-the-way place because he was going to ask her to stay the night with him. What would she do if he did? Stay with him, Nicola admitted. There was a shiver of nervousness in the pit of her stomach. It would be the first time for her. Would he mind that?

Absentmindedly, she spooned peach melba into her mouth, tasting the coldness of the icecream and the sharp flavour of the fruit, but with her mind on her unreasonable love for this man who slipped in and out of her life and didn't seem aware of the havoc he caused.

'Come back,' Ben said. 'You're a million miles away.'

Nicola looked up and flushed. 'Not really,' she said. 'I was thinking about you.'

'That's nice,' Ben said, but he did not take her up and press to know what her thoughts had been as any other man might have done.

If he had meant to ask her to spend the night with her, he would have done it then, but he let the moment pass, leaving Nicola still doubtful. Perhaps she was only imagining that Ben wanted her, perhaps he would have been shocked, even disgusted, if he had known the way she was thinking.

She made an effort to put it out of her mind.

'Mummy was agitating about my twenty-first earlier this evening,' she said.

'Are you going to have a party?'

'Got to, to please her. It will be at Berringer Hall.'

'Are you going to ask me?'

'Would you come, if I did?'

'I might, if the circumstances were right.'

'I'll put you on my list,' Nicola promised. 'I'd ... I'd rather you came than anyone else,' she added in a rush.

She went off to the cloakroom while he paid the bill already feeling the depression that came over her after an evening with Ben when they seemed to get no further forward. Deliberately, she refrained from putting on the jacket that went with her dress, but when she joined Ben he took it out of her hand and held it so that she could slip her arms into it.

'You'll find it chilly in the car,' he said. He looked at her downcast face and added softly, 'I don't need to be reminded that you're beautiful.'

It was at times like that, when he seemed to read her thoughts, that Nicola felt completely helpless. Nothing was hidden from him as far as she was concerned and yet Nicola felt she hardly knew Ben. It was not just that there were areas of his life which were a mystery to her; she accepted that unless he chose to explain it to her she would never understand the way he had built up what was obviously a thriving business. It was what went on in Ben's mind that escaped her. There were times when she was sure he desired her, even loved her, but she also felt that Ben hid himself from her and that he did it deliberately.

It was dark when they left the hotel, a moonless night. Ben did not take her straight back to London, but drove quietly along the narrow country lanes until they came to a track that ran up on to the Downs. At the top of the hill he stopped the car and turned out the headlights. Below them a few lights glittered, above them a few stars were beginning to show, and the air was fresh and cool, scented with damp grass.

Ben slipped his arm round Nicola's shoulders and she turned towards him gladly, but he did not kiss her. Instead, he stroked her hair delicately with one finger and said, 'I've been thinking about your birthday, too. In fact, I've got a present for you, if you'll accept it.'

'I'm sure I'll love it. What is it?'

'A ring.'

With his free hand he felt in his pocket and drew out a small jeweller's case.

'It's a topaz. Unusual for an engagement ring, I know, but it seemed the right stone for you.'

'An engagement ...!'

'Would you consider marrying me, Nicola?'

The surprise of it took her breath away. She could not speak. When she did manage to open her mouth all that would come out was his name.

'Ben! Oh, Ben!'

'Does that mean yes?'

'Of course! Yes! If you're really sure ... if you mean ... oh, Ben!'

For the first time, Ben laughed, on a note of deep and affectionate amusement. His grip on her tightened and he put his mouth on hers, kissing her with a passion he had never expressed before. Nicola wound her arms round his neck, with no thought in her mind but to show him how much she loved him. She pressed against him, quivering with shock and the release of the emotion she had tried to hide, until Ben very gently put her away.

'My precious, we're going to have to be a bit practical about this,' he said. 'For one thing, it's not going to be popular with your family.'

'Mummy will hate it, of course. Raymond ... well, it's not really anything to do with him and, after all, I'm nearly twenty-one.'

'What about your grandfather?'

'In many ways he's got a more up-to-date idea of the world than Mummy has and he likes you. I've talked to him about you, just a little bit, and I could see he admired the way you've ...'

'Gone up in the world?'

'Succeeded,' Nicola amended.

'Why don't you talk it over with him before you break the news to your mother?' Ben suggested. 'Get him on our side.'

'When will we announce it? At my party?'

'Before that, I think. Give people time to get over the shock before we face them. And if you agree we'll get married this summer.'

'Oh, yes! *Soon!*'

She held up her face and Ben kissed her again. As they parted, Nicola said in a very small voice, 'Ben, if you w-want me to ... you know, sleep with you before we're married, then I will.'

He laughed again, indulgently. 'Darling baby,' he mocked her. 'Of course I w-want you, but I mean to keep this very correct. No bed until we're married, baggage, so it'd better be soon.'

'You do love me, don't you?'

'Indeed I do!'

'I love you, too,' Nicola said contentedly. 'I always have, you know. You will talk to me now, won't you?'

'What about?'

'The way you feel, the things that are important to you. I never know what you're thinking.'

'If I shine a light into the dark corners, will you like what you see?'

'Yes, because they will be part of you. I love you *completely*, Ben.'

He did not respond to that, even moved away from her.

Nicola sensed an unease in him that she did not understand, not even when Ben said, 'Don't turn me into a tin god, Nicola. I'm just another human being. I was brought up differently from you, too. Never lose sight of that.'

'I know you grew up poor, but look at the way you've built up your life.'

'It wasn't just the poverty. No matter how hard you try there are always going to be things about me you won't understand.'

'If you told me, I would,' Nicola pointed out, but she got no response to that.

'I always knew where I was going,' Ben said, following his own thoughts. 'I didn't see the path clearly when I was a boy, but I knew what I wanted and where I meant to end up.'

'I'll help you,' Nicola promised. 'I can, you know. I may not have a talent for business, and I'm certainly not clever like Josie, for instance, but I know all about running a house and being a good hostess.'

'Well, of course, if I hadn't thought you'd be an asset I would never have asked you to marry me,' Ben said gravely.

'You're laughing at me. Oh, Ben ...' Nicola snuggled closer again. 'You can't think how nice it is to have someone who does that sort of loving teasing. What made you fall in love with me?'

Ben ran his hand slowly the length of her body, smiling to himself as he felt her shiver.

'You're the most beautiful girl I know,' he said, and kissed her swiftly. 'And you've got a loving heart into the bargain.'

Ben insisted on taking Nicola to visit Andrew and Bess. She saw it as a test and went with him in a mood of staunch determination to make them like her. It was not until Ben inquired afterwards. 'Can you really bear to have Bess as a mother-in-law?' that she realized that what he had been trying out had been Nicola's will to go through with their marriage.

'You still doubt me, don't you?' she said, answering his implication rather than his question. 'All right, Bess is a bit overpowering, but I'm not such a kid that I can't see behind all that loud talk. I made her feel unsure of herself. I'm sorry about it, but I did. She was full of good intentions. She'd gone to a lot of trouble to get us a meal.'

'A ham tea. I hope you realize that's the height of luxury as far as people like Dad and Bess are concerned?'

'She wanted to impress me. She gave me the best of which she was capable. That's a compliment,' Nicola insisted.

'You behaved beautifully,' Ben said.

There was a dryness in his voice which made Nicola look at him sharply.

'I was brought up to behave beautifully,' she said. 'It's one of the things I'm good at. It doesn't have to mean that I'm a hypocrite.'

She felt dismayed at the jarring note which had crept into the harmony between them.

'I liked your father,' she ventured.

To her relief, Ben's face cleared. 'Dad's the salt of the earth,' he agreed. 'The only thing he ever did wrong was to marry Bess.'

'She makes him comfortable,' Nicola insisted.

'I've done that, moving them out of the slum I was brought up in. Bess doesn't like the new house, you know. She'd be happier back in the sty, wallowing with the other fat sows.'

'She misses her old friends, I suppose,' Nicola said doubtfully.

Ben's face was taut with distaste. 'Friends! They were always fighting. One of the first things I can remember is Bess's voice yelling insults at a neighbour. Well, I'm sure of one thing now: I'm not having her at our wedding.'

'What about your father?'

Ben did not answer directly. 'We'll keep it very quiet. A quick ceremony at the Registrar's Office.'

'I've always meant to get married in the church at Berringer,' Nicola said in dismay. 'Let me have that, Ben, please.'

'I'm not religious.'

'Neither am I, not particularly, but all the same ... I shan't feel married unless it happens in church.'

'Don't worry, I'll see you feel married,' Ben promised.

Nicola edged away from him, not liking the derisive look on his face, and for once determined to have her own way.

'I give in to you all the time,' she said. 'I love you so much that I'm willing to do almost anything to please you, but I'm going to stand out against you on this. I want to be married in church and I want an invitation sent to your father and ... and Bess.'

They were travelling towards London, and driving faster than Nicola liked. A mile sped by in a way that made her feel slightly sick before Ben answered her.

'All right,' he said. 'Perhaps it's the better way. Will your mother come?'

'I'm working on her. If it's in church, and at Berringer, and she sees that we have Grand-dad's blessing, then I think she'll come round. I want Grand-dad to give me away.'

'Won't Raymond expect to do that?'

'I won't have him.'

'You can be obstinate, can't you?' Ben remarked.

'I don't want to walk up the aisle with Raymond trying to get his hand up my skirt.'

'Coarse, too. So that's why you don't like him.'

'That and the way he treats Mummy. He humiliates her in public. She may not be the world's greatest brain, but she's not a fool either.'

'Has this business with Raymond being going on for long?'

'For the last seven years. Before that I was too young to understand. I keep out of his way.'

'Nasty for you. Does your mother know?'

'Not about me. At least, I don't think so. She must know about his other women.' Nicola sighed. 'Poor Mummy, I don't think she's very happy.'

She said nothing about Marigold's outrage at the news that her only child was engaged to marry the boy who had once dug the garden at Berringer Hall, whose aunt had been her housemaid, whose uncle had done odd jobs for a pittance, but she did not need to: Ben took it for granted that Marigold's reaction had been hostile.

The only thing that worked in his favour was that Raymond insisted to Marigold that Ben was a coming man. Whatever his faults, there was nothing wrong with Raymond's nose for money; if he said Ben was making a pile, then it was true. Very reluctantly, Marigold let herself be won round.

She was offended by Nicola's insistence on having her grandfather to give her away, but even over that Raymond was able to persuade her that it might be a good thing.

'Colonel Berringer is delighted that she wants him, and there's no harm in humouring him,' he said with the easy good nature that was always in evidence when he saw some advantage in being amiable. 'I dare say he'll come down with a handsome wedding present and you know, darling, that there's not a lot I can do for Nicola. The expense of public life rises all the time; I don't know how some of our chaps carry on.'

It was not an elaborate wedding. Bess, expecting yards of white satin, half a dozen bridesmaids and hordes of smart guests, thought very poorly of it. Nicola wore a short dress of pale blue crêpe and carried a posy of rosebuds which, since she had no bridesmaids, she handed to her mother to hold during the ceremony. There were few guests, no confetti, none of the hullabaloo Bess thought appropriate when well-to-do people got married. Even the wedding breakfast was a simple cold meal she might have put together herself. Still, there was champagne and Ben had provided a car for her and Andrew. Having that pull up outside the house and a chauffeur with a cap on open the door for her was the high spot of the day for Bess.

Josie was there, but not Stan or Ethel or the two boys. Bess was surprised to see how smart Josie looked.

'You've done well for y'self,' she said, feeling generous. 'On the council, at your age! What do you get out of it?'

'Satisfaction,' Josie said crisply.

'No money in it, is there?'

'I've got a job. I get by.'

Bess sidled closer. 'Not much of a do, is it?' she asked. 'I thought they'd have pushed the boat out, an only daughter getting married. What do you think? Are they ashamed of her marryin' our Ben?'

'Nicola wanted a quiet wedding,' Josie said. 'And you can see she's not ashamed from the way she looks at him.'

Bess gave her a sharp look, quick to catch at the hint of criticism. A touch of sour grapes there.

'You'll be next, hinny,' she said encouragingly. 'I can see the best man's got his eye on you.'

'No thank you!' Josie said. 'I'm concentrating on my career.'

Chapter Twelve

Ten days after the wedding Nicola woke up early. She opened her eyes and blinked. The sun was streaming through the shutters, and the light already lay in bars of white and black across the marble floor. Beside her, Ben was still sleeping. She turned to look at him, marvelling all over again at her wonderful good fortune. She was deeply and humbly grateful for the happiness she had found with him, so much so that she had an impulse to slip out of bed and go down on her knees, except that it would feel unseemly to address God without any clothes on.

She smiled at the memory of their tumultuous lovemaking the night before. Ben had been importunate, far more so than he had been in the first few days of their marriage, when he had shown her a gentleness that made Nicola want to cry. No need for that now; she had learnt what pleased him and she gloried in giving it to him. There was a touch of complacency in her smile as she stretched and yawned. She was beautiful, and she was loved. She felt alive from head to foot, urgent with new vitality, so that it seemed as if all her life before marrying Ben she had been living like a vegetable.

He was frowning in his sleep. Nicola touched the crease in his forehead with one finger and his eyebrows twitched. She wanted to wake him up and yet at the same time she had a curious maternal satisfaction in watching him sleep.

As she moved closer to him, so that her head could rest against his shoulder, the telephone rang.

Nicola picked it up and Ben stirred. Still half asleep, he muttered, 'O.K., I'll take it.'

Nicola shook her head, holding up her hand to silence him.

'It's for me ... Mummy,' she said quickly.

She listened and Ben gathered from her look of concern that something was wrong. He sat up and then, since Nicola was still speaking, got out of bed and found his dressing-gown. He looked round when he heard Nicola say, 'Yes ... yes, of course I'll come.'

Ben was sitting on the end of the bed when Nicola put the telephone down.

'It's Grand-dad,' she said. 'He's had a stroke. Mummy sounded pretty distraught. Ben, I think he's going to die. I must go home.'

There was a long silence from Ben. At last, when Nicola was beginning to look at him questioningly, he said, 'All right. I understand how you feel. The only thing is, I can't go with you.'

He saw her dismayed look and added, 'Sorry, darling. A matter of business. I have to be here for the next few days to see a man who can't meet me at any other time.'

'On our *honeymoon?*' Nicola said.

'I kept the first ten days free for you.'

Nicola stared at him. He sounded offended, as if he had done her a favour and now she was quibbling about it.

'I didn't know you did business in Morocco,' she said quietly.

'The man's an Arab who wants to invest in property in England. It's important, Nicola.'

'All the same ...' Nicola pulled herself together. 'If you can't come with me, then you can't,' she said, stiffly because of her disappointment. 'But I must go.'

'I'll arrange a flight for you.'

'Ben, next to you he's the person I love best in the world.'

'I suppose so.'

He seemed to realize that his response was inadequate because he went and put his arms round her, holding her close. Nicola leaned against him, her eyes shut. It was all right. Ben did understand. She pulled away from him, blinking, but managing to smile.

'I must start packing,' she said.

Colonel Berringer died the day after Nicola reached

England. He was only conscious for a few minutes during the hours she spent at his bedside, but Nicola was convinced that he knew she was with him. Ben returned in time for the funeral and in his arms Nicola gave way to her grief. He held her tenderly, but she thought he was oddly silent, as if he did not know what to say.

'I'd never seen anyone die before,' Nicola said. 'It made me think ... wonder about survival, you know. I mean, one moment he was quite unconscious, in a deep coma, but *there* ... the next minute he had gone. Have you ever seen that happen, Ben?'

'Come to think of it, no, I haven't,' Ben admitted. 'Don't let it make you morbid, darling.'

'Not morbid,' Nicola said quickly. 'Just thoughtful.'

She had known nothing about her grandfather's Will, and it contained a shock. He had left a legacy to Marigold, but everything else, including Berringer Hall, went to Nicola.

'I can't understand it,' Marigold complained. 'Daddy knew how much Berringer meant to me. I always loved it. It was the place where I was always meant to live. Raymond thinks it's an outrage.'

She looked accusingly at her daughter. 'Did you know what he planned to do?'

'He never breathed a word about it to me,' Nicola said.

'I can't understand what got into him.'

'You didn't spend a lot of time here in recent years.'

'How could I with Raymond based in the south for most of the year? Honestly, it couldn't be more inconvenient. You know we only lease the house at Coryleigh and the lease hasn't long to run. I'd talked to Daddy about us taking over a wing of the Hall, coming up regularly for weekends so that Raymond can get himself better known in this part of the constituency.'

A suspicion that her grandfather might not have been enthusiastic about having his son-in-law sharing his house passed through Nicola's mind.

'I suppose we can make the same arrangement with you,' Marigold was going on. 'Or even take over Berringer Hall completely. After all, you and Ben have only just bought a house. I don't suppose he'll want to sell it.'

'I'll have to talk to Ben,' Nicola said, glad to have a way of avoiding an immediate decision.

She was not at all sure what she truly wanted. Berringer Hall was a part of her life and she had always believed that it would belong to her one day, but not so soon, and part of her recoiled from the responsibility. Besides, she had enjoyed looking at houses with Ben. The one they had chosen was a far cry from Berringer Hall, but it was pleasant, convenient for his work, modern and easy to run. Nicola had looked forward to putting her own stamp on it. Above all, she had wanted the pleasure of making a home for Ben.

'Grand-dad wanted me to have Berringer Hall and it seems wrong to go against his wishes,' she said to Ben when they talked it over. 'But he left most of the money to Mummy. I suppose he thought you could provide for me. Could we afford to run Berringer, Ben?'

'The thing to do would be to make it over to the company,' Ben said, as if it were the most ordinary thing in the world. 'We could put a good price on it, which would give us the cash to bring the house back to what it ought to be.'

'You can't be serious! *Sell* Berringer?'

'It makes sense. You don't imagine I've paid for this house, do you?'

'Yes ... of course ... I never thought about it,' Nicola admitted.

'Company property, leased to me for a nominal rent.'

'Is it ... well, legal?'

'Of course. It's done all the time.' Ben sounded amused and a little impatient. 'It appears as an asset on our books, just as Berringer would.'

'But it would mean that I'd parted with Berringer?'

'In a way, yes, it would. We'd have to tie it up so that you had the right to buy it back again, in case we ever got a divorce or something.'

'Don't say that, even as a joke.'

Nicola thought about it, but the idea was so distasteful that she said eventually, 'I can't do it.'

'Perhaps when I've explained the advantages ...'

'Not even then. No, don't try to persuade me, Ben. I know

I'm ignorant about these things and I expect logic is all on your side, but I can't let Berringer Hall pass out of my hands even if it is only a legal quibble.'

'I'll get our accountant to come along and explain it to you.'

'Ben, I've just said I won't do it and I shan't change my mind. Do try to understand. Berringer isn't just a house, it's my *home*.'

'Your home is with me now.'

'Yes, *of course*! Darling, I'd live in a tent with you, if necessary, but surely you can appreciate that I have qualms about turning Berringer into a company asset? It's such a special place and it means so much to me.'

'The most beautiful house I've ever seen,' Ben admitted. 'I always swore I'd have one like it one day. I didn't expect to have it handed to me – or rather to my wife – on a plate.'

'It's ours, not mine,' Nicola said quickly.

'But you won't accept my advice about the way to make it possible to live in it? All right, don't look so bothered. I won't press you to do the sensible thing, though I think you'll regret it. I may be able to get some help with the running expenses if we use it to do a bit of entertaining. What you're going to have to accept is hiving off a wing and letting it to your mother and Raymond.'

'I don't like Raymond.'

'I don't like Ernie Baxcombe, but I go on doing business with him, and very profitable it is, too. Look, love, your grand-dad didn't leave you a lot of cash. If we're going to hold on to Berringer Hall and you won't sell to Baxcombe and Harcourt then it's my money that'll keep it going.'

'Meaning that you can dictate what I do with it?'

'Not "dictate", never that, but I do have the right to a say in how it's run. I think we ought to do what Marigold wants, close off the West Wing and let them use it at weekends.'

'And during the long recess,' Nicola said. 'That means they'll be here all the summer months. Are we to share the garden, too?'

'Why not? It's big enough, just as the house is. It could be useful, having a Member of Parliament on the doorstep. I'll get to meet a lot of influential people.'

Nicola turned away. 'Berringer Hall means the same to you as it does to Raymond, a fine house that will give you status with people who care about such things. You don't understand the way I love it.'

'I do! It's been my dream, ever since I was a boy, to own Berringer Hall.'

Because she had said that she looked on it as their joint property Nicola bit back a reminder that Berringer Hall belonged to her, not to Ben; but that had been before Ben had let slip his expectation of using it to meet 'influential people'. The sort of people her mother and Raymond invited to cocktail parties, Nicola thought rebelliously; beautifully groomed women, all surface glitter and shallow minds, and men with hard eyes who murmured about deals and percentages. She had thought she was getting away from that world when she married Ben.

'I don't want to get involved in Raymond's political manoeuvring,' she said, which was not exactly what she meant, but went some way towards explaining her attitude.

'Nor do I,' Ben agreed. 'We can live quite separately. It's our best chance of being able to live at Berringer and I think it would be a crying shame to pass it up, even though it will land me with a sixty mile drive to and from work.'

He waited and when Nicola did not respond he asked, 'Shall I arrange for our tame architect to draw up plans for dividing the house?'

'After he's talked to me,' Nicola said quickly.

'Of course, love. I'll send him along to see you.'

The reconstruction work, arranged by Ben, went ahead quickly. As soon as the house was fit to live in again Marigold insisted on having a party and, since the larger rooms were in the main part of the house, it was held there. Ostensibly it was a joint affair, but to Nicola it seemed that she and Ben were relegated to second place. Marigold decided what food to order, where to get it, how much to allow for each guest; Raymond had seen to the drinks – at Ben's expense, Nicola thought resentfully. It was Marigold who had descended on the village and commandeered extra help. All Nicola had to do was arrange the flowers, dress herself and look welcoming.

'You look incredibly beautiful,' Ben said in a low voice as she turned away from a chattering group.

A look of dissatisfaction passed over his face.

'I didn't realize Marigold had all the jewellery,' he said. 'I must get you something of your own.'

'Please don't,' Nicola said. 'We can find a much better use for the money. The cottage in the woods and the lodge house both need new roofs and I'd like to bring the garden back to what it used to be. We might even clear the old swimming pond and use it again.'

'No!'

His shiver of distaste brought back to Nicola what had happened at the pond in the past.

'Ben, I'm sorry! I'd quite forgotten about that poor man drowning there. Don't look like that, darling.'

'A goose walked over my grave,' Ben said with a laugh. 'To go back to what I was saying – you look wonderful and I'm proud of you.'

On that occasion it pleased her that Ben took pride in her appearance, but gradually it began to seem to Nicola that he was too eager to show her off to other people. He wore her like a rose in his buttonhole and was gratified when he was congratulated on his lovely wife. Nicola grew accustomed to being inspected before they went to one of the parties she found more and more irksome, until at last she protested.

'I thought you liked making yourself beautiful for me.' Ben said.

'For you, not for other people,' Nicola told him. 'And why do we have to go to another tiresome cocktail party?'

'Because the people there may be useful to me.'

'You sound like Raymond – and you know how much I like him!'

'Meaning you'll start feeling the same way about me?'

'Meaning just that!' Nicola retorted.

She was wearing a short, full-skirted dress in blue velvet, with a wide neckline. Round her neck hung a sapphire and diamond pendant on a platinum chain. Ben had kept his word and given her something to match Marigold's jewellery, and the dress had been chosen at his request to show it off.

Nicola put up her hand and touched the pretty thing.

'Why did you give me this? Because you love me or to show everyone what a rich man you are?'

Ben looked baffled. 'For both reasons. It's good for business for people to see that I can afford to give you fine things, and it looks lovely on you, just as I knew it would. Sweetheart, you're not going to quarrel with me because I like giving you presents, are you?'

'Of course I'm not. You're very generous ... with money. I only wish you'd give me more of your time and a great deal more of your confidence. I know next to nothing about your business.'

'You know the essentials. I went in with Ernie because I wasn't satisfied with the way I was getting on. His dad was only in a small way of business, but Ernie had ideas – good ones – and I was able to put up a bit of capital. We bought up a row of houses, did them up – on a shoestring, but they've held together so far – let a couple of them to our own workmen, including Josie's dad, and sold the others. I raised more money, bought a vacant plot and went into building from scratch, in partnership with Ernie. Since then we've never looked back. Local authority contracts are our mainstay. There's been a lot of housing needing replacing. Ernie has good contacts and our tenders don't often get undercut. I've got my eye on even bigger developments, but it remains to be seen whether we can land any Government contracts. There, does that satisfy you?'

'I suppose so,' Nicola said. 'I still don't understand how you could start up a construction firm without knowing anything about building.'

'Ernie's family had been in the business, he had a qualification and you can always buy advice. Architects and surveyors are in the market to sell their services. As a matter of fact, we're big enough now to set up our own service company and it's going to be my own particular responsibility. Shall I call it Berringer Construction Services?'

'Oh, no ... I'd rather you didn't.'

'Just as you like,' Ben said, but she thought he looked rebuffed.

'It doesn't seem suitable somehow,' Nicola said tamely, trying to explain her reluctance to have Berringer linked with any commercial transaction.

'You say you want more involvement in my business life, but in your heart you believe a talent for making money is sordid,' Ben said with a restrained violence that startled Nicola. 'Money is important – as you'd know if you'd ever been without it.'

'Ben ... darling, you know I admire you with all my heart! It's just that to me Berringer stands for different values.'

'Like letting a place go to rack and ruin rather than go into the market place and soil your hands making money to put it to rights?'

'It's not making money I don't like, it's the wheeling and dealing, the people we have to be nice to, like Ernie and Raymond and their friends.'

'You can't have it both ways. Either you come in with me, look at life with your eyes open and put up with the bits you don't like, or else you stand aloof and let me run things as I see fit.'

'I have the feeling that's what you'd prefer,' Nicola said. 'To keep me in a niche like a statue to be admired.'

'Oh, don't be daft, love! You go everywhere with me, don't you? Like the party tonight – and I thought you were complaining about that.'

'I was,' Nicola admitted.

He had not understood the point she was trying to make, but while she was still looking for a way of explaining her meaning Ben went on to ask in a baffled way, 'What is it you really want?'

'To stay at home, grow vegetables and start a family,' Nicola retorted.

The thing that had disappointed her more than anything else about her marriage was that Ben was not keen to have children straight away. Now he said, with the slight frown that she knew meant that he was more displeased than he cared to show, 'You know how I feel about that. We can start a family in a year or two, when we've had time to enjoy being on our own.'

'When are we ever on our own?' Nicola demanded.

'In bed,' Ben suggested with a smile that drew a reluctant response from her. 'No complaints there, I hope?'

'None,' she admitted.

Ben was a delightful lover, as urgent now as he had been on their honeymoon, and Nicola was as passionately in love with him as ever. Perhaps it was because he was afraid of spoiling that side of their marriage that he wanted to postpone having a family? Except that he was wrong, Nicola felt it in her bones. A child would be an extension of their love. If only she could make him understand how much she longed to carry his seed inside her and bring it to triumphant life.

The first year of their marriage slipped by. Nicola busied herself with getting Berringer Hall back into something like the order it had known before the war and with a new obstinacy turned a deaf ear to all Marigold's advice. After all, she had Ben to help her and Nicola knew that he would dislike it if she appeared to be leaning on her mother instead of on him.

But it was not always easy to know whether she was doing the right thing where Ben was concerned. Their attitude towards money was completely different, quite apart from Nicola's shrinking from involving Berringer Hall in any commercial transaction. To Nicola money was something to be spent in order to give her the life she wished to lead; Ben made her a generous allowance and Nicola spent it. She would not have called herself extravagant, since everything she bought seemed to her to be necessary, but the first time she opened an envelope at the breakfast table and remarked light-heartedly, 'Oh, Lord! Overdrawn again!' she was astonished by the depth of Ben's displeasure.

'If you can't manage on the money I give you then tell me,' he said. 'Though I must say, I would have thought it was enough, considering you don't pay any of the household bills.'

'Darling, it's not important!' Nicola said in surprise. 'The Bank is used to me going into the red for a few days at the end of the month. I'll be in credit when your lovely money is paid into my account. Of course I don't want any more. You are wonderfully generous to me.'

She thought no more about it, but a few days later Ben protested about the size of the electricity bill and again she was at a loss to know what to say.

'We have to have lighting and hot water,' she pointed out.

'Could I perhaps persuade you that it isn't necessary to turn on every light in the house as soon as it gets dark?'

'I'll try to remember,' Nicola promised. She looked at him doubtfully. 'Perhaps this isn't the best moment to mention that the kitchen drain is blocked? Could you send someone to deal with it?'

'Sixty miles is a long way to send a man to unblock a drain,' Ben protested. 'Can't you find someone in the village?'

'I suppose so. Who shall I ask?'

'Nicola, for heaven's sake! You know all the local people. All you want is someone capable of scooping a few dead leaves out of an outside drain.' He glanced at his watch. 'I'd do it myself if I had the time to spare.'

'I'll ask Mummy,' Nicola said and then flinched at the look of annoyance that passed over Ben's face.

Her mother, of course, knew immediately who was the best man to send for to carry out minor plumbing jobs, but Marigold could not resist pointing out that in the old days there had always been a man employed at Berringer to do that kind of work. Nicola was left with the uncomfortable feeling that she had somehow fallen short of Ben's expectations of her and at the same time given her mother an unnecessary handle against him, and all for the sake of a blocked drain. It was all very well for Mummy, Nicola thought rebelliously, talking about how they did things in the nineteen-thirties. When she ran the house for Grand-dad they had a cook, three maids, an indoor man and two gardeners. If it hadn't been for things Ben let slip now and again about his childhood Nicola would have doubted that there had ever been a Depression.

She worked hard, rather harder than Ben gave her credit for, she thought, and sometimes harder than was necessary, because digging the garden or polishing the furniture filled up her days and stopped her from thinking about how much she missed Ben when he was away during the week, as he so often was. She still adored him, and Ben loved her – Nicola reminded herself of it frequently – but he still did not give her the full and open confidence she had expected when she married him.

All the same, he was capable of gestures which turned her bones to water. For their first wedding anniversary he gave her, not the piece of jewellery she had been expecting, but a dozen golden rose bushes.

'One for every month of our marriage,' he said.

'What a lovely thought. And I've got you cufflinks! So unimaginative of me!'

'I like them,' Ben said quickly.

He looked at her in mingled amusement and puzzlement. 'What a girl you are! Come here and let me dry your eyes. Fancy crying over a few rose bushes!'

'I'll plant them in the beds just below the terrace and we'll see them blooming and flourishing, like a good omen for us. And increasing, too, if I take cuttings.'

She gave him a mischievous look and added, 'Ben, you know what I really want from you, don't you?'

'You've told me often enough,' Ben retorted. 'All right, minx, if you're so dead set on a baby I'll see if I can manage it.'

'I'll show you how,' Nicola promised and then shrieked as he swung her off her feet.

Lying in the crook of his arm that night, drowsy and content, Nicola thought complacently of the child she might have conceived. But the months went by and her hopes were not fulfilled. She grieved about it, but secretly, since Ben was still not enthusiastic about having children and did not really share her disappointment.

The division of Berringer Hall was working better than Nicola had feared, mainly because Marigold and Raymond were both in London during the week. Marigold insisted on regarding her occupation of the West Wing as a favour to Nicola and Ben, and Nicola held her tongue even when Marigold said she hardly knew how her daughter would manage without her.

Raymond was always highly occupied and cultivated an air of busy concentration which Nicola mistrusted. He still kept his link with the City, he made himself available in the constituency and he sat on various committees. Nicola was surprised when Ben told her that her stepfather was joining the board of Baxcombe & Harcourt.

'Will he have time?' she asked. 'He seems to keep terribly busy – at least, Mummy is always complaining that she never sees him.'

'He'll be a non-executive director,' Ben said easily, skating away from the question of how Raymond spent his time. 'He won't have to do much except turn up for the occasional meeting.'

'Will you be paying him?'

'Oh, yes!'

'What for, if he doesn't do anything for you?'

'I didn't say that. We'll pay for him for his name and his advice and for the good word he can put in for us occasionally.'

He sounded abstracted and Nicola looked at him accusingly.

'You're miles away, not thinking about what you're saying to me at all,' she said.

'Sorry, I have got my mind on other things,' Ben admitted. 'I've just sent in proposals for a big Government contract to build the new university – or at any rate a large part of it. I think it's in the bag, but I'll be on tenterhooks until I know it's been accepted.'

'Does it have to be the lowest bid?' Nicola asked, eager to encourage him to talk about the business life that was still mysterious to her.

'Not necessarily. If the Ministry boys believe we can meet the deadlines and we're within the price limits that have been set then we ought to get it, but we're just tiddlers compared to the big boys and only known in this corner of England. I'm just afraid they may have more pull than we do.'

'Pull?'

'Influence. Someone to say the right word in the right ear at the right time.'

'Is that why you keep in with Raymond?' Nicola asked quietly.

'Of course.'

'And why you're making him a director?'

'He's been a good boy and if we take him on the board we can pay him for it. Don't look so disapproving, sweetie, it's the way of the world. He'll do the right thing, declare his interest and so on.'

Baxcombe & Harcourt were awarded the contract for the university. Ben was in exuberant spirits about it, quite unlike his usual self-contained self. He swung Nicola off her feet and kissed her.

'I'm almost there,' he said. 'I told Josie I'd be a millionaire one day. I haven't made it yet, but I will.'

They had Raymond and Marigold, Ernie and Phyllis to dinner to celebrate. Nicola saw that Ben wanted to impress his partner and his stepsister, but she was not at all sure that he succeeded.

Phyllis looked round the bare, beautifully proportioned entrance hall and shivered. 'It's a fine old place, I s'pose,' she said. 'But why don't you put a carpet down?'

'The floor is marble,' Marigold said.

'Perhaps it does seem rather cold,' Nicola put in hurriedly. 'Come into the drawing room.'

There was a log fire blazing in the open fireplace.

'Do you mean you haven't got central heating?' Phyllis asked incredulously. 'By heck, Ben lad, I'd see to that first thing if I was you.'

'It would mean pulling the house about too much,' Ben said. 'These fires never go out during the winter and at least we have plenty of wood.'

'That you have! It fair gave me the shivers driving along through the trees. Oh, well, it takes all sorts, I s'pose. It wouldn't suit me, I can tell you – I like a bit o' life.'

She gave herself a long, complacent look in the gilded mirror over the fireplace and forebore to mention that its surface was spotted. She was plump, as she had always been, but her flesh was firm and the remains of a suntan acquired during a long holiday in Spain gave her skin an apricot tint. Her hair had been dyed a rich chestnut. She wore a sheath of a dress sewn with green sequins. She looked vulgar and exuberant and seething with sex.

As the evening wore on Phyllis became what she believed to be the life and soul of the party. Her husband watched her with undisguised admiration, his small dark eyes glittering in his thin face. Ben remained aloof, as did the other two women – Marigold with a look on her face as if she were tasting sour fruit

– but Raymond capped Phyllis's sallies with a few risqué remarks and outrageous compliments that sent her into shrieks of laughter.

Nicola gave them coffee in the drawing room after dinner in the delicate cups she had inherited with the house and saw her mother wince at the sight of them.

'Gi' us another cup, hinny,' Phyllis said. 'There's not more than two sups in them tiny mugs. Eh, what I'd really like is a nice cup o' tea, that I would.'

'I can make tea for you if you'd prefer it,' Nicola said.

'No, no! I'll not put you to the trouble. Just top me up wi' coffee and don't stint on the cream.'

'Have you ever thought of dieting?' Marigold asked, drinking her black, sugarless coffee.

'Not me! I've never been one to watch my figure.'

She threw back her head and laughed, inviting the obvious comment, but Raymond caught Marigold's eye and refrained from the suggestion that other people would watch it for her.

They moved away together and stood for a moment by the fire. Nicola saw the way Phyllis looked at Raymond over the rim of her cup and the way he looked back. For a moment they stood staring at one another, the fleshy, highly coloured woman and florid man. Nicola had the unpleasant feeling that her stepfather was going to lean forward and sink his teeth in the apricot-coloured shoulder Phyllis was hunching towards him, but then they turned away from one another and the uncomfortable moment passed.

Phyllis gave her another disagreeable dig when she and Ernie were leaving.

'Well, like I said before, it's not my idea of heaven, but I can see Ben's suited,' she remarked, pulling her mink stole round her shoulders.

Nicola tried to smile, but something about her stiff response nettled Phyllis.

'Mind you, the luck's not all on his side. Ben's a right demon when it comes to lovin', as I know full well.' She laid a familiar hand on Nicola's arm. 'It were nowt but a boy an' girl affair, so no need to be jealous.'

Nicola recognized the spite behind her smile and tried to

look unconcerned, but she asked Ben about it when they were alone.

'Phyllis will always make trouble if she can,' he said. 'I went with her once when I was just a lad.'

He looked at Nicola's shadowed face and added with controlled violence, 'It was no more than scratching an itch. I'd forgotten about it. No, that's not true. She was the first girl I ever had and a man remembers that, enough to make me feel uncomfortable with her ever since.'

'We don't have to invite them again, do we?'

'Not here.'

He looked round the room, cluttered with cups and used ashtrays and crumpled cushions, but tranquil again, and added, 'They're not the right people for Berringer Hall.'

Josie was a more acceptable visitor. Ben ran into her shortly after her successful election to the Ferryhaven Council.

He looked amused when he mentioned it and because she thought he was belittling Josie's achievement Nicola said quickly, 'I think it's absolutely wonderful.'

'So does Josie,' Ben agreed. 'Let's have her over so that she can tell you all about it.'

Josie had changed. She had never been bashful, but now she had a cool assurance that Nicola envied. She would never have Nicola's warm, brown beauty, but on this occasion she sparkled in a way that made Nicola feel pallid.

Nicola was not, as it happened, feeling particularly well. For nearly two weeks she had been going around almost holding her breath, believing that she had at last conceived the child she wanted so much. That morning her menstrual flow had suddenly started again. She had an ache in her stomach, she felt heavy and dull and not at all inclined to enter into the quick fire conversation between Josie and Ben. She had not yet had a chance to tell Ben about her disappointment. He would be sympathetic and kind – Ben was always kind, in an offhand, automatic way as he might be to a child – but he would not fully understand her frustration.

Nicola noticed that Ben's speech broadened when he was talking to Josie, deliberately, as if it were a private joke between them.

'Eh, Ben, lad, I never thought to see the pair of us 'ere, that I didn't,' Josie remarked. 'In drawin' room, like the nobs!'

'Aye, it mak's y' think, don't it?' he retorted, and they both burst out laughing.

Because their mutual congratulations grated on Nicola she said, 'You're both more class conscious than I am. It seems perfectly natural to me to see you here.'

'That's because you don't appreciate what a hard haul it's been,' Josie said. She turned back to Ben and said, 'So you landed the contract for the university. That was an achievement.'

'Getting the contract was one thing, carrying it out is another,' Ben said. 'It's giving me some anxious moments.'

'Subcontractors?'

Ben gave her a long, hard look. 'What do you know, Josie?'

'Two of the firms you're using were close to bankruptcy a short time ago. Coming in with your enterprise has saved them.'

'What's bad about that?'

'As long as they're the best people for the job. Are you satisfied they can do it?'

'They'll do what they've undertaken to do or we'll have them out.'

'Perhaps that's the idea? Drive them into the ground, tell them they're not up to scratch, break them and take over their assets?'

Josie and Ben seemed to have forgotten Nicola, too intent on one another to consider the effect this exchange might have on her. She broke in quickly to say, 'Ben wouldn't do a thing like that!'

Ben made an impatient gesture as if telling her to shut up. 'It's been known to happen,' he said. 'All I can say is that it's not my deliberate intent, not this time. We took on the firms you have in mind on Ernie's recommendation and because they were the cheapest.'

'Last time I was home Mum told me Ernie and Phyllis were having a heated swimming pool put into their back garden.'

Nicola did not see the relevance of this remark, but Ben did.

'Damn it, Josie, we all know it goes on,' he said with

restrained exasperation. 'Someone offered him a sweetener. O.K., it's not nice, it's not ethical, but that's between Ernie and his conscience. Now do you think we could talk about something else?'

'You mentioned your mother,' Nicola said, trying to help. 'How is she? And the rest of your family?'

'Flourishing. Dad has to be away from home a lot, which doesn't please Mum. He's doing all right, but he seems to think he ought to have gone further than he has, considering he's the boss's uncle.'

'Stan's a good man, but he's limited,' Ben said. 'I don't mind giving him charge of the building of a few houses, but I wouldn't let him loose on a large site. I'm sorry, Josie, but small-site foreman is what he's likely to remain.'

'And he's not your uncle,' Josie said. 'Go on, Ben, you've left out one of your lines.'

'I don't owe anything to Bess's family,' Ben said. 'I've done what I can for her and Dad. I can't take responsibility for the whole crew.'

'Tell us about being on the council,' Nicola broke in again. 'I don't even know how it works!'

By persistent questioning she managed to salvage the rest of the evening and when Ben began to look interested and to start talking Nicola subsided. Once more she felt forgotten, left behind by these two quick-witted, experienced people. She was a child again, plodding doggedly after dare-devil, careless Josie, but in those days Ben had always turned back for her.

This time, she saw with a curious feeling of unease, he had quite forgotten her. He and Josie were absorbed in one another. Josie sat with her elbows on the table, her long, restless fingers twisting her empty glass, her eyes looking greener than usual in the soft, flickering glow she had laughed about when she had seen Nicola lighting the candles.

Why shouldn't I have candles on my dinner table? Nicola thought rebelliously. For the first time Nicola recognized Josie as a woman who was attractive to men. She had continued to think of her as the skinny, awkward girl who had been scornful of 'soppiness', but now Nicola saw, with a flash of intuition, that Josie was sexually experienced, that the movements of her rangy, angular body were those of a hunter. She had been a fool to comment regretfully to Ben that it was a pity Josie seemed unlikely to marry: Josie would choose her man and take him if she wanted him, but she would not let any incidental relationship deflect her from the path she had chosen for herself.

It was not pleasant to see Ben so intrigued by another woman, and whereas before that evening Nicola would have thought vaguely that 'it was only Josie', now she was wary, suspecting a predator in her house, even though Josie was doing no more than comment on some of Ben's business dealings.

'Shall we have coffee in the drawing room?' Nicola asked at last.

The routine question seemed to startle Ben more than was natural. He turned his head and looked at Nicola as if he had forgotten who she was and then, with a look of contrition which Nicola found she resented, he said, 'Sorry, darling, we've been leaving you out. This wretched girl has got me that riled! Why don't you defend me?'

'That would be easier if I understood what you were talking about,' Nicola said. 'I'll go and fetch the coffee.'

When Josie finally left both Nicola and Ben went out on the steps to see her go. She had bought herself a car, a rattletrap old thing, but absolutely necessary, she assured them.

As the red tail lights disappeared down the avenue, Ben said, almost to himself, 'I think she'll make it.'

'Home, do you mean?' Nicola asked, puzzled.

'No, all the way to the House of Commons. She's a bright girl, is our Josie, and determined.'

'Hard?'

'Maybe. Yes, she's got a hard streak. But then, so have I. We wouldn't have got where we have without it.'

As they went back indoors Nicola said, 'I didn't quite follow about Ernie and the swimming pool. Did she mean he'd taken a bribe to give a contract to someone?'

'That's putting it bluntly. Let's call it a favour.'

'But he's got enough money to pay for his own swimming pool.'

'Ernie would never say no to something for nothing. And anyway, how do you know how much money he's got?'

'He's given Raymond and Mummy a loan. Did you know about that?'

'No, I didn't,' Ben said, and from his frown it seemed that he was not pleased. 'How much?'

'Fifteen thousand pounds. Mummy asked me first and I couldn't let her have it. I mean, we've spent that much putting the house to rights. She wanted me to ask you and I wouldn't. You must have noticed we haven't seen much of her lately: she's very annoyed with me.'

'I'll look into it,' Ben said. 'I suppose it's all right, but all the same … Ernie should have told me.'

'If it's his own money …'

'He has a right to do what he likes with it? Mm, except that Ernie never does anything without a purpose. I wonder what he wants out of Raymond.'

Nicola put up a hand to her forehead. 'I've got a rotten headache.'

'I thought you were a bit quiet this evening.'

'You and Josie had plenty to say. Ben … I'm a bit under the weather. And depressed. No baby after all, I'm afraid.'

Her voice came out uncertainly and she looked down, biting her lips to stop them quivering, but when Ben's arms closed round her she leaned against him and cried quietly for a minute or two.

'I was so sure, this time,' she whispered.

'I know, love. I'm truly sorry. A baby would be such company for you when I'm away, and you're right, it's time we started a family. There ought to be children at Berringer Hall and I'd like a son who might take over from me one day.'

He kissed her quickly. 'Never mind, lass. There'll be other chances, and at least you'll still be beautiful when I take you down to London to meet the Prime Minister. It's going to be an important party. Having you there, looking your best, will give me a boost.'

It was then that Nicola, already feeling that she had been less than adequate in the face of Josie's well-informed convers- ation, low in health and morbidly afraid that she was going to fail to give Ben the children he ought to have, finally admitted, with bitter insight, the place she filled in his life.

Ben loved her as a connoisseur might love a beautiful statue, he valued Berringer Hall as the setting for his treasure, he enjoyed her body, she was useful to him as a hostess, he liked knowing that he was envied by other men for possessing her, but he did not look on her as an equal. Why not? Not because she was unintelligent; Nicola knew that she could have understood any confidence he chose to give her as long as he took the trouble to explain. It was because she had grown up in easy circumstances and he despised her for not knowing the hardship that had marked him for life.

Nicola closed her eyes, but the tears ran down under her eyelids. Ben thought she was still grieving for her disappointed hopes, but Nicola's despair went deeper than that. She wept for him, because by denying her the chance to be his true companion he was making do with second best. And he didn't even know it.

IV. Josie and Ben

Chapter Thirteen

'What made you lend money to Raymond?' Ben asked Ernie the next time he saw him.

Ernie shrugged, but his small dark eyes were watchful. 'He was in need, and I had what he wanted. He's been useful.'

'He's got a seat on the board and we pay him five thousand a year, which is generous. More than he's worth, in fact.'

'Ever thought we might expand abroad?'

'There was that contact with the Arabs which came to nothing, even though I gave up part of my honeymoon to chat up the sheikh.'

'We weren't in the big time then, not really big. Landing the university contract has put us into a different league. Them Arab countries have money to burn and they're beginning to think of spending some of it on dragging their people into the twentieth century – schools, colleges, hospitals.'

'You didn't think of that yourself,' Ben said slowly. 'That's Raymond talking.'

'That's right. He was in the desert during the war. He understands their ways, speaks their lingo.'

'I'm surprised he didn't talk it over with me,' Ben said.

'Perhaps he thought you'd be less receptive than me,' Ernie suggested. 'Your talk with the sheikh that time didn't go all that well, did it?'

'When I realized what he expected to make out of the deal I thought it was time to back out.'

'It's just a different way of doing business,' Ernie said. He sounded impatient. 'You have to make allowances for extra expenses in the price you quote.'

'I'm not in favour of expansion at present,' Ben said, and he spoke with a firmness that made Ernie's face crease into a bad-tempered frown. 'We've taken on as much as we can manage. Your investment in Raymond was a mistake.'

Ernie tried to pass it off with a shrug. 'I'll get my money back in due course,' he said.

'I hope you do,' Ben said.

He probed a bit further when he was talking to Nicola that evening. Nicola was still looking a bit moped, he thought. It was a pity she had been disappointed in her hopes of a baby. 'Do you happen to know why Raymond needed to borrow from Ernie?' he asked.

'Mummy's crafts centre,' Nicola said.

Some five years earlier, before her father's death, Marigold had come up against the difficulty of finding servants to run Berringer Hall and had been brought to realize that there was a drift away from the country towards the towns. She had made what everyone had agreed at the time was a praiseworthy effort to foster pride in local crafts and, at the same time, to provide employment which would keep people in the villages. In the short term the scheme had succeeded, but this success had gone to Marigold's head. She had taken larger premises, employed a young designer from art school and begun to dictate what her workers were to make and how they were to make it. Interest had begun to wane at about the time that Marigold had learnt that she was not Colonel Berringer's sole heir. He had left her a legacy, but it was not what she had anticipated, and not what Raymond had expected either. He had thought that he would be the local lord of the manor as well as Member of Parliament, with all the prestige and wealth that being master of Berringer Hall implied.

He was not a poor man, but his parliamentary duties curtailed the amount he could earn in the City, and he and Marigold led an expensive life. Marigold's legacy had been largely swallowed up in what they saw as necessary spending. The rent for the part of Berringer Hall they occupied was negligible, no more than a token, and the suite of rooms was largely furnished from existing furniture, but Marigold had insisted that anything that was added had to be of the right period to match the other pieces and they had bought some highly priced antiques.

Raymond had guaranteed Marigold's overdraft for the crafts centre, never anticipating that he would be called on to honour his guarantee. It was to finance this unexpected expense that he had turned to Ernie Baxcombe.

Knowing all this, Ben needed no further explanation. He suppressed an exclamation of disgust and said no more about it to Nicola, but he was uneasy. An alliance between Ernie and Raymond was so innately unlikely that he felt there must be more to it than had been disclosed to him: it was something to be remembered.

As for the overseas connection, Ben felt in his bones that it would be a mistake. Over the past few years he and Ernie had gained experience in the construction industry, but the truth was that they were neither of them experts, relying on the knowledge they could buy from men with the proper training, while they concentrated their own talents on sniffing out openings, buying up land and arranging finance. Ernie was the one who always seemed to know what was going on; Ben was the one who put together the package, presented the case for giving a contract to their firm, and did it extremely well.

It was also Ben who visited sites and, without pretending to know everything, kept an eye on progress and tried to ensure that standards were being maintained. Ernie, he sometimes thought, didn't care what rubbish was built so long as it stood up long enough for them to collect their money, which was why Ben worried about his over-ready acceptance of the new techniques of industrialized building.

Ben was the first to see the possibilities of system building. He approached the new idea cautiously, but Ernie seized on it with blind enthusiasm as soon as he realized that by building with pre-fabricated panels they could cut costs substantially.

'The housing of the future!' Ernie said. 'The assembly line applied to building. We can get some publicity out of that angle. Now, you get your lads in the architects' office to amend the plans we're putting out for the block of flats in Luffley, and do it quick, or the opposition'll be on to the same idea.'

'You're going too fast,' Ben protested. 'All we know about the new method is on paper. I want to see it for myself before I commit us to using it.'

'You're too slow to catch a cold. It works, doesn't it? You told me it's been in operation in Scandinavia.'

'The idea's been around a long time,' Ben admitted. 'But for low-rise buildings. I'm not sure about using it for anything above two or three floors.'

'You're the one who runs the experts. Have you talked it over with them?'

'Most of the architects seem convinced the idea is feasible,' Ben said.

'Right, then! Is there time to change the submission for the university?'

'No.'

'You said that too damn fast. You're as bad as my old dad, wedded to bricks and mortar.'

Within a week Ernie had set up a deal with the manufacturer of pre-cast concrete slabs and was deep in plans for persuading Luffley Council that they were fortunate to be getting the flats of the future. It was Ben who took on himself the job of going to the site when the flats began to be erected, taking with him a keen youngster from the architects' office who was anxious to see the new system being put into use.

Ben stood on one side and let the site foreman explain the method of operation.

'It's a standard casting, so each panel should be exactly the same as the next,' the foreman said. 'They are bolted together, you see. All the holes for the bolts are supposed to line up with one another so that they can just be slipped into place. No particular skill needed, not like laying bricks. The concrete is poured into these pillars and when it's set you've got a rigid structure. It's certainly the fastest way of putting up a building.'

'Just a minute,' Ben said. 'What did you mean when you said that the holes for the bolts are "supposed" to line up? Do they or don't they?'

'No mass production method is ever perfect,' the foreman said. 'You get the odd hole out of alignment, naturally.'

'And what do you do about it?'

The foreman looked uncomfortable. 'I talked to Mr

Baxcombe about that the other day,' he said.

'Oh, yes? What did you decide?'

'Mr Baxcombe said, and I take it he knows, that as long as most of the bolts went home O.K. we could forget about the odd few that didn't. After all, the concrete we pour will hold it together.'

'How much experience have you had of building with this method?'

'I visited the factory before we started work and had it all explained to me.'

Ben turned to the boy he had brought with him. 'Care to give an opinion?'

'I don't know much about it, that's why I came along today,' the youngster protested. He paused to think. 'All the stresses and strains, the bearing loads, must have been worked out in advance and the number and type of bolts required would have a relation to one another. I have a gut feeling that I wouldn't be happy for even one of them not to be properly in place. It would cause distortion in the fabric, at least I think it would, and place too much of a burden on the other bolts.'

'I feel the same. The trouble is, we're none of us experts, and that includes Ernie Baxcombe. Bloody hell, why didn't we stick to something we understood?'

Ben stood for a moment deep in thought. He was faced with a decision which was going to make him extremely unpopular with Ernie, though that was of no great importance to him. It was also going to cost a lot of money and that was something Ben did dislike.

'I'm leaving you here on the site,' he said to the young architect. 'Your job will be to check every pre-cast concrete panel that's delivered. Any that aren't up to standard will be returned to the factory and we'll claim compensation from them.'

He turned to the foreman, who was standing by with a face like thunder. 'No reflection on you,' he said. 'I'm giving you an assistant, that's all, but from now on I don't want any faulty materials put into these flats.'

'It'll hold the work up,' the foreman warned. 'And Mr Baxcombe's dead keen on getting the job finished on time.'

'You leave Ernie to me,' Ben said.

Predictably, his decision drove Ernie into a screaming rage.

'What do you think we're building, the bloody Taj Mahal?' he demanded. 'A block of working class flats, that's all it is.'

'Good enough for the likes of my dad and yours?' Ben asked. 'We'll have egg on our faces if they fall down, no matter who's living in them.'

'Fall down! Stuck together with enough concrete to hold up a skyscraper! Do you know how much it'll cost if we fall behind schedule? This was my project, not yours, and I'm damned if I want you interfering.'

'We're a partnership,' Ben said quietly. 'I stand to lose as much as you do if we have to pay penalties and I'm as responsible as you are if we put up a faulty construction.'

'It cost a lot to get that contract,' Ernie said, too infuriated to watch what he was saying.

Ben's lips tightened. 'I thought it all went through a bit too smoothly,' he said. 'Got it on the nod, didn't we? What have you been doing, Ernie? Buying councillors? You'll get your fingers burnt one of these days.'

'I had to ease the way a bit,' Ernie said uncomfortably. 'It's a controversial scheme.'

'Too controversial. I'm not sold on these pre-fabricated units. I don't think we should be associated with them again.'

'Don't be a fool!' Ernie stared at him as if he suspected his partner was demented. 'We'll be throwing away a fortune if we don't move with the times.'

'If you want to deal in system building then set up a separate company,' Ben said slowly.

'If I do, I'll leave you out of it,' Ernie threatened.

'Suits me.'

'You'll not be so well suited when I'm a millionaire and you're not.'

'We'll quarrel about that when it happens,' Ben said. He rubbed the back of his neck. 'I'm worn out, and I still need to take a close look at our contract with the pre-fabrication firm, just to make sure we can clobber them for supplying faulty panels.'

He was late getting home that night, as he so often seemed

to be these days. As he drove along the country roads he felt deadly tired. He was going to have a battle with Ernie about using system building indiscriminately. Coupled with his opposition to expansion abroad and his niggling worry about Raymond's financial involvement with Ernie, it all added up to a stormy situation at a time when Ben had more than enough on his hands.

The last few years had been an uphill struggle and now that his goal seemed to be in sight he was conscious of a lethargy that he would have said was quite out of character for him.

He had enjoyed the fight, clawing his way up from the gutter to within sight of the top of the mountain, but all of a sudden there seemed no fresh incentive to keep him going. Getting Berringer Hall handed to him on a plate had been a bonus he had not foreseen, and yet in a way he regretted it; he would just as soon have provided his own home, even though it might not have been so grand.

Nicola was an asset. That was why he had married her, though not the only reason. Her beauty enchanted him, and something more, a sweetness in Nicola which subdued the buccaneer in him and made him show her the best side of his character. And yet ... there was something missing. His marriage was not exciting, not once he had got used to the idea of having manoeuvred himself into the upper class of society. It had not always been easy and there were still times when he felt out on a limb, times when out of bravado he had an urge to turn up at the dinner table in slippers and shirt sleeves, without collar or tie. Nicola would have laughed, but it was not entirely a joke to Ben because he knew that was the way Marigold expected him to behave, and it was as much as he could do sometimes not to come up to her expectations, just for the hell of it.

He was neglecting his own father. He knew it, regretted it, and dismissed it from his mind. It was only when he saw someone from the past, like Josie, that he had a twinge of conscience.

Josie was one of the few people whose criticism got through to him. She had hinted at sharp practice, even bribery, in Ernie's dealings and Ben knew there were grounds for her suspicions. He had not been above doing favours himself for people whose influence he needed and accepting help from men who had an eye to future business. The point was, he had kept it within bounds. As he had said to Josie, it went on all the time. You scratch my back, I'll scratch yours. There was nothing really wrong about it; it was the way the world worked.

Berringer Hall looked mellow and welcoming as he drove towards it, but Ben was not best pleased that evening to find his home full of people. True, they were just about to leave, but he was in no mood to exchange pleasantries with the Vicar, however briefly, nor was he at ease with the neighbours from the village who were milling about the entrance hall. Too many of them remembered him as a sullen evacuee and they either treated him with a forced familiarity which put his back up or else avoided his eye and looked uncomfortab1e when he spoke to them.

'What was all that about?' Ben asked Nicola as soon as the last straggler had left.

'The final meeting of the Church Fête committee. You haven't forgotten that it's on Saturday?'

Ben grimaced. He had forgotten and the reminder was unwelcome.

'We never seem to have a weekend to ourselves,' he complained. 'There was that damn gymkhana last Saturday.'

'The rain was unfortunate. I had a look at the paddock this morning and it's in a dreadfully churned up state.'

'I'll be getting churned up myself if these everlasting demands go on. Can't we cut some of it out?'

'Not really. Berringer has always been a focus for local events. You haven't complained in the past.'

'It was a novelty,' Ben said. 'When it goes on year after year you do get a bit tired of it.'

He would not admit it, but he had been tickled at first to find himself acting as host to the local activities. Now he was bored with it and would have been glad to opt out. Nicola did not seem to realize what a strain it was being pleasant to hordes of well-meaning nonenities. She took it in her stride, but then she had been born to it and although it went against the grain to admit it, that did count.

'One of the penalties of living at Berringer Hall,' she said now, too lightly in Ben's opinion. 'There are compensations, too, aren't there?'

'I suppose so,' he admitted, but the thought still lurked at the back of his mind that Berringer was not his and never would be. Nicola's automatic assumption that everything would go on as it always had done belittled him.

'At least it gives you something to do,' he said. 'I don't know how you'd fill your days if it wasn't for all these charity things.'

'I dare say I'd manage,' Nicola said.

She looked at him thoughtfully, aware that Ben was out of sorts, and not sure how to handle his disgruntled attitude. No use asking what was wrong; he would shut up like a clam. All she could do was remain serene, provide him with food and drink and a pleasant atmosphere, and hope that the mood would pass. I spread my table in his sight, she thought, as she put the finishing touches to their evening meal. And I don't mean that blasphemously, it's exactly what I do.

'Did you never want a career?' Ben asked abruptly while they were eating.

'I thought of taking up nursing,' Nicola said. 'Mummy was against it and it was difficult to fight her. Perhaps I would have gone ahead with it if I hadn't married you.'

'I caught you young,' Ben said, with a half smile that showed that his sombre mood was beginning to lift. 'Have you ever regretted it?'

'I've sometimes wished that I'd had a bit more experience,' Nicola said.

'What – half a dozen lovers?' Ben asked in real amusement.

'No! More experience of life ... not quite such a sheltered existence. I sometimes think you hold back from telling me things because you don't believe I'm capable of understanding,' Nicola said in a rush.

She almost held her breath, willing Ben to respond.

'Such as why you were in such a black mood when you came home this evening,' she added.

'Oh, that! I had a disagreement with Ernie, and I was tired, and it was suddenly too much when half the village seemed to have invaded us. Sorry if I was a bit churlish.'

'I wanted an explanation, not an apology,' Nicola pointed out evenly.

'Well, you've had it,' Ben replied in surprise.

'Not really. Why did you fall out with Ernie?'

'Darling, if I told you it was about industrialized building systems you wouldn't have a clue what I was talking about.'

'I would if you explained.'

'I can't go into all that now and I don't want to talk business at home. Let me keep one place where I can be sure of peace and quiet.'

Peace and quiet and endless love. It was all she was able to give him. But Nicola was no longer sure that it was enough. Their placid existence might look like contentment but Nicola was afraid that Ben needed a stimulation she no longer provided, in spite of the fact that he took her to bed early that night and made love to her with a dogged, singleminded persistence that left her exhausted.

Ben felt better the next day. They had made a proper night of it and Nicola had been adorable, as always. None of his difficulties were insuperable. He could rise above them, just as he always did.

'You look a bit heavy-eyed,' he remarked as he carelessly kissed Nicola goodbye.

'Are you surprised?' she demanded.

Ben laughed and gave her a quick hug and he was still smiling as he drove away. She was a wife in a million and he'd been damned lucky to get her. Except that it wasn't really luck. He'd chosen her and courted her and the outcome had never been in doubt. He owed his marriage to his own good judgement. It wasn't Nicola's fault that he found her dependence on him irksome while at the same time resenting that the way she fitted in at Berringer put him into the role of prince consort.

She would never understand some of the things he was forced to do. Only someone brought up in the same circumstances could do that. Like Josie, for instance. Josie. Now there was a woman and a half. He ought to look her up some time, keep in touch. She was a link with the past he ought not to neglect and her presence on one of the local councils might be helpful to him.

He took the opportunity to see her the next time he was in her area. He told her that he just happened to be in Ferryhaven and had looked her up on impulse, but it was not entirely true and Josie knew it.

'Liar!' she said cheerfully. 'Come clean, Ben Harcourt. I'm a damn sight more interesting to you now that I'm a councillor than I ever was when I was plain Josie Bewley, typist.'

'You've improved since you began to grow up,' Ben said with a smile that tacitly admitted the truth of what she said.

'I'm twenty-six,' Josie reminded him. 'And I've learnt to be cautious. No use pumping me for information, if that's what you've got in mind. And, no, I won't use my influence – such as it is – to get you a fat contract, so you can put that out of your mind, bonny lad.'

'Will your principles let you have lunch with me at The Dog and Dragon?' Ben asked.

'Only because I'm fair skint until the end of the month. And I can't take more than an hour. I'm a working girl still, remember.'

She let him buy her steak and kidney pie and a pint of beer. Judging by the way she shovelled the food down she was in need of a square meal.

'I bet you don't feed yourself properly,' Ben remarked.

'You sound like my Mum! I'm not domesticated, never was. And I'm not much interested in food. Catch me fiddling around with fish mousse, like Nicola! Not that it wasn't very nice, but I'd just as soon grill a kipper. I keep body and soul together and stay healthy, that's all that matters.'

'Do you earn enough to live on?' Ben asked.

'Just about. My job's dull, but it doesn't demand a lot of me and I need that. My real life starts after working hours.'

She put her elbows on the table and looked at him with a challenging stare, her grey-green eyes brilliant.

'I'm doing my bit for the working class, my own class, which is more than you can say.'

'I keep a heck of a lot of them employed,' Ben protested.

Josie dismissed that with a wave of the hand. 'I don't imagine you pay over the odds,' she said. 'Now, Ben, while I've got you I want to pick your brains. My great interest at the moment is low-cost housing for the elderly. Do you happen to know a good young architect who'd be willing to talk to me without wanting a fee? Just talk, nothing more. I want to know if my ideas are feasible, that's all. Then, if I can get them through the council, we might be able to do business.'

'How about the labourer being worthy of his hire?' Ben inquired mildly. 'I might be able to lay my hands on someone for you. What's put this into your mind?'

'People are living longer, houses are smaller, families don't hang together like they used to – as you must know yourself – when did you last see your dad? Young people are worried about what to do with Mum and Dad. I want to do some good and be identified with a real campaign.'

'So it all boils down to promoting Josie Bewley?'

'Does that matter, so long as I get results? I do care, Ben.'

'Do you? About people, or just about your cause?'

'About people, I hope,' Josie said carefully. 'I don't ever want to be a fanatic. The man I fell for in Geneva was an out-and-out Communist and it dehumanized him. He looked like a man, he acted like a man, but the heart and mind had been taken out of him. It was a lesson I hope I'll not forget.'

'I'll find you an architect,' Ben promised. 'I might go further and take an interest in your idea myself.'

'What I need is money.'

'Why don't you start a housing association?'

'I've thought about it,' she admitted. 'I want to have some concrete suggestions to put forward to get people interested. But I really believe this accommodation ought to be provided by local government, not by a private charity.'

'I'm all for a bit of self-help myself. If the council do it they'll get the money by putting up the rates. Why not let people subscribe direct and see what they're getting?'

Josie propped her chin on her fists and looked at him steadily. 'If I get it started will you be one of the trustees?'

'I ought to have seen that coming, didn't I?' Ben said. 'You're a canny lass, Josie Bewley. I'll think about it, I won't say more than that.'

The talk drifted to other things, but Josie had Ben's promise to find her an architect who shared her views and she was fairly confident that if anything came of her ideas Ben would give her more tangible help.

It would keep her in his mind and probably mean that they would see one another again, which perhaps was not such a good idea. Josie grimaced to herself, admitting that Ben got to her in a way that few men did. She had been conscious of it after dining with him and Nicola. Driving home alone afterwards she had known a quite unexpected envy for Nicola's good fortune. The girl had everything – looks, money, a beautiful home, and Ben.

He was damnably good-looking, and he had gained in stature in the last few years. Ben as a sulky, ambitious boy had been interesting, but as a man with achievements behind him he was something more. Josie remembered, as if it had been yesterday, the jolt his appearance had given her when she had been a very young girl. It had been painful and exciting, and it still was. She wanted him, it was as simple as that, and she was not going to be able to have him.

The architect Ben sent along to her was just what she wanted: recently qualified and full of ideas, receptive in just the way she required, and very leftwing in his politics. Wet behind the ears, Josie thought privately, but that didn't mean he wouldn't be useful.

He gave her a great deal of his time, so much so that Josie was conscience stricken, until she discovered that Ben was paying him. She battled with herself and managed to refrain from ringing Ben to thank him, knowing that her real reason for the call would be to hear his voice, perhaps to arrange another meeting. I'm not in love, she told herself. Damn it, I swore I'd never fall in love again. It's more like the 'flu. I've picked up a yen for someone else's husband, but if I'm sensible and stay away from infection, I'll get over it.

Cy Maple seized on her idea of sheltered accommodation for the elderly and began to promote it enthusiastically. Her liaison with him continued in a desultory way, but she began to make excuses to avoid seeing him. With this new hunger for Ben churning her up inside she couldn't face Cy's familiar lust. Besides, she was annoyed that her pet scheme, her very own idea, was being used by the Member of Parliament for his own political ends. All the same, he got results, so Josie swallowed her pride, told herself it was the welfare of the old folk she had at heart and went along with the publicity Cy whipped up locally during the October 1959 elections.

Gradually, over the year, the idea took shape. Josie's housing association was formed. It irked her that several of the well-meaning people on the committee were as far from her political stance as they well could be and she had to endure some teasing from Ben about her new alliance with the far right.

They were meeting more often. Sometimes twice or three times in one week Josie would look up from her untidy, paper-strewn desk in the tiny office where she talked to people from the ward she represented and discovered that her next caller was Ben.

'It's on my way home,' he said in response to her reluctant protest. 'You're my halfway house.'

'Ferryhaven is considerably less than halfway between your office and Berringer,' Josie said.

'I'm not talking about mileage. If I drop in here and talk over a few problems which are different from the ones that keep me occupied all day, then it's easier to switch off before I get home.'

'Making use of me! I should have known! What does Nicola say about you always being late?'

'She's used to it.'

What Ben did not say was that he rarely mentioned to Nicola that he had called in to see Josie. Looking up he found Josie watching him. They exchanged a long, steady look and he saw that it was not necessary to tell Josie of his omission: she knew.

Josie got up from her desk and Ben watched her, stirred, as he had been for weeks now, by her unconscious, angular grace. Everything about her excited him: her independence, her acute mind, her thin, supple body, the glitter of her grey-green eyes, her suppressed sexuality.

'Stop prowling round the cage,' he said.

'You're doing too much for me,' Josie said, not looking at him. 'You come in here on top of a hard day and you've still got sixty miles to drive home. You ought to cut it out.'

'Ungrateful hussy.'

'No, I'm not ungrateful,' Josie said quickly.

'I've got more than you realize out of helping with your housing scheme – more than I've put in. You think I've forgotten where I came from, but I haven't. This is my way of giving a bit back.'

'Shouldn't you be doing it for the people where you live now?' Josie asked carefully. 'I thought you were proper Lord of the Manor at Berringer that time I came out and visited you.'

'Nicola does what's necessary at Berringer,' Ben said.

'Then what about Jarrow, where you came from?'

'This is where the chance cropped up. What's the matter? Don't you want my help any more?'

'I don't approve of you. Not of the way you've made your money nor of how you've spent it. I don't know that I like you using my scheme to salve your conscience because you've copped out of your beginnings.'

'If you only co-operate with the chosen few who pass your purity test you're going to be short of helpers,' Ben pointed out.

'You're right about that! My last committee meeting nearly sent me up the wall! The way I see it, people have a right to the sort of thing we're trying to build, but some of that lot still think of it as charity. It makes them feel cosy to do good and I hate them for it!'

'Does that include me?'

Ben stood up and held out his hand and without thinking what she was doing Josie put her own into it. The moment she felt the touch of his flesh on hers she knew she had made a mistake.

'Naturally I don't hate you,' she said in an offhand way, trying to conceal the havoc inside her. 'I mistrust your motives, that's all.'

'I'm a bit mixed up about my motives myself,' Ben agreed.

Josie could have resisted the slight tug he gave on her arm; she ought to have resisted it. Instead, she let herself be drawn towards him until they were standing breast to breast and she could feel his breath on her face. It was too late to draw back then. The slight backward movement of her head was both an admission and an invitation. They kissed with hard, hungry lips but, feeling the mounting passion inside herself, Josie panicked. She broke free, pushing Ben away so roughly that he staggered.

When she was safely on the other side of the desk, she said, 'If you ever do that again I'll scream for help.'

'Will you?'

'Don't kid yourself, Ben. I'm not here to be treated as a bit of relaxation between work and home.'

'That's *not* the way I feel about you!'

'It's the way I choose to see it. Go away, Ben, and don't come back unless you've got real business to discuss.'

He stayed away for two weeks and when he called to see her it was after a committee meeting at which his company's tender for her block of old people's flats had been accepted. That development dismayed Josie, on more than one count.

'I didn't think you meant to put in for it,' she said.

'Why not? It's all business.'

'I don't want it said that I've been drumming up contracts for my cousin.'

'I'm not your cousin. I thought you'd be pleased I was going to take a personal interest. Besides, it's the sort of small operation I can give to your dad to oversee.'

'You're making it worse. Profit for you and work for Dad.'

'Not much profit,' Ben said. 'We're doing it on a shoestring. Ernie is very put out about it.'

Josie hunched her shoulders and scowled.

'I'm damned annoyed, but I can't change the committee's decision. You'd better do a good job, that's all. Now go.'

'How have you been keeping?'

'As well as can be expected in the circumstances,' Josie said evenly.

'Me too.'

'Give my love to Nicola when you get home.'

He left her abruptly and she thought she had succeeded in putting him off, but it was not possible to avoid all meetings when she was committed to occasional visits to the building site. She could never be sure Ben would be there, but when he was he made a point of being the one who showed her round, making her wear a hard hat and helping her over the obstacles lying around.

Taking his hand was torture and pleasure at the same time. Ben seemed unconscious of the way it affected her, but once, just once, he kept hold of her hand and stood swinging it and looking at her. A workman called out and the moment passed, but the next time Josie stumbled on rough ground Ben did not turn round.

It was their last meeting for some time. Josie suspected Ben was avoiding her and was both afraid and exultant because of what that told her, and then she got a telephone call asking her to see him.

'A family problem,' Ben said, as if a meeting between them needed an explanation.

'It's a long time since you gave me lunch,' Josie said. 'I'll meet you at the Dog and Dragon at one o'clock.'

'Josie, I'd better warn you; you won't like what I've got to tell you.'

She worried about that for the next three hours, but nothing she had imagined prepared her for what Ben had to say.

'Your dad's on the fiddle,' Ben said.

She could only stare at him, not taking it in.

'Of all the jobs he had to choose it would be this one, where he ought to have known I'd be watching the last penny,' Ben said bitterly. 'Oh, it goes on all the time and we turn a blind eye to the petty thefts, but I can't afford to do that on this site. And he's been so damn stupid about it. He reported three lavatory pans damaged and then couldn't produce them for inspection – because he'd sold them, as I've found out since. There are other things, too; he's worked a couple of weekends building a driveway for one of your committee members with materials taken from the site. I can't overlook it, Josie.'

'What are you going to do?'

'Sack him.'

Josie made a gesture of repudiation and Ben asked savagely, 'Have you any other ideas? Have I got to overlook theft because he's your father?'

'Give him a chance to explain,' Josie pleaded. 'There must be some reason ...'

'He's been betting heavily and he hasn't been lucky. I picked up that information from casual gossip. But there's more to it than that.'

'It's the fault of the system,' Josie said quickly.

'Oh, Josie, come off it! Stan's got – or had – a well-paid job, a decent house at a reasonable rent, enough money to keep his wife and children fed and clothed. But there are two things wrong for Stan. One is that he can't help looking back ...'

'The fear of past poverty,' Josie said.

'That's right. His generation will never forget. I've seen it with my dad. They always make an extra penny if they can because they believe you never know when you may need it. I can understand that, even make allowances for it. The other thing is not so nice. It's envy. Stan thinks he ought to have what I've got. Every man as good as his master, that's your doctrine, isn't it?'

'Don't try to lay this at my door!' Josie said. 'I won't defend him if he's done wrong, even if he is my dad, but why don't you look into your own past before you condemn him? Moral indignation comes well from a man who stole a book worth twelve thousand pounds, doesn't it?'

For a moment they glared at one another and then Ben relaxed.

'I should never have given you that handle for blackmail,' he said. 'O.K., Josie, I won't sack Stan, but he's coming off this job and I'll demote him. He can go back to being a carpenter on the university site. And let me tell you, it's a damn sight more than I'd do for anyone else in the same circumstances.'

Seeing her downcast face he added more gently, 'Don't look so worried, lass. I won't be too hard on him.'

'I ought to have kept a closer eye on him,' Josie muttered. 'Gone home more often. He's not a strong man and Mum keeps on to him for more than he can give her. He's never got over the setback of not being able to go to Australia because of my T.B.'

She looked down, controlling a rare desire to burst into tears, and suddenly Ben's hand was warm and comforting over hers.

'It's time you forgave yourself for that,' he said unexpectedly.

She looked up, blinking hard, her eyes wide with astonishment.

'I didn't think you knew how guilty I felt,' she said.

'I know. We're very alike, Josie. We've both clawed our way up from the bottom. Different methods, different results, but the thing we have in common is that we've left people behind we think we ought to have taken up the ladder with us. I've done what I can for Dad, but I've had to accept that he's happier in a semi-detached house keeping pigeons in the back garden than he would be in a mansion.'

'I've not done as much for my family.'

'You haven't had the means.'

'I could earn more if I wasn't so keen to give my time to politics. Am I wrong, Ben?'

'You have to lead your own life. People like us ... we have a wider vision than the previous generation. It's not our fault that they can't keep up with us.'

He was still holding her hand; they had forgotten about eating. Ben's eyes were intent on Josie's face and she was unable to look away. He had strange light eyes, ringed with a darker line, clear as water, but not cold. She was flooded with helpless love, totally lost.

Ben let go of her hand and pushed back his chair.

'Let's get out of here,' he said.

She followed him blindly, unable to think, only to do what she was told. Ben's car was outside. He held open the door and Josie got in.

It did not seem to her that Ben had any very clear idea where he was going, but after driving for ten minutes he pulled up in a secluded lane and turned towards her. He put his hand on her head, smoothing down the rough, untended hair, until his hand came to rest at the nape of her neck. In response to its gentle pressure Josie leaned towards him until their lips met and then Ben's hand fell away and he snatched her to him, almost it seemed in anger.

When they drew apart Josie could hear his harsh, uneven breathing and knew that it matched her own irregular heartbeats.

'I never felt like this before in the whole of my life,' Ben said.

'Nicola ...' Josie whispered.

Looking into his face she saw that Ben was bewildered.

'I do love her,' he said uncertainly. 'But not like this. I've always gone on seeing her as outside real life. Not like us. We belong together, Josie. I've known for months, but I wouldn't let myself admit it. I'm in love with you. I don't want to be, but I am. And I'm damned if I can see what we're going to do about it.'

'There's nothing we can do,' Josie said.

She tried to keep her voice steady, but the desolation inside her came through. Ben drew her close again, but this time his mouth lingered on hers while his tongue deliberately tasted her and his hand explored the secret places of her body until Josie shuddered and clung to him in an agony of frustrated desire.

'Take me back to your flat,' Ben demanded against her ear.

'My "flat" is a bedsitter with shared bathroom,' Josie reminded him. 'And what about my job? I'm late getting back already.'

'I'll ring them for you and say you're not well enough to work this afternoon. We can't part like this.'

She wanted it so much, had wanted it for so long, that she could not refuse him. Ben turned the car and drove back. Josie felt as if every eye in the street was on them as she led him up the stairs to her first floor room. Why should she feel like that? She had never worried when she had brought Cy back with her. But this was a more serious betrayal. The thought of Nicola stayed bitterly at the back of her mind.

'Do you make a habit of this?' she demanded.

Ben stared at her and then his expression softened and Josie knew that he understood both her guilt and that she was not going to let it stop her from going to bed with him, and because he read her mind so well she was comforted.

'I have never been unfaithful to Nicola since I married her,' he said. He went to her and cupped both his hands round her chin. 'You are unique, the only one. I love you.'

He had an animal grace that for one elusive moment reminded her of Dominic, but she had never loved Dominic like this, not even in her most besotted moments. She was glad of all her past experience, glad that she understood what he wanted, and she could have wept with delight at Ben's perception of her own needs. Every movement was answered and satisfied and he knew, without being told, that she was greedy for him, had waited too long to need patient courting. They were not like new lovers, making adjustments to one another, they came together like two halves of a perfect whole, creating wave after wave of exquisite pleasure. Josie was drowning, only Ben's arms held her up, she was beyond thought, beyond reason, and then all the brightness of the world shattered into fragments behind her closed eyelids and she lay spent and separate, but not alone, never alone again while Ben was there to hold her.

'Never before,' Ben said with his lips against her throat. 'Never like this. My wild lioness, my beautiful savage.'

Josie stroked Ben's head with slack fingers, feeling the hair damp on his temples, and smiled because it was the effort of loving her that had brought that sweat to his brow.

They lay quietly together, laughing and murmuring endearments, forgetful of the time, until Ben rolled over and looked at Josie's bedside clock.

'Hell and damnation, I ought to be gone,' he said. 'Josie, my dear love, forgive me.'

'What I'd like is a cup of tea,' Josie said, sitting up. She yawned and stretched and her small breasts rose, the areola very dark round the nipples made rosy by Ben's lips.

'Don't do that or I'll never get out of bed, and I must,' Ben said.

Josie watched him lazily as he dressed, but when he was ready, she managed to bring herself to say, 'Ben, what are we going to do?'

'I don't know,' Ben admitted. 'We'll have to meet and talk it over.'

'If we meet we'll make love,' Josie said. 'I don't see any way we can go on with it.'

'You mean part ... now?' Ben asked.

'Yes. What we've just had was wonderful, but there are other people to be considered. We can neither of us afford to throw away everything we've fought for. We ought to try not seeing one another again. It will be difficult ...'

'Not difficult – impossible,' Ben interrupted her. 'You can't go through an experience like this and then say, "Well, that was very nice, now let's forget about it" – or can you?'

'We must try.'

'All right,' Ben said. 'We'll try. Am I allowed to kiss you goodbye?'

'Don't be angry with me,' Josie pleaded.

'I'm not ... yes, I suppose I am. Even though I know you're right.'

He bent over and they kissed and then he went, with nothing really settled.

Chapter Fourteen

Ben held out longer than Josie, and felt more guilty, but then he had the reason for his guilt in front of his eyes every day and sharing his bed every night. Nicola was sweet and warm and loving, as she always had been. A little withdrawn during the past year, which Ben put down to her continued frustration over not having a child. He was sure he was right about this when she told him that she was going to consult a gynæcologist in London. What threw him completely was that she asked him if he would also undergo tests.

She was apologetic when she saw that he did not like the idea, but she misunderstood the reason for his reluctance. How could he encourage her to conceive when he was consumed with longing for another woman? He felt, as if under a burning glass, the force of Josie's desire, turned always towards him, day and night.

When at last Josie telephoned him she only said his name.

'Ben …'

'Yes.'

'I can't stand it.'

'Nicola's going to London tomorrow and staying the night,' Ben said. 'I'll come to you.'

Something stopped him from telling her the reason for Nicola's visit, nor did he confide it to her the next day. They met in a rage of passion that left them weak and silent. There was no laughter between them this time. Instead, Josie burst into a storm of tears. Ben held her in his arms and tried to soothe her, but there was no comfort for either of them

When she was quiet Josie slept a little, until Ben took his arms away from her and tried to see the time by the dim light in her room.

She stirred and Ben said, 'I can't stay all night, even with Nicola away.'

'No.' Josie drew his head down and kissed him. 'Sorry I was such a wet blanket. Not like me.'

'A wet blanket is the last thing I'd call you,' Ben said, and for the first time there was a thread of amusement in his voice. 'More like Vesuvius erupting.'

'The last three weeks have been hell. I've lost half a stone in weight, fretting for you, damn you.'

'You mustn't do that, love, or you'll fade away altogether.'

He began to stroke her body with love and concern, feeling her rib cage and the way her pelvic bones jutted through the scanty flesh, until Josie shivered with excitement and pressed closer to him.

'I was going to go,' Ben protested.

'All right then go.'

'You know I can't. Oh, Josie, Josie …'

This time when they separated Josie sighed and settled against him before falling into a deep sleep. Ben was glad of it, glad to be spared the fruitless discussion of what they should do, when they should meet again. Three o'clock in the morning, when they were both exhausted by their wild lovemaking, was not the time to reach a sensible decision. He dressed quietly and crept down the stairs with the utmost caution.

As soon as he saw Nicola the following evening he could tell that something had happened to upset her.

'A bad verdict from the gynæcologist?' he asked.

'Oh, that … no, not really. He'd like to see you, but I told you that before I went. I found something out while I was in London that's really rather repulsive and I don't know what to do about it.'

For one wild moment Ben imagined that she had discovered his affair with Josie, but then he realized that she would not have spoken of it in those terms. If she did find out how would she take it? With shattering clarity Ben knew that Nicola would be heartbroken and would behave beautifully. How could he hurt her like that? How could he bear to hurt her?

'I planned to stay the night at Mummy's,' Nicola was saying.

'And didn't you?'

'I went round there and let myself in with her key. Ben, Raymond was there with Phyllis.'

'With *Phyllis*?'

'Yes. I didn't see her, but I heard her voice. They were in the bedroom. I went back downstairs, let myself out and went to a hotel. I'm sure they didn't know there'd been anyone else in the house with them.'

When Ben said nothing, she added wretchedly, 'I don't know how he could.'

'Phyllis oozes sex and you already know all about Raymond,' Ben said. 'I can't say it really surprises me. Do you think your mother knows?'

'I'm sure she doesn't. She'd be *sick*.'

'We can't interfere,' Ben said slowly. 'It's between her and Raymond.'

'I suppose so. I saw Mummy when I got back this afternoon and she asked me if I'd been comfortable and I said yes! Ben, I didn't know what else to say, but it was horrible having to lie to her about where I'd spent the night. If she ever finds out I wasn't there, she'll think I'm the one with the lover!'

Ben was stricken into silence. Nicola expected him to condemn Raymond, and he did, but what was there to choose between them? They were both deceiving their wives. It was all very well to tell himself that what he felt for Josie bore no relation to the nasty little liaison between Raymond and Phyllis; it might seem to him and Josie that their love was so right and so strong that it would be wrong to deny it expression, but in the eyes of the world they were on a par with the other couple.

There was one aspect which did add a special repugnance to Raymond's adultery.

'Did he ever repay that money he borrowed from Ernie?' Ben asked abruptly.

'I don't think so,' Nicola replied.

'Nasty.'

Ben was still brooding over it when they went to bed. He tried to avoid contact with Nicola with a morbid feeling that she might sense Josie's touch still on him. The scent of her was still in his nose, the taste of her was in his mouth, lust for her was potent in his loins. And he had to undress with Nicola, climb into bed with her, endure it when she snuggled up to him.

'The doctor pulled me about a bit; I'm still sore,' Nicola said and Ben realized with horror that she was apologizing because she did not want to make love.

'Ben, he asked me the usual questions,' Nicola went on in a small voice. 'About how often we made love, you know, and that sort of thing. I had to tell him ... it hasn't been very often lately, has it?'

'As often as most couples who've been married five years, I imagine.'

'In that case, we must have been exceptional for the first four years,' Nicola retorted.

'Are you complaining?'

'No ... there's nothing wrong, is there?'

'Of course not.'

Nothing, except that she was the wrong woman, and because all his senses were in thrall to Josie he could hardly bear to touch her.

Nicola said no more, but she did not kiss him, as she always did before they went to sleep. She turned away, lying with her back to him, and after a few wretched minutes Ben did the same.

Before she and Ben could arrange another meeting Josie had a visit from Cy Maple. She was not particularly pleased to see him at her door, but she asked him in, gave him a chair, made a cup of tea and asked how he was in a routine way without expecting him to say anything except that he was fine.

'Not too good,' Cy admitted.

Josie looked at him with more attention. He was a poor colour and he seemed more out of breath than he should have been from climbing one flight of stairs.

'Nothing serious, I hope?' she asked.

'My blood pressure's too high for one thing. I overdid things in the election last autumn. I'm going to have to slow down a bit.'

'I'm sorry.'

Josie poured out the tea, but her mind was busy with the

implications behind Cy's words.

'I'll see this session out,' he said. 'But I'm not reckoning on standing for Parliament again, Josie.'

'You'll be very much missed,' she exclaimed.

'Will I? You don't know much about politics if you think that, lass. Out of sight, out of mind. I've been useful in my day, but it's nearly over now. We were well and truly beaten last October and the Tories will hang on for as long as they can now that they've got a good majority. Next time round we'll beat them, but it'll not be before the mid-sixties, I reckon. I'll be within sight of sixty then.'

'That's not old,' Josie insisted.

'If I thought I'd get office I might hang on, but that's not likely with Gaitskell for leader, not after giving my support to Wilson last year.'

'Have you told the Party?'

'Not likely! As well write your obituary as talk about resigning when you've not long been re-elected. I'm giving you advance notice, lass.'

Josie sat and stared at him, her mouth dry with excitement, not daring to believe that she had understood him.

'Got your name down as a prospective candidate?' Cy asked.

She shook her head, unable to speak.

'That's a mistake. Get in as soon as you can. If they offer you the chance to fight a by-election, take it, no matter how hopeless it may be. It'll be experience for you. In a year or two, depending on how things are going, I'll start putting you forward for this constituency. I want you to be my successor, Josie. How old are you?'

'Twenty-seven.'

'Aye, you're a bit on the young side yet. Still an' all, they're always saying at Transport House that we ought to get more women into the House, so that's an advantage to you. If the Tories hang on for five years, say till nineteen sixty-five, you'll be just about right.'

'It's the dream of my life,' Josie said.

'It's not happened yet, but you stand a better chance with my support than without it. Just one thing, Josie – keep your nose clean!'

Her thoughts immediately flew to Ben and she felt her face reddening, but it was something else that Cy had in mind.

'You did well over the old people's flats, but it was a mistake to let your cousin bid for the contract, let alone win it.'

'I didn't know Ben was in the running until it was too late. It was only fair that he should get it and it was far and away the cheapest tender.'

'There was some trouble, wasn't there?'

'My dad tried to make a bit on the side,' Josie admitted shortly. 'Ben took him off the job.'

'I was thinking about the chap who had his drive made up free of charge.'

'He was sent a bill.'

'It may have been sent, but I doubt if it was paid,' Cy said. 'He's one of Ernie Baxcombe's cronies and when Ernie does a favour he doesn't take it back. He can't afford to. Steer clear of Baxcombe & Harcourt, Josie. There's been a bit of a smell about that name recently. I can't give you chapter and verse, but people in the know go quiet when they're mentioned. You can't afford to get mixed up in a scandal.'

He stayed a little longer and when he left Josie went close to him and they exchanged a long kiss.

'We've had some good times together,' Cy said, not quite steadily. 'That's over now. For one thing, I'm not up to it, though it goes sore against the grain to say so, and for another the last thing we want is for someone to hint that Cy Maple is promoting his mistress as future Ferryhaven Member of Parliament.'

The one person Josie wanted when Cy had gone was Ben. She wanted to tell him the news, to talk over her chances of being elected, and also to pass on Cy's disquieting hints about his firm.

She told herself that the business aspect justified a call to his office and rang him the next day, only to be told that Ben was abroad.

Josie took it up angrily with him the next time they were together. Ben had rung her from Heathrow saying he was staying the night in London and suggesting she should join him. At very short notice, and fuming inwardly, Josie packed an overnight bag and drove herself down to the safe anonymity of a small London hotel.

'I thought you'd be pleased that we had a chance to meet,' Ben said.

'I hate all this damned secrecy and I didn't know you'd gone abroad. Why didn't you tell me?'

'I didn't know myself until the last minute. Ernie doesn't normally let me loose with his foreign customers, but he'd picked up some bug that laid him low.'

'Was it a satisfactory trip?' Josie asked, slightly mollified.

'Not from my point of view. I'm against operating overseas, especially on the scale this Arabian sheikh has in mind. Ernie and Raymond are deluding themselves. They think it's going to be easy money, which it's not. Sheikh Abdul is a very shrewd customer. He's already playing one country off against another to get the best price for his massive building operation and I suspect he wants to tie it in with an arms deal with the Government.'

'That's where Raymond comes in,' Josie said.

She was sitting cross-legged on the bed, half undressed, angular and supple, her face intent as she listened to Ben talking.

'He sees himself pulling strings behind the scenes,' Ben agreed.

'Not likely,' Josie decided. 'He does a good enough job as an M.P., given that he's on the wrong side, but he'll never be anything but a backbencher. He has no real influence.'

'He's having an affair with Phyllis.'

Josie's head jerked up. 'Bloody fool! How do you know?'

'Nicola found them in the London house.'

It had been a mistake to mention Nicola. Josie's face clouded. Ben went and sat on the bed and put his arms round her and she hid her face against his shoulder.

'Does Nicola know you're back?' she asked in a muffled voice.

'I rang her and told her I was too tired to finish the journey tonight.'

'And are you? Tired?'

'Try me.'

They lay awake for a long time after they had made love, talking quietly, but not about their situation. Josie told Ben about Cy Maple's offer to support her candidature for the local constituency and sensed that he was not quite as excited about it as she had been.

'Your career still means everything to you, doesn't it?' he asked.

'The chance to *do* something,' Josie insisted. 'Until a few months ago I would have said it was the most important thing in my life. Now, I'm not so sure. You mean too much to me.'

'If I were divorced, would you marry me?'

'It would need careful timing. Yes, of course, if you were free I'd marry you like a shot, though how we'd fit our two lives together I really don't know. Let's not talk about it.'

To her surprise, when she told him what Cy had said about his firm, Ben did not take it very seriously.

'Probably a rumour started by one of our competitors,' he said. 'We're no better, and no worse, than a lot of others, but the old-established companies didn't like Baxcombe & Harcourt getting the university contract.'

'There is corruption then?' Josie persisted.

'If you do business in the part of the world I've just visited you call it following the custom of the country. Do the same thing in the U.K. and it's bribery. If a man here asks me to do him a favour – perhaps helping his son to get a job – and later on he puts in a good word for me in a corner where it's needed, is that mutual help or is it corruption?'

'It depends whether the son deserves the job and you deserve the good word,' Josie said.

'Every case has to be decided individually,' Ben agreed.

'I'm not sure it really works like that,' Josie said uneasily. 'Did the man whose drive Dad built pay for it eventually?'

'Damn. I was hoping you'd never ask me that. No, he didn't. All right, perhaps that was borderline. It was also unnecessary, because we would have got the contract anyway.'

'He was serving on *my* committee. I don't like it, Ben.'

'I don't like it either, but I've got to live with it. I've opted out of the company Ernie has set up to deal with system building even though it's a quick, cheap method of putting up houses and I may be making a mistake because that's what everyone wants. Sometimes I'm tempted to break away from him altogether.'

'I wish you would.'

'I can't until the university is finished, and that will take years. Let it drop, darling. I'm exhausted.'

Going home to Berringer Hall was difficult after the interlude with Josie. Nicola was glad to see Ben back, and she expected him to be pleased, too. She expected him to show it. Ben sensed her puzzlement, and her hurt pride, when her tentative advances brought no response. He felt wretched about it, so wretched that it even passed through his mind that perhaps the tumultuous night he had spent with Josie had not been worth it. When Nicola did not comment, at least in words, about his rejection of her, he thought he had got away with it, but the following evening Nicola brought it out into the open.

Ben had been talking about his trip abroad, making conversation, he admitted to himself, when Nicola interrupted him.

'Ben, let's stop pretending. There's something seriously wrong between us. What is it?'

'I ... I've been worried lately. I'm not sure I've done the right thing, letting Ernie go his own way over the new pre-fabrications company.'

'That's not it,' Nicola said with conviction. 'You've had anxious times in the past, but that hasn't stopped you wanting me – rather the contrary.'

'The food on this trip abroad didn't agree with me. I'm feeling under the weather.'

'A pity you didn't mention it before; I wouldn't have given you roast duck for dinner and I certainly wouldn't have encouraged you to have a second helping. Ben, stop lying to me. This isn't something that's happened in the last few days. It's been going on for weeks, if not months. Tell me what's wrong.'

She waited, but Ben did not answer.

'Is there someone else?' Nicola asked quietly.

Ben opened his mouth to deny it, but the lie stuck in his

throat and Nicola took his continued silence for assent.

'Is it Josie?'

That shook him. His head jerked up and he stared at her.

'How did you know?'

'You saw a lot of her last year over those flats. You used to come home looking different – keyed up and excited. At first you talked about it, told me when you'd seen her, passed on messages from Josie herself, then you suddenly stopped and almost at the same time it began to seem that you no longer wanted me. You've always shut me out of the things that are important to you, but you used to enjoy being with me, you used to love me. All that has gone. We live in the same house, but I feel so alone.'

'I'm sorry,' Ben muttered. It was miserably inadequate, but what else could he say?

'Is it … is it a passing thing, do you think? Are you going to get over it?' Nicola asked in the same strained, studiously calm way.

'It's deadly serious.'

When he glanced at her, Ben saw that Nicola's eyes were tightly closed.

'If I were driven to it, I could face a separation for a time and then we could try again,' she said.

'With me living with Josie in the meantime? No, that's not the right solution.'

'Do you want a divorce?' Nicola asked in a whisper.

There was something disquieting about her stillness. She was sitting with her arms wrapped round her middle, slightly bent forward, as if holding in a pain.

'It seems the only way out. I can't go on like this. I … we're desperately in love with one another,' Ben said, offering the only explanation that could excuse his behaviour.

'Are you?'

For one moment the veil of composure seemed to shiver, almost to dissolve, revealing a suffering so acute that Ben turned his head away, but when Nicola spoke again it was with the same rigorous control.

'Will Josie marry you?' she asked.

'She has said she would if I were free,' Ben said.

Nicola gave him a long look. It seemed as if, out of her own desolation, she was pitying him.

'I'll divorce you,' she said. 'But I have to make one condition.'

'Anything,' Ben said. 'Naturally, I'll support you ...'

'Ben, I'm not talking about money!' For the first time there was anger in Nicola's voice. 'It's got to be an honest divorce, that's all. I'll divorce you for adultery, with Josie named as the other woman.'

Ben's involuntary protest was stifled before it was uttered. Nicola was behaving impeccably; no scene, no fuss; and yet she still loved him, she had taken a terrible blow. How could he bring himself in the face of her blinding honesty, to plead for a divorce based on bogus evidence?

'When will you go?' Nicola was asking.

'Go?'

It had all happened so quickly that Ben had given no thought to his next move. Of course he would have to leave. The house was Nicola's. He had no part in it now. And where was he to go? Certainly not to Josie, that was impossible without warning her first. It would have to be a hotel.

They slept in separate rooms at Berringer Hall that night. It ought to have been a relief, but Ben felt strangely bereft. Anxious, too, about Nicola, who had scarcely spoken again for the rest of the evening. If she had been angry he could have understood; he had braced himself to withstand tears and reproaches and her uncomplaining acceptance of the situation pierced him to the heart. His instinct had always been to protect her and now he had hurt her so badly that she could not even speak about it.

Out of the distant past a memory came back of Nicola only six years old and the way he had comforted her after her father had been killed. She had clutched her stomach in just the same way then, as if holding in an unbearable pain.

He tried to convey something of his regret to Josie, but not unnaturally she was more intent on the news that Nicola was prepared to let him go.

'If it goes through quickly it could work out just right,' she said. 'Oh, Ben, I can't believe it! I thought it was all quite hopeless. How are you going to arrange it?'

'Arrange it?'

Josie grimaced. 'It's a bit distasteful, but I believe the usual idea is to pay someone to go to a hotel with you.'

'Nicola means to name you. That's the only basis on which she will go ahead.'

Josie stared at him and then she burst out laughing, but she was very angry.

'Clever Nicola! She knows I can't agree. Ben, are you mad? Now, when I'm just about to be adopted as a candidate? It would put paid to all my chances.'

'Divorce is common enough these days.'

'If it had been something I'd gone through a few years back I might have got away with it, but to be the guilty party in a divorce at the same time as I'm up for selection ... no, it can't be done.'

At the back of her mind was another thought, unworthy but it had to be faced: Cy Maple's support was essential to her. It might all be over between them, but would he be so eager to help her if he knew she already had another lover?

Ben's lack of response frightened her. She went to him, and stood close, looking up into his face.

'Ben, I love you. You're the only man I could ever think of marrying. The only man who comes between me and my work. I burn for you day and night. I'd give up almost anything for you ...'

'Almost anything.'

'But not my chance to get into Parliament. Nicola isn't a fool. She understands that.'

'She doesn't know how close you are to succeeding. I believe her only thought was that she wouldn't put up with any hypocrisy over our divorce.'

'The way I see it, she's pretending to let you go but making conditions to keep you on a string.'

'No, that's not the way Nicola does things.'

'She's a damn sight more human than you give her credit for. Take her down off her pedestal and realize that Nicola's as capable of scheming to keep her man as any other woman.'

'I was hoping that if I took a flat you would move in with me.'

'I can't. Ben, it's not that I don't want to ... I *can't*.'

Watching Ben's unresponsive face, Josie said, 'If you don't understand why it's impossible then you don't know me as well as I thought you did.'

'I see your point of view,' Ben admitted. 'I'm a bit thrown, that's all. I've left Nicola, I'm without anywhere to live, she will only divorce me if she can name you, and you won't hear of it. We've reached a dead end.'

'I'll talk to Nicola.'

'No!'

'Don't be silly, Ben. I'm not going to quarrel with her. If I can get her to realize that we're totally committed to one another and there's no chance of getting you back she might agree to going about the divorce in a different way.'

For the first time that night their lovemaking was strained and awkward and each of them blamed it silently on the other. When Ben got out of bed and began to dress Josie pretended to be asleep. She felt Ben bending over her.

'I know you're awake, you obstinate little cuss,' he said. 'Promise me you won't go near Nicola.'

Josie opened her eyes. 'I run my own life and make my own decisions,' she said. 'If you don't like it, get out!'

In spite of the way she had spoken of it to Ben, Josie had a sick feeling in the pit of her stomach as she drew up outside Berringer Hall. The house was at its best in the late evening sunlight, mellow and peaceful, the creamy stone taking on a golden glow from the setting sun. There were yellow roses in the garden and the lawn had been freshly mown in even stripes. The scent of cut grass drifted towards her.

It suddenly came to Josie that Ben had given all this up for her and Nicola had lost her husband, but Josie was not prepared to make the sacrifice that was demanded from her. Was there any way she could get Nicola to see that it was totally impossible?

She was shocked by Nicola's appearance. Her manner was quiet, almost submissive, but her face was drawn and there were dark hollows under her eyes. In the face of so much dumb suffering Josie's fluent words faltered and died away.

'I love him,' she said helplessly. 'I can't help it, I just do.'

'I know,' Nicola agreed.

'And Ben loves me.'

'Does he? He's in love with you at the moment, I can see that, but you're not the woman for him, not permanently.'

'I was right, you are trying to hang on to him. You knew I wouldn't want to be named in the divorce.'

'I thought you might object and I thought it would give Ben a jolt. Ben is used to a wife who sacrifices everything to his convenience.'

'I'll never be that sort of doormat.'

'That's one of the things that attracts him to you. He's excited by your independence, the fact that you can hold your own with any man.'

'We're two of a kind, Ben and I. We belong together.'

'You strike sparks off one another because you're alike,' Nicola agreed. 'But Ben is the one who understands compassion, for all he seems hard at times.'

'I've given my whole life to helping other people,' Josie said, really stung. 'That's why it's important to me to get into Parliament.'

'People in the abstract,' Nicola said. 'The suffering poor. I honour you for what you've done and I think it's absolutely right that you should be given a chance to help govern the country.'

'I'll lose that chance if you name me in your divorce!'

'You have a choice – Ben or a seat in Parliament. Not both.'

'But *why*, Nicola? You've already lost Ben ...'

'Not irrevocably.' A strange little smile flickered for a moment on Nicola's lips. 'My poor Ben, he's going to be so very uncomfortable without me.'

'Oh, you've got all the domestic arts, I know that,' Josie said impatiently.

'And you despise me for it. Try for a bit of humility, Josie. What you've achieved is marvellous, but there's nothing wrong in being good at cooking and keeping house and providing clean shirts when they're wanted.'

'If you don't mind being a glorified servant.'

'I took a pride in it and Ben owes some of his success to me.

He's going to miss having me to back him up.' Nicola sighed suddenly. 'He got me too easily, that's always been the trouble. There's never been any man for me but Ben. I doubt whether you can say the same.'

Josie ignored that dig. 'If you think he'll give me up for a bit of domesticity, you're wrong,' she said.

'Perhaps, but the thing that will work against you is that Ben will never really forgive you for making him hurt me.'

Josie went home with nothing achieved and with the uncomfortable feeling that Nicola had shown a far more acute insight than she had expected. A lot of what she had said was true, especially about Ben not wishing to hurt her. Josie felt disgruntled at having been very firmly put in the wrong. Well, of course, it was wrong, committing adultery, except that Josie took the view that there was no point in two people who had outlived their first commitment to one another staying together. If it had not been for the complication over the parliamentary nomination she would have had no scruples about living openly with Ben. It irked her to be driven into hypocrisy.

She was disquieted, too, by Nicola's hints about Ben's male helplessness on the domestic front. For one moment she thought rebelliously that she would rather be free to lead her own disorganized life without Ben, eating whatever came to hand, flinging her washing into the launderette when it became an absolute necessity, going out and coming home at any hour that suited her, able to respond to a sudden call without stopping to consider anyone else. But Ben understood the sort of life she led. He admired her for it; even Nicola had said that. He would adapt – if they were ever able to live together as man and wife.

Chapter Fifteen

It took very little time for the news to get out that Ben and Nicola had separated. Ernie spoke to Ben about it during Ben's second miserable week at a hotel.

'What's this I hear about you leaving home?' he demanded. 'Is it permanent?'

'Probably,' Ben said.

'Don't tell me Nicola went off the rails? I thought she was a straightlaced little piece.'

'It's not Nicola's fault.'

'You then? Go on! Who is she?'

With an effort Ben kept his temper, but it showed in the thinning of his lips and the way his eyes glittered.

'My wife and I have agreed to live apart,' he said. 'That's all I'm going to tell you. It's our business, not anyone else's.'

'Don't talk to me about "my wife and I" in that namby-pamby way, Ben lad. And it is my business. Her mum and Raymond aren't going to like it and this isn't the time to put Raymond's back up.'

'His usefulness is limited, if you ask me.'

'That's all you know.'

'If you've got the development abroad in mind then I'm telling you, once and for all, that I won't go along with it.'

'You've already put the kybosh on that. I should never have let you handle that contact. They could see you weren't going to co-operate.'

'I'm glad to hear it.'

'I've got something else lined up. You've heard about the plan to refurbish the Maxton shipyards?'

'A rumour,' Ben said.

Shipbuilding had boomed in the post-war years. Customers had queued up to place orders with British shipyards. Now it seemed as if the first wave of enthusiasm was subsiding. Orders were going overseas to places where there were modern yards and fewer restrictive practices. There had been persistent talk of a modernization programme at Maxton's. A scheme of that sort would take Baxcombe & Harcourt into the field of civil engineering. They weren't equipped for it, but they could be. Almost against his will, Ben's mind began to turn over the possibilities.

'It'll go ahead if they can get Government money into it,' Ernie said. 'There's a parliamentary committee being set up and Raymond's sitting on it. He'll keep us posted.'

'Won't he have to declare an interest if we're in the running for the contract?'

'He's going to resign from the board.'

'In that case, what's in it for him?' Ben demanded.

'Don't worry, I've got Raymond where I want him. He owes me money and he's been laying my wife.'

'You knew?'

'I always know when Phyllis has been having a bit on the side. It's over now. I told her I'd cut her tits off if she didn't give him up.'

The unwilling suspicion came into Ben's mind that Ernie had seen the crude sexual attraction between Phyllis and Raymond and had cynically closed his eyes to it until he could use the knowledge to advantage.

'A little bit of scandal won't do Raymond much harm,' he said, with his mind on his own dilemma.

'It will if his wife divorces him,' Ernie said. 'Raymond likes being married to the late Colonel Berringer's daughter and living at Berringer Hall, even if it is courtesy of your Nicola. He'd find a difference if people knew he'd done the dirty on her with a woman who's come up from the slums and shows it. Phyllis suits me, but she's not everyone's cup o' tea. There'd be eyebrows raised at our Raymond's vulgar taste. And he'd be strapped to find the fifteen thousand he owes me. Very expensive, adultery, as you'll find out, my lad.'

Again Ben's mouth tightened, but he said nothing in

response to that taunt. For the hundredth time he wished he could be free of Ernie. He had said 'when the university is finished', but now it looked as if they might get involved in something equally big and of vital importance to the area in which he had grown up. The fact that it concerned Maxton's yard was of particular interest to him. It would be sweet to confer as an equal with the man who had once rejected him as unsuitable for a minor administrative post. As for Raymond's part in it, that was distasteful. Putting it at its crudest, Ernie intended to blackmail him into revealing confidential information and, presumably, to use influence to get Baxcombe & Harcourt the contract.

Ben would have liked to have talked it over with Josie, but not while their relationship was in its present delicate state. Josie had not told him the outcome of her visit to Nicola, which Ben took to mean that it had been unsatisfactory, as he had expected.

When Josie telephoned him a few days later she sounded strained and cautious.

'I'd like to see you,' she said.

'Yes, we must meet,' Ben agreed.

'Come to my place about six o'clock tomorrow evening.'

When she opened the door to him Josie was looking pale and untidy, as if she had been caught only half prepared.

'I overslept this morning and I was later getting home than I expected,' she said, and the fact that she bothered to make excuses was a symptom of her new uncertainty with him. 'I've only just washed up my breakfast things and made the bed.'

'Let's unmake it,' Ben said.

He reached out and pulled her to him. Josie flung her arms round his neck and pressed tightly against him.

'We shouldn't have parted the way we did last time,' Ben said unevenly. 'I've wanted to get in touch, but I thought I ought to leave it to you. It's been hell, not knowing whether you still cared or not.'

'I care,' Josie said. 'Ben, I love you so much I break up into little pieces every time you lay a finger on me. Even hearing your voice over the telephone ...'

'I know. Talking to you yesterday unsettled me for the rest of the day. I want you. Now. I can't wait.'

'It's the same for me. I couldn't sleep last night, thinking about you and wanting you to come to me.'

They were as urgent with one another as they had been the first time, even more so because they both knew that the fact that they still loved one another brought them no nearer to a solution to their difficulty.

Eventually Josie stretched with lazy voluptuousness and yawned.

'I'm hungry,' she said.

'I've worked up a bit of an appetite myself,' Ben said. He bit gently at her shoulder. 'I could eat you.'

'You very nearly did.' Josie snuggled closer, complacently aware that their lovemaking had been splendid.

'There's still time to go out and get a meal.'

'I can't be bothered to make myself look respectable. I've got some sausages. I'll cook those.'

'Do you mind if I take a bath?' Ben asked.

'Do, darling, if you don't mind walking along the corridor carrying a towel and probably bumping into all the other tenants.'

'Oh, damn. I wish you lived in more civilized surroundings.'

'My surroundings are me,' Josie said shortly.

He hung around, watching her while she fried sausages, bacon and tomatoes. While her attention was on the sizzling pan he slipped in the question he had been wanting to ask.

'Did you talk to Nicola?'

'I did, but I got nowhere. She's more devious than I thought.'

Ben frowned. Devious was not a word he would have applied to Nicola.

'She's not going to let you go easily,' Josie said.

'So we're no further forward?'

'Worse than that. We've taken a definite step backwards. Here, take your plate over to the table and I'll tell you why I wanted to see you.'

'I thought you already had,' Ben said with a half smile.

'Apart from being crazily in love with you, damn you. Ben, my dad is going to make trouble.'

'Does he know about us?'

'No, or he wouldn't have told me. He's got a grudge against you for putting him down from being foreman and he means to get even.'

'It was only for your sake I kept him on.'

'I know, but he still feels hard done by. He says there's corners being cut on the construction work for the university and he means to report it to the County Surveyor. That's why he told me, he wanted to know how to get in touch with him.'

'And you told him.'

'I did, but it'll take him a while to get round to it. He expected me to offer to write the letter for him and I didn't.' She looked at Ben with a frown. 'That's how far you've demoralized me. If anyone else had been involved I wouldn't have hesitated.'

'How serious are these "corners"?'

'Difficult for me to judge, not being an expert. Dad said something about shoddy materials which I didn't understand.'

'It's supposed to be a quality job, within reasonable limits,' Ben said. 'I'll look into it.'

Josie relaxed, the unease which had haunted her since Stan had spoken to her beginning to subside.

'I was afraid you might already know about it,' she admitted.

'My name's not Baxcombe,' Ben said.

With Ben's assurance that he would investigate Stan's suspicions Josie dismissed the matter from her mind, until her father spoke to her again.

'I saw that man you told me about and he got in a rare old state,' Stan said.

'I thought you were going to write!' Josie exclaimed.

'Aye, I had it in mind to do that, but I'm not handy at letter writing, as you well know. Mr Luke came to the site an' I tackled him there. He were pickin' his way round, like he were on eggshells, castin' an eye here and there. That's no way to see what's wrong, and so I told 'im.'

Stan chuckled in a satisfied way. 'Very 'igh and mighty wi' me he were 'till I told him I'd a daughter on the council. He knew your name all right. That shook him.'

Still Josie did not take it very seriously, not until she had a visit from Mrs Luke.

Since becoming a councillor Josie had made herself available one evening a week for local people to come to her and air their grievances or ask for help with their problems. She had a tiny office at the Labour Party headquarters in Ferryhaven, with a rickety desk and three chairs, and there she dispensed advice, filled up forms, explained their rights to people who clung obstinately to a belief that they were being done out of something, and sometimes arbitrated in a quarrel that threatened to disrupt lives. It was exhausting, painstaking work, but it was one of Josie's few direct contacts with the people she represented and she welcomed it for that.

Mrs Luke was rather different from the pathetic women who usually sat in the chair on the other side of Josie's desk. She was in a highly nervous state, but that was not unusual. She was also affluent and intelligent, the sort of woman who could afford to employ a solicitor or who was capable of filling up her own passport application. A comfortable, motherly looking woman, with a round, rosy face, now puckered in distress.

'I'm that worried about my husband I don't know what to do,' she burst out.

Josie fingered her address book, ready to turn up Alcoholics Anonymous or something of that sort, but Mrs Luke's problem was more far-reaching than that.

'He thinks you're going to cause trouble for him,' Mrs Luke said. 'He's a good man, Miss Bewley. He doesn't deserve it should all fall on him. It's that Ernie Baxcombe. He ought to be hung.'

For the first time Josie connected this plump, worried woman with the surveyor responsible for checking the work on the university site. All the uneasiness she had felt when Stan had first spoken about it woke up.

'Tell me about it,' she said.

It was an involved story. Josie had to help Mrs Luke along by patient questioning and all the time the cold horror inside her was growing.

It had started mildly enough. Basil Luke liked to play golf. There was a very good local golf club with astronomical fees, the sort of place the great shipping tycoons had kept to themselves in the past. Ernie Baxcombe, with his strange ability to have a finger in every pie, had offered to put Basil Luke up for membership and had laughed away Mr Luke's reluctant excuse that he could not afford it. Basil Luke became a member of the golf club and nothing was ever said about paying for it.

'I was pleased at first,' Mrs Luke said. 'Basil loved his game of golf. It got him out in the open air, he was fitter than he'd been for years. Of course, it meant me being at home on my own more, but I used to go and meet him at the club house for a drink, or we'd sometimes have a meal there. We met some very nice people.'

It was pleasant, but it was expensive, and when the very nice people began to ask the Lukes to their homes their hospitality had to be returned.

'I've always been a good cook and I enjoyed having a crowd in for a meal,' Mrs Luke said. 'But, of course, our place wasn't up to the other houses we visited. We talked of moving, though we both knew we couldn't really manage it, but there was a bit of waste ground next door to our bungalow. Next thing I knew, Basil had bought it and we were having an extension built.'

'By Ernie Baxcombe,' Josie said through stiff lips.

'By Baxcombe & Harcourt,' Mrs Luke agreed, and Josie winced at the use of Ben's name. 'I worried about the expense till Basil told me Ernie had loaned him the money and wasn't asking much in the way of interest.'

'He collected in other ways?' Josie suggested.

'Aye, that he did! I didn't catch on at first. Basil's never been one to talk about his work. I wouldn't have understood it, you see. It was a long time before Basil got really worried, too. Ernie just asked for a few little favours, nothing really out of the way, and Basil was glad to oblige him.'

'Until the new university came along,' Josie said.

'That's what's turning Basil grey,' Mrs Luke admitted. 'Let alone that he reckons Baxcombe & Harcourt didn't ought to have got the contract in the first place, though I don't know how true that is, Basil is worried sick about the work that's being put into the place. I couldn't make it out at first, the way he's changed lately; then your dad tackled him, threatened to report the shoddy work to you, and Basil broke down and told me all about it. He tried to crack down on it, you see, and Ernie just laughed.'

'The idea being that he'd call in his loan if your husband insisted on better quality work?'

'Worse than that. He'd accuse Basil of being bent and supply the evidence to prove it. He'd say Basil knew all along that Ernie was paying him to keep his eyes shut.'

She leaned forward, her eyes fixed urgently on Josie's face.

'Miss Bewley, we didn't look on it like that, not either of us. Ernie was a friend. I didn't connect it with Basil's work.'

But Basil Luke must have known what was in the wind, Josie thought. He'd started by being a fool and ended up as a knave, but without Ernie Baxcombe's stomach for depravity.

'It was always Ernie Baxcombe your husband dealt with?' Josie asked and waited with a dry mouth and beating heart for Mrs Luke's answer.

'Oh, yes!'

But even as Josie sank back in her chair in relief, Mrs Luke added, 'The way Basil sees it, Ernie does the dirty work and they keep the other one as a respectable front. Very high and mighty is Mr Benjamin Harcourt. Do you know his father is nothing but a ship's riveter and still lives in Jarrow? But the son got himself an education and married a lady. He keeps the nobs happy while Ernie stays in the background, but it's Ernie who's the brains of the outfit.'

'I know Ben Harcourt well. We were children together,' Josie said. 'I don't think ... I'm *sure* he wouldn't be party to the sort of thing his partner has been doing to your husband.'

'If you're friends with him you would think that,' Mrs Luke said. 'Just like we thought Ernie was a real nice man when we first knew him.'

She left Josie with an appalling dilemma. Mrs Luke wanted Ernie brought to book and her husband rescued from the tangle he had got into, but she wanted it done without any retribution falling on his head. When Josie hinted that Basil Luke was almost bound to lose his job once the story came out, she was indignant.

'It's my Basil who's going to help you clean up this mess,' she said. 'Why should he suffer?'

'Does he know you've come to see me?' Josie asked.

She saw from the way Mrs Luke reddened and looked down that she had not told her husband what she meant to do.

'He knows we can't go on like this,' Mrs Luke said. 'I was told you were good about helping people in trouble, and your dad having told you already, I thought I'd appeal to you. Help my Basil, Miss Bewley. If he's done wrong – which I suppose some people might think he has – then he's learnt his lesson.'

The thing that gave Josie a sleepless night after this interview was making up her mind whether she should tell Ben about it. It was confidential, between her and Mrs Luke, and she had in any case already given him a hint that trouble was brewing. Strictly speaking, both Ernie and Basil Luke should be prosecuted, and it might yet come to that, but it would mean the end of the firm Ernie and Ben had built up together. Grimly, Josie recognized that she and Mrs Luke were in the same position: they both wanted Ernie brought down and they both wanted to shield the man they loved.

How far was Ben implicated? When she had told him about Stan's complaint and asked if he had known, Ben had said that his name was not Baxcombe. She had been reassured at the time, but now Josie saw that it implied that Ben knew that Ernie's dealings were crooked.

He had said he would look into it. If he did that and uncovered all the ramifications, then he might take action himself to clear up the unsavoury mess. Or he might not. With a sinking heart Josie recognized that if she had been totally sure of Ben's reaction she would have had no hesitation in going straight to him.

She had a duty as a public servant, but surely she could take some private steps before coming out in the open with all she knew? She would tell Ben, she would insist that he made a proper investigation, but keeping it within the firm to begin with.

With that decision in her mind she fell asleep, only to wake up the next morning with another insidious thought in her mind. If the affair was hushed up and at some later date her part in it became known her credibility would be destroyed. What price then her chances of becoming a Member of

Parliament? She was Ben Harcourt's mistress, she was the reason he had left his wife. That had seemed like scandal enough to ruin her hopes, without the nasty whiff of corruption added to it.

If Ben had not been involved she would not have hesitated, that was what lacerated her. With the clear intelligence Josie brought to all the problems in which her emotions were not involved she saw that to be at the forefront of a campaign to clear up corrupt practices would do her political career nothing but good. Her name would be made. So which should she betray – her love or her principles?

People first, Josie told herself grimly. Ben deserves to be given the benefit of the doubt. Before she could change her mind again she rang him and arranged a meeting.

She arrived at the country pub she had chosen looking so ill that Ben exclaimed in concern. A suspicion darted into his mind and he said, 'Love, you're not pregnant, are you?'

Josie stared at him. 'Of course not. I told you you could leave all that to me,' she said.

'A pity, in a way,' Ben said. 'It would have forced your hand.'

'Destroyed me, you mean,' Josie retorted. 'Not that I'm not in a fair way to being ruined anyway if it ever gets out that I'm tipping you off about what's going on in your precious company.'

She looked round the crowded bar. 'Not here. Take me somewhere quiet in your car and I'll tell you.'

They parked off the side of a quiet lane by the opening into a field. With her eyes fixed on the rows of golden stubble in front of them, Josie poured out Mrs Luke's story.

'You didn't know, did you, Ben?' she said. 'Tell me you didn't know!'

'No one could do business with Ernie without realizing he had a shady side,' Ben said.

'And you've associated with him for years.'

'I didn't know he'd got his hooks into Luke.' Ben's face darkened in bitter anger. 'Damn him, I see now why he's got me so steamed up over the Maxton project – to divert me from the university. And he succeeded. God, that man's a bloody genius, in his way.'

'What are you going to do?'

'I'll get an independent assessment of the work that's been done. Your dad's complaint will justify that. If there are faults I'll ask Ernie why Luke didn't put in a report. He'll probably tell me. He's proud of the clever way he arranges these things.'

'And then?'

'I'll insist on the work being done properly. It won't be the first time I've had to interfere. That will put Luke in the clear.'

'It sounds almost too easy,' Josie said.

'Don't you believe it! If work has to be re-done we'll overrun our deadline and it'll cost a fortune in penalty payments.'

'Good! You deserve it – Ernie for being a criminal and you for being careless. But I don't like it. Ernie's dealings with Basil Luke are only the tip of the iceberg, aren't they?'

'You may be right.'

Very clear in Ben's mind was the recollection of Ernie's gloating over the way he had fixed Raymond. The Maxton contract might depend on Raymond's influence, and Ben wanted that contract.

'You know darn well I'm right,' Josie retorted. 'Ernie's no straighter than a corkscrew. He ought to be put out of business.'

'If Ernie goes bust, I go bust. Do you know how many men we employ? Not to mention the sub-contractors. What about your dad? Will he thank you for throwing him out of work?'

That silenced her, but only for a moment.

'The university will still have to be built. Someone else will come in and finish it.'

'Over my dead body! Leave it to me, Josie, please. I promise I'll do everything in my power to clear it up and if I frighten Ernie into thinking he's going to be exposed it may pull him up.'

It satisfied Josie for the time being, but she was still uneasy and she felt compelled to say, 'Ben, until this affair has blown over I can't see you.'

Ben started his car with a grinding of the gears that betrayed his state of mind.

'I thought that was coming,' he said. 'Still putting your career first, aren't you?'

'I've put my future in jeopardy by telling you Mrs Luke's story,' Josie said. 'I've given you the chance to get out of a very nasty hole. A bit of gratitude wouldn't come amiss.'

The thing that Ben had not gone into with Josie was that the architects for the university were Harcourt Construction Services, his own firm, set up specifically to give the parent company the expert help it needed, and what Ben wanted to know was why no one from inside the company had alerted him that things were going wrong.

Without saying why he wanted them he commandeered a set of plans and specifications and spent a grim two days with the head architect in tow examining all the buildings under construction, at the end of which he had a long list of complaints.

'Sorry about this,' the architect said. 'We were told these faults were being rectified. Some of them are trivial, but there's no way anyone could pass the plumbing for the chemistry building.'

'Keep this to yourself for the time being,' Ben said. 'I don't want it blabbed around that we've been doing a botched job. It's in my hands now and I'll see things are put right.'

'It'll be a relief,' the architect admitted. 'I've been wanting to talk to you, but I never seem to be able to get hold of you, and Mr Baxcombe ... well, he doesn't have your grasp of what makes a good job.'

Ben opened his mouth to protest about his unavailability and then decided to say nothing. It ought not have been that difficult for one of his own staff to get a word with him.

He tackled his secretary about it when he got back to his office. She looked flustered and then defiant.

'You've been out of the office a lot lately,' she said. 'Mr Baxcombe asked for all calls from the architects' office to be routed to him so that queries didn't get delayed.'

'I'm here now,' Ben said. 'And I've never been one to let work pile up, as you well know. What did Ernie promise you in return for keeping complaints away from me?'

She cried and protested, lost her temper and gave in her

notice, which suited Ben very well. In the end he established that she and her fiancé had been promised a new council flat being built by Baxcombe Systems, even though they did not qualify for the housing list, which must mean that Ernie had squared someone in the council housing department.

Josie would have thought that Ben was proceeding slowly. She would have stormed into Ernie's office in a blaze of indignation and challenged him. Ben took his time. His next step was to spend a day with the accountants. Then he went and saw Ernie.

'I dare say your spies have already told you what I've been doing,' he said.

'We're partners,' Ernie said. 'I've no objection to you taking an interest in the business, but I would have expected you to tell me first if there was something bothering you.'

'I've stopped work on the chemistry building.'

'So I heard. The contractors were round here complaining that they're going to fall behind schedule.'

'You insisted on employing them and they've been cutting corners to an extent I'd call almost criminal. All the plumbing will have to be pulled out, which will mean damn near gutting the place.'

'Don't be a bloody fool. We can get a certificate for that building at the drop of a hat.'

'Because you think you've got Basil Luke in your pocket. Well, let me tell you that he's started to talk. You've pushed him too far and he's going to break. If we can show that his main objections are being met then I think he'll hush up. I hope so, because otherwise you're going to find yourself in the dock.'

'You, too,' Ernie said in a hissing whisper. 'You're as much involved as I am.'

'I've shut my eyes for too long to your shady little deals, but you've always known that there are some things I won't go along with, which is why it was necessary for you to bribe my own secretary to keep me in the dark. Oh, yes, I know about that! This is where we call a halt, Ernie. I'm giving orders for all the faults in the university buildings to be rectified.'

'What about our penalty clauses?'

'I've seen the books. I know we've got a cash flow problem. We're running dangerously close to the edge, but we'll go right over if you're prosecuted for bribery and corruption.'

Ernie's eyes glittered, but he said nothing, not even when Ben added, 'I'll see the Bank. We can probably get our overdraft extended.'

He did not take Ben's next pronouncement so quietly.

'We're not putting in for the Maxton contract.'

'But we've got to!'

Ernie was so incensed that he leapt to his feet, his thin body quivering. He's ratlike, Ben thought dispassionately; all he needs is whiskers. A nasty little man. Why the hell have I gone on with him for so long?

'The way you're playing it, we'll make hardly any profit out of the university. We might even end up with a loss,' Ernie was saying.

'I've gone into it with the accountants and the figures say that the worst that can happen is that we'll break even.'

'And what use is that? What are we going to use for money if we don't get the Maxton contract? It's in the bag, I'm telling you. With local pull and inside information from Raymond ...'

'We're not using Raymond. And to make absolutely sure that it's seen that we're not using him we won't tender for the job.'

'I'm not putting up with this! You can't dictate to me!'

'You can't apply for the contract without my consent.'

'Oh, can't I! Raymond hasn't resigned from the board yet. We'll vote it through without you.'

'Not after I've talked to Raymond you won't.'

Ben went out of the office, the door crashing behind him. He was so angry that he dared not stay in the room any longer. It had been as much as he could do to keep his hands off Ernie. An insane desire to take the little rat by the throat and shake the life out of him had come over Ben as he had realized how confident Ernie had been that he only had to show Ben that their profit was at risk to win him over to his side. It had been that way in the past, but no more – and not only because of Josie.

Without giving himself too much time to think about it, Ben

put through a call to Berringer Hall, but when he heard Nicola's voice at the other end he hesitated until she repeated inquiringly, 'Hello? Who is it, please?'

'It's Ben,' he said. 'Nicola ... it's not about us, it's business. I ought not to have rung you, but I need to speak to Raymond. Can you tell me where he is?'

'He and Mummy will be here tonight, arriving about six o'clock,' Nicola said. He could not tell from her voice whether she resented his call or not.

'I'll come over and see him,' Ben said. 'I won't ... I needn't bother you.'

'Don't be silly, Ben. I'd like to see you. Come in and have a drink with me when you've finished talking to Raymond.'

'Does he ... do he and your mother know about us?'

'Only that we've agreed to part. Not about Josie.'

It was a constant source of irritation to Marigold that the front door to the wing of the house she and Raymond inhabited was the old servants' entrance, but that evening when she opened it she said with mock approval, 'How nice to see you coming in by the right door for once.'

Ben ignored the deliberate insult. Poor Marigold, how degraded she would have felt if she had known that her husband had been bedding Phyllis.

She took it badly when Ben asked to see Raymond alone, but Raymond seemed to be expecting it.

'Has Ernie rung you?' Ben asked.

'He thinks you've taken against the idea of going for the Maxton contract,' Raymond said. His eyes flickered to Ben's face and away again.

'It's in your interest to back me,' Ben said. 'True, it means that Baxcombe & Harcourt will be short of money, but as you're coming off the board that's of no interest to you. It will let you off the hook Ernie's got baited for you.'

'He says that if the contract doesn't go ahead he's going to be so short of cash that he'll have to press for repayment of the loan he made me,' Raymond said.

'A man of your standing shouldn't have any difficulty in raising fifteen thousand pounds. Get Marigold to hock some of her jewellery. I noticed when I came in she was still wearing her diamond brooch.'

'She'll see me in hell first if Ernie tells her about Phyllis.'

'Tell her yourself. Come on, Raymond, you must have been in the confession business before this. It's over, isn't it? Tell her the woman tempted you. She won't find it hard to believe, having met Phyllis.'

'It didn't work out that way for you and Nicola,' Raymond suggested, an edge of spite to his voice.

'That's our business,' Ben said, his face closed. 'We're still friends. I'm going in to visit her when I've finished with you.'

Raymond still wriggled, but in the end Ben got him to admit that he would be glad to be free of Ernie, that even the reduction in income would be preferable to a charge of corruption. Ben went through the green baize door to Nicola feeling that he had done a good evening's work.

Nicola was looking better than she had the last time he had seen her. It was a relief to see her with colour in her cheeks, looking calm and relaxed, even smiling at him almost as if nothing had happened. Almost, but not quite. There was a reserve in the way she greeted him which did not begin to disappear until they had finished their drinks and Ben had glanced at his watch.

'Do you have an appointment? If not, stay and eat with me,' Nicola said. 'I put together a meal that will stretch to two in case you were able to stay.' She smiled with wry amusement. 'No arsenic in the soup.'

There were roses in a silver bowl reflected in the dark polished wood of the dining table; the linen napkins were crisply clean; and the plates were part of the Minton service that had been one of their wedding presents. The food was more appetizing than anything Ben had eaten in the last few weeks. After the meal Nicola gave him coffee in the exquisite Sèvres cups. The last time they had used them had been when Josie came to dinner.

It occurred to Ben that Nicola was trying to show him what he had thrown away. There was something childlike about the display, as if she were setting out her treasures and asking the grown-ups to come and buy. And yet Nicola was not that naïve. In her own way she was a clever woman, for somehow that evening she had created an atmosphere in which he found himself able to relax in spite of their own situation and his desperate anxiety about his firm. He would have liked to have told her all about it, which was strange considering how he had kept her in the dark in the past. Why was that? Because Nicola would not have agreed with all his dealings and he shrank from exposing anything shoddy to her honest candour. Josie would not have approved either, but she would have understood the urge to succeed that drove him down the path he had chosen. Nicola would have said it was better to be poor and above reproach, but then she had not been deprived as Josie and he had been deprived.

He owed it to Josie to bring up the question of divorce again. While he was still searching for the right words Nicola did it for him.

'Josie will have told you about our talk,' she said. 'Not very satisfactory from her point of view, I'm afraid.'

'She thinks you don't understand that doing it the way you want means the end of her ambition to be an M.P.,' Ben said.

'I understand perfectly. My offer still stands. I'll divorce you, but only if Josie is named.'

'Why, Nicola?' Ben asked quietly.

He thought she was not going to answer him, but in the end Nicola explained.

'I'll only let you go to a woman who loves you enough to put you first.'

As Nicola had done. The unspoken words hung in the air and embarrassed them both. Josie did not put him first. Nicola knew it and so did he, but Ben was less sure than Nicola that he had any right to expect it.

He left soon after that. It had been an odd evening, but at least he had sorted Raymond out – or thought he had. For once he had the whiphand over Ernie and he would use it to good effect. From now on he would breathe a cleaner air.

Chapter Sixteen

It seemed to Josie that the Luke affair had been marvellously well resolved, especially since she had Ben's promise that he would make a clean sweep of all Ernie's shady dealings. She was put out when Mrs Luke muttered that it was all being swept under the carpet. Josie suppressed her own reluctant agreement that this was true and pointed out with some sharpness that she had done what she had pledged herself to do and had saved Basil Luke from a very nasty situation.

She saw nothing of Ben and even though it was her own choice the lack of him was a constant ache of unsatisfied need. They spoke once or twice on the telephone, very guardedly, and she gathered that he was working every waking minute to try to put right the faults that had been committed, no longer leaving the contractors to get on with the job, but supervising their every move. He seemed so taken up with his work that Josie had a piqued feeling that the question of his divorce had taken second place.

Her name was safely down on the list of prospective parliamentary candidates, but nothing had been said about her standing in Cy Maple's place and in her heart Josie knew that she would be very lucky indeed to be selected for such a safe Labour seat. She was not even sure that Cy had yet signalled his reluctance to stand again and so she kept a discreet silence and put her energy into keeping her name in the forefront of local politics. It would all have been very satisfactory if it had not left her wanting Ben so badly. There was a hole in her life that only he could fill and sometimes Josie thought she would go crazy from the frustration of keeping herself apart from him.

The summer came to an end and Parliament was sitting again. Because the start of a new session was a busy time and he usually spent more time in London and less in the constituency after the long recess, Josie was surprised when Cy dropped in to her little office one evening.

'Thought I'd catch you here tonight,' he said, sitting down heavily in the chair opposite her. 'Josie, love, those old people's flats are well and truly finished, aren't they?'

'Ages ago,' Josie said.

'Satisfactorily?'

'Yes, indeed. They're all occupied and everyone seems very happy.'

'No complaints about the way they were put up?'

'None,' Josie said. She had an unpleasant feeling that she knew what was coming next.

'Good,' Cy said. 'Then your connection with Baxcombe & Harcourt is finished?'

'Except that Ben Harcourt is still a sort of step-cousin and a very close friend,' Josie said evenly.

'A pity about that. I've picked up a rumour that's got me hopping mad. The story I've heard is that Raymond Wadsby is asking for an investigation into corrupt practices in this area.'

'*Raymond?*'

'Makes you sick, doesn't it? A bloody Tory, and not even an M.P. in this county, let alone the constituency. The trouble is, it looks as if he's got an inside story, having been on the board of Baxcombe & Harcourt.'

'I can't believe it,' Josie said. 'I just can't believe it.'

What she meant was that she was unable to take in that Raymond had taken this incredible step, but Cy misunderstood her.

'Always difficult to believe that a friend has been underhanded,' he said sympathetically. 'Thought I'd tip you the wink, mainly so that you can keep clear. Better not see anything of that cousin of yours until we know how deeply involved he is.'

It was the moment for Josie to be frank with him and she could not do it. She saw the abyss in front of her and shrank back. But she must say something. If it came out, as it must if there were a full investigation, that Mrs Luke had approached her, then Cy would want to know why she had not spoken out. Come on, girl, she thought wildly, you're supposed to be able to think on your feet.

'Cy ... I've heard something of the sort before, but I thought it had all been cleared up,' she said.

'Oh? Tell me about it.'

'I'd rather not. A constituent approached me ... I took it up on her behalf.' Josie swallowed. 'Ben was very co-operative,' she said firmly.

Cy looked dissatisfied, but to Josie's relief he did not press her.

'Sounds a minor matter compared to what Wadsby's alleging,' he said.

He lumbered to his feet and even in her preoccupation Josie registered that he was moving more slowly than he had done the last time they had met. He was not well, worse perhaps than he had told her. If he didn't last out the life of this Parliament her chance might come sooner than she had expected. If she hadn't messed it up for good.

Josie struggled with miserable indecision all the evening and then, late at night, gave in and put through a call to Ben.

'There's bad trouble brewing,' she said. 'I need to see you, Ben.'

'Drive to some tourist spot on Saturday, book a room and I'll come and join you,' he suggested.

'I suppose ... yes, it's probably the only way,' she agreed. 'I'm so on edge I feel as if there were eyes spying on us behind every window.'

She knew from Ben's long silence what he was thinking: that if she would live with him openly there would be no need to fear detection. But now, more than ever, it was impossible to do that.

They met in Keswick in a small hotel overlooking Derwentwater. It was the end of the season, but the town was still full of cars and people taking advantage of the fine autumn weekend, perhaps the last of the year. The sun sparkled on the water, the hills on the far side of the lake were grey and purple, and there were still boats pottering about. A white-sailed yacht skimmed over the surface in the fitful breeze.

'I can do with a break,' Ben remarked, looking at the pleasant scene.

'Make the most of it,' Josie said. 'You may find yourself in the dock before many months are past.'

By the time she had finished telling him about Raymond's call for an investigation Josie was almost incoherent with rage.

'Raymond Wadsby!' she exclaimed. 'A *stupid* man. A hidebound Tory from his wooden head to his nylon socks. And it could have been *my* story! I could have been the one pushing for a clean-up campaign. The Conservatives will use it for propaganda, of course they will – hard graft in a Labour-controlled area, it'll be meat and drink to them. We ought to have cleared it up ourselves, and would have done if I hadn't been so keen to save you. It makes me sick to think of Wadsby licking his lips over the juicy scandal. Does he know about Basil Luke?'

'No, and if Luke will co-operate we can probably suppress that, since Ernie's blackmail didn't succeed. Raymond was in Ernie's clutches himself. I went and saw him and warned him to get out.' Ben gave an odd little laugh. 'It was a mistake to forget that he's a politician.'

'You went to Berringer Hall? Did you see Nicola?'

'Yes.'

'What did she say about us?'

'That she will only let me go if she's satisfied you will put me first,' Ben said.

They looked at one another steadily and then Josie turned away. 'I can't do it,' she said. 'You know that, don't you?'

'I'm beginning to see it,' Ben said. He sounded immensely tired.

Josie went to the window, looking down on the people strolling along by the lakeside. 'Look at them,' she said. 'Happy and contented, well-fed and well-clothed, money in their pockets, and probably most of them came by car. Then think back to what it was like when we were children. There are still people who live like we did, Ben. You have to know where to look for them, they don't get noticed like they did in the nineteen-thirties, but they exist. My whole life is dedicated to helping them. I can't betray ...' In a very low voice she said, 'I can't betray a couple who set out to walk to London with a baby to start a new life.'

She started when she felt his hand on her shoulder and then she sensed his understanding and turned and leaned against him.

'Are we still staying the night?' Ben asked.

'Yes. Take me out to dinner. Let's have an expensive meal and lots of wine and to hell with tomorrow.'

She kept up a good front for the rest of the evening and if her air of gaiety did not deceive Ben he made no comment on it. Back in their hotel Josie clung to him in a frenzy of passion, her long, narrow body twining about his, her lips and hands importunate, urging him on to fresh assaults until Ben dropped blindly into a black hole of oblivion from which he awoke hours later to find Josie beside him racked by sobs.

He gathered her close, trying to soothe her, but when Josie was quieter he said in a low voice, 'It's goodbye, isn't it? That's why you brought me here.'

Josie was beyond speaking, but he felt the assenting movement of her head.

'Is there no other way?' Ben asked.

'None that I can see,' Josie muttered. 'There's no way we can be together unless I destroy my life's work and even now, lying here with you, loving you so much, my dear, dear love, even now I can't bring myself to do that.'

'As my wife you could still help people,' Ben said. 'There are charities, voluntary work, social services ...'

'No! I don't want to put ointment on sores. I want to change the system.'

Josie went off first thing in the morning. Ben stood and watched her battered little car until it disappeared round a corner. It was early and there was a Sunday morning calm in the town. The sun shone as it had done the day before and the lake and mountains were as lovely, but Ben did not see them. Looking blindly over the tranquil water, ruffled by the morning breeze, he took stock of his situation. Within the space of a few months he had lost his wife, his beautiful home and now his lover; his company was in jeopardy, his name was being whispered about, and the next thing he faced losing was his liberty.

There was no doubt in Ben's mind that the investigation Raymond was instigating would uncover enough to bring him to trial, even though he looked upon himself as less culpable than Ernie. Recently, Ben had made an effort to keep his hands clean, but in the earlier years he had not been so scrupulous. At the time it had seemed an almost inescapable fact of business life that no one did anything for nothing. Ben was hard put to it to remember all the little deals that had been done. A tip-off that a certain piece of land would be considered for council development, followed by an anonymous case of whisky which Ben himself had put in the boot of a car; a 'consultancy fee' paid to a man who had not disclosed his interest when Baxcombe & Harcourt's next contract came up for discussion; a luxury holiday abroad, all expenses paid, followed by a recommendation that Baxcombe & Harcourt should be used to build an extension to a Public Library.

As for the university development, there had been some underhand dealing there, involving disclosure of tenders from other firms which should have been confidential. Ben had not been a party to whatever bargain Ernie had struck over that, but neither had he asked any probing questions, too excited by the immensity of the project to query the expenses Ernie had incurred, too carried away to be either prudent or honourable.

Now, faced with the probability of being charged with conspiring to corrupt local government officials, Ben cursed the way he had allowed himself to go along with the tide of favours given and received. He had offered bribes to people holding public office in order to obtain advance information about building projects and to make sure that his firm's tenders were given favourable treatment, and the only thing that might tell in his favour was that he had genuinely struggled to put right some of the wrong that had been done.

V. Nicola and Ben

Chapter Seventeen

It took months for the case to come to trial. Work on the university buildings went on and Ben slaved to get as much as possible finished before the axe could fall. Money was a constant anxiety: with the possibility of corruption charges hanging over the company the bank manager was no longer co-operative and the useful link with Raymond's City interests was severed. Ernie was savage; if he had reminded Ben in the past of a rat, now he was a rat cornered.

They were both interviewed by the police and Ben took legal advice.

'I'm afraid there's little doubt that there's a case to answer,' his solicitor said carefully. 'There'll be a preliminary hearing, but I have to warn you that you will almost certainly be sent to trial.'

'And the outcome?'

'Impossible to say. If you've been frank with me ...'

He shot a look at Ben and Ben kept his face as smooth as if he had nothing to conceal – but he had; there were aspects of the Luke involvement which he had not revealed and had no intention of revealing.

'As I'm sure you have,' the solicitor went on, sounding as if he were trying to convince himself, 'then you are less culpable than Mr Baxcombe.'

He shuffled his papers and added, 'There's just one point ... you're no longer living with your wife?'

'No.'

'And Mr Raymond Wadsby, the prosecution's most important witness, is your father-in-law. Did you and Mrs Harcourt separate because of these allegations?'

'No.' Ben hesitated and then added, 'There was another woman. But that's all over. I don't want her brought into the case at all.'

'You'd better tell me about it,' the solicitor said. 'These things have a nasty way of coming up unexpectedly.'

'I'm not prepared to give you her name.'

'You're making a mistake, Mr Harcourt. I want to instruct Counsel, even for the preliminary hearing, and I'm sure he will press you for this information. It's a question of character, you see. The prosecution will attack you on every angle.'

Ben shook his head. There was no question in his mind that he must keep Josie's name to himself. Once let it be spoken out loud and it would wing itself to the listening ears.

When he got back to the hotel where he was still living Ben found an unexpected visitor: his father. Andrew sat on the edge of a chair in the reception area, his eyes fixed on the door, his cap held between his hands. When Ben came in he got up with a look of relief on his face.

'Thought I'd come an' see how you were, lad,' he said awkwardly. 'Things are going against you, seemingly.'

'You've read the newspapers,' Ben said.

'Aye, we all have. Someone's got it in for you.'

'Raymond Wadsby,' Ben said. 'Come into the bar, Dad, and I'll buy you a drink. It'll be quiet in there at this time of day.'

They sat by the window on the far side of the bar, out of earshot of the barman, who had nothing to do but listen and who was eyeing Ben with the curiosity he was beginning to recognize everywhere.

'It's a bad business, Dad,' Ben said. 'Ernie ... but I mustn't throw it all on him. I've shut my eyes to things that I ought to have seen were dangerous.'

'The Baxcombes were always a rum lot,' Andrew said. 'I had my doubts about our Phyllis marrying Ernie, but the women wanted it and he did well by her while the good times lasted.'

Ben had nothing to say to that and Andrew went on, 'It were through Phyllis that we heard you an' Nicola were separated. It surprised me, that did. I thought Nicola was a staunch lass.'

'It wasn't her fault, it was mine,' Ben said quickly.

'Well, whatever the rights and wrongs of it, it isn't fittin' you should be living in a hotel at a time like this. What I've come to say, lad, is that you're welcome to come home. It's not what you've been used to since you went up in the world, but when you're in trouble there's nowt like your own folks.'

There was a constriction in Ben's throat that made it difficult for him to speak. He swallowed some of his beer and said gruffly, 'Thanks, Dad, I appreciate it, but it wouldn't do. I'm scarcely on speaking terms with Ernie and Phyllis and I dare say Phyllis still visits her mum. You don't want us quarrelling in your kitchen. And you'd be badgered to death by reporters leaning on the gate and the neighbours dropping in to catch a sight of me. You don't know what it's like.'

'You look poorly, lad.'

'I'm tired,' Ben admitted.

Tired, and sick at heart. Josie's defection was constantly in his mind. At all sorts of incongruous moments he would remember that he would never hold her in his arms again and it was as if someone had jolted against a broken limb. If he had been happy in his work perhaps he could have lost himself in it, but that solace was denied him. If he had been living a normal life, not cooped up in a hotel, bored and lonely, then he might have spun a comfortable cocoon to cushion his raw nerves. As it was, there was nothing to save him from memories that drove him out of his bed to pace about the room for hours on end, nothing except the horror of the proceedings which were going to ruin his business and take away his good name.

It never occurred to Ben that his father might do anything more than accept the excuse Ben had made for not taking up Andrew's invitation to return home, but he underrated the worry Andrew felt after seeing his son's white, tense face. There was only one person who could help Ben, in Andrew's opinion, and that was Nicola, and so he went to see her.

'I thought you wouldn't mind,' he said apologetically. 'It always seemed to me that you were devoted to our Ben when you were together and he told me 'isself that it were his fault you'd parted. He's in a bad way, lass. I don't know how long it is since you saw him ...'

'Too long,' Nicola said. 'I haven't changed, Mr Harcourt. I'd take him back tomorrow, if he'd come.'

'He's got an obstinate streak: he won't ask to come, not Ben,' Andrew said. 'You'll need to push him into it.'

'He was … alone?' Nicola asked.

'Aye. He told me he'd made a fool of 'isself with another woman, but she's dropped him now, that's obvious.'

He looked round him in a baffled way.

'All this, and a lovely young wife, what did he want that he 'adn't got?'

'Excitement.'

While Andrew puzzled over this, Nicola sat for a moment in thought and then came to a decision. There was more than one thing holding Ben back from returning to her: pride, his love for Josie and Raymond's continuing presence at Berringer Hall. There was nothing she could do about Josie, but she could, if necessary, ride roughshod over his pride and she could see that Raymond did not intrude on him if he returned to Berringer Hall.

'I'll do what I can to bring him home,' she promised Andrew.

Before her resolution could weaken, Nicola went through the green baize door into her mother's part of the house.

'Our present situation can't go on,' she said to Marigold. 'Keeping you and Raymond here in my house looks as though I support his campaign against Ben, which I don't. I'd like you to move out.'

'Darling, you can't be serious!' Marigold's wide blue stare of astonishment was something Nicola had been familiar with since her childhood. 'We have an arrangement …'

'A very informal one. I'm bringing it to an end.'

'But all our furniture … the alterations we've had done … '

'Ben paid for the alterations and the bulk of the furniture came with the house and belongs to me.'

'Daddy's Will was so grotesquely unfair,' Marigold complained.

'You got most of the money.'

'As if that counted, by the side of Berringer Hall. I don't know how you can have the heart to take my home away now, when it's so important to Raymond.'

'I don't happen to like Raymond. I never have and he

certainly hasn't made me feel better towards him by trying to ruin my husband.'

'What husband? I thought he'd left you ... and a very good thing, too.'

'I love Ben,' Nicola said. 'Never forget that. I'm bringing him back here again.'

'You must be mad! Now that you are free of him you could make something of your life. Darling, you're still young, and a beautiful girl. You could marry anyone. Someone of our own sort, just as I always planned for you.'

'I think your plans were for yourself,' Nicola said sadly.

'How can you say such a thing? I could have been so proud of you.'

'If I'd scored the right number of points by marrying someone your friends would have liked for one of their own daughters. I never wanted to play that game.'

'I don't know where you get this odd streak. I gave you every advantage ...'

'Except one. Do you know one of the strongest links between me and Ben? He had a deprived childhood and so did I. I understood his loneliness. Unfortunately, I never really got him to understand why. He thought, like you, that because I was fed and clothed I was all right, but what about the days I spent with no other children to play with because you didn't think the village children were suitable, even though you let me go to school with them? What about the holidays when Grandfather was the only person who wanted me? I loved him, and I loved coming to Berringer, but did you ever consider what there was for me to do with myself here?'

Nicola paused for breath and saw that her mother was too shocked by this outburst to think of a proper reply.

'You made friends at school,' Marigold protested feebly.

'Not really. I'd got out of the habit by then.'

'You can't say I neglected you. It's too ludicrous. If I do have a fault it's that I care too much about other people.'

'I wasn't "other people" I was your own daughter, too close to home to be noticed. Oh, yes, I know you did a lot of good work, and still do. I don't know where the local Conservative Association would be without you.'

'That's it, you see. I've always had claims on my time quite outside ordinary domestic duties.'

'Heaven preserve me,' Nicola said bitterly, with her mind on Josie, 'from women with a mission in life.'

'I don't understand you in this mood,' Marigold complained. 'I suppose you're feeling the strain of this dreadful case, as we all are, but now you've got this extraordinary tirade off your chest I hope you'll think better of turning Raymond and me out of our home.'

'No. I stand by that. I can't fetch Ben back here while Raymond is living practically in the next room and Ben is coming home if I have to knock him over the head and kidnap him.'

Three days after his father's visit Ben returned to the hotel after his day's work and asked for his key.

'Mrs Harcourt has already taken it up, sir,' the receptionist said brightly. 'Oh, and here's your receipt. Mrs Harcourt forgot to wait for it.'

Ben took the receipted bill and stared at it. The receptionist was looking at him curiously. She knew about the investigation, everyone knew about it. Ben turned away from her interested eyes and ran up the stairs.

Inside his room Nicola was packing.

'Your father came to see me,' she said. 'He said you were looking ill and I ought to be looking after you and I agree with him. I'm taking you back to Berringer Hall. Hand me those shirts.'

'Nicola, you must see that's quite impossible ...'

'I gave Mummy and Raymond notice to leave and their part of the house is empty,' she interrupted. 'If you really can't bear to live with me then you can have their quarters, though it will make housekeeping simpler if you come into the main part of the house.'

She hesitated and then added, 'Separate rooms, of course. I'm not trying to force myself on you.'

'It's unbelievably generous of you,' Ben said. 'But I can't ... you must see that I can't accept. You do realize I may go to prison?'

‘That’s what Raymond thinks,’ Nicola agreed. ‘I believe the Court will have more sense.’

‘I’m not pretending to be a hundred per cent innocent.’

He heard her sigh, a sad, acquiescing sound, but she went on packing.

He had had a gruelling day. He was chilled to the bone from standing in the rain, tired and dirty, and he had given yet another statement to the police which left him feeling as if a layer of skin had been stripped off him. The thought of Berringer Hall was almost unbearable. Peace and beauty and, above all, privacy. He longed for it with a physical ache as strong as his craving for Josie. But of course it was impossible.

‘I can’t do it, after the way I’ve treated you,’ he said.

‘We were married for five years,’ Nicola said. ‘That counts for something.’

‘I’m still in love with Josie.’

He thought that would silence her, but Nicola said with unanswerable logic, ‘But she’s not here, is she? It’s all right, Ben, I understand why. I think I always saw more clearly than you what a conflict there’d be between Josie’s idea of duty and the way you felt about one another. The way I look at it is that if she doesn’t feel able to look after you while you’re going through such a difficult time, then that leaves the way clear for me to do it.’

When he still stood in the middle of the room looking mulish, Nicola said in exasperation, ‘Do be sensible! It will look far better for us to be living together again.’

‘You sound like my solicitor,’ Ben said.

‘Take this suitcase,’ Nicola said. ‘I came by taxi so that there’d only be one car to worry about. Will you drive or shall I?’

‘I will,’ Ben said.

The timeless calm of Berringer closed round him. It was like stepping out of the harrowing everyday world into a place untouched by the sordid transactions that had enmeshed him. That night Ben slept for an unbroken eight hours.

He wandered down to breakfast in his dressing gown and yawning.

‘It is Sunday, isn’t it?’ he asked. ‘I’ve lost all count of the days.’

'It is and I've made kedgeree for breakfast,' Nicola said. She gave him a long, considering look. 'You look a bit more human than you did yesterday. Or will do when you've shaved.'

Ben rubbed his bristly chin. 'Indulge me. I haven't had a sloppy breakfast for months. I smelt the coffee, that's what brought me downstairs. No one makes coffee like you.'

It was not an entirely fortunate remark. Ben pulled himself up and the look of strain came back to his face.

'If we're going to have to watch every word we say there's no point in your being here,' Nicola said. 'You missed my coffee. Well, it's nice to be missed for something. I told you before I married you that I was a good cook. I'm planning to go to church later. Are you coming with me?'

'I'd rather not. Though it looks as if prayer is about the only thing that can help me now.'

'Don't be flippant about it,' Nicola said. 'I happen to believe and I'm sorry now that I let my churchgoing slip while we were married.'

'You insisted on being married in church,' Ben recalled.

'Because it meant something to me. It still does. I'm married to you for life, Ben. Even if we are divorced I shan't marry anyone else.'

'Are we going to be divorced?'

'That's up to you. It always has been.'

By the time Nicola got back from church a fine, drizzling rain was falling. Ben had lit the wood fire in the room he had always used as a study and was stretched out in one of the armchairs reading Dickens.

'Don't you have the Sunday papers any more?' he asked.

'I thought we could live without them,' Nicola said.

Ben guessed why she had stopped the papers.

'There's not much point in trying to shield me,' he said. 'They've already done their worst and in any case the whole thing's what they call sub judice now.'

'I'll just go and give the joint a poke and do one or two things in the kitchen,' Nicola said. 'Pour me a sherry, will you?'

It was the nearest they came to discussing the case all day

and Ben knew that Nicola was deliberately trying to keep him from thinking about it. When she came back he was standing by the window with a glass in his hand looking out over the formal garden, half hidden in a soft, smoke-like rain.

'I love this place,' he said.

'Yes, but it might have been better if you'd had to provide us with a house,' Nicola said, with one of the flashes of insight that took him by surprise. 'Grand-dad meant it for the best, but he did me a bad turn when he left me Berringer. You would have been happier fighting your way up from a cottage to a villa, from a villa to a country house.'

'But I've just said, I love it,' Ben protested.

'We never quite hit the right balance. If you made a decision I reacted against it – like I did about taking in Mummy and Raymond – and if I acted without you, then you felt you were being shut out.'

'It was like a foreign country to me,' Ben agreed reluctantly. 'You were at home, but I was always feeling my way.'

'Money, too. We never quite saw eye to eye about that.'

'Where I was brought up it was the women who managed the money. Bess, with all her faults, always knew to the last half penny how much she had in her purse and how to spend it to the best advantage.'

'My carelessness annoyed you.'

'It surprised me. When I saw that you expected me to be the money manager I fell in with it because I wanted to do what was seen as the normal thing in your world. I think now I ought to have given you a few lessons in book-keeping and forced you to handle things. It's been worrying me since we parted in case you haven't been managing. Are you all right?'

An idea, half formed in Nicola's mind, of getting Ben to take an interest in Berringer again by presenting him with her jumbled mass of unpaid bills was hurriedly discarded.

'I can cope,' she said with an inner dismay she hoped Ben could not see.

When they were able to talk to one another like that Nicola felt that they were making some progress, but all too often their conversation was stilted. They were not at ease with one another – how could they be? – and she thought that Ben sensed how ceaselessly she watched him for some sign that he was recovering from his infatuation for Josie.

Nicola was determined to get him back. The hardest thing she had ever done had been to let him go, without fuss, without reproach, with nothing to guide her but an instinct that a bird freed from a cage might come winging home of its own accord. If Josie had proved her wrong, had thrown up her career to join her life to Ben's, Nicola would have bowed her head in bitter acceptance, but in her heart she had been sure that would not happen.

Nicola believed that Ben and Josie were essentially in conflict with one another. It might make for an exciting love affair, but she did not see it as a basis for marriage. Ben, for one thing, had an appreciation for the finer things of life which Josie entirely lacked, even thought immoral. His love for Berringer Hall had stemmed from this. He enjoyed music, he had an eye for a good picture – Nicola had seen him pick up a piece of porcelain and hold it, quite absentmindedly, but with instinctive pleasure. Josie would have sold it and given the money to charity, and however worthy that might be, Nicola felt that Ben would have been the poorer for it.

Josie had dazzled him with her intellect, her independence, her sexual daring and, above all, the clarity of her aims. Until she had fallen in love with Ben, Josie had had no doubts about the way ahead. Nicola suspected that she had had only one playtime in her life, in Geneva, and that had turned sour. Since then Josie had dedicated herself to her work and Nicola was sure that if she ever chose a permanent mate it would be somebody who would work by her side, and he would have to put up with the discomforts and shortcomings, for Josie would never be a homemaker.

This was the point on which Nicola based her hope: Ben needed a home. She had given him that and it was in the belief that he would miss it that she had sent him away to join Josie.

Judging by the way he had reacted since Nicola had fetched him back to Berringer Hall, she had been right, but that did not mean that he was any nearer to turning back to her. He had lost something of the gaunt look which had worried her when she had seen him at the hotel; he ate the meals she put in front of him, and Nicola wondered whether he realized how much anxious thought went into their preparation; he said when she asked that he slept well, which she suspected was not entirely true; and he made an effort to talk to her, but not about anything that really mattered.

He had always been a solitary person, Nicola thought with resignation. His aloof, self-sufficient air was part of the attraction he had for women; each of them thought she would be the first to discover him; they were all sure that inside the palisade there was a different man, warm and human and passionate, and they were right. Nicola had known the joy of union with this hidden man, but she had been over-sensitive and had waited for him to reveal himself. Josie had crashed through the barriers and taken him by storm, and Ben not only suffered because his defences had been destroyed, but was determined to make the walls stronger in future.

They lived side by side like strangers and Nicola wept over it in secret, all the more so because she knew that his long celibacy did not come easily to Ben. In the years of their marriage she had discovered him to be a man with a strong sex urge. She had known that he was sleeping with Josie almost as soon as the affair had started because Ben had stopped making love to her, and that was not natural for him.

As the date for the preliminary hearing drew nearer Nicola saw the tension grow in Ben. She wanted to comfort him, to give him release, and to find it herself. And Ben wanted it, too. She knew him too well not to be able to read the signs. He avoided any unnecessary physical contact with her, turned his eyes away when she made an effort to look attractive, drank more than usual, though not to excess: that had never been an escape for Ben. If she went one night and got into bed with him, he would take her, but would he forgive himself afterwards?

'I'll come with you to the Court, of course,' she said.

'I'd rather you didn't,' Ben replied.

'I want to be seen to be supporting you. Raymond will be giving evidence, won't he?'

'Oh, yes! Milking the publicity for all it's worth. Very much our blue-eyed boy, is Raymond. The nasty man lent him money and then tried to blackmail him into leaking secrets, but Raymond couldn't be tempted. He told all, insisted on an investigation and uncovered a network of corruption – that's his version.'

'What about Phyllis?'

'That may or may not come out. There are two ways of looking at it. Either Raymond is a nasty character who will lay any woman weak enough to let him or else he's a Sir Galahad who fell for a sexy temptress put in his way by the man who was trying to corrupt him. It can be twisted round to be very damaging to our side.'

'To Ernie's side,' Nicola said.

Ben looked at her with a half smile that was the warmest expression she had seen on his face for weeks.

'You're very loyal,' he said.

It was the opening Nicola had been waiting for.

'I love you,' she said.

'Still?' Ben asked.

'Always. In every way. Ben, you're still my husband and I want you. The way we're living is unnatural and it's putting too much of a strain on you – on both of us. Start sleeping with me again.'

Ben shook his head. 'I can't use you like that,' he muttered uncomfortably.

Nicola went to him and put both her hands flat against his chest, looking up into his face.

'Are you ever going to be able to marry Josie?'

'No.'

'Are you going to go on living like a monk for the rest of your life?'

She got the same slight smile as before. 'It's unlikely,' he admitted.

'Am I still attractive to you?'

'You're beautiful and kind, and far better than I deserve.'

'And familiar,' Nicola said. 'You know me. I'd much rather you "used" me, as you say, than went to a stranger.'

She could tell by the tension in the muscles under her hands that it was only by an act of will that he stopped himself from reaching out for her.

'Damn it, Ben,' she cried in exasperation. 'In five years of marriage there were times when you wanted it and I didn't, and it never took you long to persuade me, and you didn't have any scruples about it either. Do stop pretending to be such a perfect gentleman and act naturally.'

She knew that she had won when he laughed. She moved closer and let her arms slide round his neck. Ben seized her and held her so tight that she could scarcely breathe, but he did not kiss her.

Nicola cast a distracted thought to the dinner cooking in the oven, but now that she had got him to this point she was certainly not going to lose her opportunity.

'Come upstairs,' she said. 'Now.'

She saw Ben watching her as she undressed and she exaggerated her movements, deliberately provocative. His own fingers seemed unnaturally slow, fumbling over buttons and zip, but when he turned to face her, naked, there was no doubt about his reaction. Nicola held out her arms and he fell on her like a man possessed, but in all the striving of their bodies Ben spoke no word of endearment. When he had finished and they fell apart, Nicola turned to him, but Ben rolled away from her and lay on his other side, quite separate. As the langour of satisfied desire receded Nicola began to be aware of the first stirrings of a terrible pain. Tears gathered and rolled down her cheeks.

'Why are you crying?' Ben asked.

'Just reaction,' she lied.

But it was more than that. Ben had done just what she had invited him to do: he had used her. And it had solved nothing.

All the same, he did move back into the same room with her, mainly because Nicola, obstinately determined, took all his things out of the bedroom he had been using and restored them to their accustomed place. Ben made no comment. They lay side by side in the same bed and sometimes he turned to her in wordless need.

Just once she got from him something more than the blind impulse of a demanding body. Instead of turning away, Ben gathered her close and said, in an oddly moved whisper, 'You're so good to me.'

'We'll come through these bad times,' Nicola said.

'After the case is over, even if I'm free, I shall go away.'

'Ben, dear, no! What have I been doing all these weeks if I haven't been showing you that your place is here?'

'I have to get away,' he repeated. 'I have to decide what I'm going to do with the rest of my life.'

Just as they were keyed up to attend Court within a few days Ben returned home one evening in a state of exasperation and despair.

'The hearing may be postponed,' he said. 'Some fresh evidence has come up.'

'Good or bad?' Nicola asked.

'How could it be good? It was the one thing I'd hoped wouldn't come out. A man called Luke has been interviewed and instead of sticking to the story he agreed with me he's offered the prosecution entirely new evidence about Ernie. Why the bloody man had to have a crisis of conscience now, considering what he's swallowed in the past, I really don't know. Damn him, I was *helping* him by letting it be thought that he'd pointed out faults and I'd had them put right. My legal men are furious because I misled them. We're having a meeting tomorrow to discuss it. Oh, God, I ought to warn Josie!'

'Tell me about it,' Nicola said.

Hesitantly at first, and then in a rush, Ben poured out the story of Basil Luke's involvement with Ernie and his own desperate efforts to repair the damage.

'But surely this is to your advantage?' Nicola said, puzzled.

'Josie ought not to have told me.'

'But the outcome was good.'

'The law says corruption exists if a gift is accepted, even if the act for which it was a bribe is not carried out. Basil Luke took plenty from Ernie and Josie ought to have known that baulking at passing a faulty building didn't put him in the clear. Why did she conceal it? To help the Lukes or because I was her lover?'

Ben went to the conference with his solicitor and counsel and found his own shortcomings forgotten in the news they had for him.

'I'm relieved to see you,' his solicitor said. 'Did Mr Baxcombe get in touch with you?'

'I've not set eyes on him.'

'Nor spoken to him?'

Ben shook his head.

'He's disappeared,' the solicitor said. 'His wife believes he's left the country. Did he have unlimited access to your company bank account?'

'For cheques over a thousand pounds we both had to sign.'

'Just as well, though you'd better inquire how many thousand pound cheques Mr Baxcombe has made out to himself in the last few days. Apparently he's taken everything that was in his joint account with Mrs Baxcombe, and all her jewellery.'

'He won't have taken much out of the company account,' Ben said grimly. 'Because there's precious little in it. How does this affect me?'

'It reinforces the basis of our defence – that the greater part of the guilt lies with Mr Baxcombe,' the barrister said. 'It seems likely that the fresh revelations from Mr Luke were more than he could face. You really should have told us about that sooner.'

'You know now why I didn't,' Ben said. He sat in deep thought for several minutes. 'Will Luke be prosecuted?' he asked.

'If he is it will be the merest formality. He's made a voluntary statement; he will undoubtedly be advised to plead guilty and no doubt will get off lightly.'

'Will he give evidence at my hearing if I plead guilty?'

'But his evidence strengthens your case!' his solicitor exclaimed.

'All the same ... I'll do anything to make sure Josie Bewley's name isn't mentioned in Court.'

The two lawyers looked at one another and at last the barrister said, 'A guilty plea – which will now, of course, have to include your knowledge of the corruption of Basil Luke – will save the expense of a hearing in a higher court. Given that, and the fact that Mr Baxcombe has absconded, it might be possible to get a reduced sentence. It will need careful handling.'

When Ben returned home and told Nicola what he intended to do she stared at him with as much dismay as his solicitor.

'Plead guilty? Oh, no! Surely this is the time when you should start fighting!'

It took her a moment or two to understand the reason for his refusal to listen to reason.

'It's Josie,' she said. 'Is there nothing you won't do for that woman?'

'If she's dragged into the case and disgraced then all the unhappiness we've been through will have been useless,' Ben said. 'I can't undo anything I've done, but I can rescue one small thing out of the wreckage.'

Nicola stared blindly into the fire, the flames leaping and blurring in front of her eyes.

'If her ambitions failed then she might turn to you,' she pointed out.

'You don't know Josie! She'd never forgive me. We'd never be able to live together.'

'And neither can we,' Nicola said wearily. 'I thought I could make you turn to me again, but I can't. I'm defeated. You're right: after the case is over you'll have to go away.'

Chapter Eighteen

Nicola looked upon Ben's decision to plead guilty to the greater part of the charges against him as a piece of pigheaded gallantry. She was both angry and jealous that Josie, who had done so little to deserve it, should have inspired such devotion, but in spite of her reservations she insisted on going to Court with Ben. She was sick beforehand, something she concealed from Ben. It was only nerves, she told herself. She sat in the bathroom for a little while, drank some cold water and waited for her nausea to subside.

The courtroom was cold and yet airless. Nicola, still feeling queasy, shivered and nervously took off her gloves and then put them back on again. Ben seemed calm, but he was wearing the wooden look which meant he was uncomfortable. She was struck by the casual way everyone behaved, leaning over desks to talk, lounging in their seats and looking bored, quite at odds with their formality towards one another once the case had started.

It took far less time than she had expected. Ben pleaded guilty to almost everything that was charged against him. The prosecution had forborne to press any allegations of conspiracy in connection with Basil Luke. Instead, Luke – who had already been given a minimum punishment – was cleverly used by Ben's counsel to bolster Ben's character. Nicola realized that Ben was on tenterhooks, but Basil Luke was anxious to keep his own wife out of the case, he had already been through his story several times, and they managed to get it across without any mention of Josie, leaving an impression that Ben and Luke had co-operated to put right some of the damage Ernie had done.

Nicola saw Ben give him a look of acute dislike, even though his evidence had been helpful. His obsequious manner irked Nicola, too, and she could see that the way he wallowed in his guilt was pushing Ben into an attitude that might be dignified, but also looked arrogant.

The thing that seemed to tell most against Ben was the deal Ernie had pushed through for building a block of flats in Luffley. Two councillors had already been found guilty of accepting favours from him, in one case a prolonged holiday abroad for himself and his family, and in the other case a brand new car, and the gifts had been shown to be linked to the processing of Baxcombe & Harcourt's bid for the contract for the flats.

The charge of conspiring to corrupt these two men was the one point that Ben contested and it was the one that proved most damning to him. His counsel would have liked to have alleged that the acts of bribery had been carried out under the aegis of Baxcombe Systems, which was entirely Ernie's concern, but unfortunately the contract had gone through before the new company had been formed.

The magistrate intervened with a question that at first seemed harmless.

'I don't understand why there was this split between you and your partner,' he said to Ben. 'Why was a separate company formed to deal with the new style of building and why were you not concerned in it?'

'The new system was not proved to my satisfaction,' Ben said carefully. 'I preferred to be concerned with the more traditional building methods.'

He might have got away with that simple explanation, but the prosecution pressed the point.

'A housing authority faced with these radical proposals would require greater persuasion to accept the designs?'

'Possibly.'

'Possibly. Come now, Mr Harcourt. Is it not true that an untried building system requires a greater degree of expertise in the art of selling to put its merits across?'

'It wasn't "untried".'

'I stand corrected. Will you accept "unfamiliar"? An unfamiliar method of building is more difficult to sell?'

'Yes.'

'Did you wish to distance yourself from the methods of persuasion your partner might use?'

Fatally, Ben told the truth.

'Yes.'

Prosecuting counsel let the implication hang in the air. Then he put the knife in.

'The arrangement was that your own company, Harcourt Services, supplied expert advice to Baxcombe Systems for a fee? You were concerned in all their contracts?'

Too late Ben saw the trap he had dug for himself.

'Yes.'

'And made a profit from them?'

'Yes ... but this isn't what I'm here to answer! I'm charged with corrupting Biggs and Olyphant and I didn't have anything to do with it!'

'But you were sufficiently suspicious of the way your first industrialized building contract had been obtained to insist on this unusual distancing operation between you and your partner?'

'I *knew* nothing,' Ben insisted.

'And continued to know nothing while making an excellent profit out of your ignorance?'

There was no possible reply to that. Ben's baffled shake of the head might have been a denial, but he knew only too well that it was the exact truth.

In the event, the magistrate accepted Ben's 'not guilty' plea to the conspiracy charge, but there was no telling how much he had been influenced by the exchange between Ben and the prosecution when it came to pronouncing sentence on the string of minor charges to which he pleaded guilty. He took into account the saving of a further hearing in a higher court, he noted Ben's partner's defection, Basil Luke's favourable evidence, and the fact that the prosecution admitted that Ben had been 'co-operative'. Nevertheless, he could not overlook the acknowledged gifts and favours which had eased the path of Baxcombe & Harcourt and which Ben knew about. Ben was fined £2,000 and sentenced to three months' imprisonment.

'Not quite what I'd hoped for,' Ben's solicitor admitted to Nicola. 'I anticipated a longer sentence, but suspended for a period, which would have meant Mr Harcourt would have been free as long as he committed no further offence. Still, three months ... that's not too bad.'

'When ... when does it start?' Nicola asked through stiff lips.

'Immediately, Mrs Harcourt.' The lawyer looked at her compassionately.

'You mean, Ben can't come home first?'

'No, he's already in custody.'

'Can I see him? I *must* see him.'

In the bleak little room at the back of the Court Nicola found Ben sitting at a plain wooden table. He got up when Nicola was shown in, moving stiffly as if he was not quite sure that he had the use of his limbs. Even in the short space of time since he had been sentenced he had begun to look different. His face looked gaunt, his eyes seemed to have sunk back into their sockets, he had a remote, detached air about him as if he were forcing his mind away from the knowledge of what had happened to him.

Nicola choked and moved forward quickly, but Ben stepped back, as if he did not want her to touch him.

'I can't believe it!' Nicola said. 'That *stupid* magistrate! I thought he'd let you go free. It didn't seem to me as if you'd done anything very dreadful.'

'That was what I thought at the time,' Ben said. 'Just oiling the wheels, that's all it seemed. But I was playing Ernie's game, I can see that now. He'd got me on a piece of string, just like all the other fools.'

'It was all Ernie's fault!'

'Not entirely. He was active, I was passive. I let him get away with murder – practically – as long as the profits kept rolling in. I knew, of course I knew, that some of the jobs we got must have meant underhand dealing, but we did good work. We deserved our success. It wasn't until he got too greedy that he started authorizing shoddy work that I took a stand.'

'You could appeal,' Nicola suggested.

'No, I think not.'

He passed a hand over his forehead, obviously trying to marshal his thoughts.

'Paying the fine will take most of my spare cash. Are you all right for money, for the moment?'

'Yes, of course,' Nicola said quickly, without pausing to consider that she had no idea how much money she had in the Bank.

'I'll get my accountant to work something out – provided they'll let me see him,' Ben promised.

'Ben, please don't think about things like that. Not now! Isn't there anything we can do?'

'I think I'll take my medicine and get it over. Three months ... the lawyers keep saying it's a short sentence. You can tell they've never been faced with it, can't you?'

'I'll come and see you,' Nicola promised, half choked by the sobs she was trying to keep back.

Ben protested, but Nicola was quick to hear the half hearted way he spoke. He did want to see her, even though he told her to keep away, and once she had got that idea into her head nothing would have prevented her visits.

It was a grim business. Nicola scolded herself for shrinking from it, especially when her weekly visits became a routine and the other women waiting to see their men recognized her and greeted her as one of them. As she was, of course, Nicola reminded herself in a moment of painful humiliation. She was the wife of a criminal, except that nothing would persuade her to think of Ben in that way.

With thoughts like that in her mind it was difficult to greet him cheerfully, though she made an effort to talk constructively about the future.

'In a few weeks you'll be able to put this behind you, make a fresh start ... '

'I'd like to know how!' Ben retorted and she saw that her well-meant words had irritated him because there was nothing solid behind them.

'The company is being wound up, the work on the university handed over to another firm,' Ben went on. 'What I'll be when I get out is penniless and unemployed. And who will give me a job? A smart-aleck with dirty hands, too clever for his own good.'

'If no one else will employ you, you'll have to start on your own again.'

'No money. I'd need a sizeable sum for even a modest start and, believe me, no one is going to lend it to me situated as I am.'

Nicola drove home in a mood of desperation after that interview. Somehow she had to lift Ben out of his despair, but she had no idea how to do it. How could she be expected to know, with her ignorance of financial affairs? Josie would have been more use to him and her astringent tongue would have roused him as Nicola seemed unable to do.

Glancing in her rear mirror she saw that she was being followed up the drive by another car. Nicola pulled up in front of the curving, shallow steps of Berringer Hall and waited.

The young man who got out of his car was obviously ill at ease.

'My name's Guy Parkes,' he began.

'You're not a reporter, are you?' Nicola demanded.

'Good Lord, no! I'm an architect. I work ... I worked for Ben ... for your husband.'

'You'd better come in,' Nicola said. Deliberately she added, 'I've just come from the prison.'

When she saw how he winced she relented and went on, 'I'm dying for a cup of tea. Come and join me.'

Over the tea cups Guy Parkes poured out his shock at Ben's conviction.

'The thing is, Mrs Harcourt, some of us who've worked with him think he's had a hard deal. There are plenty of people who've done worse than he did still walking round without a stain on their character. It's damned unfair.'

'I agree – more or less. Ben, you'll find, doesn't take quite the same view.'

'We wanted him to know that we'd still be willing to work for him if he thought of making a fresh start. I've got an option on a piece of land with planning permission next door to my parents' house in Sussex – which is a good long way away. They'd like me to buy it and arrange for it to be developed because they could trust me to design houses that wouldn't offend them. If I could only raise the money I'd go ahead and ask Mr Harcourt to put together a team to do the building.'

'It would be ideal,' Nicola said. 'Have you any hope of getting the money?'

He grimaced in a way that made him look comically young.

'My assets can be measured in hundreds, and we're talking about prime building land with planning permission. There's a big consortium breathing down my neck, just waiting for my time to run out. The only reason I've got an option to buy is that the land belongs to an old friend of my father's. It was daft of me to dream of anything so ambitious.'

'Your Bank ...'

'There might be difficulties,' the architect said uncomfortably.

'If Ben is associated with the scheme,' Nicola said, remembering Ben's own words, and the young man's silence answered her.

'I wondered – if you knew that there was this chance – if you might be able to help,' he admitted.

'Like you, I haven't any money,' Nicola said sadly.

Guy Parkes looked round him in a puzzled way. They were in the drawing room, surrounded by antique furniture upholstered in pale gold silk brocade, with fine pictures hanging on the walls; the tea pot was silver, the cups and saucers were eggshell china.

'I'm sorry, we all had the impression that Ben was married to someone rich,' he said. 'Oh, gosh, I suppose I shouldn't have said that.'

'Don't apologize. I'm rich in possessions – at least, I suppose I am when I come to think of it, though I've always thought of all these things as belonging to Berringer, not to me – but I'm terribly short of cash.'

'You don't think ... perhaps you could raise some capital?'

'Would Ben want that, do you think?'

She saw the moment when Guy remembered that there had been some estrangement between her and Ben, which was not as it happened what had been in her mind, and it reduced him to incoherent embarrassment.

'I ought not to have come,' he said miserably. 'Putting my big foot in it. I'm sorry, Mrs Harcourt. I thought, knowing the way you've been standing by him, that you'd want to help if you could ...'

'Of course I do,' Nicola interrupted him. 'It's just that at the moment I don't see how.'

She sat in silence for a moment before asking, 'How long have we got before your option runs out?'

'Until the end of June.'

'Don't do anything until you hear from me again,' Nicola said.

'Shall I go and talk to Ben about it?'

'Not on any account! Not unless I give you the go-ahead. Above all, don't give up your option until I've seen what I can do to raise the money.'

The next day Nicola went to see her solicitor, not the firm employed by Ben for his defence, but the old family firm who had dealt with her grandfather's affairs.

'I want to raise some money, a lot of money, for a building project,' she said. 'Can I do it by mortgaging Berringer Hall?'

'You can, but I certainly wouldn't advise it,' the solicitor said. 'Unless the money you raise is going to bring you in a good income how are you going to pay the interest?'

'I hadn't thought about that,' Nicola admitted. She frowned in dissatisfaction. 'I wish I understood more about money matters.'

'I take it you want to go on living at Berringer Hall?'

'I haven't considered doing anything else,' Nicola said. 'Could I raise money on the house and then let it to someone for income?'

'There might be difficulties about a mortgage on a house in which you were no longer living,' the solicitor said cautiously. 'And if, as I conjecture, you want to lend the money to your husband, then I have to tell you that no one is likely to consider it a very good risk. Besides, tenants for houses like Berringer are few and far between. Certainly you could ask a substantial rent, but you would have to be patient and wait for the right person to turn up.'

'I can't wait,' Nicola said. 'I desperately need to raise this money as soon as possible.'

She went away with nothing settled and with a feeling of

inadequacy that depressed her. The cost of running Berringer Hall had begun to frighten her. She blamed herself for the careless way she had left everything to Ben in the past. If a bill had come in she had passed it to Ben and he had paid it with only an occasional joking complaint that he was being ruined. Nicola had never considered how much electricity was burnt, the cost of the log fires in every room, the general rates, the water rates, the wages for the gardener and the women who helped her in the house. When flowers from the garden had been in short supply, Nicola had ordered what she wanted from the florists to adorn her lovely rooms, if she wanted something special in the way of food she thought nothing of telephoning to London for it to be sent, when linen had needed replacing she had gone to the best shops as a matter of course. Above all, she had never stopped to consider the constant minor repairs needed by a house over two hundred years old. It had been Ben who had seen that there were no leaks in the roof, that the gutters and drains were kept clear, that the decoration of the house was carried out, while all Nicola had had to do was to decide on colour schemes.

It was true that Ben had had the workmen and resources of his company at his command, but looking back Nicola was ashamed of her slender grasp of the practical aspects of running Berringer Hall. She had prided herself on being a good housekeeper, but now it seemed she had been something less than that. For the first time it occurred to Nicola that Ben might have grown impatient of her dependence. She had complained that he did not treat her as an equal, but had she really behaved like one?

When the gardener came to her and asked whether he should send the lawn mower for its annual check up she said 'Yes' weakly because she did not know what else to say, but when he suggested ordering a load of gravel to repair the drive she made an equally arbitrary decision and came down against it.

Because she hoped it might rouse him from his apathy Nicola consulted Ben about her problems the next time she saw him.

'I doubt whether there's any harm in letting the drive go for the time being,' he said. 'But I've got it very much on my mind that something will have to be done to get you some money.'

A small, ironic smile appeared on Nicola's lips for a moment. You and me too, my darling, she thought to herself.

'You'll have to let the wing Raymond and Marigold occupied,' Ben said. 'It ought to bring in a good rent, not the pittance they paid. I'd be glad to think of you with some company in the house, too.'

'You'll be home before long,' Nicola said and held her breath as she waited for his reply.

'No,' Ben said deliberately. 'I can't do that, my dear. As soon as I get out of here I shall go away. I'll find a job, some sort of job. At least I'll support myself, even if I can't keep you as I meant to do when we were first married.'

'You won't lose touch completely? Promise me that, Ben. It would be too cruel to drop right out of my life and leave me wondering what had happened to you.'

'I won't do that,' Ben promised.

He glanced round at the long room, at the tables with men and women on opposite sides, heads down, voices kept low to preserve some degree of privacy.

'You ought to divorce me,' he said.

'You had my answer to that a long time ago.'

'Circumstances were different then.'

'At least Josie is out of the picture now,' Nicola said with the new asperity that seemed to have come to her lately.

She got no reply and Ben's silence drove her into speaking of the one thing she had promised herself she would not mention, not here in this sordid room, surrounded by other people discussing their problems.

'Josie ought to have been in court,' she burst out.

'How could she be?'

Ben's response was swift, but Nicola thought from his curtness and the way his mouth tightened that he had hoped that Josie would take the risk of being in the public gallery.

'You're still besotted with her,' Nicola accused him.

'No. Being in here has had a strange effect on me, as if I'd cut myself loose – from Josie, from you, from everything. I'm free of her now, as free as I'll ever be. It's not a pleasant sensation. Like floating in limbo. I don't seem to care very much for anyone, not even you, kind though you've been.'

There was a finality about the way he spoke that made Nicola feel chilled to the bone. He was going to go away and leave her. Now, when she needed him more than ever. But, in all fairness, Ben did not know about her overwhelming preoccupation and she had made up her mind not to tell him, not unless he showed signs of turning back to her of his own accord.

She was still grappling with her problem when her solicitor telephoned her.

'Quite fortuitously I've had news of some people who are looking for a property of the size and quality of Berringer Hall,' he said.

'Marvellous! How much rent do you think they'd pay?' Nicola asked, even though her heart sank at the thought of moving out.

'They are only interested in a property they could own outright. Would you consider selling, Mrs Harcourt?'

'Sell Berringer? You must be mad,' Nicola said with conviction.

'I wish you'd think about it. My dear, I've known your family a very long time. No one would be sorrier to see Berringer Hall pass out of your hands, but you must remember that I also know how much your grandfather left you and it is not enough to maintain such a property. Unless your mother can take it over ...'

'No, she can't afford it any more than I can.'

'Or your husband is able to contribute substantially ...'

'He's not.'

'Then I don't see how you are going to manage.'

Since Nicola had been coming to the same conclusion she had no reply to that.

'I'll think it over,' she said unwillingly.

Nicola spent a sleepless night. Sell Berringer? Her lovely home, the house she looked upon as being in trust for the next generation, it was unthinkable. And yet, she had said that there was no sacrifice she would not make to help Ben. Was she going to make reservations now that the chance had been offered to her?

She got in touch with the solicitor again the next day.

'How much will they pay?' she asked.

'I believe they are looking for a property worth around four hundred thousand pounds.'

'I'll have to find out if that's enough,' Nicola said. The young architect was ablaze with enthusiasm as soon as she spoke to him. 'That would secure the land,' he said. 'After that everything would depend on wangling enough credit to start building.'

'I'm not throwing four hundred thousand pounds into something that may never get off the ground,' Nicola said with a sharpness that surprised both of them. 'I can raise more by selling the contents of the house as well – if I decide to sell, which I'm not at all sure about. There are more difficulties than you realize. I feel terrible about even considering the idea of selling a place that was left to me by someone who thought I would look after it and pass it on. If I do it, I have to be sure that it will be worth while.'

'Can I tell Mr Harcourt about the project? I'm sure he'll see what a good deal it is.'

'He must never know where the money has come from,' Nicola said swiftly.

'But he's bound to know that you've sold up and moved out,' the young man said.

'No, he won't. I want you to get him away, down to Sussex, so that he won't pick up any local gossip. And I want your promise not to give me away.'

She got his reluctant promise even though she could tell he saw no sense in it. After a second night spent pacing the floor, Nicola reached a decision.

'I'll sell,' she told her solicitor abruptly. 'But I have to be sure that the new people are suitable.'

'I was afraid you might make that condition. I have to tell you that the prospective purchasers are not a private family but a company who want the premises for a staff college. They are a multinational concern with a very good reputation. I think Berringer would be very well looked after in their hands.'

He looked at her pale face with the concern of an old friend.

'Forgive me, but you don't look at all well,' he said.

'I'm a bit under the weather,' Nicola said carefully and he reflected on the strain under which she had been living and said no more.

'This news about the people who want Berringer not being a family isn't entirely unwelcome,' Nicola said. 'If they're going to run the place as a staff college they'll be wanting a housekeeper, won't they? I'll offer to take on the job.'

She saw that she had really startled him and went on, 'No one knows more about running Berringer than I do, even though I see now that I've neglected the money side. I'll need a job, and it's the one thing I'm good at.'

'But won't you find it difficult ...painful?'

'Probably, but that's not important. I need to do this. I have to find out whether I'm capable of doing a proper, full-time job and I want to keep busy, quite apart from finding the money welcome.'

'You don't anticipate being with your husband?'

'No.'

In spite of that uncompromising denial, Nicola was blankly astonished to get a letter from Ben just before his three months were up to say that he had already been released.

'I kept quiet about the remission I earned because I didn't want you there to meet me,' he wrote. 'You would have tried to get me back to Berringer Hall and I've made up my mind that now is the time to make the break that must come. I won't leave the district without letting you know and I'll see that my solicitors always have an address where you can reach me. Think again about that divorce. You'd be better off without me.'

She wept over it, but in the end she came to accept that, given Ben's pride, it was inevitable that he would shrink from the sight of her waiting for him at the prison gates. In many ways his decision was a relief, even if it was painful. Ben was wrong in thinking that she would have urged him to return to Berringer Hall. That was one thing she was anxious to avoid. Indeed, it was not advisable to meet him at all. In the inhibiting surroundings of the prison interview room it had not been difficult to keep him in the dark, but Ben would soon recognize the deception she was practising if they met now face to face.

The transfer of Berringer Hall was not as easily accomplished as Nicola had hoped. There were long negotiations, surveys, offers and counter-offers. Some of the contents were sold with the house, others went to auction and fetched rather more than Nicola had anticipated. She kept back very little, just enough to furnish a small house.

'I want to retain the little cottage in the woods,' she told her solicitor. 'Will you arrange that for me?'

She had a meeting with the Chairman of the corporation which was buying her home and discussed her situation with him with the utmost frankness. At the end of their interview she knew that she had impressed him.

'The circumstances are, to say the least, unusual,' he said. 'But I respect your desire to help your husband – I've met him, by the way, and thought well of him until ... well, I suppose we're none of us perfect. I agree to your keeping the little cottage back out of the sale and I think we can employ you in the New Year if you're sure you can do a satisfactory job. If it becomes too much for you then I shall expect you to resign.'

'I'll keep going,' Nicola said. 'It's a matter of self respect. I have to prove that I can do something hard, really hard, and do it well.'

It was heartbreaking, seeing the familiar household treasures disappearing. She had a visit from Marigold which tried her sorely.

'Raymond should have thought what the outcome might be before he set out to destroy Ben,' Nicola said, her face set and cold. 'Without Ben's support I can't run Berringer Hall.'

'But all our lovely things? How could you sell them?'

'Grandfather left them to me unconditionally. It's my right to sell them if I see fit. I've kept back his portrait for myself and I thought you would like to have your own picture.'

'Too good of you,' Marigold said sarcastically. She looked at the painting of herself as a young woman, unmarked, carefree, ignorant of the years to come and her face crumpled. 'I was so happy then! If I'd known what was going to happen! Even my own child has turned against me!'

'I haven't done that,' Nicola said wearily. 'I'm fond of you, as fond as you've ever allowed me to be, but I have different priorities now. I have to make a home for myself and ...'

'And your precious husband, I suppose? Once you've got a nice nest-egg together – and you must be making a fortune out of the sale of Berringer – then you hope he'll come back to you.'

'If Ben ever comes back I'll welcome him, but that's not why I'm selling Berringer.'

'Why then? If you couldn't afford to run it then surely you could have let it, not parted with it irrevocably?'

'I'm buying the future. I can see you don't understand and I'm not going to explain. Don't come and see me again, Mummy. I'm going to settle down here, live quietly, do a job of work.'

'If you mean to take a job you'll need to attend to your appearance,' Marigold said, looking with disfavour at her daughter, attired in old slacks and a fisherman's smock loosely belted round the hips. 'I've never seen you look such an utter mess!'

'If you'd warned me you were coming I wouldn't have spent the morning clearing out the attics,' Nicola retorted.

'Totally unnecessary! I could find you a woman to see to all that.'

'I'll do things my own way,' Nicola said and her new obstinacy completely defeated Marigold.

Nicola thought it fortunate that she was at Berringer Hall supervising the removal of the furniture she was keeping when Ben eventually telephoned. Her heart leapt at the sound of his voice and then panic swept over her as she realized how inopportune his call was.

'It looks as if I may have the chance of some work in the south,' he said. 'I've seen the site and it looks promising. I'm moving down there, but I didn't want to go without talking to you first. How are you managing? Are you all right?'

Nicola, leaning against the only table left in the room, looked round her. The bare, dusty floor was littered with packing cases and rolled up carpets; there were faded patches on the walls where the family pictures had hung, naked light bulbs covered in dust hung from the ceiling.

'I'm fine,' she said. 'Everything's going well.'

'Can I come and see you before I leave?'

'Better not,' Nicola said in a panicstricken hurry.

She could tell by the long silence before he spoke again that she had disappointed him. She shifted her weight from one foot to the other. Her legs felt like lead and her back ached. She longed to see him, but that was a weakness she could not afford.

'As you wish,' Ben said at last, very stiffly. 'There were things I wanted to discuss with you. Money, for instance. I hope to be earning a wage soon. I want to make you some sort of an allowance. It won't be much, but I feel I ought to make some contribution, knowing how expensive Berringer is to run.'

'I've ... I've sold one or two things,' Nicola said. 'I've had advice and I'm investing the money.'

'I hate to think of Berringer losing any of its treasures. What have you got rid of?'

'Pictures and silver. I was surprised how much they fetched.'

'I see. You don't want my help then?'

'Yes, I do,' Nicola said, trying to think while she talked. 'I'll accept what you feel you can afford.'

'I'll let you know – by letter.'

'All right. How are you, Ben? Are you getting over it?'

'If you mean getting over being in prison, yes, I suppose so. It's not so easy to get used to not being my own boss.'

'Perhaps this new job ...' Nicola suggested very tentatively.

'It does look quite hopeful,' Ben admitted. 'Does the fact that you don't want to see me mean that you're having second thoughts about a divorce?'

'On what grounds?' Nicola asked, thinking that would dispose of the question.

'A charge of cruelty might stick.'

'Cruelty? Don't be silly, Ben. As if I'd do such a thing. Come back and see me in a year's time. We'll get ourselves sorted out then.'

She cried after he had rung off, but the removal men claimed her attention and she had to stop. They tactfully ignored her tear-stained face, being accustomed to women getting emotional when they were breaking up their homes, and Nicola was able to find some relief in making decisions about the furniture she wanted taken to the cottage.

As the long slow months went past Nicola set her house in order and waited. Until Berringer Hall had been modified and redecorated there was little for her to do, which was just as well. She was achingly lonely, shut away in her little cottage in the woods. The local people were kind, but she shrank from their curiosity. She had cut herself off from her husband, her mother and all her friends. There were times when the plans for the opening of the staff college seemed more important than the actual loss of Berringer or the changes in her life.

She heard from Ben, stiff, cautious letters, as if he were not quite sure that they would be welcome, and she wrote back with as much spontaneity as she could manage when she had so much to conceal. She knew from other sources that the project in Sussex was going well, but she did not let Ben know that.

From time to time she saw news of Josie in the newspapers. In the national press now, Nicola noted; Josie was becoming a well-known personality. Nicola tried to imagine her state of mind, and could not. It was beyond her understanding that anyone could have been as much in love with Ben as Josie had been and given him up, especially at a time when he had needed support. Josie might be the coming woman in politics, but Nicola judged her fiercely and obstinately as a woman who had failed to meet the standards Nicola set herself. Sometimes she knew that she was illogical, that Josie lived her life by a different set of values, but Nicola clung to her belief that her way was right, because if she was wrong what was the point in the sacrifices she was making?

She avoided any contact with Ben's family. There was nothing to take her to Jarrow or Ferryhaven, but on one occasion she did have to go to Newcastle in connection with the sale of some furniture and she took the opportunity of visiting one of the larger shops. As she walked through the fashion department, with a touch of wry amusement at how little attraction the clothes displayed had for her, she caught a glimpse of a mane of bright chestnut hair and an ample figure in an electric blue coat. It was Phyllis: the last person Nicola wanted to see. She stepped quickly behind a rail of cocktail dresses, ducked down her head and pretended to be interested in a choice between silver lamé and magenta sequins. Glancing up cautiously she saw that Phyllis was holding a dress against her and looking in the mirror. While her attention was apparently fixed on her own reflection, Nicola made a quick exit through the fur department.

That was the last time she went anywhere for some time. Berringer was her world. She immersed herself in it and the only person she wanted unceasingly, day and night, was Ben.

She thought perhaps he might come home for Christmas and braced herself to deal with his shock at the changes in her life, but Ben did not leave Sussex. He sent her a present, a small bottle of her favourite perfume and Nicola was divided between tears and laughter because he had remembered and because it was so remote from the life she now led.

She would give him a year, one whole year from the time he had gone into prison. It would be April then. Spring, the time for new beginnings. She would have been housekeeper at Berringer for over three months, an independent woman, able to manage her life without him if that was what he wanted, though considering the revelations she had in store for him, Nicola looked forward sometimes with misgivings, sometimes with hope, to a fresh start for them both.

VI. Bright Tomorrows

Chapter Nineteen

When Ben came out of prison his first intention had been to cut himself off from Nicola, apart from letting her know where he was to be found, but something had made him write to her after he was settled in Sussex and they exchanged several letters during the year. Nicola's letters were not particularly informative. She said she was well and she wrote about the garden, particularly mentioning how well the roses had done that year. Ben wondered what he should read into that. Was it a reminder of the golden roses he had given her for their first wedding anniversary or had Nicola forgotten that gesture?

Neither of them brought up the question of divorce again and Josie's name was not mentioned. As for Josie, she had kept her resolve to stay away from him. It was no more than Ben had expected after her avoidance of him during the trial. He tried not to blame her, to see it from her point of view, but from time to time the thought slid into his mind that Nicola would not have deserted him like that.

Reading one of Josie's speeches in a newspaper Ben recognized all her old clarity and force. It cost him something to admit it, even to himself, but she would have been wasted as the wife of a disgraced builder.

He rented a small flat and fended for himself during his months in the south. He told himself that it was better than living in a hotel, that it was paradise compared to the house he had grown up in, but it was a far cry from Berringer Hall and he could not help thinking with nostalgia of what he had lost.

When Nicola wrote in that strange, conscientious way, about the flowers in the garden, Ben closed his eyes and remembered the warm scent of wallflowers against old brick, Nicola cutting the grass when they were short of a gardener, wearing shorts and a sleeveless blouse, her arms and legs beautifully brown, the tip of her tongue showing between her lips as she concentrated on keeping the lines straight; Nicola, dressed for a party, stirring a jar of potpourri and the drift of perfume in the air; Nicola in the kitchen, her cheeks flushed and her hair ruffled, proud of the skill he had not believed she possessed.

Ben woke one night from a confused dream and wondered why it was Nicola who haunted him and not Josie. He decided the next day, when his mind was clearer, that it was because the break with Josie had been decisive, whereas his marriage to Nicola lingered on in a way that must surely be as unsatisfactory to her as it was to him.

The summer visitors to Sussex disappeared, the autumn gales lashed the coast, wilder than Ben had expected here in the soft south. During the cold, still days of winter he took to visiting the beaches and walking for miles along the edge of the sea, but as the first hints of spring began to appear he went up to the Downs and discovered a new freedom in the sweep of the empty hills.

He became more and more restless. There were too many things in his life that still needed sorting out and he ought to have the courage to face up to them. He must see Josie again, for one thing. When he had told Nicola that he was no longer in love with Josie he had believed it to be true, and yet there was a nagging feeling that until he saw her face to face he could not be sure that the old feeling for her had really disappeared.

He was still hesitating about how he was to approach her when he saw her photograph on a political poster. There was to be a by-election in a Sussex coastal town and Josie was billed as one of the speakers at a rally in support of the Labour candidate. Not that he had much chance of getting elected, not in that Tory stronghold, but Josie, judging from the set of her jaw in the photograph, was ready to do battle on his behalf.

Ben went to the meeting. He hoped that Josie would not spot him in the audience in case the sight of him put her off. He was glad to see that the hall was nearly full; he was nervous for her, he realized, which was fairly stupid because she must be an experienced public speaker by this time.

When Josie began to speak Ben saw that his fears had been unfounded. It would take more than the sight of a former lover to put Josie Bewley off her stroke when she was in full flight. She was a first class public speaker, better than the candidate himself, infinitely better than the agent who introduced her. With a feeling almost of anger against himself Ben began to realize how much he had underestimated her. He had said she would go far, but he had said it in a patronizing way; he had never really appreciated how good she was.

He had always known that she believed passionately in the rightness of her cause and because of the depth of her feelings he had come to think of her commitment as emotional. Now he recognized the clear, analytical mind behind the forceful speaking and was startled by Josie's grasp of facts and figures. Not that she was a dry speaker, far from it. She roused her audience to enthusiasm and she made them laugh; she got them on her side, and Ben was not the only one there that evening to see that she was a more worthwhile candidate than the official nominee.

At the end of the meeting Ben deliberately stood up a little ahead of the rest of the audience. Josie, on the platform, caught the movement and looked towards him. Ben saw her eyes widen and the way she became very still. Without haste he disentangled himself from the departing crowd and went towards the front of the hall.

Standing below the platform and looking up at her, he said to Josie, 'Can we have a word?'

'Outside,' she said. 'I'll get my coat.'

In the street, with the last stragglers looking at them curiously, recognizing Josie, she huddled her coat round her shoulders in a gesture that brought back a hundred memories.

'I'm staying the night with the agent,' she said. 'I told him an old friend from the north was in the audience, but I can't spend too long with you because he and his wife are expecting me back.'

'Can we go somewhere for a coffee or a drink?'

'Let's just walk along the front. I can do with some sea breezes.'

They walked side by side without saying anything. There was

a moon, but the sky was overcast, and its light shone fitfully from behind wisps of ragged clouds. Below them the sea sighed against the shingle beach.

'The tide's just turning,' Ben said.

'I hope that's a good omen,' Josie remarked. She paused and stood leaning against the railing looking out towards the faint line of foam on the edge of the waves.

'You were very good tonight,' Ben said abruptly.

'Thanks. It's a dress rehearsal for me, in a way. Cy Maple isn't going to be able to carry on much longer and I've been told officially that I'll be adopted in his place. But keep that to yourself for the time being.'

'Congratulations. So everything's going your way?'

'You could say that,' Josie admitted. 'How about you, Ben?'

'I get by. I was lucky enough to get some work in my own line, here in Sussex. It's worked out rather well and may lead to other developments.'

'I'm glad about that. Have you forgiven me for not standing by you?'

'I suppose, in a way, I'll never do that,' Ben said slowly. 'But I always understood your reasons and tonight I began to see that you were probably justified. You've got a great future ahead of you, Josie.'

'I hope you're right.' She gave an excited little laugh and Ben realized that in spite of the shock of seeing him, in spite of what she had just said, Josie's mind was still on the speech she had made, on the success she had achieved that evening.

She did make an effort to detach herself from her preoccupation.

'How about Nicola?' she asked. 'Are you back together again?'

'I haven't seen her since I came out of prison,' Ben said.

From Josie's silence he gathered that she had understood the way he had emphasized 'prison'. It was not a pleasant word, it had been a nasty experience, and there was no harm in making her face up to the reality of what he had been through.

'I'm sorry, really I am,' she said. 'But it's all behind you now, Ben.'

'Is it? Don't be too sure of that, and don't let yourself feel too safe. If Ernie is ever tracked down the whole thing will be opened up again.'

'Do you think he'll be found, after all these months?'

'He might get tired of living abroad – if he is abroad – and give himself up. Someone might have a crisis of conscience, like Basil Luke, and confess to helping him.'

'To get away, do you mean?'

'Of course. Didn't it ever occur to you? Ernie's disappearance was too timely and too damned convenient to be anything but a put-up job. Someone – perhaps several people – wanted him out of the way. The matter of Ernie Baxcombe has been swept under the carpet. I wonder how long it will stay there?'

Josie shivered. 'Damn you, Ben,' she complained. 'I was feeling on top of the world and now you've spoilt it. There's still corruption, then?'

'Our case was the tip of the iceberg. When he decided to put his investigation in hand Raymond started uncovering a mess that's so unsavoury that the smell of it will be with us for years. You'd better make up your mind to it, Josie lass; if you take over the Ferryhaven constituency then you're taking on trouble.'

'I'll handle it,' Josie said. 'I suppose I should thank you for the warning.'

'It wasn't what I had it in mind to talk to you about when I brought you out here,' Ben admitted.

'What then?'

'I had to see you, talk to you. I had to know whether the fire had really gone out.'

'And has it?'

For answer Ben moved closer. Josie turned towards him and they clung together in a long kiss.

'It wouldn't take much to set it alight again,' Ben said in a low voice.

Josie shook her head in a helpless gesture.

'I can't afford to get involved,' she said. 'I can't let all that start up again.'

'I know. We've got to part and this time it really will be for good. I'm going to try to go back to Nicola, if she'll have me.

She needs me, far more than you ever did, and perhaps I need that, too, that feeling of being responsible for someone. God knows how she's been managing this past year, but she's never complained.'

'That's her strong suit,' Josie said and in spite of herself she could not keep the sharpness out of her voice. 'Nicola's played a waiting game and she's won.'

'Not entirely. I'll never be wholly free of you, my dear, my very dear.'

'Oh, God! Ben, go now. Leave me here and walk away. Get out of my life and don't come back.'

He hesitated for one long moment and then he did as she asked, and Josie stood leaning against the railing, listening to his footsteps growing fainter, and the moon came out from behind a cloud and dazzled her because of the tears in her eyes.

Ben did not write to warn Nicola to expect a visit from him. Instead, because he had been unsettled by his meeting with Josie, he put it off, going first to see his father and Bess.

'You've been able to make a fresh start then, lad?' Andrew asked awkwardly.

'In a small way. I'll never get into the millionaire class now, Dad.'

'As long as you get by,' his father said vaguely. 'People like us, we were never meant to go that high.'

In the past Ben would have contested that. Now he held his peace, even though he was surprised by the strength of his conviction that his father was wrong.

There had been no word of Ernie. Whatever bolt-hole he had gone to, it had proved safe. As for Phyllis, she was living with her mother and Andrew, and Ben braced himself to withstand her malice.

'I'm gettin' a divorce, of course,' she said. 'Good job the house was in my name; at least I've got a bit of money to keep me going.'

She had kept her flashy wardrobe, but she had put on weight and her emerald green skirt was creased across her ample hips. She eyed Ben, tall and self-possessed and maddeningly good-looking, with bitter envy.

'I don't know why you don't do the same and get shot of Nicola,' she said.

'It's up to Nicola,' Ben said. 'I'm the one at fault.'

'D'you still think so? You're far an' out! Your Nicola lost no time in consoling herself once your back was turned and no way she can hide it either. I saw her a few months ago in Newcastle, big as a house. She didn't see me, or pretended not to, more likely.'

'Nicola ...? You must be mistaken,' Ben said with total conviction.

'I know a pregnant woman when I see one, and is it likely I wouldn't recognize your Nicola?'

'I don't believe ... she wrote to me ... she said nothing. Phyllis, *when* did you see her?' Ben demanded.

'I was doing some Christmas shopping, not that I had much heart for it, but I thought it might cheer me up. November some time, I s'pose. She looked as if she might drop the brat at any moment.'

'Last spring, a year ago, we were living together,' Ben said slowly. 'If it's true, if Nicola has had a baby, then it's mine. God in heaven, why didn't she tell me?'

'Because it isn't yours,' Phyllis said impatiently. 'She kept quiet because she didn't want you to know. You've been sending her money, I bet. The funds would have dried up fast if you'd known she'd had a little by-blow.'

Ben shook his head, trying to clear his mind. Nicola and another man? A man who had given her the child she had always wanted? So soon after she and Ben had been together and she had shown him how much she loved him? No, it wasn't possible.

'I must see her,' he said, thinking out loud.

He gave Phyllis a look of acute dislike. She was preening herself, pleased by the sensation she had caused.

'Why the hell didn't you let me know?'

'None of my business,' Phyllis said with a shrug.

'You saved it up until you could tell me to my face,' Ben said.

'Perhaps I did. You looked proper dumbfounded. Don't let that stuck-up bit pull the wool over your eyes, Ben lad. She's no better than any of the rest of them, including her stepdaddy.'

'We had a Christmas card from Nicola,' Andrew said. 'No word in that of any baby.'

He looked shyly at the tall man of thirty-five, almost a stranger to him now, who had been his Gwyneth's boy.

'If you think the little 'un could be yours then I'd say you were right,' he said. 'I always thought Nicola was straight as a die. If she'd taken up with anyone else and got hersel' with child she'd have told you.'

Ben set off for Berringer the next day. No question now of getting in touch with Nicola first and telling her to expect him. If he was to get to the bottom of this mystery he would do better to take her by surprise.

Because he had previously arranged to have a talk with his solicitor that day it was late afternoon before he reached Berringer Hall. He drove in through the tall wrought-iron gates and noticed, without really thinking about it, that they had been newly painted. The drive, too, was looking particularly trim. Nicola had been spending money on the place.

As he got out of the car Ben heard voices in the garden. A damn nuisance if she'd got visitors. It was then that he realized how much he was counting on seeing Nicola on her own.

He still had his keys, but he felt a certain diffidence about opening the front door and walking in. It had been a year, after all, and if there were strangers about it might be awkward. He rang the doorbell and waited. It seemed a long time before it was opened by a young man who looked surprised to see Ben on the doorstep.

'The door's not locked until eleven o'clock,' he said. 'Go straight in. Reception's in the hall on the left.'

Reception? Ben felt as if his mouth must be dropping open.

'I wanted … er … is Mrs Harcourt here?' he asked.

'She'll have finished work and gone home,' the young man said, adding to Ben's disorientation.

'Gone home?' he repeated.

'She lives in the cottage in the woods. If you ask at the desk they'll fix an appointment for you to see her tomorrow,' the young man said helpfully. 'Unless it's something personal?'

'Yes, it is,' Ben said. 'I'm ... I'm a relation.'

'Oh, in that case I expect it'll be all right if you walk through the gardens and take the short cut. I'd show you the way, but I'm late for a lecture.'

'I know the way,' Ben said.

The gardens were the same, except that someone had laid out a clock golf course on one of the lawns. Half a dozen young men were playing and it was their voices he had heard. There were some thick plastic files on a wooden seat by the side of the lawn. Ben squinted at them as he passed and saw the label, 'Berringer Hall Management Training College.'

The path was familiar, the one he had trodden so many times as a child. Nicola had clung to his hand and Josie had raced ahead. The dusk was gathering under the trees. The way still went by the side of the pond where Paul had been drowned, but it looked as if they were making an attempt to clear it up. The reeds had been cut and the remains of the old jetty cleared away. Would it be used once more as a swimming place? Would anyone remember that a man had died in that water?

There was a light on in the cottage. It had always been a dark little house. There was some washing on the line, small garments and white squares which were undoubtedly nappies. As Ben put his hand on the gate the door opened and Nicola came out. Without seeing him she went to the line and felt the washing, then she took the prop away and began unpegging it. The simple, homely actions struck Ben like a blow over the heart. He could neither move nor speak.

Nicola sensed that she was being watched and turned. They stood, looking at one another, forgetful of their surroundings, and then Ben opened the gate and went in.

'Nicola ... ' he said uncertainly.

Nicola recovered her self-possession first.

'Help me to take in the washing before the air grows damp,' she said. 'Then we'll talk.'

'A baby,' Ben said helplessly. 'You've had a baby.'

'Wait till we get inside.'

In the kitchen she took the washing from him and laid it in a tidy pile ready for ironing.

'I'll go and fetch him,' she said.

Ben stood in the middle of the room waiting. Some of the furniture looked familiar. It must have come from Berringer Hall. But what was Nicola doing in the cottage?

He heard Nicola coming down the stairs, moving slowly. The staircase was narrow and steep. She would have to be careful if she was carrying a baby. He still couldn't take it in, not until she was back in the kitchen with the child in her arms.

'He's just been bathed and fed, so he's almost asleep,' she said. 'A pity to disturb him, but it isn't every day a boy is introduced to his father.'

'He is mine?' Ben said.

'Oh, Ben! Can you doubt it? Look at his lovely dark hair and he's got your chin and nose exactly. Besides ... you know perfectly well there was never anyone else for me. Only you.'

'A boy,' Ben said, still dazed.

'William Andrew Harcourt.'

'William Andrew.'

'After his two grandfathers. I call him Billy. He ... he hasn't actually been christened yet.'

She flushed and looked away. 'I was waiting ... '

'Hoping I would be there,' Ben said. 'How could I, when I didn't know? Oh, Nicola, you should have told me.'

'I know, I know, but there were reasons ... complications. Would you like to hold him?'

With infinite care she transferred the child to Ben's arms. He clutched the soft weight and sat down on the edge of a chair. The baby opened his eyes and looked up into Ben's face. Gravely they considered one another and then Billy's lip jutted out, his eyes screwed up, his face turned scarlet, his little body stretched and he bawled a protest at being manhandled by a nervous stranger.

'Instant judgement,' Ben said. 'And who can blame him? Here, you'd better take him. I don't seem to have a knack with babies.'

He spoke carelessly, hiding his emotion, but Nicola smiled and her own eyes were moist as she took her son back again. In her familiar arms Billy was soothed. She patted him gently, rocking him to and fro, murmuring softly in his ear.

'He's nearly asleep,' she said. 'I'll put him back upstairs.'

When she returned Ben was still looking stunned.

'I had no idea,' he said. 'Why didn't you tell me, Nicola? You must have known ...'

'Before you went away,' Nicola admitted. 'It might have come to nothing. You know how often I'd been disappointed in the past. But apart from that, if you'd known you might not have gone and I thought it was absolutely necessary that you should.'

'I've had a good year,' Ben admitted. 'I'm back on my feet again. I can't say my name is cleared, but I've put the prosecution behind me and made a fresh start. When the houses we've built are sold, and that won't take long because they're good value, the people who put up the money are going to finance another development and my same team will get the job.'

'I'm glad about that,' Nicola said.

'Nicola, you're making talk, trying to put me off talking about the baby. I can't get over it, you know. How old is he?'

'Four months.'

'And you were on your own. It wasn't right. You should have told me.'

'You might have looked on him as an encumbrance.'

'Never!'

'Or felt obliged to come back to me.'

Ben did not reply to that and Nicola said, 'Yes, you would have done. I didn't want that. But I did take your money. I thought you'd want to feel you were supporting your child.'

Ben shook his head helplessly, not following her complicated logic.

'You've been getting up to other things, too,' he said. 'Why are you living in this cottage. And what's happened to Berringer Hall?'

'I sold it.'

'*Sold* it?'

'It was far, far beyond my means to keep it going. We poured money into it, Ben. I couldn't go on doing that. Just at the moment I was in despair I heard of a multinational corporation who were looking for a property in this neighbourhood so I put it on the market.'

'But you *work* there!'

'It was an absolutely perfect arrangement. I kept this cottage out of the sale because I wanted somewhere independent to live, and they agreed to employ me as a housekeeper. I was able to work almost until Billy was born and I've gone back again since. I take him with me, of course.'

She spoke with an airy unconcern that for a few minutes almost deceived Ben, burdened as he was by all he was having to take in. He sat, grappling with it, until Nicola said, 'I had my lunch at the College, but I was going to make myself an omelette. Would you like one?'

'No, I wouldn't,' Ben said. 'Not until I've had a few more answers out of you, my girl. Sit down.'

'We can talk while we're eating,' Nicola said nervously.

'No, we can't. Do you think I can keep my mind on food with all this hanging over me? Berringer Hall was almost unencumbered. We had a small bank loan when we modernized the kitchen, but that was negligible compared with the value of the whole property. Good God, girl, you must have got a fortune for it!'

'Quite a bit,' Nicola admitted.

'So why are you living in a tiny cottage and working for your living?'

Nicola did not reply.

'What did you do with the money?' Ben persisted.

'I invested it.'

'So I should hope! How much?'

Again an obstinate silence.

'You might as well tell me,' Ben said. 'You know perfectly well I won't rest until I find out.'

'Five hundred and fifty thousand pounds,' Nicola said reluctantly.

'Whew! You drove a hard bargain. O.K., now let's have the rest. You ought to be living very comfortably indeed on the income from half a million pounds. Why aren't you?'

'It was a ... a long term investment,' Nicola said, looking harassed. 'I was thinking of Billy's future.'

'If you'd been doing that you would have held on to Berringer Hall,' Ben suggested.

'Oh, no! Ben, it was outdated. Who can afford to live in that style these days? Truly, I began to see it as a millstone round my neck ...'

'Nicola, look at me.'

Miserably, Nicola lifted her head and looked Ben in the face.

'You're lying,' he said with conviction. 'You loved Berringer Hall. If I'd been asked I would have said you would have sweated blood to keep it, especially with a son to hand it on to. Why did you sell?'

She shook her head, mutely protesting at being questioned so closely.

'If you'd let it as a temporary measure I could have understood it,' Ben said. 'But to *sell* ... it's beyond belief!'

'Letting it wasn't enough. I looked into ...'

'What did you do with the money?'

Ben got up and stood over her, waiting for her answer and unable to believe that the suspicion that had come to him could be true.

'I told you.'

'Come on, Nicola, you haven't told me a thing.'

'I invested it in ... in a man I believed in,' Nicola said.

'God Almighty!'

Ben sat down heavily.

'The Hope Trust. That was it, wasn't it? You provided the money to buy the land so that I could have a job again.'

'I wondered whether you'd remember my name,' Nicola said. 'Nicola Rosemary Hope. It seemed appropriate.'

'Half a million pounds!'

Ben passed a hand over his forehead.

'You'll get it back, of course,' he said. 'The houses are selling well.'

'You're forgetting, the money we get back is to be re-invested.'

'*We*? The money *you* get back.'

'I just provided the cash, you put in the brains and sweat. It was a joint investment, Ben.'

'The thing I like about that remark is the way you use the word "just",' Ben said. 'Half a million pounds! As for making use of it again, of course I can't accept.'

He sprang to his feet, too agitated to sit still, and began pacing about the small room while Nicola watched him with troubled but determined eyes.

'If you refuse you'll be throwing all your team out of work,' she pointed out. 'Besides, what else am I to do with it? I can't buy back Berringer Hall.'

Ben came to a halt by the window with his back to her, staring out towards the darkening woods.

'That you should have made such a sacrifice ... It's unbearable,' he said in a thickened voice.

'I've done quite well out of it, actually. I expect to make quite a profit. If we go on it will make a nice inheritance for Billy.'

'Money! It can't compare with what you've given up. Do you think I don't know you would rather have camped out in one room in Berringer than have had gold ingots in the bank?'

'There are other houses in the world,' Nicola said, watching his rigid back. She was beginning to be worried about the way Ben was taking it. She had always known it would be difficult, but she had underestimated his sense of outrage.

'I still can't take it in,' Ben admitted. He turned round to face her, searching her face as if he had never known her before.

'I came back thinking you needed me,' he said. 'I've spent the last year imagining you scraping to make ends meet, but happy because you were still living at Berringer. And all the time ... Nicola, it's not just the money, though God knows that's been a shock, it's the fact that you had a child, our child, and kept me in the dark.'

'I didn't want you to be worried,' Nicola said nervously.

'I had a right to be worried. Didn't it occur to you that I might want to be around when my son was born?'

'Ben, be reasonable! Before you went away you were so remote and unreachable. When I visited you ...'

'Yes! Week after week you came and sat opposite me in that damned prison and never once did you hint that you were carrying my child. If I was unreachable, as you say, that news would have got through to me all right. Can't you see what an incentive it would have been, to know that ... that ...' His voice faltered and stopped.

'You never seemed that interested in having a family,' Nicola said helplessly. 'I was the one who was keen to have a baby.'

'In the abstract a baby didn't mean all that much to me,' Ben admitted. 'But once he was on the way ... now that he's *real* ... '

'You think you might come to love him?'

Nicola was frightened by the way Ben looked at her, in bitter anger and resentment.

'A fine idea you must have of me, to ask a question like that,' he said. 'Yes, I do feel I might come to tolerate my own son. If I'd known he was on the way I would have stuck around, helped you, supported you. When I think what it must have been like for you, not only selling Berringer Hall, but pregnant into the bargain and everyone wondering where your husband was – well, no, I'm wrong about that, aren't I? They knew where he was – disgraced and in prison. Perhaps you thought I wasn't good enough to father your child, that's why you kept quiet?'

'Ben, no, no. This is all going wrong! All I wanted to do was to spare you an extra anxiety!'

'I don't need to be spared, not in that way. I may have been a fool, a bit of a villain, but I never had to be spoon-fed, *pampered* like that. I would have faced up to my responsibility if I'd known it existed.'

'I didn't want you to think of me, or Billy, as a responsibility. I wanted ...' In a very low voice Nicola said, 'I wanted love.'

A silence fell between them. At last Ben got up.

'I need time to think,' he said. 'All this, coming on me so suddenly, it's too much to take in. The baby ... Berringer ... finding out that you've been supporting me all this year when I've been worrying about how you were managing without me ... I've got to think of some way of repaying you.'

'Ben, no! That's the last thing I want!'

He looked at her with a slight, twisted smile.

'You still don't understand, do you? The last, the really final blow to my pride. I came back meaning to tell you that I thought I could offer you a future, only to find that once again you're the one who's done all the giving. I can't take it, Nicola, I just can't take it!'

Chapter Twenty

When Ben left Nicola he knew that she was close to tears, but he was too angry, too mixed up in his head, to stay any longer. Nicola, his sweet, dependent Nicola, who had looked to him for help in everything, had taken the shattering decision to sell Berringer Hall, and apparently carried it through with considerable success. Singlehandedly, she had rearranged her life to cope with living in a tiny cottage, having a baby, doing a job. It was all so wildly outside his expectations that he did not know how to deal with it.

As he walked back through the woods, scarcely knowing where he was going, Ben began to realize how much he had counted on taking up his life with Nicola again. He had pushed it to the back of his mind, told himself with a touch of complacency that he was doing the right thing in trying to patch up their marriage, but all the time, ever since he had had his final talk with Josie, the one thing he had wanted was to get back to Nicola.

He stopped by the swimming pond, looking at the water, so clear and still, remembering with half his mind the delight he had taken in swimming in it when he was a child, remembering too the way Paul had died on an icy winter night. Did he fall or did he step deliberately into the black water? Ben had never known. The one thing he was sure about was that it was the legacy that Paul had unwittingly left him that had started his rise in the world. Rise or fall? Now there was a good question. For the first time in years Ben thought about the *Book of Hours*.

The following day, after a night spent tossing endlessly on his uneasy bed, Ben went in search of that *Book of Hours*. It was something to do, something to pass the time while he wrestled with the problems to which he had not yet found an answer.

He had not wanted to stay with his father and Bess and so he had booked himself into a Newcastle hotel for a couple of nights, always, he realized now, with the idea in his head that once he had seen Nicola again he would not need a hotel bed. Now he asked them to extend his booking and was disgusted with himself because of the way his heart sank at having to do it. Then he went out to look for the museum to which he had once loaned the *Book of Hours* and which had bid for it successfully when he had put it up for auction.

The museum looked brighter than he remembered it. It came to him suddenly that the last time he had been there the windows had been stuck up with strips of paper because the war had not long been over and no one had got around to removing the precautions against flying glass. He was none too sure where to find the mediaeval manuscripts, but he discovered them at last.

The book he still thought of as 'his' was displayed on its own in a glass case. It was open at a page Ben recognized, a page which had a small, leering devil peeping round the tail of the initial letter. On an impulse Ben went in search of the curator.

To Ben's astonishment, though he tried not to show it, it was not only the same man, but he remembered Ben.

'Not that I would recognize you,' he said with a smile. 'But of course I remember the circumstances perfectly. You left the *Book of Hours* with me for safekeeping and eventually we were able to buy it. The price seemed a little high at the time, but the value of these things has been rising lately and I now wonder whether perhaps we didn't get something of a bargain.'

'Would you let me have it out of the case?' Ben asked.

'I think that could be arranged. I can perfectly well understand your wanting to look at it again. A lovely thing, though *not*, of course, the original cover.'

'So I remember you telling me, all those years ago,' Ben said in some amusement.

He was given space at a desk in the crowded room belonging to the curator and the precious book was put down in front of him. Slowly, Ben began to turn the pages and as he did so he grew more and more interested, even excited. He had always liked it, but as a boy he had not really appreciated the delicacy of the painting, the glowing colours. He had learned to value fine things since those days, and a small voice at the back of his head pointed out that he owed some part of his education to Nicola, who had always lived surrounded by beauty; beauty she had given up for his sake.

Nothing could really take his mind off that for long. Ben closed the book with a sigh.

'Finished?' the curator asked.

'Yes. I only wanted to refresh my memory.'

'I hope you don't regret parting with it?' the curator inquired with a smile.

'It seemed the right thing to do at the time. Now ... I suppose I do wish in a way that I still owned it. Thank you for letting me see it.'

As Ben walked out of the museum, at a loose end once more, his mind played with that question. Did he regret what he had done? The *Book of Hours* had not belonged to him, he had not had any right to sell it. He had argued that Paul would have wanted him to have that legacy, and he still thought that was probably true, but would Paul have approved of what he had done with the money? He had stolen that thing of beauty and used the proceeds to buy his way into a shady deal with Ernie Baxcombe. A bad beginning, and although Ben still thought that he had done a lot of good work, he wondered uneasily now whether that one false step had not set him irredeemably on a path which led into a quagmire of deceit.

He passed through a room of antique statues, looking at them with unseeing eyes until one caught his attention and brought him to a halt. It was only a fragment, the head and torso of a young girl, but something about the way her head was set on her long, graceful neck, something about the sweet, forward thrust of her rounded shoulders, reminded him of Nicola. Nicola, another thing of beauty he had thrown away. Except that he could have that back for the asking, if he could only sink his pride sufficiently to ask.

Standing, apparently absorbed in studying a Greek statue, Ben smiled wryly to himself. What pride? He ought to have learned humility by this time, he had had enough lessons in it.

But for Nicola to have turned the tables on him as she had done was so unlike his image of her that he had been thrown into total confusion. His smile deepened, he almost laughed out loud. Fantastic, ridiculous, unpredictable woman. How could she have treated him like that and then expected him to say 'thank you very much' and settle down to live with her again? Still, he ought not to have walked out in the way he had done the previous day; he would have to go and see her again.

Without giving himself too much time to think about it, Ben went back to the hotel and got his car. It was only when he was on the road to Berringer that he realized that Nicola would still be working when he arrived. He idled an hour away over lunch, went for a walk, and then in desperation bought an evening paper and sat in the car to read it.

The by-election in Sussex was very fully reported because, against all expectation, the Labour man had scraped in with a majority of seventeen. There was a photograph of him and behind him in the crowd of wellwishers was Josie. Ben recognized her wide, triumphant grin and knew with absolute certainty what she was thinking: next time – Josie herself. Whatever regrets she might have had about parting with Ben had been forgotten in this victory, and it would always be like that for Josie. She would get into Parliament, there seemed little doubt of that, probably in time she would get office in a future government, and her private life would take second place. She might marry one day, and Ben rather thought she would, but it would be a fellow politician, someone who would share her own overwhelming interests.

When he grew too impatient to wait any longer Ben drove on towards Berringer, but this time he went up the rough little lane which led to the cottage in the woods. He was still too early, there was no one at home, and Ben was forced to sit in the car once more.

The cottage had been newly painted and looked fresh and pretty, but the garden was in need of tending. He guessed that Nicola was finding it rather too much to look after with all her other tasks. Ben got out and looked in the small lean-to shed where Stan had always kept his gardening tools. The lawn mower was in there, looking as if it could do with a good clean.

Still Ben hesitated. If he cut the grass would it look as if he were trying to move in? On the other hand, the grass needed mowing and it seemed a small thing to do for Nicola, who obviously needed some assistance.

When Nicola's own small car drew up at the gate Ben was in his shirt sleeves pushing the lawn mower over the front lawn.

'I got bored, waiting for you to come home,' he said. 'So I looked round for something to do.'

'I couldn't be more grateful,' Nicola said. 'I usually cut the grass on Saturday or Sunday, but last weekend was wet.'

'Where's the baby?'

'In his carry-cot on the back seat of the car. Could you bring him in for me?'

Neither of them had commented on Ben's reappearance. While Nicola carried a bag of shopping indoors Ben lifted the carry-cot out of the car. It was heavier than he had expected, and more awkward. Billy was awake. He kicked his feet in the air and waved his arms and Ben had a vague feeling of being welcomed.

'He doesn't seem quite so disgusted with me as he was yesterday,' he remarked.

'I'm going to bath him, feed him and put him to bed. If you want to talk you'll have to wait until that's done.'

'I could finish the grass,' Ben offered.

'It would be a help,' Nicola admitted. 'Lovely to think I could sit in the garden tomorrow without feeling guilty.'

Ben went back to his grass cutting, neatened the edges, cleaned up the lawn mower and went indoors. He could hear the soft murmur of Nicola's voice coming from the old back scullery which had been converted into a bathroom. Ben went through and stopped in the doorway. Nicola was sitting on a low chair, Billy on her lap, a blue plastic bath full of soapy water at her feet, and a covered enamel pail by her side. She was buttoning up the front of her dress and it came to Ben with a little shock that she had been breastfeeding the baby. Somehow he could not associate Nicola with that earthy natural function.

Her hair was untidy, and needed cutting, she wore very little make up, her hands were slightly reddened and instead of the pearly nail varnish she had worn in the past her nails were cut short and bare. And yet this slight air of dishevelment was infinitely becoming. Everything about her was subtly different. Her figure was fuller. She had a look of maturity she had never had before. But the curve of her neck as she bent over the baby was the same as Ben had recognized in the statue at the museum, and the line of her mouth had the old, remembered sweetness.

She looked round and as their eyes met Ben felt that somewhere deep inside him a stroke had been sounded as if on a gong and the reverberation shivered right through his body. He was speechless, struck dumb by astonishment. So this was love. Not the wild passion that had flamed between him and Josie; not the carefully exploited affection he had felt for Nicola in the past; not even the desire she had aroused in him because she was young and fresh and beautiful; this was something that changed the entire world. If any danger threatened Nicola and Billy he would defend them to the last drop of his blood; if he could be given the chance he would work for them, hold them and cherish them for the rest of his days.

Still watching him, Nicola lifted the baby and put him up to her shoulder and even that small, competent action struck Ben as amazing. Did she realize the change that had taken place in him? Ben thought not, or if she had seen it she was not going to say anything. Instead, her words were prosaic – perhaps deliberately.

'I doubt if you're used to burping babies or I'd hand him over to you,' she said. 'Are you planning to eat with me?'

'I don't know ... I suppose ... if you'll have me,' Ben said.

'Then perhaps you'd like to go and peel some potatoes.'

Ben found the potatoes, and the knife, still in a daze. The cold water tap at the kitchen sink dripped. He made an absentminded note of it as something he would have to see to. If Nicola would let him stay, that was. She must, it was unthinkable that she should send him away now.

Was this the way she had always felt about him? If it was then no wonder she had been prepared to make sacrifices. He would have done the same – now.

He heard Nicola take Billy upstairs and then she came down and began to move round him in the kitchen. From upstairs came the sound of a loud, insistent voice.

'Is he all right?' Ben asked nervously.

'Oh, yes. Just determined not to be put to bed without a protest. He's very strong willed – obstinate, like his father.'

The crying continued.

'Just listen to him,' Nicola murmured. 'Bawling his head off. Would you go up to him? Tell him to shut up. Perhaps he'll listen to the voice of authority!'

The little back bedroom had been newly decorated, too. Ben was glad that Nicola had had the sense to provide herself with some comforts. The blue and cream room was delightful, much lighter and more airy than he remembered it.

'You're a lucky fellow, little as you seem to appreciate it,' Ben informed his yelling son.

The sound of his voice was a novelty. Billy's face changed from an alarming shade of puce to a lighter scarlet, his screwed up eyes opened and he looked at Ben curiously. Very carefully, Ben bent over the cot and picked him up.

'Come on, old chap, give me a break,' he said. 'I want to make love to your mother. In twenty years time you'll feel for me.'

Billy gave an uncertain hiccup and his lower lip trembled again. When Ben extended one long finger and tickled him experimentally under the chin, Billy made a grab at the finger and held on. Ben sat very still until that soft determined grasp slackened and Billy's eyes closed. The curve of his eyelids against his cheek was so perfect that Ben was enthralled. He smelt of warm milk and baby powder. He had gone off to sleep in utter trust and once again Ben was smitten by helpless love.

Back in the kitchen Nicola looked round with a smile.

'You picked him up,' she said accusingly.

'Oh, well, it did the trick,' Ben excused himself. 'Anything else I can do?'

'Lay the table, please.'

Obediently, Ben began to spread the cloth and put out knives and forks, but there was an amused gleam in his eyes at the crisp way Nicola issued her orders.

'You've made the place look quite different,' he said. 'More homely. In fact, quite comfortable.'

'I like it,' Nicola said. 'You can sit down. I'm just going to dish up. I put this casserole in the oven at lunchtime.'

'Do you come home to lunch?'

'No, I usually stay at the college, except when I want to put a match to the gas or something like that.'

She put a plate in front of him and for the first time in months Ben's food looked appetizing to him.

'Eat it while it's hot,' Nicola said absently and wondered why Ben laughed, even though she was glad to hear it.

It was difficult to find anything to talk about while they were eating, since they tacitly agreed to postpone their most important discussion until the meal was over. Several times Nicola looked up and caught Ben watching her and she flushed and looked away. Too late, she wished she had taken the opportunity while he was upstairs with Billy of washing her face and combing her hair.

She gave him apple pie and cream and Ben ate it with every appearance of enjoyment. Whatever he had come back to say to her, it didn't seem to have spoiled his appetite.

'Do you mind if we wash up and have coffee afterwards?' Nicola asked.

'Anything you say,' Ben agreed.

He made the kitchen seem small. Having him standing behind her with a tea towel made Nicola nervous, so that her hands were clumsy and the china clattered in the bowl. If Ben noticed he made no comment.

'Real coffee,' Nicola said. 'One of the luxuries I allow myself.'

She regretted the careless words as soon as they were out, especially when Ben said deliberately, 'You'd be able to afford a great many luxuries if you didn't have such an expensive husband to keep.'

It was on them, the moment she had been dreading. Once again she was going to have to justify what she had done and since talking to Ben the previous day Nicola was no longer so sure that she had been right. She had kept it secret because the thing she had dreaded more than anything was that he might think she was trying to buy him. She had always known that one day sooner or later he would find out that she was behind the Hope Trust, but she had seen it as a more formal occasion, over an office desk, not coming on her unawares as it had done yesterday.

'Are you going to throw it all up, just because you don't like where the money came from?' she asked.

'I can't do that, the job's unfinished and there are other people to be considered besides myself,' Ben said. 'No, as far as finance is concerned, I'm prepared to let the present arrangement stand – up to a point.'

It was more than Nicola had expected, even though she had begun to hope when Ben had come back to talk to her again.

Ben was absorbed, thinking aloud. 'The present project is near completion. We'll sell the houses and make a tidy profit. The next step has to be thought about. Guy is a good chap, but having an option on that bit of land was a fluke. He's a decent architect, but he's not a property developer – in fact, he's not allowed to be; he has to stick to his profession. I'm the one with the flair for finding openings. I'll scout round and see if I can discover another place ripe for development, but if I do I want the whole thing put on a proper basis. We'll form a company.'

'And you'll be in charge,' Nicola said.

Ben looked at her steadily.

'It's the way I am,' he said. 'I suggest you become chairman of the company and I'll be managing director. I'll expect to be paid a salary, but the bulk of the profits will come to you. It's up to you, but I think you should start some sort of fund to safeguard Billy's future.'

He drew a deep breath. 'I've forgiven you for selling Berringer Hall behind my back.'

'Thank you,' Nicola murmured and even the irony with which she spoke was something new for her.

'I know what you're thinking,' Ben admitted. 'You've got more to forgive than I have. I'm an adulterer and an ex-convict. I dragged your name through the mud and yet you've given up everything for me.'

'That's not what I really meant,' Nicola said quickly. 'Just for a moment I was a bit nettled at being forgiven for doing something I thought was right.'

'Some of what you did was so generous it takes my breath away – and why you think I'm worth it is more than I can understand. But I do begin to have a glimmer of an idea of how you felt. I didn't see it yesterday, but today I understand that sometimes it's necessary to make profound sacrifices. The thing I still disagree with is keeping quiet about the baby. You should have told me.'

He seemed to be waiting and at last Nicola brought herself to say, 'All right, I admit it. I should have told you. Oh, Ben, if you knew how much I *wanted* you ... wanted you to know, all those long months of waiting. But I didn't want you to come back to me because you were sorry for me. Not pity, Ben, never that, please.'

'I don't pity you,' Ben said. 'On the contrary, I admire you profoundly. For a girl who didn't know how to read the gas meter when I married her, you seem to have made remarkable strides.'

'Oh, Ben, that's not fair! You only had to show me once. As for the past year, it's not been easy, but I'm holding down quite a responsible job and enjoying it, I'm coping with Billy, I've come to terms with losing Berringer. I'm ... I'm not quite the same person as I was when you left, Ben.'

'I can see that. What I want to know is, how are you going to manage when Billy is older? You take him to work with you now and although it can hardly be ideal I suppose he's reasonably quiet and easily managed. What will happen when he's a two-year-old toddler?'

'I haven't got as far as thinking about that,' Nicola admitted with her head bent. 'I suppose ... if there are profits to come from this business you want to run then I can either pay someone to look after Billy or give up work until he goes to school.'

'Good, that's what I wanted you to say because I hoped it would make you realize how necessary it is for you to take the profits I'm offering you.'

It sounded as if he meant them to go on living apart, that was the only thing that Nicola could think about.

'If we're still separated, that is,' Ben said, as if he had read her thoughts. 'Tell me again why you sold Berringer and gave the money to me.'

Nicola jerked her head up, suddenly angry.

'All right, I'll tell you. I love you. I've gone on loving you all the time, even when I saw that you despised me, even when you were making love to Josie, even when you admitted to the sort of double-dealing I would have condemned in anyone else. I plotted to win you back by putting Josie into an impossible position, I humbled myself to bring you home when I thought you needed me, I seduced you into going to bed with me again, I sold my most precious possession so that you could make a fresh start and I went through miserable lonely months of pregnancy so that you shouldn't be disturbed when my plan started to work. So now you know.'

'I do indeed. What does a man do to deserve a love like that?'

'You don't have to "deserve" it,' Nicola said sadly. 'It just happens. Sometimes I wish it didn't. It would be a lot easier just to be free of you, but I know I never will be.'

'Any more than I'll be free of you,' Ben said steadily. 'I chose you for my wife because you were the kind of girl I'd made up my mind long since I would marry. What I never realized was that you were always the pattern I measured the others against. I was proud of you, and proud of myself for having won you, but I did love you, too. You were more to me than the prize for winning the race, but I was too busy admiring my own cleverness to admit it. There was always a touch of guilt in my thinking about you. That was why I fell for Josie. We were equals, or so I thought, and I had no need to hide my worse side from her.'

'Nor from me,' Nicola said quickly.

'Yes, my dear. I always knew your moral standards were higher than mine. I resented it and told myself that it was because you'd never known hardship.'

'A different sort of hardship,' Nicola said with a sigh. 'My grandfather was the only person I ever knew who really loved me. Except you.'

'You do believe it, then? That I loved you?'

'I want to believe it,' Nicola said, but she had noticed that he had used the past tense and it made her response sound wooden.

'I've been very lonely this past year,' Ben said. 'I spent a lot of time on my own. And the person I thought about was you.'

'What about Josie?'

'I saw her a week or two ago.' Ben paused, struggling for honesty. 'There was still something there,' he admitted. 'I could see *why* I fell for her so violently, but there's no place for me in her life and I can truly say that I no longer want it. After we'd talked I felt free to come back and see whether there might be some hope of our trying again. Of course, I didn't expect all these shocks you've been giving me. Yesterday ... perhaps I was ungenerous, but I was shocked to the core.'

'I meant it for the best,' Nicola said. Her eyes searched his face anxiously. A new feeling of hope was struggling inside her.

'Ben, if you really want to try again we're not going to let a thing like money come between us, are we? Couldn't we be partners and husband and wife as well? I know I said I wasn't trying to make you come back to me, but it wasn't true. I do want you.'

'What may come between us is my feeling of unworthiness,' Ben admitted.

'That won't last long,' Nicola said, and now she was smiling. 'I know you, Ben Harcourt! Humility is not your strong suit!'

'I'm trying to convince you I've changed,' Ben protested. He looked down, almost as if he were afraid to look at her.

'I *have* changed,' he repeated. 'So profoundly that I can hardly believe it myself.' He raised his head, a look of exasperation and amazement on his face.

'Damn it, Nicola, I've fallen in love with you! All over again, completely differently; I'm so dumbfounded I don't know how to handle it. I want you back as my wife. I'm so determined to get you back that I'll camp at the gate and lay seige to you, if necessary.'

'I don't think you need go to those lengths,' Nicola said unsteadily. 'My dear, I've told you – I'm here, ready and waiting.'

They looked at one another, both nervous of the next move,

and then Ben held out his arms and Nicola went to him.

It was a clumsy embrace and they broke apart, half amused and half regretful that they should have forgotten how to hold one another.

'I haven't made such a hash of kissing a girl since I was a teenager,' Ben remarked. 'We can do better than that, my dear.'

He shifted to hold her more comfortably and Nicola put her arms round his neck, her breasts sliding upwards against his chest. Ben's grip tightened and this time their lips met in mutual delight. Ben's hands moved over her back and Nicola broke away from his mouth and sighed, burying her head against his neck.

'You still smell the same,' she said in a voice of utter contentment.

'Pleasant, I hope,' Ben said unsteadily.

'You know what I mean.'

'Mm. Darling Nicola.'

They kissed again and broke apart laughing.

'It's going to work,' Ben said. 'It is, isn't it?'

'If you'll do your part. Don't leave me out, Ben – please. Tell me what's going on, even if it's bad. I can take anything as long as we're sharing it.'

'That's one of the things you've made me understand. You left me out of the decisions you made and I was outraged, but I'd kept you in ignorance of my business dealings for years, made a point of it, in fact. From now on I'll consult you, not just because you're entitled to know what's being done with your money, but because I want you to be involved in the whole of my life.'

'That's all I ask,' Nicola said with a satisfied sigh.

Ben held her loosely in the crook of his arm, his lips brushing the silky hair that sprang from her wide forehead.

'When is this new arrangement going to start?' he asked.

'It's started, hasn't it?' Nicola said in surprise. She looked up into his face and recognized the amused quirk to his mouth, the familiar glint in his eyes.

'Oh, I see what you mean! You haven't changed, have you? Two kisses and you want to go to bed.'

'Yes, please. If you're sure ... '

'I'm sure,' Nicola said. 'You are my dear, dear husband. My lovely baby's father. I've loved you all my life, ever since I was a little child. How could I ever stop. I tried, but it wasn't possible.'

'I don't deserve it,' Ben said. 'God knows I don't. But I will try. Er ... is that little devil upstairs going to wake up and disturb us?'

'Probably. One of the disadvantages of being a family man, my dear.'

'I'll have to learn to live with it. Still, he's quiet at the moment, isn't he? I mean, I know it's barely eight o'clock, but ...'

He broke off when he saw Nicola's face, alight with laughter.

'What makes you think I need persuading?' she demanded. 'How fortunate that we got the washing up done early!'

'In another moment you'll have me believing you planned the whole thing,' Ben said. 'You're a scheming woman, Nicola Harcourt, and I'm beginning to think you might be a very clever one.'

Nicola leaned against him, blissfully aware of the hard strength of his body.

'No, I'm not clever,' she said. 'Not in the sense of being able to look ahead and plan to make everything work out like this. I acted out of instinct and some of the time I can see I was wrong. All I know is, I always wanted you back, but not out of any sense of obligation, not because of money, not even because of Billy, only because you wanted me in the same way.'

'And that's what has happened,' Ben said.

As they went out of the room with their arms round one another he said in a low voice, 'I know now who my true love is, and it's you, my darling girl, my dear wife.'